*R*osemary
*F*riedman

The Long Hot Summer

HOUSE OF STRATUS

This edition published in 2001 by House of Stratus, an imprint of Stratus Holdings plc, 24c Old Burlington Street, London, W1X 1RL, UK.

www.houseofstratus.com

Typeset, printed and bound by House of Stratus.

A catalogue record for this book is available from the British Library.

ISBN 0-7551-0120-0

FOR
CHARLOTTE

I've travelled the world twice over,
Met the famous: saints and sinners,
Poets and artists, kings and queens,
Old stars and hopeful beginners,
I've been where no one's been before,
Learned secrets from writers and cooks
All with one library ticket
To the wonderful world of books.

PART ONE

One

She liked the house in the early morning before anyone was awake, particularly in the summer. In the hall the leaves of the monstera and the ficus shone with the slanting rays of the sun which had been up since five. In the lighted tank the Black Mollies and the Rosy Barbs glided back and forth with rhythmic certainty in their own perpetual daytime. She must remember to tell Joey to do something about the water.

In the Poggenpohl kitchen everything was as she'd left it the night before, except for the cereal trail bearing evidence of Joey's night starvation. Mechanically she cleared away the packet with its 'Free Inside' and the sugar and mopped up the puddle of milk. Cassius stretched and shook himself, then walked sedately to the garden door, knowing the pattern. She unlocked the three security devices insisted upon by the insurance company after their burglary and let him out. The garden, ravaged by the drought, was not its best, the lawn bald and browning, the roses fatigued. There had never been a summer like it. Not that she could remember. Day after day with the mercury over seventy – over twenty rather, she never could get used to it, any more than she could the grams and the millilitres, having to refer to her conversion tables every time she cooked.

She did not like the heat but took care not to complain too much because Derek, who tolerated it better, said it was 'her age', a comment guaranteed to send her into an inner rage belied by the outward tolerant smile. Everyone was suffering. Joey could not sleep, Derek carried a spare shirt in his briefcase, and even Cassius lay dormant all day under a tree. Only Anne-Marie seemed happy, lying out, whenever she could, in the full heat of the sun, in the briefest of bikinis.

The unprecedented heatwave was the major topic of conversation. People discussed the discomfort of it and exchanged hints on how to keep cool. London had taken on an air of New York with men in shirtsleeves. The tube trains were unbearable. No one wanted to go to bed and the streets were still busy at midnight. Soft drinks were at a premium, as were ice creams which scarcely survived the journey to the mouth. Ice had run out but not the beer. The TV newscasters reported the soaring temperatures nightly and showed strange scenes of Londoners adapting to the heat. Hoses were banned both for gardens and car washing. Small boys flaunted their dirty necks as chauvinistic evidence of their efforts to save water. Some said it was the end of the world.

If one had to cook, early morning was the best, the only time. After that the heat in the kitchen became intolerable. Derek berated himself for not having put air-conditioning into the house, but how was one to know?

It was the end of term and Camilla was coming down. Lorna had got up to make a chocolate cake. She always made one at the beginning of each term for Camilla to take up to Warwick with her, and one when she came down. It was a tradition, like so many other things she had started, and it was expected of her. Half the campus seemed to wait with anticipation for her chocolate cake. It was always the same one; enormous and quite a feat of cooking; enough for dozens of mouths hungry for the sweetness of homes they had left behind.

It didn't seem like two years since the first chocolate cake. She and Derek had taken the uncertain Camilla up to her new home in the Midlands. It was the first time she had been away except for holidays. She remembered the bare room on campus which had seemed so impersonal, so cell-like, with its narrow bed, its single cupboard, its window looking out on to other curtained windows shielding what she afterwards discovered were the Sunday afternoon couplings. What else was there to do? They had brought coloured bulrushes in the market and a green vase to put them in, and a Degas poster which Derek fixed to the wall with Blue-tak. The room began to look a bit better and Camilla put her name in the slot outside her door, her groceries in the locker in the tiny kitchen, and her butter in the fridge which she had to lock.

The corridors had been full of activity, everyone staggering in with heavy cartons in which all that could be seen were stereos and giant boxes of cereals. Grown men hidden behind the Sugar Puffs and the Cornflakes and the Frosties. They'd left her listening woefully to 'Abbey Road' and felt like executioners, forgetting that this was the moment they had striven for through the struggles with O-levels and with A-levels and the trials of the interviews. Derek and she had not spoken on the way back down the motorway, each choked with the emotions engendered by their firstborn flapping her sticky little wings and leaving the nest.

They had adapted quite quickly. She had cleared away the half-eaten apples and the crumpled Kleenex and the woolly hat Camilla had left around and found it pleasant to have the house tidy and receive the unexpected phone calls cut off by pips in their prime so that they never did discover what she had swapped her balalaike for. The second year had been different. She had moved to a flat off campus. Flat! Well, three rooms, kitchen and bath shared with two others in an old house in

Leamington Spa. The stairway was strewn with bedding and divan legs and motorcycle engines. Her mattress was on the floor. She had her teddy bear by her side and Marx on the mantlepiece. She had been driven up by a young man with a red beard and held her deck on her lap all the way as if it were Sèvres.

She was an old hand now. They were all old hands, used to the comings and goings. They visited and tried not to show their distaste of the ice-cold bathroom and the rings inside the mugs from which they had to drink their tea. Camilla was reading philosophy but they heard more about Wreckless Eric, the Damned, the Clash and the Jam than Cartesian meditations and Wittgenstein.

Sometimes Lorna wondered if it was right for her to have gone away. From a conventional schoolgirl whose world was pretty well circumscribed Camilla had made the transition into one of the world's myriad blue-jeaned semi-adults who shot their mouths off about society without having had the experience which would qualify them even to hold an opinion. The whipping boys were familiar. The Establishment, nuclear deterrents, the phoney values, the megalomania and the capitalism of the middle-classes. The arguments went round and round like skittles at a fairground. Camilla and her friends, who had never had to work from nine till five most probably never would (they would not after all be up in time), knocked them down from their vantage point on the floor where they sat in the small hours (what other hours were there?), drinking from the rivers of coffee which flowed through the campus.

She was sure that the chocolate cake was a symptom of her own maternal needs and kept the recipe in her kitchen 'File-It'. The children had given this to her for a birthday. A ring file, such as they used for school, it had inspired her originally to organize her culinary data as they did their work. The good intentions persisted for several weeks. *Hors d'œuvres* and Starters were followed by Soups and Entrées, with Puddings and Pastries bringing up the rear. The good intentions lasted no longer than her determination, at various times, to keep her drawers tidy, to take up needlepoint, or to learn a new language. Scraps of paper torn surreptitiously from magazines in the hairdresser's began to infiltrate the pages. Backs of envelopes on which she had scribbled 'Unusual Cucumber Salad' and 'Watercress Soup' slid hither and thither. Bon Viveur and Katie Stewart were seconded from the *Telegraph* and *The Times* to make bedfellows for Lois' kipper pâté and Irene's strudel. The whole caboodle swelled hideously with time, and lost its pristine whiteness in blobs of cake mixture, smears of oil, and various splashes of this and that. 'University Chocolate Cake', now nestling incongruously between 'Lemon Sorbet' and 'Sukiyaki', was well endowed with cocoa, the ink running down the page in dried purple tears. She got as far as '400 grams butter' when Cassius yelped to be let in. He sidled past her as she held open the door, leaving hairs on her dressing-gown. He made for his water-bowl and lapped noisily.

Her relationship with the dog was ambivalent. The depressed-looking collie represented for Derek the obedient child he did not have, perfectly trained, never arguing, no complaining at the longest walk in the foulest of weathers. He did not, however, have to wash the muddy paw-marks off the floor on winter days, dry the shaggy coat when he came in from the rain, open the smelly cans of meat and remember to order them, cope with the occasional manifestations of digestive disorders as they appeared, restrain him from molesting the window cleaner in intimate places and attend to his daily exercise. Derek had bought him and took him over at weekends. He had, however, attached himself unequivocally to Lorna. He moved where she moved, stood when she stood, sat when she sat. The house, she knew, smelled of dogs, especially when it was wet outside. She had never been an animal lover and every autumn when he shed lumps of fur over the furniture she vowed to get rid of him. Only occasionally, while walking him, did she feel virtuous and that he served some purpose. Over the common, woman and dog; without him she would certainly not have walked; it helped her with her weight problems.

He padded back and forth to the larder and cupboards as she got out scales and tinfoil, sugar, eggs, flour, milk, and cocoa. The butter and the sugar went into the Magimix, a present from Derek for Christmas. Her kitchen was so mechanized that often she felt the penchant for labour-saving devices had come full circle and that the labour saved was now equivalent to the labour involved in terms of breakdown, maintenance, nuisance, and service. Because Derek was an architect he insisted that she had the benefit of every convenience that was going. He liked 'toys' and he liked leading weekend visitors on a tour of the gadget-oriented kitchen. Proud as he was, however, of the built-in, self-clean automatic cooker with its roast-guard (bells ringing when the beef was rare), rotisserie, simmerstat and lights (all that was lacking was the music), he was unable to make himself an omelette as he could not operate the banks of controls. There were times when Lorna herself found it menacing. A kind of science-fiction kitchen round which she felt she should be walking in a space-suit. There were days when she loved its smooth efficiency (provided everything was working) and others when she fantasized about scrubbed wooden tables and stone sinks and Aga ranges bearing simmering stock-pots. Surrounded by her automatic waste-grinder, can-opener, dishwasher, clothes-washer, fruit-juicer and coffee-grinder, each vibrating with its own particular rhythm, she felt she needed a conductor's baton to harmonize the cacophony, or that she was a spider caught in a web of its own making. On headache days she could not stand the noise and fled from the kitchen, tightly closing the door. Today, with another certain eight hours of unbearable heat, Camilla coming down with her friends, people for drinks, Grandma for tea, she was at momentary peace with the teak formica and the dark red ceramic tiles.

The butter creamed easily, changing in seconds from hard yellow squares which she'd fled into the Magimix to pale, sugary foam. She ran the spatula round the bowl and, sliding her finger down what remained on the white plastic blade, put it in her mouth. The sweet creamy taste of the mixture reminded her that she had had no breakfast. She filled the kettle and cursed as the orange rubber sink-swirler dropped into it from the tap. She fished it out. It always reminded her of an orange penis. It was past its prime and had stretched. She must remember to get a new one. She started again with the water, then switched the kettle on and wrote on the plastic memory-board with the special pencil, 'sink-swirler', underneath 'greaseproof paper' and 'carpet cleaner'. She broke the eggs into a clear Pyrex basin, looking with disgust at the two rusty globules of embryo chicken. She never quite knew how to cope with them. Sometimes she ignored them and simply added them to whatever she was making, pretending that she hadn't really seen. On other occasions she fished them out meticulously with the half eggshells, to which they seemed to be mysteriously attracted, as she had been taught to do at 'Advanced Cookery'.

Today she pretended they did not exist, and, overcoming her revulsion at the new life they represented, she added the eggs to the butter and sugar and in a few whirrs the mixture was amalgamated and her conscience salved. She sifted the flour with the cocoa, feeling irritated with the lumps which conglomerated in the bottom of the sieve. She pushed the last of them through with her fingers, then heard the newspaper thud on to the mat and had a moment of regret at getting up so virtuously early. She went to pick them up and wondered whether to take them to Derek or if he was still sleeping as he had been when she had slipped out of the bed. She decided he was and left them on the hall table on the brass tray they had brought from Istanbul. She left a cocoa thumb-print on the front of the *Sunday Times*.

7

There was something about the Sunday newspapers. She liked to read them in bed with Derek. They did not quarrel about the sections. Derek read the news, the comments on the news, the letters. She read the *faits divers* and the Review Sections with their surveys of the Arts: books, plays, radio and television. She also read the adverts – all of them. Houses, holidays, for sale, wanted; Special Offers for which she sometimes sent away (her sorbetière, the briefcase she had given Derek for his birthday), the fashion pages, and the account of 'One Person's Day' which she generally thought extremely dull. She was aware that the dichotomy was due to the fact that Derek lived in the real world while she lived mostly in her head. She believed this a circumstance which had come about because of the life she led, and had lately felt that the consequences could be dangerous. Something to do with a thin line which she must be careful not to cross. Its definition was not absolutely clear and she did not think about it too much. Later in the day they swapped sections and she would read about 'New boosts to industry', 'Railways expect to halve freight loss', and the latest extradition of terrorists, proclamation of rights, and denials and affirmation of defence cuts. On most Sundays by the time she got out of bed, her face grubby with newsprint, she had bought a flat in the south of France, contemplated a holiday in the Western Isles, and vowed to attend an exhibition of watercolours in Bond Street, an Arts Council lecture at the Serpentine Gallery, and at least six concerts at the Festival Hall. Lying in bed in the terylene and cotton 'Patience Rose' sheets (Harrods sale), none of it was any trouble at all. By the time Monday morning came it was a different story.

The cake was too large for any of her cake tins. Irene, who had given her the recipe, had suggested a roasting tin lined with tinfoil and that was what she always used. She took the long silver baton out of the drawer and tore off more than she needed. She thought, as she often did, how extravagant, and that her grandmother had cooked without silver paper and Snappiwrap and Handiwrap and silicone paper and plastic bags, just as she had managed without electric fryers and pressure cookers and thermostatically controlled everything. There had been a grey gas-cooker, she remembered, and big black saucepans and the food seemed to smell more like food. She glanced at her shelf of recipe books, Elizabeth David through Claudia Rodin to Muriel Downes and Rosemary Hume. She couldn't remember her grandmother's having a recipe book at all, she just cooked out of her head, throwing in handfuls of this and that and tasting from a wooden spoon. She ground salt too from huge oblong blocks and made butter into patterned balls with wooden bats you dipped into cold water. The butter had been served in Sainsbury's by ladies with muslin turbans who weighed it and slapped it into shape on the marble slab before wrapping it with a few deft movements to individual order. There had somehow been time. Time to wait at the counter for butter, then at another for eggs; to pass the time of day with friends and neighbours not caught in the frenetic rush there was today. There was little of either leisure or pleasure in shopping now. Charging round Sainsbury's with laden trolleys, everyone absorbed in her own little grand prix, in and out of the sections, delicatessen and soap powders, and into the straight for the final lap to the checkout. They bent and stretched and stood mesmerized and pondering, struck into ghastly frozen moments of indecision between the long grain and the pudding rice. The trolleys assumed lives of their own as they grew increasingly unmanageable with their rapidly growing loads of drunken, double-pack toilet rolls and spaghetti hoops and jumbo soap powders. Often she thought of it as a ballet; arabesquing for the tomato chutney and pliéing for the water-crackers (3p off). It could at times be quite aesthetic, the higgledy-piggledy load of packets and tins finally passing in dignified order along the conveyor belt to be packed neatly in cardboard boxes while she stood with her chequebook in her teeth trying to prevent the boursin being crushed into unrecognizable shape by the relentless arrival of the bullying tins of peaches and of sauerkraut. It was quite a feat of strength. Shelf to basket, basket to check-out, check-out to boxes, boxes to car, car to kitchen, kitchen to store cupboard and to fridge. You needed the strength of an ox these days. Some women had small children as well, perched on their trolleys. She always felt sorry for them and for herself when Derek said what have you been doing all day as though she'd done nothing more strenuous than sewing samplers. Sometimes she looked at the load and the long snake of paper itemizing what she had spent, which seemed to add up to more and more each week, and thought thank God I won't have to shop again for a month, but in a day there was tomato purée and bay leaves chalked up on the memory-board and she had run out of bleach and whole black peppers.

She turned the oven on and put the creamed mixture into her other mixer which was better at mixing then creaming and had the motor turning gently as she added the milk and the eggs and the cocoa and the flour which spurted up out of the bowl in a soft brown mist.

She watched, fascinated, as the mixture became blended into a glossy, beige mass and, tasting some, wondered whether she was going to eat any when it was done. She wasn't the only one with a weight problem. It was one of the many crosses of middle-age. It didn't seem fair that up till the time Joey was born she had been stick-thin like Camilla and tucked into everything she could lay hands on without gaining an ounce. Now there was nothing for nothing. She had to pay for every excess with too-tight trousers and skirts, an uncomfortable feeling of heaviness and the thickening round the waist that brought problems of guilt and depression, which could be alleviated temporarily by chocolate and apple pie and cream, eaten furtively, which added more pounds and more guilt and depression... There was no winning. Life, without a doubt, was on the side of the young. They were not punished for beer or chocolate bars. Never thought about it; neither had she or Derek once. Now the morning weigh-in had become a daily ritual. Sometimes she forgot and stood on the scales with the shower-cap, then took it off as if it could make the slightest difference. Often she cheated, adjusting the dial to just under the correct reading, aware that she deceived only herself. She did try. She went to exercise classes run by a skinny Viennese of indeterminate years who rolled on the floor in a black leotard, twisting herself into all manner of knots and exhorting her ladies to do the same. The exercises helped with her thighs and her 'hanging bottom'. They did nothing for her weight which was a problem of sheer self-control. At times she had it; sitting virtuously before pallid mounds of cottage cheese, knowing full well that a sudden shift in equilibrium brought about by unexpected stress or strain or the dark machinations of her hormones would send her running for the French bread and butter, the mashed potatoes she made for Joey, and the comfort of the chocolate bars whose wrappers littered her car.

It was hard to be a woman. Apart from the difficulties common to both sexes, one had to cope with the appalling cataclysm of adolescence, the trials, great and small, of child-bearing, and before one had time to turn round the tumultuous finale of the fertile years. Sometimes she wondered if there would ever be any peace except that brought by death from the extortionate demands of her own body.

The bowl, with its great mass of mixture, was heavy to lift. She was about to tip the lot into the silver-lined roasting tin when she suddenly remembered with horror that she had forgotten to add the beaten egg-whites. Typical of her memory lately. Lucky she had remembered or the whole lot would have been wasted. It had something to do with concentration. Lack of it. There was so much clutter in her mind, like a junk room that needed a good sort out, that there seemed no room for some of the things she tried to retain. Irene found the same. She'd waited an hour at the bus stop for her daily help who came on Tuesdays before she had realized it was Wednesday.

She used to have a good memory. She had been clever at school, only in those days one never did anything with it; took a secretarial course and had a job for a while or was finished in Switzerland, passing the time as best one could while waiting for Mr Right and marriage. Judging by the troubles a great many of her friends were having, it had turned out to be Mr Wrong, but that was beside the point, it was marriage that was the operative word, the be-all and the end-all. It was expected. Now it was university degrees for all; it had become a *sine qua non* like A-levels and fitted you for as little. It provided and excuse, however, for three years of lazing around with no responsibilities to either state or parents who provided the grants, at the end of which one had become used to being thoroughly idle and iconoclastic.

The egg whites took moments only. At cookery school it had been a balloon whisk and a copper bowl, probably better, but the chocolate cake would be eaten anyway, not too closely analysed. It was a question of air and volume but one could not be too pedantic.

She cut the white clouds into the chocolate mixture in figures of eight with a metal spoon. When it was done she sloshed the lot into the roasting tin and levelled the surface. The light on the oven had gone off, indicating that it had reached the required temperature. She put the cake in and set the timer for sixty minutes.

Looking round the kitchen with distaste she wondered whether to leave the mess for Anne-Marie, then decided it wasn't worth the long face and collected the bowls and spoons and spatulas and wiped the chocolate pools and rivers and opened the dishwasher, only to find it was full of dishes from the night before. She closed it again and stacked the things on the draining board.

It was eight o'clock and, despite the open windows, already warm in the kitchen. She didn't know how people managed in hot countries; didn't think she'd survive five minutes.

On Sunday mornings Anne-Marie brought them breakfast in bed. There were no signs that she was stirring so Lorna, after listening outside her door for a few moments, opened it. Her room was the smallest in the house but pleasant. The blue and white wallpaper matched the curtains and the bedspread. The carpet was scarlet. The au-pair girls liked it.

Because of the heat Anne-Marie had removed her blankets which she had folded neatly on the chair. She slept on her stomach. The ink-black hair with which she could do so many things lay over the sheet like a jet curtain. She was dead to the world and Lorna knew it would take more than calling to wake her.

"Anne-Marie! Anne-Marie! Eight o'clock, Anne-Marie!" She sighed and pulled back the curtains. There was no reaction. On the dressing table were Christian Dior nail varnish and expensive face creams. On the bedside table the latest in Swiss travelling clocks and transistor radio in maroon leather.

She shook the shoulder tanned from days of lying in the sun. "Anne-Marie!"

She began to grow angry with the girl, as if she were doing it deliberately to annoy. She shook her rather more roughly. "Anne-Marie!"

"Eight o'clock, Anne-Marie."

A slim arm reached for the clock.

"I was sleeping," Anne-Marie said.

"You were. You're nearly as difficult to wake as Camilla. It's Sunday. Will you bring breakfast? There are people for drinks and lunch. Camilla's coming down."

In their own room Derek was stirring. He lay naked on top of the bed, running to fat round the middle.

"What time is it?" he asked.

"Eight o'clock. I've already made a cake."

Two

At eleven o'clock Lorna, in blue jeans, was hoovering the living-room while in the kitchen Anne-Marie, still in her house-coat, dreamily cut radishes into perfect flowers. It had been a mistake to give her salad to prepare. She knew it the minute it was out of her mouth, by which time it was too late. She had been at it since ten o'clock and there were now a dozen radish flowers opening their petals as dreamily as Anne-Marie herself, in a cut-glass bowl.

She was a sweet girl, sweet and kind. She did anything Lorna asked but it took her all day. She seemed to live in a trance from which it was impossible to wake her. Sometimes, especially when she was harrassed as today, Lorna longed for one of the efficient bitches they had had in the past. She didn't like giving house-room to other people's problem daughters at all, feeling that she had enough trouble with her own, but now that Camilla was away it meant that without someone in the house she couldn't go out in the evening with Derek or away for the weekend because of Joey, whom Anne-Marie adored.

She noticed him now at the door of the living-room in his striped pyjamas. He was mouthing at her. She switched off the Hoover.

"...steel wool."

"Under the sink."

"That's got soap in. It's for the fish."

"You're not going to start with the fish this morning," she said unreasonably.

"There's green on the glass. I think they're having too much light. It'll come off with steel wool."

"Have you had your breakfast?"

"No."

"There're people coming."

"Who?"

"Aunty Irene and Uncle Dick…"

"He can look at my thumb."

"What's the matter with your thumb?"

"I told you. I banged it in woodwork. It's swollen."

"Show me."

He came to her holding up his thumb, which was inflamed.

"I'll bathe it in hot water."

He snatched it away. "I can do it."

"You do it then." She kissed the top of his head, which smelled of warm boys. "And some friends who are staying with them, and the Pearsons…"

"I don't like the Pearsons."

"They are neighbours and we owe them…"

"Who else?"

"Camilla will be here for lunch with two of her friends, we'll have it in the garden, and Grandma for tea…"

"You'll want the fish to be clean for Grandma."

"Go and have your breakfast."

"I need some steel wool. Without soap. Just a tiny bit will do. And have you seen my syphon tube?"

"On the shelf with your rugby shirt last time I saw it. Have your breakfast and I'll have a look for some steel wool. There may be a bit in the utility room that Daddy had for the rust on the car."

"What time's Cam coming?"

"I don't know. Lunchtime. You'd better put her records back."

She put away the Hoover. Her face was beaded with sweat and her shirt sticking to her back. She made stuffed eggs, a dip with boursin and garlic and chives and aromat, and washed celery and carrots and cut them into strips. She took the pirog filled with mincemeat from the freezer and made a potato salad.

Anne-Marie in her yellow sprigged housegown was on her twenty-fourth radish.

"I think we can take some things on to the terrace when you've finished that," Lorna said pointedly.

"Yes, of course. I quickly have my *douche* and wash my hair and dress myself."

Lorna sighed, knowing that that was her for the rest of the morning, and wondered why she bothered. There was no denying she was good-hearted. When Lorna had had flu and was dying for drinks and someone to answer the door, Anne-Marie went out for two hours and came back with three perfect apricot roses on the longest of stems which she had arranged in a vase by her bed.

The chocolate cake, an uninspiring slab, stood waiting to be filled and iced. Sometimes she saw herself as a kind of magician. Nauseating parcels of meat and poultry arriving from the butcher's, spewing forth bones and giblets, to be transformed within a few hours into parsley-strewn daubes and elegant blanquettes. She told herself that it was better than painting. At least you didn't have to hang your mistakes on the wall for all to see.

She looked at the chocolate cake, remembered she needed cotton which was upstairs in her sewing-basket and opened her mouth to ask Anne-Marie, then shut it again thinking it would take half an hour, and called Joey.

There was a wail from the hall and she went running. Joey was retching and there was a dark puddle on the carpet. The fish were swimming back and forth in agitated confusion in the tank.

"What is it?"

"You made me swallow it!" He held up the syphon tube. "I was getting the sediment out."

She looked at the puddle. "Joey, please!"

"You shouldn't have called me. You made me jerk and it's upset the guppies." He coughed tank water up into the bucket he had on the floor.

"Do you have to suck it?"

"To get it started. I'll have to start again now."

"Have you had your breakfast?"

He had his mouth round the rubber tube.

Upstairs in the bedroom the door to the bathroom was open. Derek, in shorts, the hairs on his chest white with talcum powder, had his mouth round one end of the green garden hosepipe, the other end of which was in the bath. She wondered if all the men in her house had gone mad. She did not speak to him and wondered which was more disgusting, fish-tank water or dirty bath-water.

It was Irene who had taught her the trick with the cotton. It was hard enough to slice a small cake into two latitudinally, let alone the jumbo-sized chocolate one which would have been impossible.

She cut a length of cotton longer than the perimeter of the cake, then held it round the cake in the centre of its thickness, crossing over the two ends in front of her. Holding her breath she pulled the two ends firmly, crossing them over. The cotton cut softly into the sponge, slicing it neatly in two. She lifted the top half off and set about making the filling and topping.

She was absorbed, smoothing away with a palette knife and listening to a Brahms concerto on the radio, and didn't hear Derek come in.

When she looked up he was standing, hands in the pockets of his shorts, staring at the garden.

"I've watered the roses. I hope they like Imperial Leather. I think they look better already. Wish I could do something about that lawn. Just look at it."

17

He really suffered for the parchedness of it, the brown, arid patches.

"It'll take a month of rain to put that right. If it ever gets right."

He watched her icing the cake. "Why don't you come outside?"

"The cake," she said, "lunch…"

"Too hot to eat much. It's already seventy in the shade…"

She put down the palette knife and stared at him, wondering if he really thought she was in the kitchen for preference and whether to point out that if people were invited for drinks you had to give them something and that after they'd gone he'd look at his watch within ten minutes for certain and say how about a spot of lunch, what have we got, as if it appeared by magic, besides which Cam and her friends…

"…drink's more the order of the day." He opened the cupboard and held a bottle to the light. "We're a bit low on vodka. What do you think? Got to keep Dick tanked up."

"If you didn't give him so much he wouldn't drink so much. Then Irene wouldn't have to keep shouting at him."

"When did Irene not shout at him? If she stopped he'd probably collapse into the silence. I thought she'd burst a blood vessel last night when she yelled at him for opening up that treble."

"Poor Dick. He wasn't to know I was nursing 'zlotys'."

"Poor Dick, I think, will not be allowed to forget it in a hurry."

He stood the bottle on the tray she had put ready for the cake. She moved it mechanically.

"Ice," he said. "We'll need buckets of it."

She watched him get the ice with neat, precise movements. He was a neat, precise man. He kept his cupboards and his life in apple-pie order. His ties were folded in neat, precise rolls, points to the front, ranged like soldiers on the shelf. There were shoe-trees in his polished shoes; shoe-trees even in his slippers.

On his desk at the office there was never more to be seen than her photograph in its silver frame, a desk diary open at the correct page, a virgin memo-pad, and half a dozen perfectly sharpened pencils. If there was a stain on his clothes it upset him. There were, as far as she knew, no stains on his life. If there had been he would get the Thawpit and a pad and, using circular movements, rub them out. He was a kind man. Kind and fair. The children knew where they were with him. If they transgressed they had to pay the penalty. If they pleased him they were rewarded. The system applied to herself, too, although the rewards and the punishments were more subtle; an extra show of affection, a studied withdrawal. She could mark her behaviour on the chart of his responses. It had not always been so. In the early days of their marriage, when he'd been struggling as a newly qualified architect, she could do no wrong.

Starry-eyed, he had taken her to Blenheim Palace, Bath, Greenwich, King's College Chapel, the cathedral at Hereford. He had shown her vaults and ceilings, columns and plinths, and she had learned to distinguish between Greek and Gothic, Elizabethan and Jacobean, classical and baroque.

Somewhere, snuffed by the economic climate of Britain, the spark had gone out. He had built sterile office blocks of concrete and glass, town houses like luxury pig-pens, factories in the cheapest finishes. He liked his work and he liked his home and he kept them in separate compartments as he did his socks and handkerchiefs. He brought home no papers nor talked very much about what he was doing. At home he was absorbed by his garden, his golf, and his weekend drinks with the neighbours. They did not go out much. When Derek came home at night, if they weren't playing Scrabble he liked to put his feet up and watch television. Once a week, to get her out of the kitchen, they had dinner, usually with Irene and Dick, in one of the restaurants which had sprung up in the vicinity and which were occasionally written up in *Harper's and Queen*. The menus were adventurous and the prices high. Derek didn't mind. He had never been mean. They had one long holiday a year, in spring or autumn, and three or four weekends in the Cotswolds, log fires and home-made bread, the Lake District, or Wales. Usually they went with another couple because of the golf. Occasionally on a Sunday night Lorna went to a concert with Irene, leaving the 'boys' with devilled chicken legs or smoked salmon sandwiches to play each other at Scrabble or gin-rummy.

"We're getting low on tonics," Derek said, squatting in front of the fridge. "Will you get some?"

Lorna wrote 'Tonics' on the memory-board. "Slimline?"

"Half and half. Might as well have some bitter lemons while we're at it."

She added 'Bit. lem.' And wondered if Derek realized that you couldn't park your car in the High Street, it was all double yellows, and that tonics and bitter lemons were heavy and had to be lugged and that it was easy to say and difficult to do.

The cake was now transformed from a heap of ingredients to an appetizing entity. Wiping her forehead she thought, silly really, chocolate in this weather, and perhaps Derek was right, would anyone want cake anyway? Cold drinks and ice-cream were more likely. She had plenty in the freezer, blackcurrant, and blackberry, and grape and walnut, made in her sorbetière.

Derek was carrying glasses and bottle out to the terrace. She picked up her radio and went upstairs.

In the bathroom she stripped and stepped into the Sahara beige shower cubicle. There was no messing about with water that was too hot or too cold or that dribbled or drowned you in a deluge. Being married to an architect had its compensations. Everything in the house worked or was repaired as soon as it was necessary. They had no missing tiles or clogged gutters. The rooms were decorated in rotation and the outside of the house painted every two years. The house was functional, decorated in 'good' colours, filled with furniture from Heals'. Built-in units from Scandinavia and shaggy carpets in autumn colours. She had wanted blue and rose and antique bits and chintz, such as she had been brought up with in Dorset, but Derek had built the house and the inside had to be as perfect as the outside, and she had given up the struggle quite early on, trying to think only of the cupboards which sprang open at a touch and the bed which raised its head at the press of a button, and not of the glass and chrome which mirrored the sterility of the thing in their shining faces.

The concerto ended and the clapping of the audience mingled with the rushing of the shower water. She turned off the thermostatically controlled tap. 'With that performance of the Piano Concerto in D Minor, Opus Number Fifteen, by Brahams, we end this concert...' She switched it off, not wanting to listen to the panel game which she knew came next. The radio was her lifeline. She listened to the music and the talks and the afternoon plays, to *Woman's Hour* with 'Suma Gregor' or 'Junox More'. At times, too lazy to switch off, she heard *Listen With Mother* and thought what an insult it was to the two-year-olds and how would they ever learn to speak correctly when the BBC told them 'Goodbye till termorrow'.

Cool again, for five minutes, she put on a cotton skirt, shirt and sandals, feeling the sensuous summer pleasure of bare legs and no bra. Her figure wasn't bad for her age. Her age. Her age. The roaring forties. One would think it was some sort of crime to be heading for the end of them. Good for a laugh anyway.

The terrace looked like a picture from *Homes and Gardens*. Derek had arranged the table and the chairs, white with brown and gold cushions, and the umbrella, gold with a white bobble fringe, and one long chair and the bamboo drinks trolley and the tiny bamboo tables. She brought out the dip and some nuts and olives and pickled cucumbers and the stuffed eggs flavoured with curry. Normally at this time of the year the garden was a picture. Now it looked sad, cracked, craving for water. The heat was like warm flannels. It was hard to believe this was England.

" 'Morning all!" Dick in pale blue shorts and shirt and pale blue ankle socks appeared round the side of the house. Irene, also in shorts and looking, Lorna thought, faintly ridiculous, followed behind. In their wake came a tall, emaciated-looking couple, he in a tweed sports jacket and tie – Lorna wondered how he could bear it – and she in a long cotton skirt that looked as if she had made it herself and cheesecloth blouse. Jewellery, hand-made from ethnic places, was at her throat and her fingers.

"Sebastian and Lola," Dick said, presenting his friends. "Lorna and Derek."

Lorna knew, because Irene had told her, that Sebastian was an anaesthetist from Guildford and had been at medical school with Dick, and that Lola taught English for the Open University. They shook hands. Sebastian's hand was limp and dry, his face was limp and dry, too, a lock of pale hair falling over his forehead. His approving smile was as unexpected as it was charming, beautiful white teeth illuminating an intelligent oval face. He likes curvy blondes, Lorna thought, and wondered why he had married his thin, pale stick of a wife.

Dick rubbed his hands. His eyes were on the vodka.

"Smirnoff! That wouldn't be bad on a treble."

"Too many letters," Derek said. "Ladies first anyway. Lola?"

She smiled at Derek. "Whisky?"

Lorna guessed she would take it neat.

"Ginger ale?"

"No; nothing."

"Usual for you, Irene?" Derek asked, reaching for the jug of tomato juice. She had trouble with her bladder which was irritated by alcohol.

He took care with it, adding Worcestershire sauce and celery salt and ice and lemon.

"Gin and tonic?"

"Please," Lorna said.

There was a wasp on the curried eggs. She brushed it away and handed them round. Sebastian took one, and Dick.

"You're supposed to be dieting," Irene said.

"Tomorrow."

Derek held up a bottle. "Punt e Mes," he said for the benefit of Sebastian and Lola. "My favourite drink. There's a story in how its got its name."

Lorna closed her eyes.

"Turin 1786. Antonio Carpano opened a bar next to the Stock Exchange. At that time…"

Sebastian and Lola were listening attentively.

"…one ordered one's bitter by *points*. Well, one day prices on the Borsa went up one and a half points. A broker dashed in from next door, absent-mindedly ordered a 'Punt e Mes' – a point and a half, in Piedmontese dialect, of course…"

She noticed that both Irene and Dick were looking as interested as if it was the first time they had heard the story.

"…The drink that resulted became so popular that Carpano's stuck to the name and have been producing Punt e Mes ever since," Derek unscrewed the cap and, holding up his glass, poured some out. "In the summer I like it long…"

With a slice of orange, Lorna said to herself.

"…with a slice of orange."

"Cheers. Why don't we sit down?"

There was a shuffling of chairs. Lorna handed the dip, brushing the wasps away.

"Little buggers," Dick said, putting his feet up on the *chaise longue* and trying to adjust the back to his satisfaction.

"That one wasn't for you, Dick," Irene said.

"Why not?" Dick said. "Talking of chairs, have you heard the one about the woman who went to the dentist? She said, 'I'd rather have a baby any day than have a tooth filled.' 'Well, hurry up and decide,' the dentist said, 'Because I'll have to alter the position of the chair.' "

"Dick!" Irene said.

23

"I wish I could remember jokes," Sebastian said. "There's a chap at the hospital who tells them non-stop while he's operating and I can never retaliate."

"Don't put your feet on it, Dick," Irene said.

"Why not? That's what it's for."

"Not shoes."

"It's all right," Lorna said. She always felt sorry for Dick. She handed him a pickled cucumber.

The doorbell rang.

"That'll be the Pearsons." Derek got up. "Where's Anne-Marie?"

"Washing her hair."

"I'll go."

"Our neighbours," Lorna said by way of explanation to Sebastian and Lola.

Derek led the Pearsons out through the sliding windows, which were opened right back so that the terrace became an extension of the house.

Pauline was wearing a pink silk suit and pearls, for all the world as if she were a memsahib and this was India. Her pink leather strapped sandals matched. She was wearing tights, or stockings probably. Lorna thought, my God, how can she in this weather? Hugh was dressed correctly too, in blazer and white flannels, open-necked white shirt with a spotted silk scarf at his neck.

"Poor bloody lawn," Hugh said, looking at it. "Never had such a lazy summer. All right for you boys, play golf, the only exercise I had was walking up and down behind the mower."

"You don't know Sebastian and Lola," Derek said. "Dr and Mrs Mackenzie, Colonel and Mrs Pearson. What will you have, Pauline?"

"Gin, please," Pauline said. Looking at her, Lorna thought that it was probably not the first of the day.

There were a dozen wasps over the table.

"What about a jam jar?" Lola suggested.

Lorna fetched one with apricot jam in the bottom. She put it on the low wall well away from where they were sitting.

The wasps stayed with the dip and the curried eggs.

"Give them a curried egg," Dick said.

"At a shilling each!" Pauline looked shocked.

"Don't give your age away, love," Dick said. "By the way, have you heard the one about the man who was bothered by inflation? He came home one day and said to his wife, 'If only you would learn to cook, darling, we could get rid of the housekeeper.' 'You're absolutely right,' she said, 'and if only you would learn to make love we could sack the chauffeur.' Any more vodka?"

"Dick!" Irene said.

"Yes, my sweet?" He gave his glass to Derek.

"Not too much," Irene said.

"You live in Guildford?" Derek said to Sebastian.

"Outside," Irene said. "Right in the heart of the country."

Derek waved an arm. "Blast these wasps. I used to have a client out there. Shamley Green."

"Shamley Green's not far from us."

"I used to go down quite often at one time," Derek said. "The A3 to Guildford, the A281 to Bramley, left at the mini-roundabout, right at Wonersh…"

"We don't usually bother with Guildford. We turn off to Merrow and through Farley Green. Lousy roads but a prettier route."

"That wouldn't suit these two." Irene waved at Dick and Derek. "Shortest distance between two points is their motto. You'd think their lives depended on it."

"Incidentally," Hugh Pearson said, "I've got a new little trick for the mornings. Come off the North Circular at Neasden, down Dudden Hill Road to Willesden High Road, turn right into Brondesbury Park and out into the Edgware Road through Carlton Vale. Cross the Edgware Road, wriggle round through St

John's Wood and Camden Town, King's Cross and Grays Inn Road, and you're laughing!"

Lorna listened with one ear, wondering what men always found so fascinating in routes and times as if five minutes off made them morally superior. A wasp hovered over Derek's left ear. He brushed it away.

Anne-Marie, her white shirred-top sundress showing off her brown shoulders, came out with newly washed hair on to the terrace. It hung like rich, dark silk. Hugh forgot the short cut to the office and leaped to attention. Sebastian and Dick stood up.

Dick put an arm round her shoulders. "Give Uncle Dick a kiss!"

"Dick!" Irene said.

Anne-Marie wrinkled her nose and kissed his cheek.

"When are you coming to look after us? We'd treat you much better than these two. We'd give you something to eat." He put a hand round her tiny waist. "Look at you!"

Lorna thought of the pounds of cheese and tubs of yoghurt and Blue Mountain coffee and oranges and apples and best black cherries consumed by Anne-Marie each week.

"She's half starved," Dick said. "And she needs a drink. So do I."

"Dick!" Irene said.

Lorna moved to sit next to Lola.

"It must be nice to live in the country." She could see her in a cottage garden surrounded by children who were called Tristan and William and Lucy. "Do you have a family?"

Lola shook her head.

"Lola's an authority on Victorian poetry," Irene said quickly, as if to compensate for her lack of family.

"I used to love poetry," Lorna said. These days there was no time. One was too busy just living. "We did the Victorians for School Certificate. William Morris..."

"One up to you," Irene said. "I used to think of him as wallpaper. Lola's disgusted with me, but then she gave me up as a bad job years ago."

"You must admit it's a pity" – Lola was smiling – "to be architect, poet, painter, house decorator, weaver, dyer, printer, tradesman, politician, stump orator and militant Socialist, and only remembered for one's wallpaper."

"It's very *nice* wallpaper," Irene said. "We've got it in the downstairs loo."

Joey came out. He was wearing swimming trunks.

"Uncle Dick, will you have a look at my thumb?"

"We can't have any children," Lola said, watching him. "I've got funny tubes."

"Come and see me in my surgery and I'll lance it for you," Dick said, looking at the thumb.

"I think it's getting better." Joey snatched it away hurriedly. He took a curried egg in one hand and some dip on a piece of celery in the other.

"Hand them round," Lorna said.

"I can't. The wasps will chase me."

"Mrs Mackenzie teaches English, Joey."

"I got C for English. Multiple choice."

"What's your favourite subject?" Lola said.

"Haven't got one."

"Nothing you like?"

"Chess. And tropical fish. Do you want to see my Gouramis? I've got two females and a male. You can tell because the female has yellow fins and the male red. They're the thick-lipped ones. I had a Dwarf Gourami but it died. That was mauve."

"I'd like to."

The doorbell rang. Lorna looked at Anne-Marie. She was discussing alpine flowers with Sebastian, who leaned over her like a bent willow.

"I'll go," Lorna said. "It'll be Cam."

Three

She got a shock every time Cam came down. She should be used to it, she knew, but was not. Cam stood on the polished step, thin, dark rings under her eyes, pale face almost obliterated by a mass of unkempt hair. Her jeans were frayed and not very clean, her nipples protruded through her brown vest top.

"Hi!"

"Hallo, darling," Lorna said.

"This is Armand."

Lorna thought at once of Robert Taylor but her mind boggled at Cam and Greta Garbo. He was no taller than Cam and slight as a girl with long straight hair to below his shoulders. It looked shining and clean and his shirt was clean too.

"Hi!"

"Hallo, Armand."

"Hi," Blake said. She was Cam's *éminence grise*. A sad, Modigliani girl of few words and many cigarettes. She seemed to live in a dream world of her own, moving like a zombie, speaking, when she did, so softly it was hard to catch what she said. She made Lorna feel uncomfortable, but she had no parents so Cam often brought her home.

There was a smell of sweat. It was a hot day and the drive had been long.

"We're in the garden," she said. "Irene and Dick are here, and the Pearsons."

They walked straight through to the garden. How sure they were of themselves, Cam's generation. They did not need the constant reassurance of mirrors, cloakroom, or handbag. They wore no make-up and there seemed not to be paraphernalia such as sunglasses and diaries and handkerchiefs and keys and other small luggage to be carried about the person. Camilla didn't even wear a watch although they'd given her enough of them over the years. As long as she knew what day it was, she said, that was enough. Lorna didn't know how she managed to turn up at lectures on time, if she bothered to turn up at all. It all seemed so casual, undisciplined, paid for, too, by the taxpayers. How were they going to get the world out of the ghastly mess her lot had got it into when they didn't even know what time it was?

On the terrace only the Pearsons looked askance. They had one son who was an accountant. There had been no freaking out for three years in a sea of paper cups beneath the cumulus of stale smoke. She felt Pauline look the young people up and down then retract herself a little, tightening her thighs and drawing the pink sandals in beneath her chair.

Armand squatted down and stroked Cassius tenderly.

"You like dogs?"

It was a superfluous question. The rapport was tangible.

"What are you going to drink? Derek asked.

Cam said, "I'll get some beer."

Lorna followed her into the kitchen.

"Everything all right, darling?"

She opened the fridge. "Why not?"

"Who's Armand? Anyone special?"

Camilla laughed. "You never give up. He had his sister's car. Gave us a lift. The least I could do was lunch. Any shandy?"

"In the larder. It'll be warm." She didn't suppose they chilled the drinks on campus.

"Anything been happening?" Cam said.

Lorna wondered when she had last had a bath.

29

"Daddy was stung by a wasp. There's a plague of them. Joey did appallingly badly in his exams. We're going to speak to his headmaster. Life goes on."

"What is for lunch?"

"Pirog and salads; in the garden. We've been eating in the garden all the time. Grandma's coming for tea. Are you going to clean yourself up a bit?"

"I'm clean."

"I expect you are. You just don't look it."

"Same old record. I don't know why you worry about me."

"You never will until you have children of your own." Motherhood was like Freemasonry, she thought. You didn't know what went on until you joined.

"I'm not going to have any children."

"Why?"

"What's the point?"

Lorna tried to think. "I don't know. If you have to ask that perhaps you shouldn't bother."

"I've no intention of bothering. It's a trap. Like marriage."

Lorna ignored the bait. "You're terribly thin, Cam. Are you eating?"

Cam clutched the beer cans in one arm and put the other round her. "Look, Mother, get it all off your chest in one go then we can relax. I know I'm skinny, grubby, scruffy, etcetera, etcetera, but give me a few days here and I'll probably be walking around in a clean cotton dress like Looby-Lou, beautifully scrubbed with my hair in bunches. Where are the beer mugs?" She noticed the chocolate cake. "You made a chocolate cake!"

"Yes."

"For me?"

"Yes."

"And I'm so beastly. I don't mean to be."

"It's all right."

She was ambivalent about Cam's homecomings. With the fashion for late, if ever, marriages, one was left with disinterested twenty-year-olds sharing one's home. They were no longer children who could be told what to do, nor house-guests who might reasonably be expected not to bring their dirty laundry and to make some attempt to fit in with the family. They turned up whenever they happened to feel like it, together with 'meaningful relationships' or friends who were passing through 'identity crises' or who couldn't touch anything with egg in it and had to have special pillows. Lorna's generation seemed to have managed to grow up and leave home quite quickly, claimed generally by somebody else. Today the sons and daughters seemed to be around, sometimes for years, like lost property. It was not a natural situation. It did not work.

They went into the garden. Cam told Sebastian that she was going to Israel with Blake. They were going to work on a kibbutz, at the end of the week. By then the pleasure of having Cam at home would have worn off. Lorna would have grown weary of the anti-social hours, and picking up after them. A week was enough.

Armand sat cross-legged on the ground at Lola's feet. Blake sat on the low wall of the terrace, her beer mug in her hand, smoking and talking to no one. The wasps had found the jam-jar.

"Did I tell you we were changing to gas?" Irene said. "And we're having a battery generator in case there's another strike this winter."

"When hasn't there been?" Dick said. "Bloody unions are running the country."

"There's only one answer to it," Hugh said, getting his fist ready to bang the table.

Lorna hoped he wasn't going to smash any glasses.

"Send the army in!" Crash.

Anne-Marie jumped.

"It worked in 1926. That's all they understand…"

31

Lorna could see he was working himself up into, 'What we need in this country is discipline, run it like we ran the army. First sign of disloyalty, first sign, mind you, even at the top and' – another bang on the table – 'out!'

It was too hot for a confrontation and Cam and Blake were bound to explode and say something tactless and Hugh would get upset and sound off again and 'young people, what they needed was discipline, a spell in the army…'

The sun had cut a wedge across Irene's shoulder.

"Can you move the umbrella, darling?" Lorna said, "Irene's burning."

"No," Irene said. "Dick will do it. Dick, the umbrella."

Derek shifted the heavy umbrella stand. "How's that?"

"Now Pauline's in the sun."

She put a hand to her blonde waves and Lorna knew she was worried about her tint.

By the time they'd settled the umbrella to everyone's satisfaction Hugh had forgotten what he had been going to say, and was strolling up the garden with Dick discussing his sciatica to save a visit to the surgery and shaking his head over the scorched earth.

Lorna, hugging her glass, listened and watched. Next weekend they would go to Irene's, the following one to Lois or Estelle. In the winter the drinks were in the living-room. In the summer, outside. The talk, in any one season, was interchangeable, except when some new scandal or fresh wave of gossip overtook Home Farm Close. Sometimes she thought she would scream at the predictability of it all, as if at a play she had seen too many times.

They stood at the far end of the garden for some time, not minding the sun. When they came back Dick picked up the vodka bottle.

"Might as well finish it."

"Dick!"

"It's all right, darling, you can drive."

They lived five houses away.

The last of the curried eggs had a brownish, dried crust.

"It's a bit pathetic," Lorna said, offering it.

"If nobody else…" Dick said, cramming it into his mouth.

"Dick, it's almost lunch-time!" She looked at her watch. "I think we should be making a move…"

"We ought to be off, too," Pauline said. "Hugh?"

"We'll see ourselves out," Irene said, getting up. "Don't move. It's too hot. We'll go round the side."

"We playing tonight, Lorna?" Dick said. "I've got the most superb word."

"I don't know…" Lorna said. "Cam…?" She knew quite well Cam wouldn't need her. "If you like."

"You still playing that game?" Cam said.

"It's all that's left to the old," Dick said. "Scrabble."

"I shall never grow old."

They had lunch outside, trying to keep everything and everyone under the umbrella. She walked in and out a dozen times for Anne-Marie's once, carrying the iced borsch and the pirog.

It wasn't restful. The wasps kept up an attack on the food and it was too hot even under the umbrella.

She cleared away with Anne-Marie, whose movements grew even more languorous after the wine Derek had plied her with.

She was soaked with sweat again by the time the kitchen was tidy, and dragged herself upstairs for her third shower of the day. In the house it was comparatively cool. The fish, in newly clear water, swam back and forth in the lighted tank, unconcerned about the vagaries of the weather. For them there was neither summer nor winter, neither night nor day.

From the bedroom window she looked out on to the garden. On the terrace Derek slept on the *chaise longue*, his mouth slightly open, on a sea of Sunday newspapers. On the lawn, in bikinis, Cam and Blake and Anne-Marie lay supine, as if they had been dropped. Cassius was curled up beneath the shade of the apple tree which never bore apples. By his side Joey played himself at chess.

She took off her clothes and felt the dampness at the back of her neck. She was striped brown and white from the hot afternoons and her bikini. She opened the bathroom door and stopped dead. Facing her, Armand, naked, stared.

Her first thought, almost preceding the shock, was, he's not like a girl at all despite the hair. His body was taut, slim, beautiful.

"I'm sorry," Armand said. "I wanted a shower. Cam said upstairs…"

"Cam has her own bathroom…" too lazy even to show him.

"I didn't know. I'll get my things." He bent to take his jeans and shirt and underpants and sandals from the floor. She realized she was still staring. Then that she was blocking the doorway because he was standing in front of her.

"Sorry." He moved to pass her and she moved too in the same direction, as one did in the street, executing a little dance. Their flesh touched, his cool from the shower, hers hot. Their eyes met. He stopped and dropped his clothes. She went to the window. It would be hours before any of them moved. He was behind her. She turned to him, not knowing why nor caring.

It took no more than five minutes. There was no love. Only lust and the torpid heat of the afternoon. When it was over the bedcover was creased and damp; from her body, sweat; from his, damp, from the shower. There was a small stain where his semen had dripped out of her. He was in the bathroom. When he came out he was dressed and she saw how slim his hips were, the jeans disguising the hardness of his muscles. His hair was tied in a ponytail.

"I'm sorry," he said.

"It was my fault. I'm not sorry. I enjoyed it."

"Yes, but…"

"It doesn't matter. Really."

He squatted by the bed, easily.

34

"Are you sure?"

"Sure."

He looked at her. "It was great."

Great. Words. How one word could make you feel guilty. It suddenly hit her. My God. The sun must have made her crazy. With a friend of Cam's. With anyone. Out of sheer lust on a Sunday afternoon. Like on campus with the curtains drawn. But this was Home Farm Close and she was old enough to be his mother and the curtains were open.

He had gone downstairs. She looked out of the window. The scene was the same as if time had not moved. It scarcely had. Not time. It was an aeon in her life, as if she had made a decision, given an answer to a question she had not formulated. They all slept. It was her piece of the pattern that had altered. She wondered if she would still fit in and if she wanted to. The picture wouldn't be the same with a great, jagged hole.

She spent a long time in the shower, letting the water cascade over her. She decided not to allow herself to think. Just to accept. If acceptance was denial. OK. The feelings were too painful, too complex to examine. He had used Derek's towel. That seemed to be the biggest problem. She stood with it in her hand for some time, then dropped it in the laundry box.

She straightened the bedcover, dabbed at the stain with a damp flannel, it would soon dry in the heat, put on a sun-dress with flat sandals, some cream on her face, and went downstairs.

She hadn't expected him somehow to be sitting in the kitchen. Had thought he would avoid her. Remembered he was not her generation, was not bound by the *mores* imposed by her conditioning.

He was drinking beer and feeding Cassius peanuts that had been left from the morning.

"We don't feed him. Only once a day."

"Sorry."

It was the second time he had apologized. It was an all-embracing word covering illicit sexual relationship and feeding peanuts to the dog. She realized the two things had equal substance in his mind.

"I'll brush him if you like. Where do you keep the brush?"

She understood there was to be no talk of what happened. She was beginning to feel it never had.

"In the utility room."

He looked puzzled.

She pointed to a door off the kitchen. "Where we keep the washing machine and the wellingtons and the flower vases."

He looked surprised that there should be a special room for these things.

"I hate utility rooms!" she said.

She was startled at her own vehemence and thought perhaps it had something to do with the heat of the day. When Derek had built the house he had carried on about the importance of the utility room and how it would take the pressure off the other rooms. She had grown up without a utility room, not feeling its lack. The wellingtons had laid drunkenly on the back porch, there had been no washing machine, and the flower vases were kept in the outside cupboard next to the outside lavatory. It wasn't only the utility room. It was the whole house. An open prison; architect-designed. There were no locks on the doors, yet where was there to go? Sainsbury's? Cash and Carry? The kitsch little shops selling boutique clothes, or the delicatessen with its pissaladière and aioli bringing Provence to the wastelands of Hertfordshire? The library with a waiting list as long as your arm for Margaret Drabble? The self-conscious art gallery offering sticky oils painted on holiday in the Jura by local artists? After ten o'clock at night you could dance naked in Home Farm Close and no one would ever know. True, geographically, as Derek often pointed out, they were not far from London. He did not take into account the traffic or the sheer fatigue of leaving the car at the station car park (20p or tokens to get out), then taking the train and the smell of Baker Street station and the futility of trying to find a taxi. Added to which she had to be back for Joey and to prepare dinner so that there was virtually no day, and when she did make the effort she invariably flitted from shop to shop in sheer panic at the passing of the hours, achieving nothing except sore feet.

Armand was finishing his beer.

"Are you in Cam's year?"

"I graduated last year. English."

"Where do you live?"

"Cornwall Terrace."

"Regent's Park?"

"In a squat."

She'd always read the riot act to Camilla about squatting.

" 'Property is theft' and all that?"

He nodded.

"You must enjoy Queen Mary's Gardens."

"I'm too busy." He seemed not to notice the sarcasm.

"Doing what?"

"Writing my book."

"You were telling Lola."

"I have a theory. I have put Proust, James, Flaubert, Dickens, into the centrifuge of my mind and have come up with an amalgam. It can't fail."

"I've never heard such conceit." She smiled.

"I've given the matter a great deal of thought. I think about nothing else. What do you think about?"

Lorna looked round the kitchen. "Chocolate cake and Joey and Cam and whether the freezer needs defrosting and what to have for dinner."

"I suppose you would if you're a housewife."

She looked at him. He had not intended to deprecate her role. It was the term that had come into disrepute since the career cult had hit the suburbs. These days the implication was that the woman who stayed at home to look after her family was a kind of lazy half person. You noticed it at social gatherings. The imperceptible switching-off when you admitted to being wife and mother. Irene called herself a 'home economics expert' and had written it in her passport. In the years since Cam was born the whole concept of motherhood and homemaking had been degraded, or at least down-graded. You could admit to typing a man's letters or drafting his will, pulling his tooth or testing his blood samples, but not to washing his socks, cooking his dinner, or smoothing out the rough patches in his life with an experienced and loving hand.

"Where's your real home?" she asked.

"Wales. My father is a miner."

She thought of D H Lawrence; his mother washing his father's back at the end of a long day at the pit. There had been a play on television. She could almost smell the soot.

"It's not like that," Armand said

"Like what?"

"Like you think."

She blushed at his intuition.

"There's no poetry in it; none at all. I shall write my book and get them out. You'll see, it will be a great success."

"I'm sure it will."

"It's pretty grim where we live. They live."

"No utility room?"

"No running water." He tweaked at Cassius' coat. "Come on, old friend. Why Cassius?"

"He had a 'lean and hungry look'. We chose him from the litter." She saw him looking at her. "It hasn't always been chocolate cake and washing cut knees."

"I'd like to read you my novel; some of it."

She felt flattered.

"I think you would understand what I'm trying to say."

"I'd like that." She meant it. There was a sincerity about him. In the middle of the kitchen she felt that she was on a desert island with him, the Poggenpohl receding into the distance.

Noises in the garden, Cam calling, "What time is it?" Derek answering, "Three-thirty, Grandma will soon be here," brought her back to reality. She stood up.

"I'll find the brush for you."

Derek brushed Cassius as he cleaned the interior of the car, methodically, capably. Armand did it with love, speaking to the dog in a soft voice all the time, his own hair mingling with the dog's coat, down on his haunches...She felt desire for him stirring.

"I'll be out in the garden."

Perhaps there was something in her voice. He looked up at her, as if for the first time acknowledging what had happened between them. She didn't want him to apologize.

In the garden nothing had changed since she'd looked from the bedroom window. She gazed at Cam and Blake and Anne-Marie and wondered how they could, out in the direct rays of the sun like that. You'll burn. Come in. She wanted to warn, caution, protect. She turned away and pulled a chair into the shade.

Derek slept again, unaware of her last, adulterous hour. Unaware of her. He'd mind, oh yes. It was not the sort of thing one could confess to. Cam, yes. One accepted it. She was on the pill, ostensibly for dysmenorrhoea. The standards were different.

Her mother would be arriving soon. There would be much ado about chairs in the shade and Joey saying, 'Good afternoon, Grandma,' politely with a peck on the cheek and having to explain for the millionth time how she could let Camilla 'go about like that'.

She loved her mother, or thought she did, or thought she should. She was never absolutely sure. Why did relationships have to be so complicated; especially in the heat? Alone with Cam her role was defined. Her mother's presence shifted the balance. She became at the same time mother and daughter, extending both backwards and forwards, feeling that her life was spreading over generations. It gave her a conviction of being outside time, and awareness of immortality.

Sometimes, listening to her mother, she heard herself, talking to Cam. It brought back painful memories of childhood. When Derek was angry with Cam she suffered for her, with her, as if it were her own father chastising her for some misdemeanour. Her father had died from lung cancer. His last words to her had been, 'Look after your mother.' To her, not Pam – there were only the two of them. It was a cruel legacy and played on her mind, making the guilt, which was never very far away, plague her each time she was short or angry with her mother, which was – although she tried to control the anger – often.

By presence alone her mother had the capacity to turn her back into a small girl trying to please. Had her mother not been coming, tea would have been a 'do-it-yourself' affair. Coke or milk-shakes as they were needed; the chocolate cake cut in the kitchen and brought out in sticky fingers, leaving crumbs for the birds on the lawn. Shortly now she would lay up a tray with a drawn-thread traycloth and the Royal Albert cups and silver teaspoons and pastry forks and diaphanous tea napkins. She'd make the tea in the silver pot, aware of Blake looking at her with amusement as if she were watching a Noël Coward matinée. Her mother, sitting upright on one of the chairs which belonged to the table, which Derek would have put under the umbrella, would put the side of her thumb against the tea-cup, testing to see if it was hot. She would take a sip, then looking reproach-fully at Lorna say: 'I wonder whether I could have a spot more milk, dear.' Lorna, who had been waiting for it and who had in fact added the spot more milk when she was pouring out, would act out her enforced part in what she always called to herself 'the tea charade'; there were others. She would take the cup and with clenched teeth add more milk, not too much, otherwise she would be accused of 'drowning it' and would have to start all over again.

Derek, as far as her mother was concerned, could do no wrong. He represented the son she had never had. He took her to the station and collected her when necessary and had long discussions about the roses. Instead of being pleased when she saw their two heads together, it made her angry. So much made her angry. Particularly lately. She wondered if it was, as Derek suggested lightly but too often for comfort, her age. She was only forty-five and her periods were still regular as clockwork. She had almost been able to tell not only the day of the month but almost the time by them. She didn't have any hot flushes, like Lois, nor sleepless nights like Irene who confessed also to sexual difficulties, needing lubricants. She would have to get a book out of the library on the subject. She wasn't at all sure that it was that which was bothering her lately anyway. It was more a kind of general dissatisfaction, as if life were passing her by. It had been OK at first, for a long while, marrying Derek; the children; she had felt very physical about it all. Sex and birth and breast-feeding and shovelling in groats and cleaning extremities and cuddling up to read stories about cats or steam engines. Camilla was gone now, however – seven-eighths at any rate – Joey hardly needed her, having enough to occupy him with his chess and fish and football and friends. He was a sociable little fellow, well adjusted like his father, not full of dark moods like herself and Cam.

The heat was impossible, even under the umbrella. She moved her legs, which were sticking together. An image of Armand came into her mind, lean, like a colt, muscles rippling like a Leonardo drawing; funny how the long hair was not synonymous with femininity. Derek had once been virile like that, coming in a moment. Now he took his time over it. For the first time she began to feel ashamed, the familiar guilt, that she had made a fool of herself, of Cam. How could she? Must have been mad. The heat. It affected everyone.

"Lorna." Derek was shaking her. She must have dropped off. "Lorna. Mother's here."

She struggled to get off the chair, to wake herself up.
"Don't get up, dear," her mother said.
She knew that there'd be murders if she didn't.

Four

Thinking about it the next day she had to laugh, although it wasn't really terribly funny.

The worst moment had been when they were going to bed, totally exhausted, or so she'd thought, sapped by the heat.

Derek had gone into the bathroom. After a few moments there was a yell. "Where's my towel?"

She had intended to replace it. My lover had a shower.

"Use mine."

"It was here this morning." He worried at everything.

"I put it in the wash."

"It was clean."

And now it's soiled. Like your wife.

He liked a big towel, hers was small. He came in wearing it round his middle. His belly flopped over it. She thought of Armand.

"She probably used it to dry the bath," Derek said, annoyed.

"Who?"

"Anne-Marie."

"If you think she cleans the bath on a Sunday. The most she could run to this morning was twelve radishes."

"You're always on at her."

"So would you be if... It doesn't matter." It didn't.

"I think she's rather sweet."

It was useless arguing. She knew Derek had a soft spot for her, and in Anne-Marie's eyes he could do no wrong.

To her horror he wanted to sleep with her. It was the heat. She was conscious of his weight, the sheer bulk of him, and thought of Armand's firm, round buttocks.

"Good, wasn't it?" he said, satisfied.

"Very."

You could lie to men. She wondered why they were so simple about such things. Vanity, perhaps. If you told them they pleased you you could have anything. She had learned that long ago. It was a pyrrhic victory.

His hand was on her shoulder. "Nice having Cam home."

"Mm."

"Does she have to look like that?"

Lorna lay still, tense.

"Why don't you talk to her?"

"She's not a child."

"Still…"

He liked everything to be neat, tidy. It upset the order of things to have Cam and her trail. After a few days of her the sparks would fly. She would side with Cam, identifying.

"That fellow gone home?"

"Armand? Didn't he say goodbye?"

"He was out with Cassius when I came up. Looks like a girl…"

Doesn't feel like one.

"…Felt like getting a pair of scissors…"

It had lain, sweet smelling, over her face.

"You asleep?"

"Mm!"

He kissed her. "Good night, my love."

Waking every morning was like waking on holiday. The sun streamed through the open window on to their bodies covered only by the sheet beneath which they had fallen asleep.

She got out of bed to cook breakfast, knocking at Joey's door as she went by. He came down without washing. She sent him back.

"Grandma's going to buy me a Swordtail. She gave me the money. I'll get it after school."

"Don't be late."

"I will be if I'm buying my Swordtail."

"Of course." Mother jargon. Don't be late. Take care. Mind how you cross the road. Put your cardigan on. Take off your wet socks. Don't bold your food. Wash behind your ears. Manifestations of one's own anxiety.

Derek read *The Times* while he ate. He saved the *Guardian* for the train.

"What are you going to do today, dear?" He was reading the leader.

"Rob the bank."

"You'd better put some air in your front off-side tyre. It looked a bit flat to me. Pass the marmalade." He reached out his hand for it, not looking.

Joey was stuck in his comic.

"And you might take the shears to be sharpened."

"The sound's gone on the television," Joey said. "It's the Bionic man tonight."

"I'll ring them. I've got to get the waste-grinder people as well. There's something down there."

Derek looked out of the window at the thirsty garden. "What's wrong with Cassius?"

He stood in the middle of the lawn, coughing.

"Grandma fed him chocolate cake," Joey said.

Armand had given him peanuts. She wondered if she would see him again.

She kissed Derek goodbye, wandering out to the garage with him, in her dressing-gown. It was already warm. He carried his tie and jacket over his arm.

"Tell Joey to hurry." He gave him a lift to the station. He was never ready.

"Joey!"

"Coming."

Anne-Marie was turning the sleeves of his mauve-and-black striped blazer the right way round. Lorna noticed there was a button missing.

"Don't keep Daddy waiting. I don't know why you can't be ready."

"I'm ready. Hold on a sec. I've forgotten Grandma's money." He went upstairs three at a time.

Derek hooted.

She hovered at the door, feeling for them both.

He came down like a herd of elephant.

" 'Bye, Mum!"

"Take care."

She watched them go. Her men. The father mirrored in the son. There was a kind of pride. What did she want? She didn't know. Only that she hadn't got it.

The house was quiet. Peaceful, not empty. Cam and Blake were asleep upstairs. The disturbed *Times*, the crusts from Joey's toast – she was always telling him – told that they had been and gone. Anne-Marie was reading her letter. She got them almost every day, minute black writing almost covering the flimsy paper.

"Boyfriend?"

She nodded. He lived in the same village. She had known him since childhood. They were going to get married. Lorna wished it was as simple with Cam.

Blake glided into the kitchen. A cigarette hung from her lips. She groped for the kettle. Her name was B Lake. Lorna had never discovered what the 'B' stood for.

There was no 'Good morning'.

"Good morning!" Lorna said brightly, realizing that she sounded like a gym mistress. She thought she detected a grunt in reply.

"Cam still sleeping?"

"Mm." She coughed into the coffee jar. Her fingers were stained yellow. She didn't know why she gave her houseroom. Cam said she was terribly clever. Talking didn't seem to be one of her best subjects.

"Monday." Lorna said to no one in particular. "Washing day."

"In Berne it is raining," Anne-Marie said without looking up from her letter.

"Someone I know just came back from Juan-les-Pins and it was raining there," Lorna said to no one in particular. Anne-Marie stayed with her letter. She got the impression that Blake was not frightfully concerned about weather conditions on the Côte d'Azur.

The milk was still on the back step.

"You should take it in immediately in this heat," she said to Anne-Marie. "It goes off."

There was no response.

She wrote 'Shears' and the name of the television rental company and 'waste-grinder' on the message pad they kept by the telephone, then added 'library' – she wanted to look for a book on the menopause – 'tonics' and 'bitter lems'.

"Can you get me some ciggies?" Blake said.

"You ought to stop." She felt it her duty. *In loco parentis*. "It's five and a half minutes off your life each time you smoke a cigarette."

Blake shrugged. She had already tried suicide twice. On one occasion Cam found her in the bathroom and been instrumental in getting her washed out quickly. Inspired by her own altruism she had joined Samaritans and Night Line. It hadn't lasted.

"Players Number Six." There seemed no money forthcoming.

"It's against my principles."

Upstairs she emptied the washing boxes in her bathroom and in Joey's. She looked at the unappetizing pile on the floor in the corridor. It was like the butcher's meat, waiting to be processed. She took it down to the utility room to sort it. Shirts, Derek had been wearing two a day, handkerchiefs, pants, briefs, cotton dresses, Joey's socks rolled into balls as he had taken them off. Her grandmother had had a copper and a board against which the clothes were rubbed by hand. Afterwards they were mangled. She didn't suppose Joey would know what a mangle was.

She sorted her load carefully. Her grandmother with her copper had not had the worries of selecting the correct cycle and in careless, unthinking moments seen her entire washing shaded blue (Joey's games shorts) or socks reduced to Lilliputian size.

Cassius walked over the sorted humps of washing to see if she was going to take him for a walk. She shooed him away. She poured out soap powder and water softener and set the machine off. Through the porthole she watched for a moment as Derek's blue and white striped shirt assumed a life of its own, dancing first this way, then that. She could understand why people sat for hours in launderettes watching their own programmes as if it was 'Kojak' or 'Dad's Army'.

Anne-Marie was folding her letter. She put it in the envelope and stuck it behind the tea-caddy. Another of the words that had fallen into desuetude.

"Bernard is coming," Anne-Marie said.

"That's nice." She didn't think it was nice at all, knowing that it would mean the disappearance of Anne-Marie for as long as Bernard was in England.

"You must ask him for dinner."

"Thank you. Also my mother and my father and my grandmother."

"All coming?"

"Yes. With the car."

"Well, let me know the date."

Often she thought they were more trouble than they were worth, the au pair girls. She got them through an agency who vetted the families they were to go to as thoroughly as they did the girls, and made it abundantly clear that you were privileged to have one of their young ladies at all.

It started with a photograph, two by two, from which Ingrid or Caterine or Chantal stared unequivocally. There were few clues although Derek, who prided himself on the understanding of human nature of which he had very little, said he could always tell. Long hair or short; eye make-up or as God had given them; cross round the neck; smiling or serious. The questionnaire they filled in was not much help. Cooking: a little. From experience Lorna knew this applied only to fondue. English: a little. Have you a stamp? I must go to school. Experience: babysitting with nieces and nephews. Father's occupation: Représentant. They were always 'représentants' or civil servants. She imagined Switzerland overflowing with them. Mrs Steiger from the agency marked the questionnaires with one star or two or three according to her own assessment of the applicant. The more stars the better. Lorna had learned to disregard them. She had had three stars who made toast like cardboard and eggs like bullets, and one stars who whipped up soufflés and sewed like dreams. Most of them were spoiled or had troubles at home. It became obvious quite soon why they had left or were thrown out. They were rounded up by Mrs Steiger or her assistant in Switzerland and shipped, like cattle on the hoof, to England.

Twice a year she met them at Victoria Station. The familiar record started on the way home. This is London. It is not a very nice part. Just for trains and buses. There are no good shops here. We have a big traffic problem. Not like in Switzerland. Where we live it is nice and green. No, it is not near Piccadilly. Yes, quite a long way from Piccadilly. No, there are not many families living in Piccadilly. Yes, you can buy a cashmere scarf for your father's birthday, but not today. No, there is no disco where we live but there are some very nice Swiss girls. Were you sick on the boat? My daughter is the same age as you; well, a little older. Yes, she speaks French; she is at the university. Joey is nine. Do you like small boys? You have never seen one? I thought your nephews...? They live in Antwerp! I see. No. It is not much further. It's not a very far really. It's the traffic. No, this is not Cambridge. We are still in London.

She left them in the bedroom while she made herself a cup of coffee, wishing it were whisky. When they were ready they came down bearing slabs of Swiss chocolate thick with honey and hazelnuts in mauve and blue wrappers. She always pretended to be surprised.

After the chocolate came the tour of the house. When it was finished it was time for photographs. She had to admire the smiling, technicoloured, foreshortened puppets that were 'my mother, my father, my grandmother, my aunt from Geneva, the wedding of my sister'. She was relieved when, exhausted by the journey, they slept the clock round. When they awoke she took them round the district pointing out 'my friend's house, the station, the supermarket, the church (are you a Catholic and do you go to mass?), the post office'. She fixed up English lessons for them and took them on the first day; found classes for yoga or potting or table-tennis or whatever their interests happened to be. They generally saved up their teeth for the National Health Service so she took them to the dentist. Invariably they became constipated, and concerned because they did not have their regular menstrual periods. She sent them to see Dick in the surgery, who said it was the change of air. They took pills and brewed teas. It generally took two months to get over the 'Annie's knickers are in the airing cupboard' and 'do not make the bed my husband is still in it' stage. By the time they really had the hang of things and were familiar with such institutions as redcurrant jelly with lamb, and notes for the milkman, the six months was nearly up and they flung themselves into a display of hidden talents ranging from macramé wall-hangings to tempting roesti. The tears of coming almost mingled with the tears of parting. They clung as if they could not bear to leave, swearing eternal friendship. Sometimes they did write; at ever-increasing intervals. More often there was nothing to indicate that you had shared your intimate moments with them except a wedding announcement years later when you had forgotten exactly which one Josephine was (the one who rose at five each morning to run round the Common in a tracksuit or the one who was exclusively preoccupied with her long, red nails) but sent effusive congratulations none the less.

Irene no longer bothered with them. Fed up with working fifteen hours while the au pairs worked five, she had imported a Filipino girl like a little brown monkey who beavered away happily all day with no nonsense about going to school or crochet classes just when you wanted to go out. Lorna might have done the same but knew she would have to cope with Camilla on exploiting the Third World.

Anne-Marie and Blake were still at the kitchen table, a pall of smoke hanging over the coffee cups, when she was ready to go out. She realized that this was not breakfast but elevenses at ten. The downstairs had been hoovered. She had rung Buckingham's about the waste-grinder, calling 'p.m.; no, madam, it was impossible to give a time, our engineers are very busy' (did they know it meant staying in all afternoon?); the TV rental company did not deign to answer the phone at all until she had hung on for almost half an hour. She gave her name and address to the girl who said, "Oh is it for a service call I'll put you through the line's engaged will you hold?" (She always thought hold what?) "I'm trying for you." She didn't want to ring back and start all over again. Still engaged. Ten minutes. No wonder the phone bill was so enormous, it wasn't all Joey and Cam with her reversed charges. "Puttin' you through now." She repeated her name and address and the nature of the fault, then held again while they found out when the engineer could call. The closest they could get was 'some time tomorrow'. Not today? It had been the same day service when they'd signed the contract. "We've got two engineers off sick." Joey and Derek would not be too pleased.

She went out to the garden shed for the shears and put them together with the dry-cleaning and Joey's shoes for the menders. He only seemed to get two or three weeks' wear out of them; they didn't seem to be constructed for walking. Something in the living-room caught her eyes. She went in and inspected the carpet. Cassius had been sick. Grandma's chocolate cake or Armand's peanuts. Wretched dogs. They were more work than children.

In the kitchen Anne-Marie looked at her questioningly as she walked through with the bucket.

"Cassius. He's been sick on the carpet."

Anne-Marie stroked his head. "It is too 'ot for 'im."

Outside felt more like California than England. She opened the car roof. It started first time which pleased her. She was dependent upon it. Hated it when it went wrong, failed her. Felt she needed a new one, not just the plugs cleaned or the mixture adjusted. She knew little about such things, regarding her car as a means of getting from A to B, not an object to be loved, cherished, polished, admired, as Derek did.

They were queues at the bank and the post office. She always seemed to land in the bank behind someone with a suitcase full of cash to pay in and be counted; in the post office someone drawing family allowance for the whole street in addition to a request for forms the clerk had never heard of and assistance in filling them in. At the ironmongers she waited with the shears while a woman she knew by sight debated the respective merits of a non-stick and cast-iron frying pan. They accepted the shears and wrote her a ticket, then said they had to send them away and that they would be six weeks. The summer would be over. She didn't know whether she should leave them and stood there in an agony of indecision. It was something which had come upon her lately; the indecision. It was like a pain. Worse than a pain. Embarrassing too. Crushingly embarrassing. She had been in Harrods and seen a handbag that she liked while walking past the handbag counter. Her old one was worn out. It was Italian. Soft brown leather. We've just had them in, the assistant said, in all colours and all sizes. They sell like hot cakes. We can't get enough of them. He showed her a large size with a zip and a smaller size with a flap; some had two handles, some had one; you could have a shoulder strap or one that could be either, and was adjustable, and one with a special pocket for a pen. Funnily enough it was the pocket for the pen that floored her. She had never considered you could buy a handbag with a special pocket for a pen, which she was always losing, or that she would want one. But the one with the pocket for the pen was the shoulder bag, not with one strap but two, which seemed not very comfortable and the large size was rather unwieldy but fine for holidays and the smaller size fine for everyday but not large enough for holiday guide books and things and then the flap would be useful rather than the zip which was a bit of a nuisance but if she had the flap then there wasn't the pocket for the pen and she fingered them, stroking in an absolute agony, conscious of the tall young man standing there patiently as he had been trained to do and she could not, could not, make up her mind about the straps or the flaps or the zips or the pockets or the size or even the colour and she had felt mad and ill and finally said weakly, pointing to the largest, I'll take that, and it was more than she wanted to pay and didn't even have the pen pocket but just to get out. The next week she had taken it back hoping that the same young man wouldn't be there. He was. She didn't care. She cared. Wanting to explain that she hadn't always been like that but women of a certain age, perhaps he had a mother. He didn't look as if he had a mother. He wrote her credit note with obvious disdain. Yes, madam, I remember the name and address. How could one forget?

She clutched the shears and closed her eyes, picturing Derek coming home in the evening. Did you take the shears, dear? Yes, they'll be ready in six weeks. Fine, I don't need them. Did you take the shears, dear? Yes, they wanted six weeks so I didn't leave them. Well done. I need them. Better blunt than nothing. She left them. She had been such a decisive young woman. Now she could spend an hour in the mornings dithering about what to have for dinner, an endless list of possibilities kaleidoscoping through her mind.

Unnerved by the shears, she stood in front of the serried rows of drinks in the supermarket unable to remember whether they had dozens of tonics and were out of bitter lemons or dozens of bitter lemons and were out of tonics or was it ginger ale Derek had asked her to get? She looked for her list compiled from the memory board and the pad next to the telephone. She found the receipt for the shears and the prescription for her new glasses and her paying-in book and the credit note for the handbag and Cam's last letter but no list. She put bitter lemons and ginger ales in her wire basket on top of the Flora and mangetout. They had the fans going but it was unbearably hot. Women in summer dresses filled the aisles like sweet peas, queued with baskets on tanned arms at one of the only two check-outs which were manned. They inched forward. Two trolleys of a week's shopping. As you were while the price of a tin of tuna fish was verified, the cashier holding up her hand like a small girl at school wanting to be excused.

In the High Street the sun was bright. Her shopping bag heavy. She passed the dry-cleaner's and remembered she'd left the cleaning in the car which was in the car park, too far from the shops. She got Blake's cigarettes and only on the way home remembered the library and Joey's shoes.

It was after midday when she got back, the strap of her sandal was rubbing her big toe and she was thirsty. Cam, in a long T-shirt that served as a nightie, was coming down the stairs clutching a bundle.

"I've brought my washing down."

"Cam! We put the machine on hours ago. We're supposed to be saving water."

"What's the time then?"

"Nearly lunch-time."

She followed Cam into the kitchen, picking up the tired underwear and done-to-death jeans she dropped as she went.

"I looked in 'Trend'. You know, that new one next to the Abbey National. They had some pretty sun-dresses. Not expensive. I'll take you tomorrow if you like. You'll need them if the weather…"

"I'm going up to Warwick tomorrow."

"You've just come down. What for?"

"To sign on."

"You mean the dole?" Walter Greenwood.

"Social Security." She let the washing fall in a heap on the floor of the utility room.

"You know Daddy doesn't approve."

"Look, it's silly to throw away all that money."

It was the system that was wrong.

"Where's Blake?"

Lorna looked. "In the garden. She's been up for hours."

Cam ignored the reproach. "Where's the chocolate cake?"

"In the tin."

She opened the fridge. "Any shandy?"

"For breakfast?" Lorna noticed the fridge was full of ginger ales.

"Did Armand ring?"

"I told you I've been out. He didn't ring before I went. Ask Anne-Marie. Why?"

"He's going to lend me a rucksack."

"She wondered if he would bring it over.

Cam sat at the table, her hair wild, her knees to her chin, with the shandy and chocolate cake.

She's tried several times to think of Armand. Making it real.

The phone rang. She answered it.

" 'Land of Lobelias and Tennis Flannels'?" a liking voice said. It was Armand.

"You want Cam?"

"I'd rather have you. How's my friend Cassius?"

"He's fine. No, he isn't. He was sick. You shouldn't have fed him peanuts."

"Apologies."

"I'll put Cam on."

"Don't rush away."

She held the receiver out to Cam.

"Armand."

"He had a lot to say."

Five

She liked hanging the washing in the garden. There was pleasure in the bending and stretching, the securing of corners, the gentle sway as the light breeze caught the clothes. There was the smell of the clean washing too, the sun at the back of her neck, the colours of the shirts and the towels and summer dresses; the shapes, like flags and like scarecrows. She was, she thought, probably a throwback. The embattled, embittered leaders of Women's Lib, whose army seemed to consist entirely of generals, would have laughed with contempt at the satisfaction the simple task never failed to give her. It was neither efficient nor paid for; merely satisfying some primeval need these indomitable ladies seemed not to have, or to have repressed, and having to do with living and caring for families. She watched them on television; read their books; and came to the conclusion that they were muddled intellectuals, often with deprived childhoods, who attempted to project their hang-ups on all women. They claimed to represent the sisterhood but to Lorna there seemed nothing very feminine about them at all. It was stupid to say that the nature of men and women was identical when everybody knew that it was not. She had never heard of a man who at certain times of the month was capable of putting his wallet in the fridge, the milk bottle in his briefcase, and leaving an empty house to go shopping without the keys.

"Bucking Hans," Anne-Marie said, coming, out barefoot.

"Oh, yes! For the waste-grinder. I'll be in in a minute."

She pegged up the last shirt and stood back for a moment to admire her handiwork. It would be dry in no time in this weather. Too dry; impossible to iron. She would have to keep an eye on it.

"Did you get my ciggies, Mrs Brown?"

Blake, from her garden bed, was eyeing her through the bushes.

"I did; yes." She wondered if she wanted them brought out. Room service. Probably did. God, they were lazy.

Cam was still talking to Armand. She felt jealous. She had said he wasn't a boyfriend. Probably wasn't. She had plenty of friends who happened to be to boys and confided in them as she in her day had done only with girls. Then there had been a sharp line dividing what could and what could not be discussed with a member of the opposite sex. She remembered preferring a hasty death to her father discovering when she was having her period. Such niceties no longer existed. Reproductive and alimentary function were discussed with no more reticence that Freud or Sartre.

Anne-Marie was refreshing the waste-grinder man with coffee, and explaining where she came from. He told her he had been in Italy during the war long before she was born.

"About the waste-grinder," she said, knowing from experience that time was money. Her money.

"Problems?"

"Yes, it seems to be jammed."

He went out to the van for his tools, whistling. Came back with a bag. "Let's have a look at her then."

Anne-Marie stood watching. It was nearly time for her to go to school.

She took the fruit she had bought our of her shopping basket. Raspberries, strawberries, peaches, bananas, pears.

"Will you help me with this, Anne-Marie? Fruit salad for tonight."

Cam hung up the telephone and with it her vision of Armand. "We'll be out tonight," she said. "Me and Blake."

"But you said you'd be in. I've defrosted a leg of lamb."

"Jed's got tickets for a gig."

"They're all the same," the waste-grinder man said from under the sink where he had his head. "No consideration. Think it's a bleedin' 'otel. Drives the missus mad. My boy's at Reading. Politics and economics. Politics and economics! I 'ad a spanner in me 'ands when I was fourteen and lost me kneecap in North Africa the time I was 'is age. Don't know what it's all about, they don't." He emerged, clutching the waste-grinder. "Talk, talk, talk, that's all they know. Well, I feel sorry for 'em when our lot's gone. You can't run a bleedin' country sitting on your arse and talking. Job of work? They don't know the meaning of it. State this and state that, from the orange juice to the old age pension. A spot of the old Churchill's what they need; some o' the old blood, sweat and tears. I'll take 'er out in the garden."

Lorna realized he meant the waste-grinder.

"Can I have my ciggies?" Blake, damp hair clinging to her face, pale from the heat, stood limply at the door.

"Sorry." She couldn't think why she was apologizing. She looked in her basket.

"Thanks." Blake opened them feverishly.

"Armand's got the rucksack." Cam told her. "He wants me to collect it."

"I'm going to town on Wednesday," Lorna said.

Cam looked at her. "You won't carry a rucksack."

"I don't mind."

It was another self which spoke. She certainly minded carrying a rucksack. It was said now. She couldn't go back. Well, she could.

"All right then." Cam looked at her again, she thought oddly.

She cut up the bananas and the pears and the plums. Anne-Marie was on her first peach.

Cam was looking at the fruit salad. "There was a band, Fruit Salad. In Coventry. We hired a coach. It was pretty amazing."

The waste-grinder man stood silhouetted in the doorway. He held up what once had been a teaspoon triumphantly. "There's your culprit!"

Lorna looked at Anne-Marie.

"You'll 'ave to 'ave a new unit. This one needs putting out to grass. You'll only 'ave trouble."

You never knew. It was like taking your watch to be repaired. You were in their hands.

Derek wasn't going to be pleased.

"I've got one on the van. I go on 'oliday tomorrow."

You couldn't win. "All right. I suppose so." It was an endless drain. Parts for this, repairs to that. Eight or nine pounds just for calling at all.

"I'll fetch 'er in."

Cam had her fingers in the bowl, taking slices of peach.

"Cam, please!"

"I won't be having any tonight."

"Will you be in this afternoon?"

"Yes, I have to see to my brown. I've got strap marks on my back."

"There's a parcel to go back to Harrods. I'll leave it in the hall."

"Where are you going?"

"Exercise class."

"I don't know why you bother. Exercise is so bad for one. All those sweaty women."

"It wouldn't hurt if you took a bit more. I don't know what you're going to do on a kibbutz."

"I'll get by."

She probably would. She had a way of getting by.

Lorna looked at her. "Would you like me to make an appointment for you with my hairdresser?"

"I'd like you to leave me alone."

The bell rang. "That'll be Julia," Cam said.

They had been at school together, Cam and Julia, and had kept up the friendship. Julia had trained as a beautician and now had a private and exclusive clientèle.

She came in groomed like decorated china on display. Beside her Cam, still in her T-shirt/nightie topped with the bird's-nest hair-do, looked grotesque.

"Hallo, Mrs Brown."

"Hallo, Dear."

Her hair was short in the latest style, burnished and shining, her skin clear and matt, her apricot mouth luscious, her lashes long and black beneath taupe shadow. She wore a white camisole dress with a rope of jade beads and white shoes with very high heels on her tanned legs.

She kissed Lorna, leaving her in a cloud of 'Opium'.

"You look gorgeous," Lorna said. "As usual."

"I think she's about to make odious comparisons," Cam said.

"Can't you do something about your friend?" Lorna asked.

It wasn't the first time.

"I told you," Cam said, yawning. "How's Robert?"

Julia lived with a married man who could not or would not leave his wife. He had four children.

"Fine." She sat on the table.

"What's new in the beauty world?" Lorna said. "I'm thinking of having my face done." She touched her skin. "This weather is drying it up."

"Money down the drain. Why don't you give it to me instead?" Cam said.

Julia laughed. "She's right."

"Doesn't it really do any good?"

"Not facials."

"I always feel better."

"That's because you're relaxed. Feet up, soft lights, sweet music. You could do the same at home."

Cam put a tea-towel round her neck and leaned back in her chair with her head in Julia's lap. "My husband doesn't like my face," she said. "What can you do about it?"

Julia fingered her face, with the apricot tipped fingers, smoothing down the nose, beneath the eyes.

"A treatment," she said seriously. "Your skin is suffering from neglect. It's starving and we have to feed it."

"A treatment then."

" I must be honest with you, Madame. I don't think you will see very much result with *one* treatment. The skin is a delicate structure. We have to nurture it, slowly, like a fragile plant. A course of twelve is what I would recommend, and of course you save a little if you have the whole course."

"What does it do?"

"Well, I have these special creams prepared for me from the stomach of crocodiles. The proteins in the creams are identical to the proteins which lie directly beneath the skin. By applying just the correct amount in the right manner the proteins interact and we get a neutral reaction resulting in a clear skin. I can supply you with some of the cream and some of my special lotion which you must apply afterwards and you can keep up the essential protein levels between treatments…"

The waste-grinder man was standing, spanner in hand, spellbound.

"Does it really come from crocodiles?"

Julia laughed. "No. A chemist in Ilford."

"And is all that stuff true?"

"Not a word," Julia said cheerfully. Putting the tea-towel over Cam's face and pinching her nose through it. "I have to live."

Cam sat up. "It's immoral."

"It depends which way you look at it. People believe what they want to believe. They feel better, therefore they look better. It's cheaper than psychotherapy."

"Will you do my blackheads and massage my shoulders? Blake's here, you can do her too."

"I can do with a bit of a massage meself," the waste-grinder man said.

Lorna covered the fruit salad and put it in the fridge.

"Let's all go in the garden," she said pointedly. The waste-grinder man was never going to finish with all the distractions. "We'll have lunch outside."

She was ambivalent about the exercise class which she went to every week. It was held in a large room next to the library. It had a bright green carpet like a tennis court. They left their shoes by the door and hung their clothes on pegs like at school. Mostly they were middle-aged women, although there were always one or two au pairs like gazelles who Lorna thought should not be allowed. It was bad for morale. Looking at herself in the mirror – there were mirrors everywhere – she thought she looked quite presentable in her black leotard.

Ilse put the music on. It came from a tape, the theme music from 'Match of the Day'.

"Right, ladies. Circle in the middle. No. We wait for Lois."

All eyes turned to Lois who gorged and dieted and gorged and dieted by turns. Her breasts hung almost to her waist as she struggled with her leotard.

"Lois must concentrate on her bosom. Have you ever seen such a bosom? And Lorna" – she kicked Lorna's behind with her toe – "on her hanging bottom. Tighten the bottom, Lorna. Always tighten the bottom. Right!" She clapped her hands. "If Lois is ready? Arms above the head, feet togezzer, knees bent, and sving and sving and sving, let yourself go, and again and again and again, to the music…to the music…that's better…don't stop… I said don't stop!"

After the limbering up, stretching waists and loosening backs and shoulders and necks, they had exercises at the bar. Bounces which made the thighs ache, bends which brought forth the moans and groans of agony and "Vy don't you work? You haf to vork, Estelle, hold it zere, where it hurts the most, for vun and two and sree and four and five!"

They did rhythmic movements of the pelvis. Hertfordshire housewives making like Egyptian belly dancers, forward and backwards and to the side in wild frenzy, urged to greater efforts by Ilse. Afterwards they attempted what Ilse called 'The Happy Marriage', which involved holding on to both feet and balancing on the coccyx until the legs were straight in the air.

Coming away from the class Lorna always felt more energetic, pleased with herself for having made the effort.

They went to the Cherry Tree, Lorna and Irene, Lois and Estelle. It had become a habit.

Lorna wanted to go to the library for her menopause book.

"You can order for me," she said. "I won't be long."

The library was set back from the road with a green sward in the front and a bench for senior citizens. The posters were wilting in the heat. How to Enjoy the Rest of Your Life. The Transcendental Meditation Programme. Local maps and views. Fostering. The Acorn Tennis Club. College of Further Education: full-time courses. Help the Aged. Plenty there for the civic minded.

She pushed the swing door and held it open for a hot-looking mother with shopping and a child in a push-chair, remembering how it felt. She let the smell of wax polish and books wash over her and walked through the vestibule, where they no longer stamped your books with the old purple ink-pad but waved a magic pen over the stripes and dots on the inside cover. The display of the week was hobbies. Baskets and basketry. Paper sculpture. Knitting. Tatting. Seed collage. Seed collage! You had to be desperate.

She glanced at the returned books trolley; Jean Plaidy and Nora Holt, Painting Technique and the Companies Act.

She suddenly realized she didn't know which section to look under and glanced vaguely round. Social Sciences, Economics, Philosophy, Religion... So much choice. She became almost paralytic in the library, as she did in the large department stores with their rails and rails of garments. The sheer amount of it all was enough to precipitate an attack of migraine.

The young librarian was passing, a stack of books balanced beneath his chin. She waited while he put down the load on his desk and started to sort it. She stood in front of him and opened her mouth. No words came. She would not have minded asking him where she could find a book on childbirth, pregnancy, adolescence, old age. She could not ask him for a book on the menopause.

In the more likely-looking shelves she examined the titles. *The Ulcer Diet Cookbook; Rheumatism; Preparing for Retirement. Deafness. Blindness. Cancer.* Nothing remotely like.

She would try on Wednesday at Hatchards in Piccadilly.

The sunlight blinded her. The babies waiting outside in the prams were naked, waving their emancipated limbs.

The Cherry Tree was empty. People were in their gardens or at the swimming pool. They sat a table in the window.

"We ordered ice coffee for you," Lois said, eyeing a sweating chocolate éclair in the display counter. She was obsessed with her weight and needed to be. Her sun-dress was wrapped round her like a bandage. She maintained that at home she never ate a thing, not even when Geoffrey came home at night. They had all seen her leaving the Cherry Tree carrying the tell-tale pink and white boxes tied with string.

"How's Jane?" Lorna asked.

"Working herself to a frazzle. I don't think exams should be allowed in weather like this."

"Jeremy has hay fever," Estelle said. "I mean his eyes never stop running, poor child, and itching. I feel so sorry for him..."

"I'm glad Polly's finals aren't until next year," Irene said. "Perhaps we shall be in the ice age again by then. We had such a marvellous letter…"

"Andy writes super letters. She's asked us to keep them all for her, they're more like a diary, so that when she comes down she'll have a record…"

"Jeremy does that on holiday. That dig he went on. His descriptions of all that archaeology were so vivid you really felt you were back in the past…"

"Cam does too…"

They spoke of their children, each one thinking only her own special. To Lorna's mind Andy was a cold fish, Jeremy gangly and unattractive like his father. Probably destined for dentistry too. Archaeology, well, it was the same thing really, digging around among the cavities. They swelled with pride as they recounted the activities of their sons and daughters, listening with half an ear, each waiting to make her own contribution. Their faces glowed with pride as if it were they who had a new boyfriend, were expecting to get a two-one, were making plans to cross the Sahara in a Land-Rover.

"Cam's going to Israel on Friday," Lorna said. "To work on a kibbutz…"

The waitress came with their order. Four pairs of eyes swivelled to the tray with its tall dark glasses topped with the white floating islands.

"My God, look at that whipped cream! Did you ask for it, Irene?"

"I did not!"

"But you knew!" Lois wailed.

"You could send it back." Lorna felt cruel.

Lois pretended she hadn't heard and picking up the long spoon dipped it lasciviously into the cream. A dreamy look came into her eyes. You could see the richness of it, the sweetness of it, compensating for a need unfulfilled by Geoffrey, by Jane or

Andy, by her huge house with ancient oak tree and the new swimming pool on to which it shed its leaves.

"Anyone seen Yolande?"

The cream blocked the straw. Lorna picked up her spoon. "Not like her to miss a class."

"I don't mind if she does. Miss, I mean. Never puts on an ounce. I don't know how she does it."

"Her mother played hockey for Glamorgan."

"What on earth's that got to do with it?"

"Talking of mothers," Lois said, leaving Yolande, "Geoffrey wants to turn the billiard room into a granny flat. I don't honestly think I could cope, but you know Geoffrey and his mother."

"If my mother-in-law came to live with us I'd leave," Estelle said. "Simply leave. It couldn't work no matter how hard I tried. Sunday afternoon tea is just about my limit. I feel like a piece of chewed string after that and Jonathan and I invariably have a row on the way home. It takes me until next Sunday to recover."

"Mine is still convinced I'm incapable of looking after her little boy. After twenty-five years! It's not surprising really, because every time she comes to dinner every damn thing goes wrong because I'm so unnerved…"

"My mother ruins Joey. She's forever giving him money when we're trying to teach him the value of it and to budget. I'm sure she does it deliberately."

"It's hard to imagine we shall be the same."

"We shan't have any grandchildren, darling the way things are going. It's become a dirty word. They're all enjoying themselves too much, can't see the point of children."

"Is there a point?"

"Lorna!"

"I mean, just between ourselves. All this time and money and heartache and love we put into it, then they don't need us and they go, and you can be damned sure the question of a granny flat in the billiard room won't even arise. There won't be a billiard room to start with."

"The trouble with us" – Lois had cream round her mouth – "is that we weren't educated for anything."

"Marriage."

"You don't have to be educated for that. Can you imagine a diploma in grazed knees and 'being there'?"

"There's always the Open University."

"We are the superfluous generation. There should be special scrap heaps."

"There are, darling. They call them committees."

"In my opinion," Lorna said, "things have now gone the other way. Our kids are over-educated. They are so busy passing exams and collecting degrees they never actually have to *do* anything. Or if they do they're almost middle-aged by the time they get round to it."

"Lorna's right," Lois said. "My niece wants to be a librarian. At one time you just had to have a certain amount of common sense and to love books. These days you have to be a computer. I'm going to have that éclair."

"Lois!"

"I'll take the dog for a walk."

"You have to walk for about three hours to use up the tiniest number of calories."

"Making love uses up eight hundred."

"Where did you hear that?" They looked at Lois.

"Read it. Under the dryer."

"What else did it say?"

"Eating yuck improves the skin."

"Eating what?" Estelle said.

"Yuck. Come."

"Eating it!" Estelle looked puzzled. They teased her in the group for her naïveté. It was said she had never seen Jonathan undressed.

"I'll have an éclair," Lois said firmly to the waitress who had beads of sweat on her upper lip. "That one!" She pointed to it. "Anyone else?"

They all looked longingly, particularly at the strawberry tarts, and shook their heads.

"How do you mean, eating it?" Estelle said.

"Watch Lois."

She opened her mouth and closed her lips round the éclair. There was an expression of bliss on her face.

"What's it got to do with Lois eating an éclair?"

They laughed.

"I really don't see…"

"It doesn't matter, sweetie. It's too hot. Can we have the bill, please?"

They paid, twittering over the VAT and the service and Lois' éclair which threw the calculations out.

When they'd gone the Cherry Tree was empty except for the chilled pastries and the hot waitress.

Six

Lorna stood on the terrace shielding her eyes from the sun. Cam and Blake lay naked on the rug, Cam on her front, Blake on her back. They had firm breasts, and bottoms which did not hang. The roses were faded, overblown and tired, Cassius was under his tree.

"Did Harrods come?"

Her voice could not be heard above the transistor.

"Cam! Did Harrods call?"

A hand reached out. The music faded away.

"What?"

"Harrods. Did they call for the parcel?"

"Nope." She lay down again and adjusted the volume.

She could not see inside the house, blinded temporarily by the sun. When her vision returned she noticed a slip of paper on the doormat. Harrods had called for her parcel but received no reply. She felt anger rise within her. One thing. Just one thing she had asked Cam to do. There was no consideration for anyone, anything. Totally absorbed with their fascinating selves. It was the crass assumption of the unimportance of everything that needled. Harrods would come another day, Cam would say, no panic. True. But first there must be the telephoning and the wrong numbers and the hanging on and the holding and the wrong departments and the making sure they would call when someone was in. Not Cam for sure. Sometimes she felt it was their way of making certain you would not rely on them for anything. Simply being reliable. A defence against responsibility.

"I got my Swordtail!" Joey stood beside her holding aloft a water-filled plastic bag in which a bright green fish was suspended.

"Very nice." Her mind was still on Cam.

"You haven't even looked!"

She hadn't. His face was red and damp from the heat and his tie trailed from where he had stuffed it into his pocket.

"He's a nice little fellow. Do you want some tea?"

She babied him, realizing she needed it. He was quite capable of getting it himself. She made a sandwich with lettuce and cheese and a glass of Nesquik with ice. There were ants in the cupboard where they kept the Nesquik and the jam and the marmalade, and no ant powder. She wrote 'ant powder' on the memory-board and took everything out of the cupboard and washed the shelves, squashing the ants as they darted hither and thither, thinking of Albert Schweitzer who would go out of his way rather than tread on one. She boiled a kettle of water and took it out on to the terrace.

"What on earth are you doing?" Cam called.

"Looking for the ant's nest. They're in the house. All over the place. Why don't you put some clothes on? Joey's in. I think you've had enough sun anyway."

There was a dark movement between the cracks of the stones. She bent down. Ants were swarming from a grass-tufted hole. She directed the stream of boiling water into it, causing the panicked exodus of a thousand scurrying ants. She thought how cruel and what a horrid death and carried on pouring, a sudden image of Hitler and concentration camps in her mind. There was no more water in the kettle. The treatment had not been very effective. Ant powder was the only thing. Today, if possible, or she would have to clean the cupboard again. She looked towards Cam. She would certainly not run an errand.

71

"Joey!"

"Yes?"

"What are you doing?"

"Seeing to my Swordtail."

"Would you like to go round to Auntie Yolande for some ant powder?"

"I've got sixteen irregular verbs to learn. Ask Cam. She never does anything."

She called Cassius, who opened one bloodshot eye and pretended not to hear.

"Walkies!"

He heaved himself up and stretched his back legs and shook his head, then trotted towards her.

She took the lead, although it was not necessary.

Home Farm Close was an estate of superior houses; a poor man's Beverly Hills. The roads were gravel, private. The Reeses, next door but one, had two Rolls; a white and a red, his and hers. The Spanish houseman washed the outside windowsills every morning. She was on nodding but not on ant-powder terms. They kept themselves to themselves. There were the sounds of children playing, and splashes, and tennis balls. The fronts of the houses, neo-Georgian and mock Tudor, stared blankly at the sun. Empty garages waited for the evening or the children to come home from school.

Yolande and Leonard's was one of the few post-war houses. Derek had built it for them. The land had originally been part of the garden of 'High Trees' next door, which still had more than sufficient for its needs. It was long and low. 'Yonard' in wrought iron was spelled out on the white wall like a Spanish hacienda. Yolande's yellow Alfa Sud was in the drive. She was probably in the garden. Lorna went round the side of the house, exhausted by the short walk in the heat, the sun burning her shoulders. She looked back for Cassius. He was lifting a leg on Leonard's copper beech hedge. There was no one in the garden. The hammock and the Spanish tubular garden furniture were tidy. There was no evidence that Yolande had been sitting outside. She looked through the kitchen window in which busy lizzies and avocado stones and pineapple tops were growing. There were no signs of life. She tried the door, which opened, and felt a furry sensation on her bare leg. Herod, the classy Burmese cat, brushed past. That would be the undoing of Cassius. He wouldn't come in now. He would go home and bark until Joey opened the door.

The remains of a boiled egg and the toast rack were on the table. She thought, Yolande's lunch, and then, no, Yolande of all of them did not cheat and ate only yoghurt, or a piece of cheese and an apple. There was a glass too which had had orange juice and a cup stained with coffee. Leonard's breakfast remains at what was nearly dinner time? And where was Clare? The hall was quiet, tidy.

"Yolande!" She thought her voice echoed. If Yolande had gone out, why had she left the gate and back door open? The car was outside anyway, unless she'd gone to Irene's or Estelle's.

"Cooeee!"

Must have gone to borrow a tomato or a lemon. Probably bump into her on the way home. She stopped in the kitchen again, something worrying her. The boiled egg. There was nothing more sordid than the remains of a boiled egg. Yolande was so houseproud.

She went up the open tread staircase. The door of Clare's room was ajar. Neat rows of dolls of all nations and a patchwork bedspread. Tidy. She tried not to think of Cam's.

The master suite stretched across the back of the house. There was white carpet into which you sank up to your ankles. There were towels on the floor of the bathroom. Strange. The house did not seem to have been tidied since the morning.

In the bedroom Yolande was in bed, her red hair contrasting prettily with the green pillow. She was sleeping. It seemed stupid to wake her for ant powder.

"Yolande!" Why did she then? She looked pale. The white skin whiter than usual.

"Yolande!"

There was no movement. Leonard's pyjamas were on the bed, not folded.

"Yolande!"

The freckled arm lay over the sheet. She took the manicured hand. The fingers were cold and stiff. She shook the bony shoulders, knowing there would be no response. There were no words to crystallize what she knew because it was not possible, she had only come round for some ant powder. There were pills by the bed, or had been, the bottle was empty, and an empty glass; next to them a small photograph of the mother who had played hockey for Glamorgan.

She did not remember the sequence of events. Only that Dick came and Leonard and Clare, and Irene and the Lombards from next door. She heard herself saying, "Dick, are you sure? Are you absolutely sure?" when she'd known as soon as she'd touched the pink-tipped hand.

Waiting downstairs in the living-room she could see Yolande, in her leotard at Ilse's, skinny arms outstretched; at the wheel of the yellow Alfa Sud; picking the sweet peas which grew against the fence; moving, always moving.

There was talk of anti-depressants, which they'd all taken at one time or another, unable to cope temporarily with the world they had created, and Dick asked Leonard, poor Leonard, if anything unusual had happened that morning before he'd left for his chambers. There had, of course, to be a post mortem but they knew. They all knew. It had happened to Thelma Barrington three months ago, unable to sleep and getting in a panic and taking more and more of her pills till she forgot how many she had taken...

In subdued voices they discussed Yolande and who had seen her last, and what she had said, and what she had done, and how, seeking to find some clue, some precognition of what had happened.

Leonard stood in front of her, pot belly straining at his damp shirt, blinking at her through his glasses.

"God, Leonard, I don't know what to say." She put out a hand which he took and squeezed with moist, eloquent pressure. She thought of the boiled egg and tried to reconstruct the morning scene. Had it gone as usual? Goodbye, darling. Goodbye, have a good day. Don't forget to order the fertilizer for the lawn. I won't. See you tonight. Or had they quarrelled, over the children or the joint account, or, nothing at all? One of those familiar quarrels unique to marriages, purporting to belong to day-to-day issues but stemming from fears and anxieties buried deep.

They'd never know. One never really knew. Not what went on between consenting adults in private.

"Derek will come round when he gets home," Lorna said.

"My brother and sister are on their way. I think we'd rather be alone tonight…"

"What about Clare?"

"She knows that if she wants…everybody…so kind…"

Not kind enough. None of them had heard her cry for help.

Outside Irene said, "There seems to be an epidemic round here. Thelma Barrington; Yolande. It's like the ten little niggers. Sure you're all right?"

Lorna smiled. "You needn't worry about me."

"I should have rung her to see if she was coming to Ilse's."

"It would have been too late. Dick said so."

Irene looked back at the house. "I can't believe it. I still expect her to appear at the door in her blue sun-dress. Bugger my bladder! I'm going to pour myself an enormous vodka. Coming?"

"I have to get dinner. We're seeing you later."

"Do you want us?"

"We may as well huddle together for comfort."

It seemed to take her hours to get home, and all her energy and concentration.

Joey was in the hall, busy with his fish. He looked at her.

"Where's the ant powder?"

"The what?"

"The ant powder."

It seemed a lifetime ago. She dragged herself up the stairs.

"Didn't Auntie Yolande have any?" he asked cheerfully.

In the shower she thought they were all like candle flames, burning brightly, the aura was all that anyone ever saw, was allowed to see, never the wick. Yolande's flame had burned as bright as anyone's. How bad she must have felt and no one knew. She had the soap-on-a-rope round her neck and twisted it; tighter, very tight, biting into her flesh. Letting it go again she thought she couldn't, not ever, was not brave enough, even on her bad days would carry on putting one foot in front of the other. Looking down at her body gleaming through the running water she had a sudden vision of Armand. It flashed on and off as if in lights, his body, the young teeth, the fresh mouth. She relived the sensations he had provoked in her. Making love with Derek, feeling the middle-aged weight of him, the neck no longer young, made her aware of her own disintegration. The towel she wrapped round her was sand-coloured. It matched the bath. She greeted herself in the mirror and knew what she was going to do. It had to do with Yolande. Poor darling Yolande. She lay on the bed where she had made love with Armand and opened the towel. Viewed from above her breasts looked not so bad. With fascination she watched the nipples become erect. Her legs opened automatically and her hand went down between them. Thoughts and images darted into her head of Armand and Yolande and Cam and Blake naked on the lawn and a river bank on which she lay entwined with Armand and his long hair flowing among the buttercups and his lips and his pale body on the green grass which was like a carpet and she rolled on to her front and on to her hand which went inside her own body and she cried for Armand and Yolande and the tears clouded her vision and the river bank as if a mist had fallen but she was rising above it to where there was sun and bird-song and everything bursting with beauty… A noise stopped her. The door was being rattled. Damn. Damn. Damn.

"What is it?" There was agony in her voice.

Joey. "Will you test me on my verbs?"

"Later."

"Daddy will be home."

She knew that what he meant was that she should be too busy.

"I said later!" she shouted angrily.

"Can I come in then?" He rattled the door again.

"No. Go away."

"What are you doing?"

"Resting."

The river bank had gone. She tried to get it back. It was no use. She was aware only of the reality of her damp body and the fact that she must put the potatoes on.

Cam and Blake were in the kitchen ready to go out. Cam opened the fridge.

"Can we have some of those cherries?"

"They're for tonight. Auntie Irene and Uncle Dick are coming."

"They won't eat all those."

"Leave them alone. Something frightful has happened, Cam."

"I thought you looked odd."

"Auntie Yolande. She's dead."

"You've got to be joking. What was the matter with her?"

"Nothing. As far as I know." Nothing that showed.

"What then?"

"No one knows. There has to be a post mortem. I found her. When I went round for the ant powder."

"You never said."

"I don't know what I'm doing. I can't believe it."

"O-D'd! My God! Who'd have thought it! In Home Farm Close! Poor old Clare."

"We don't know until after the post mortem."

"People just don't die. Where did you find her?"

"In bed. I thought she was sleeping. The pillowslip was green. She looked so pretty." From the corner of her eye she saw Cam and Blake exchange glances.

"Look, would you like me to stay with you?"

Perhaps the Harrods parcel hadn't been important.

"No. Thanks. I'm fine. Daddy will be home soon."

"Till he comes?"

"No. You go. Joey's here."

Cam put an arm round her and she buried her face for a moment in the mop of hair, getting it in her mouth.

She put the water on for the potatoes and went into the garden to pick some mint.

The rug was still on the lawn, indented with the imprint of two bodies. There was suntan oil and a pair of sunglasses and two tumblers with crumpled straws. She felt irritation surging inside her, cancelling the moment of rapport she had had with Cam. She'd better clear it up before Derek came or there'd be murders. She spent half her life protecting the children from him. Small things for which, like a mother duck, she interposed herself.

After twenty-four years of marriage she still looked forward with anticipation to Derek coming home in the evenings. It was the high-spot of her day. There was always so much to tell, small happenings, the nuts and bolts of life, which often, lately in particular, turned out to be tales of woe concerning things gone wrong with the house or with the children. Today she had to tell about the shears and the waste-grinder, and the TV man not coming till tomorrow, and Yolande. Strange about Yolande. She kept forgetting and had to force herself to remember. Derek would be shocked. She would have to lead up to it gently. So often when there were things to tell she had to gauge his mood, wait until he had relinquished the problems of his own day to make room for hers. Sometimes she forgot and, overwrought, started on him before he was over the doorstep about the gardener having wasted the entire morning because he couldn't start the mower or her mother was coming to dinner and she'd taken apple purée out of the freezer thinking it was lentil soup and water had come through the newly painted kitchen ceiling because the cistern upstairs had overflowed, then had wondered why he appeared not to listen or shouted because the light had been left on in the den in broad daylight and how he wasn't made of money although everybody appeared to think he was. Sometimes she fantasized how it would be, should be; Derek coming home and putting his arms round her and saying poor darling, what a busy day you must have had, tell me all about it; then he'd come in, his face crumpled with fatigue, and complain about his latest tax demand, they must surely have made a mistake, and Joey's roller-skates in the drive, he could have broken his neck, and the last of the Bristol Cream he'd been looking forward to and which she'd sloshed into the trifle, and she was unable to help feeling let down, disappointed, cheated even. A part of her knew that life was not the movies and that he had had to contend with traffic and unfulfilled promises and inefficient secretaries and non-functioning public services and the enormous difficulties of scratching a living in order to go on scratching a living.

She heard a key in the front door but it was Anne-Marie in her cherry embroidered sun-dress, the hair which she had piled on the top of her head for coolness straying down in tendrils. She put her straw basket in the table and took a glass of water.

"I was in the park. It was good."

"Will you lay the table?"

"Of course. I must wash myself and take another dress. It is more 'ot than Switzerland."

"Humid. I'm going to test Joey on his verbs."

79

He was reading *Battle Action*. His room was the opposite of Cam's. Neat and orderly. He took after Derek. He lay on the bed with his knees up.

"I thought you had sixteen irregular verbs to learn."

"Done it."

"I came to test you."

His eyes did not leave the comic. "After this."

"Auntie Yolande is dead."

"How do you mean dead?" He tore his eyes from 'Hellman on the Russian Front'.

"No one knows. I found her in bed. She was dead."

He looked at her. "She wasn't all that old."

Forty-three.

"Will they fetch Simon home from school?"

"I expect so."

"Golly! He'll be in the middle of his exams." He had reached out to the boundary of his experience. Exams and football, cricket and chess and tropical fish.

She heard the front door slam.

"That'll be Daddy."

Derek kissed her, his face moist, and went to the fridge for beer. He took it out into the garden.

"It'll never recover. Not now." She knew he meant the lawn.

"We didn't get the South Bank job. That tender cost us a hundred and fifty thousand pounds. It was rock bottom. I swear no one could have done it for a penny less."

She walked round the herbaceous borders with him. He was looking at the wilting delphiniums and the tobacco plants but his mind was on the South Bank.

She wanted to tell him about Yolande but you couldn't just say 'Yolande is dead' like that. If she left it until after dinner he'd say why didn't you tell me, what are you keeping it for? She couldn't decide whether it was better for him to lose his appetite or get indigestion. She often felt, with Derek lately, that she was going up the down escalator.

"You've never seen anything like the traffic tonight," he said. "Dozens of breakdowns; engines boiling over. Even the tar on the road was melting. You don't know how lucky you are being able to sit in the garden all day."

She let it go. "I've something to tell you."

He stopped. "Not the car again! We can say goodbye to the no claims bonus."

"Not the car, Yolande."

"What's she done?"

"Nothing. She's dead."

He turned from the flower beds to face her.

"I'm sorry. I couldn't say it any other way."

She told him the story, starting with the ant powder.

When she'd finished he said, "Poor old Leonard."

We weep for ourselves. Cam had thought immediately of Clare, Joey of Simon, Derek of Leonard. For herself she was Yolande in her hour of despair.

It cast a pall over dinner. Only Joey was hungry. It took more than death to dull the appetite of a small boy. He rattled on about the cricket scores which did little to relieve the heaviness of the atmosphere.

"I wonder who'll be the third," Lorna said when Joey had left the table and Anne-Marie was washing up.

"How do you mean?"

"Things always go in threes. Thelma Barrington. Yolande…"

"Don't be ridiculous!"

"It's not. You know it."

"It must have given you quite a shock, finding her."

She started to cry at the sympathy in his voice. "It was the boiled egg that was so horrid…"

He stood behind her and put his arms round her, cradling her head. "What about a little brandy?"

The warmth of his body was arousing her.

"Shall we go upstairs?" It was strange. She had felt the same after her father died.

"I thought Irene and Dick were coming?"

"There's time."

"I'm awfully tired," he said. "This heat…"

Armand had not been bothered by the heat. Derek patted her head. "What did I do with the evening paper?"

During the evening she kept having to remind herself that Yolande was dead. As if it were imperative that she did not forget for one moment.

When Irene and Dick came they felt that Scrabble might take their minds off what had happened at 'Yonard'.

"It's not so bad for Leonard," Irene said. "All the world loves a widower. If it was Yolande who was left on her own it would be tough titties."

"I thought women were liberated," Dick said, handing out the letter racks.

"You must be joking. There's a lot of hot air but when it comes to the nitty-gritty such as women on their own nothing has changed at all; never will. It's in the nature of things."

"Let's get started," Dick said, feeling the subject should be changed. He put his hand into the bag of tiles and withdrew one. "A," he said, putting it face up on the table.

"Don't throw away your advantage now," Irene said.

"I haven't done a thing yet!"

"I'm only pointing out that it can influence the entire game."

"I can only do my best."

"Just remember not to open up any trebles."

Lorna and Derek exchanged glances. Irene and Dick were always bickering but Scrabble brought out the worst in them.

"Let's get cracking," Derek said.

They played on the terrace on the circular, slatted wood table which Lorna painted with teak-oil every summer. The air was warm and still; a Mediterranean night. The smoke from Dick's cigar kept the midges at bay. The bowl of cherries was on the table together with the Scrabble word guide and the dictionary.

On the board they made corpse and bed and drug and suicide.

Seven

Going to town in the train, Lorna reflected that Yolande's death had cast a pall not only over herself and the household and Home Farm Close but over the entire neighbourhood. When she'd taken Joey's shoes, which had stared at her accusingly from the floor of the car, to be repaired, the shoe-maker had said such pretty shoes, she always had, and always so cheerful. The girl in the paper shop said: Only was in last Friday to pay the bill. Who ever would have thought...? Even the TV repair man knew: the lady with the red hair and the set that swung out from the cupboard in the bedroom. Fair turned you up. Mind you, there was quite a bit of it about these days; as if it were measles. There were whispers, unpleasant rumours really, about Leonard, dear old Leonard, and the Chinese pupil in his chambers; about what went on at the evening class Yolande went to on Tuesdays, about the fact that she had confessed to having had electro-convulsive therapy. It was all quite horrid. Several times on the previous day she had to stifle the impulse to ring Yolande as she often did. She owed her half a jar of sesame paste. She could have got some in town today but when would Leonard ever make hummous? The thought was ludicrous. Who was going to look after them anyway, him and Clare? Would they sell the house, Yonard, where they had been so happy...? She pulled herself up. You did not take your life if you were happy. Of course they couldn't be certain if she had until after the post mortem. The ambulance had taken Yolande's body away. They had all stood in the road, impotent, thinking that Yolande should have been out with them in the burning sunshine rather than on the way to the mortuary where they would probably put her in a fridge. Afterwards they had sat in Irene's kitchen, drinking coffee into which they had cried. Not even Lois had touched the biscuits. Leonard and Clare had had dinner at Irene's last night. Tomorrow they would come to Lorna. She was going to buy some pâté for them at Robert Jackson's. She wondered how long they would go on being passed from one house to the next. Already they were mentally linking Leonard with various widows and divorcées of their acquaintance.

She disliked the journey to London. By the time she got to the car park it was practically full with the cars of the commuters. She had to leave hers at the far end and walk back over the pot-holes, the gravel damaging her town shoes. In summer it wasn't quite so bad, in winter the pot-holes were full of water. Up the wooden steps and across the bridge to the ticket office. Cheap day return. Cheap. That was a laugh. You usually had to wait for a train, they seemed not to hurry themselves once the rush hour was over. Other ladies going to town like herself waited on the platform. Railway personnel ambled by, swinging lamps. She had to resist the chocolate machine from which as a schoolgirl she had bought red-wrapped bars of Nestlé's milk for a penny; an old penny at that. It didn't even taste the same today, despite the fact that it was goodness knows how many times the price. When the train arrived, bringing with it the smell of tunnels and of stations, she sat in a non-smoking carriage. Sometimes she brought the newspaper to read; sometimes just made her shopping list. It usually said things like hair, teeth, things back to M & S, wedding pres., cricket socks. Today it was hair and specs, the buttons for Joey's blazer, Robert Jackson's, Hatchards for the book, and of course Armand. She had her prescription and needed to choose some frames. Thankfully she did not have to wear them all the time but when she did it was to be bifocals, a fact that she found faintly depressing. The older one got, the more time one had to spend on oneself. It was like the preservation of an ancient monument. More expensive in terms of labour and money as the years went by and disintegration speeded up. Her general health was good which was something to be thankful for, although she was aware that she was entering the danger zone when big 'C' came to get you or high blood-pressure or heart trouble or arthritis. She'd read an article which said that if you fell over at her 'age' there was an increased risk that you would break something as the bones were inclined to develop little holes in them and become more brittle. A jolly prospect. No, it wasn't the major things with her, but the minor ones could be pretty irritating. Take teeth. They had been good once. Now there were items such as bridges and root canal fillings and caps and crowns and long sessions in the chair which were necessary in order to preserve them. She had developed a callous beneath her foot and a corn on one toe which needed expert attention every six weeks. What with that and her hair, covering the grey and keeping it in good condition and shape, and having her legs and underarms waxed, it was getting to be a full-time job. Recently she had noticed to her horror three or four whiskers which despite plucking grew obstinately on her face. She knew she would have to come to electrolysis at some point. Until now she had skimmed over the discreet advertisements telling about it, congratulating herself on the fact that she had no need of such information. One day, she supposed, it would be colostomy bags and chairs that lifted you automatically up the stairs. It came upon one so suddenly. There were years between twenty and forty when you simply didn't think about such horrors. Everything functioned; you never got tired or irritable or depressed, you looked good with the minimum of effort, the jawline was firm, as was the bosom and the stomach and the neck.

There was a young man opposite. His striped shirt had a white collar which he had loosened because of the heat. He had his jacket and his briefcase on his lap and hadn't cleaned his shoes. She looked up at the wrong moment and met his eyes and felt herself blushing which she thought was ridiculous for a woman of forty-five with a grown-up daughter. She knew that she was still tolerably attractive and wore her blonde hair shoulder length, not having succumbed to the traditional, layered, chrysanthemum cut of the 'older woman'. It was the double chin and the bulge around the middle that would give her away. Her legs were good and she generally wore high heels which made them look even better.

Much as she loathed the train with its rattling and bumping through dreary suburbs, it was good to get out of the house and the district. She felt like a child on a spree. There were fields and trees round Home Farm Close, but when you stepped outside the house nothing to stimulate the imagination, revive the tired senses. Often she had suggested a move to Derek, but he wouldn't have it, despite the fact that it was he who had to do the daily journey to his office in London. It was worth it, he said, to step out in the evenings into his garden, to breathe the clean air after the pollution of the city, to stroll round to his friends, gather for walks and drinks and golf at the weekends. It was all right for him. He got away every day. Sometimes she thought she would die from sheer boredom; one couldn't after all do this train journey just for the hell of it. She was aware of herself rotting little by little in the wilderness, her highs provided by the return of Derek each evening, visitors, and Cam coming home. Northwood Hills. Preston Road, Wembley Park. Not names to conjure with. Schoolgirls who were late, and daily helps. The carriage was grubby. Chocolate and cigarette packets, newspapers which had been abandoned, and a layer of general grime over everything. No matter how fresh she was when she started out, she always felt grubby by the time she arrived at Baker Street. She had always had a fear on trains, on buses too for that matter, that she would not get off in time. As it drew into the station she felt herself rooted to the spot and had to will herself to move, hanging on to the hooped straps as she did so, afraid she would fall with the jerking of the carriage. The very worst that would happen was that she would be carried on to Great Portland Street, but that wasn't really the point. Rationalizing didn't help in the slightest. There was a gap between the train and the platform through which you could see the rails. 'Mindthegap!' It yawned like the Grand Canyon. She looked at it doubtfully then forced herself to stride over it, surprised to find herself safely on the platform. There were people swarming up the steps like ants. She felt life stirring within her. A sense of excitement as to what might happen to her in the big city.

Hair first. She was a bit sorry really as she never really liked herself fresh from the hairdresser's like a parcel done up in gift-wrapping. The set and the newness of it and the exhaustion engendered by the frustrating experiences in the salon always made her feel at her most unattractive and middle-aged and she wanted to look her best for Armand. Best was not oldest. She'd got on a black linen dress which slimmed her, and black patent shoes. She mightn't have bothered with her hair but there was half an inch of grey root showing and the sun had turned the remainder of it brassy. Besides, it was time for a trim.

She stood outside the station in the shimmering heat and looked at her watch. Hailing a taxi, she told herself, as she usually did, that it was cheaper in the long run as by not waiting for buses she could get everything done in one day which would save the time and the money in not having to come up for another. It was expensive enough anyway, the fares and the transport and the lunch to which she always treated herself even if it was just a sandwich. If only she could persuade Derek...a flat in town and a place in the country would have suited her better. Just a little place where they could go at weekends. Derek said they had the best of both worlds where they were and that he couldn't stand packing up every weekend. He had the best of both worlds, she admitted. For herself she had the shitty end of the stick. Often she would have liked just to wander. To go to a gallery or an exhibition. But there was always so much to do in the way of shopping and appointments, whether for herself or the children, that she never actually got round to very much else.

She paid the taxi in Albemarle Street, as usual not knowing quite how much to tip, and consequently overdoing it. She had achieved nothing and already the money was beginning to flow.

"Hallo, Mrs Brown!" The girl at the desk who had been there for years crossed her name off in the appointments book. They always left a letter addressed to Lady This or the Countess of That in a prominent position on the reception desk to remind the Mrs Browns of their place.

The cloakroom lady, a squat Italian with a moustache, handed her a tan and white checked gown which matched the tan suède wall-covering. Because of the heat she went into the cubicle to take off her dress. The gowns were short and she was glad her legs were nothing to be ashamed of as she went, mini-skirted, downstairs to the tinting bay. Women with pale mauve heads and oily black ones held out their fingers or toes for the manicurists. Others, with a million tiny rollers in their hair, drank coffee. The highlights, like silver porcupines, sat patiently waiting for them to take. They were discussing a wedding.

"She looked ever so nice," Angela, the head tinter said, "really summery. I didn't half feel sorry for her though, in all that heat. Good morning, Mrs Brown. How are you today? Take a seat, I'll be with you in a minute. Steven, give Mrs Brown a tinting gown and some books, then mix me some forty-one with half of thirty-three as quick as you can."

She sat in front of the mirror which she could swear was made of some sort of flattering glass, quite different from her mirror at home, and ordered coffee. When it came it was Rombouts with a little container of cream and brown-wrapped lumps of sugar on a wooden tray. She gave the boy the extortionate thirty pence and five pence for himself although it was only himself anyway.

It was an hour and a half later by the time she was tinted and colour-bathed and washed and rinsed and conditioned and upstairs again to look for Clive who had been doing her hair for a very long time. He saw her in the mirror and indicated a seat. He seemed not very far through a cut which she thought had probably also to be blow-dried. She looked at her watch and felt the day slipping away from her and the first stirrings of a migraine headache. She ordered more coffee and looked through the latest blue-covered copies of *Vogue* and *Harper's* and *Country Life*. A woman in the next chair, clutching a poodle, held her cigarette so that the smoke drifted in Lorna's face, increasing her irritation. She made exaggerated movements of her arm to waft it away but the woman seemed not to notice. They never did. Inconsiderate lot, smokers. She read an article on 'How to Keep Your Man Happy in Bed' and another on 'Summer Desserts'. She wanted to tear out one of the recipes but didn't like to, although everybody did. Perhaps while she was under the dryer, unless she could be bothered to copy it out. Every now and then she glanced towards Clive, willing him to hurry. She knew perfectly well that it would make no difference. He was quite impervious, giving his full attention to each client. She knew that she would appreciate his single-mindedness when it was her turn.

Another forty-five minutes had gone by the time he dusted the hair off his chair with a towel which made her think of attendants in ladies' lavatories. She sat down and looked at herself, with Clive standing behind her, in the mirror.

He combed her hair tentatively. "What are we doing today, cutting?"

"I think so. It's about time."

He tucked the towel into the neck of her gown.

"Head down, please."

You couldn't hurry him. Each length had to be measured against the last, checked and rechecked. When it came to the rollers, enormous red ones, they were wound and secured with care. When he was satisfied he said, "Put Madam under the dryer," to a junior, and to Lorna, "See you soon," then was away to his next clients who had been giving him dirty looks.

Under the dryer she ordered an egg sandwich on wholemeal bread although she should have had cottage cheese or yoghurt. She picked up every last bit of mayonnaise that dripped out with her coffee spoon.

When she was dry and unable to sit there any longer because of the heat, her gown sticking to her back, she eased herself out and stood behind Clive.

"I think I'm dry."

"Take Madam's rollers out, Linda. Won't keep you long."

He had just started a blow-dry. She powdered her nose.

It was two o'clock by the time she emerged into the sunshine of Albermarle Street, having paid the bill and insinuated a pound note into the pocket of Clive's skintight jeans and tipped the shampoo girl and Angela and the cloakroom lady who had a glass ashtray of ten-pence pieces displayed ostentatiously in front of her.

Three hours remained of her precious parole and she had to apportion them carefully.

She was near Hay Hill so thinking glasses next, made off in that direction.

They were displayed round the walls. Rows and rows of them; every size, shape, and colour. She looked round vaguely.

There was one girl, younger than Cam. She was on the telephone and took no notice of Lorna. She put down her handbag and helped herself to some frames. She discovered that she could not balance them back on the little racks on the wall so she left them on the shelf feeling guilty for her untidiness. She was old enough to remember when assistants in shops had assisted. How they knew exactly what sort of sugar for marmalade and whether a dress suited you and which size of needle for darning. They should really call them cashiers now, not assistants, although even that was inaccurate. They no longer needed to be able to add up, just press a few buttons and when the whirring stopped examine a dial to determine the cash total and the correct change to give and the day's date. If you were stupid enough to consult them on a minor point they would look at you blankly and say it's a matter of personal preference, as if one didn't know that in the first place. The frames did nothing for her. The heavy ones made her look like a schoolmistress, the pale ones like a granny. On their own they looked fine. So did she. The symbiosis was fatal.

"Did you want any help?" The girl had her hand over the mouthpiece of the telephone.

Lorna smiled ambiguously. She could manage without the kind this child could give her.

There were more than a dozen pairs of frames scattered over the shelf. She was becoming despondent. Perhaps she would leave it for another day, although it was awkward in the evenings when she wanted to knit and watch television at the same time. Perhaps somewhere she would find a frame made just for her, matching her illusion of herself.

The girl put down the phone and brought a frame from the display in the window.

"These are new in. Christian Dior. They're very popular."

They were mauve and enormous. She wondered whom they could possibly have been popular with.

"Or these." She held out a gold-rimmed frame that popularity had done to death.

There was a clock on the wall. She still had to go to Robert Jackson's and Hatchards and get the buttons for Joey's blazer. After lunch-time, when she was in town for the day, the hours seemed to slip away more quickly. Sometimes she got in quite in a panic as mid-afternoon approached, feeling that she would never get everything done, as if it were a matter of life and death.

She put on a thin, imitation-tortoiseshell frame, preferring to be a schoolteacher than a granny; she did not, after all, have to wear them constantly.

"How do these look?"

"Very smart. They really suit you. Quite lightweight too."

"I'll have these."

"You'll need to see Mr Pocock about the lenses. I'll see if he's back from lunch. Have you got your prescription?"

She hoped he was back from lunch. She was rapidly losing interest in the whole affair. Everyone was always at lunch or at tea. She had been trying to ring the china supervisor at Selfridges for a week now and seemed always to catch what appeared to be a permanent tea-break.

Mr Pocock's lunch smelled as if it had been drunk and not chewed. He examined her prescription and explained at length about the various permutations of bi-focal lenses which were available.

"It all depends," he said, "on the purpose for which you need them…"

She was aware of the minutes disappearing. He was consuming her precious store from the afternoon.

"…In your case what I would suggest is the small 'D' shape. We call them 'housewife' bi-focals…"

She felt her irritation surge at his sweeping assumptions.

"Look straight at me."

She looked into the piggy eyes as he held a finger to his nose.

"Fine."

He hoped they would be ready in two to three weeks if luck was on their side. She had no wish to be allied with Mr Pocock under any circumstances and attempted to make it clear by the haughty demeanour with which she left the shop.

She walked up Bond Street towards Piccadilly, enjoying the dressed windows and wishing she had the time to linger at

Raynes and Aspreys, Elizabeth Arden, Cartier and Ferragamo. She had the distinct impression that London had been taken over by a tourist coup, the natives confined to their homes by curfew. Snippets of conversation in a dozen languages floated by as she walked quickly, wishing she had not worn the patent shoes which attracted the heat of the pavement.

It was four o'clock by the time she had the duck pâté and some mozzarella cheese and dried apricots and a book called *No Change*, which she thought a pleasant euphemism for the menopause, in her black nylon shopping bag. She wondered whether she should trouble about Joey's buttons, then knew she must, she could not get the right colour locally, and took a bus down Regent Street to John Lewis. The bus stood stationary in the traffic. Lorna sweltered and dabbed at her face and looked at her watch.

In Oxford Street you could scarcely move for the crowds and there was the fulvent stench of humanity.

In John Lewis she fought her way through impediments of human flesh which seemed to have nothing better to do than stand and stare in the aisles.

For the second time in a few hours she longed for the old days. At the haberdashery counter, she remembered, the assistant took the sample button you had brought and showed you a card with the colour and sizes and, when you had together agreed the nearest match, noted the number and pulled out a little box with dozens of the buttons you wanted and you said, one, or two, or three, according to your needs. Now they were hanging from hooks on roundabouts in cards of ten which you had to buy even if you only wanted one and there was very little selection. It was the same with screws or cup-hooks, three or four times as many as you needed and then in plastic bubble packs which tested one's ingenuity to open and could not be reclosed.

She chose a card of ten of almost the same colour and size as the mauve button in her purse and stood in line at the Pay Here desk.

She stood in line again for the Ladies' where she wanted to freshen up before she went to Armand.

Outside, aware that her hair was too set and that she had powdered over the dirt on her face, she stopped a taxi.

The taxi driver dropped her at Cornwall Terrace. There were coloured rugs over the railings, drooping sheets at the windows, and an air of desolation over everything. The steps were dirty, and there was an overflowing dustbin on them. She rang the bell wondering whether she should have come. A slim young man in a vest and tattered jeans with a headband round his forehead opened the door and smiled at her. Beyond him she could see a bicycle, the grubby lino in the dark corridor, and the staircase.

She smiled back. "I'm looking for Armand." She realized that she didn't know his second name.

"Are you his mother?"

She looked at him sharply and was sure she should not have come.

"No."

"Sorry." He did not look sorry. He was still smiling.

"That's all right."

"I'll get him. You don't mind if I close the door?"

Perhaps he thought she was the police. She considered crossing the road and disappearing as fast as she could into the park...

The door opened again. Armand had no shirt on. You could see his ribs with their covering of translucent flesh.

"Hi!" He seemed neither pleased nor sorry.

"Hallo. I came for the rucksack. Cam..."

"Come in."

She followed him upstairs past the bicycle. There was a smell of damp and cats and unwashed bodies and clothes.

The music hit her. The same sounds as those with which Cam surrounded herself.

What had once been the drawing-room had two mattresses on the bare floor. There was a deck and two speakers, the leads snaking over the floor like brown spaghetti. The young man who had opened the door was sitting cross-legged in a corner, still smiling like a Cheshire cat. Another, with wild black hair, sat in the centre of the room, smoking and playing himself at cards.

"You've met Eugene."

He smiled from his corner.

"And Jed?"

She thought she had seen him once with Cam.

"Hi!" He did not look up from the cards.

"Hallo!"

She felt ridiculous in her black linen dress and patent shoes with her new hair-do and her nylon shopping bag. No wonder Cam had thought it strange when she'd offered to come.

Eugene was still smiling, although she failed to see what at. She looked at him nervously.

"Do you want to sit down?" Armand said.

His bed was at the end of the room. It was strewn with books and papers and a portable typewriter. He cleared a few of the papers. She sat down awkwardly, wishing they'd turn the music off. Her skirt was tight and she did not know what to do with her legs.

Armand indicated the papers. "My novel."

"How's it going?"

"Great."

She looked round the high, beautiful proportioned room, with its ceiling rosette and the crystal chandelier someone had left behind, perhaps as a reminder of things that should be.

"Can you just live here? I mean doesn't anyone…"

"They can't touch you. Not if you change the lock. It's the getting in that's difficult. If they catch you breaking and entering, that's it. After that…" He shrugged. "It's convenient."

"I'm sure it is." People paid hundreds of thousand of pounds for the convenience of Regent's Park.

"You look amazing," Armand said.

He seemed not to be joking despite the fact that she felt so desperately out of place.

"I've been to the hairdresser's."

He touched her hair. "It's pretty."

She looked at Jed who was bent over the cards. Eugene was still smiling but into the distance. It was as if they were alone.

Kneeling, Armand took the shoes from her tired feet. She tucked her legs beneath her.

"I'll tell you about my novel," Armand said. "I'll dedicate it to you if you like."

Eight

She should have been home, walking Cassius, making a plum crumble, sewing the button on Joey's blazer. Instead she learned that the subject for a good novel had to come all in one piece, in a single jet; that the important thing to a writer was not his experience but his range; that it was the fundamentals of his personality that kindled the creative spark.

Armand spoke of Flaubert, of Austen, of Hardy, and of Proust, names rarely bandied in Home Farm Close. She did not notice when Jed and Eugene left the room or that the music had stopped. Only that they were alone.

"I'm boring you," Armand said.

"No!"

"Do you realize that man is the only animal that *can* be bored; or discontented."

"I seem to spend a lot of my time being both," Lorna said.

"The most important problem we have to solve is that of our own existence."

"How do you do that?" Lorna asked.

Armand took her hands. "Stay here with me and we'll talk about it; all night."

"We're going out to dinner," Lorna said. "In Hatch End."

"You can have Steve's bed." Armand indicated the mattress at the other side of the room. "Steve's in Germany."

Lorna laughed. "I have to cook dinner for Joey and Cam before I go out; and sew the button on Joey's blazer. He'll get a hundred lines from Mr Snell…" It sounded ridiculous.

"Please stay," Armand said.

Lorna uncurled her legs. "I have my life; in Home Farm Close."

"What's the use of it if you aren't happy?"

She was silent.

"Are you happy?"

Lorna thought. "Sometimes."

"Not enough," Armand said. "Don't you want to live?"

"What is it that I do?"

"Repeat patterns."

Lorna stood up, her legs numbed from sitting on them. "Women like me," she said, "have responsibilities. You can't just walk out."

"Think about it."

"There's nothing to think. Honestly, Armand. You're very sweet and it's very tempting…" She looked at her watch then shook her wrist. "My God! Do you realize it's six o'clock!"

"I don't have a watch."

"Of course."

"A bit early to turn into a pumpkin."

"Not in Home Farm Close. Derek will be going mad!"

She did not understand how two hours had passed without her noticing, except that in them she had not been expected to attend to the needs of those around her. Armand had talked to her as if she had a mind of her own. It compensated for the housewife bi-focals.

She pushed her feet into her shoes which seemed to have become two sizes smaller.

"I'll get the rucksack," Armand said.

She had completely forgotten. Would have gone without it.

She held it awkwardly. It was heavy and not terribly clean.

They stood in the room, separated by a shaft of sunlight.

"Good luck with the novel."

"I'll see you again?"

"I don't think so; no."

"I'd like to. I love you."

"Thank you," she said. "For the rucksack. I'll give it to Cam."

He came with her to the front door.

A taxi with its flag up was passing. She hailed it, her third of the day.

Armand's face was framed in the open window.

"See you!"

"Baker Street station," she said to the driver, but her eyes did not leave Armand's until the taxi was out of sight.

It was years since she had travelled in the rush hour. The mood of the homeward-bound travellers was not good. Exhausted by a day of suffocating heat and work, they were not disposed to be accommodating towards a smartly dressed middle-aged lady carrying a rucksack, even though her legs were still good.

The platform was dense with people, the trains more so. She darted up and down searching for a carriage into which she felt she had the ghost of a chance of insinuating both herself and the wretched rucksack. She began to panic, feeling hot and tired and thirsty and guilty and that she was never going to get home.

She had to stand all the way and was pleased when she turned the car into the peace and quiet of Home Farm Close; hysterically pleased almost, her face clammy and dirty, her legs banged to bits from the rucksack.

Derek opened the door before she could get her key into the lock.

"What happened to you? I was worried. Cam said you told her you'd be back at five. It's quarter past seven." He looked at his watch although he must have known. "Irene and Dick are here, you know we're supposed to be going out, the table's booked for seven-thirty. Joey and Cam didn't know what to have for dinner."

"I'm sorry."

"Where have you been?"

She held out the rucksack.

"I had to fetch this for Cam."

Joey came out of the kitchen. "I was starving so Cam made fish fingers and Mr Snell says if the button isn't on my blazer by tomorrow…"

She stood stock still. She heard Irene call her from the living-room and Derek fussing about drinks and tables and remembered that she must have left her nylon shopping bag with *No Change* and the duck pâté and the buttons for Joey's blazer on Armand's bed.

"Are you all right?" Derek said.

"Yes, of course. Just tired."

"The heat. It was foolish to go to town."

"Yes."

"I was really worried about you."

He was worried about himself. Her failure to appear on time had upset his routine, the tidiness of his day. She was never 'not there' when he came home. For the first time she wondered why on earth she should be.

"You did get my button?" Joey said.

"I went up specially."

"Great."

"I left it behind though."

"Where?"

"Somewhere. I don't know."

"What am I supposed to tell Mr Snell?"

"I went specially to get it."

"How do you mean, you left it behind?" Derek said. "On the train?"

"No. I …I left it in the shop. I'm always doing that. You know I am. I pay for things then leave them on the counter. It's a symptom. We all do it. You do it too …don't you, Irene?"

"What's that, dear?"

Lorna walked into the living-room. "Pay for things in shops and leave them behind?"

"Frequently. The day I'm dreading is when I forget to pay for them and you'll be reading about me in the local paper. *Black Chiffon* and all that. Peggy Ashcroft, wasn't it?"

"Anyway, it doesn't really matter," Derek said. "You can always get another button."

"What about Mr Snell?" Joey said.

"It does matter," Lorna said, meaning because she had left the buttons at Armand's and that she must go back to the Union Jacks on the railings and the grinning Eugene.

"He'll go absolutely mad," Joey said.

"What shall we have for pudding?" Cam called from the kitchen.

"Do you think they'll keep the table?" Dick said. "You know how busy they get. Perhaps we ought to ring and say we're going to be late."

Cassius was jumping up at her and howling because she had not said 'hallo', made a fuss of him. She pushed him away. She did not want to placate Derek, the dog, think of Mr Snell, pudding for Cam…She was hot, weary, wished she was back with Armand.

"What shall we have for pudding?" Cam came out of the kitchen.

"I heard you the first time. I've only just come in."

She knew it was a feeble excuse. One was expected to produce puddings at will.

"I brought your rucksack." It lay on the floor.

"You brought that?" Derek said. "What on earth for?"

"I was going to town. I offered."

"No wonder you're exhausted." He glared at Cam accusingly.

"It's not her fault," Lorna said. "I offered. I was going right by."

"What's the code for Hatch End?" Dick called.

101

Upstairs she took off the black dress. The morning, with the car park and the train, seemed years away. She tried to mind that Joey was going to get a hundred lines from Mr Snell and felt it odd that for the first time she didn't feel guilty for not replacing the button, only detached. Perhaps it was the heat, but nothing seemed quite real, nothing belonged. Not Cassius nor Cam nor even Derek. They had been wildly in love, she and Derek, or so she had thought twenty-four years ago. He had supplied the missing bits of her. She had been grateful. One either married, she thought, one's mirror image, or the missing half of a jig-saw. It was the latter in her own case. Her own weaknesses were compensated for by Derek's strengths. Sometimes she wondered if this inhibited her from developing strengths of her own. Certain parts of her personality remained undeveloped, stunted. Like a vampire, she had fed on Derek to compensate for certain deficiencies in herself. In the same way he had fed on her. Often she wondered if she was any longer capable of functioning on her own. They had been heady days, the early ones, neither of them happy except in each other's company, when they were not together having endless conversations on the phone. If they did not see each other he wrote to her by express post, sometimes three times a day. It no longer seemed like that with young people. Perhaps because the sexual urges were not frustrated. If they wanted to be together they simply were, at all hours of the day or night, just like that.

There had been no telephone in the squat. There wouldn't be. She would have to wait until Armand got in touch about the shopping bag, or make another journey to get it back.

Cam came in without knocking and sprawled across the bed, the mass of hair obliterating her face.

"I opened a tin of rice pudding," She said. "Joey wants syrup on it. We must be out of it."

We. She had been in Warwick for the last two years yet 'we' were out of golden syrup and bought the wrong sort of apples. She should be grateful, she supposed, that she still regarded

Home Farm Close as her home; at any rate somewhere to store her winter coats.

"There's raspberry jam. He likes that."

There was no movement.

"Aren't you going to give it to him?"

"He's nearly ten years old. It's time you stopped treating him like a baby."

She said nothing. The criticism was justified. Joey was her baby and would be until he left home and probably after that too. She was aware that the clinging was neurotic but it was essential she have something to love; something small, something hers. She tried to hide it from Joey, knowing her excessive concern was unhealthy. She could not hide it from Cam.

She changed the subject.

"You can come to the restaurant if you like. Anne-Marie will be in soon."

"You must be joking!"

"It's quite nice."

"With Irene and Dick!"

"Aunty Irene and Uncle Dick!"

"I don't know how you can stand them. She never stops shouting at him. I don't know why he puts up with it."

"I don't criticize your friends."

"At least they're not stereotyped cabbages; there's nothing wrong with my friends."

"That's a matter of opinion."

"What do you mean?" She was getting prickly.

"Nothing."

"What's the matter with my friends?"

She wanted to say 'A lot of scruffy layabouts,' but she said: "Cam, dear, go and see to Joey's pudding."

"F— Joey's pudding. I'm sorry Mummy. I forgot where I was for a minute. I'm really sorry. It just slipped out."

She was a little girl again. She got off the bed and put her arms round Lorna.

Lorna felt her thin body and had her hair in her mouth and thought my God, how you bear them and love them and worry when they're sick, and get up in the night, and melt with pride and die a thousand deaths from anxiety, then they grow up and away and you don't know them any more and Cam wondered why she worried about Joey's pudding.

She detached Cam's arms. "Daddy's waiting."

"You don't love me; only Joey."

"Cam, you're twenty-one. It's different. I'll always love you."

"Can I borrow the car?"

Lorna stood still. She didn't like lending her car to Cam who treated nothing with respect.

"Where are you going?" She played for time.

"Sally's."

"Where does she live?"

"Harrow-on-the-Hill."

"All right." Her nature got the better of her. "You'll be careful?" She visualized herself tomorrow stranded in Home Farm Close with no car, the prison doors closed.

"I'm only going to drive it!"

"You don't take care of anything! Look at the way you gave me back the cardigan I lent you."

"I couldn't help it. I told you. I didn't know the paint was wet."

"And my white sandals?"

"How was I to know it was going to rain?"

It was the same with everything. She wanted to help her, give her things, but somehow the gestures turned sour. She took her best umbrella and lost it, her eyebrow pencil and sharpened it away to nothing, her last stamp and forgot to mention it.

"What time will you be back?"

"How do I know?"

"Well, please be back by twelve if you're taking my car."

"OK."

Sometimes she listened to herself talking and was appalled. Twelve had been her father's witching hour. Everything that happened afterwards was wicked. It was the hour when all good people retired to their beds. She looked at Cam who was pleased to get the car at all.

"I'm off then." Cam looked at her reflection in the mirror behind Lorna.

"Do you think I'd make a good model?"

She wished she was twenty-one; her life before her, uncharted, unchannelled.

"Do you?"

"I don't know Cam."

"One day you'll see my name up in lights. You'll be so proud. Where are the keys?

"Hanging up. Take care."

Downstairs Joey said: "I can't eat it without syrup so I took a choc-ice. Have you seen what's happened in the freezer?"

"No. What?"

"There's this enormous bulge of ice. You can hardly close the door."

"There can't be. We've just defrosted it."

"Look then."

She looked. A solid white mass ballooned like ice-flow from the top shelf. She shut the door on it with difficulty and turned the key.

"Don't open it again." Just the weather for the freezer to go wrong. She wrote 'Freezer man' on the memory-board. Her life was full of men. Men for the waste-grinder and the washing machine and the dish-washer and the cooker and the fridge and the television and the Hoover and the gas and electricity meter readers and the gardener and the window cleaner and the milk-man and the man who delivered the oil. One day she would write a book about the men in her life.

"They really won't hold the table," Derek said.

"I'm ready."

They went in Dick's car because he was on duty and had left the number of the Dolce Vita with his call service. Lorna sat in the back with Irene, an arrangement they had adopted over the years.

They were comfortable with each other. They had moved into Home Farm Close at the same time and had been friendly ever since. Polly was the same age as Cam; and Michael, who was a medical student, a year younger. Often she wished that he had been older, then he and Cam might have fallen in love, despite the fact that he played squash and jogged every morning and preferred the Proms and Kenwood to The Average White Band and the Vibrators. He was going into general practice like his father, and hard as she tried Lorna could not visualize Cam as a doctor's wife snugly secure in a Home Farm Close.

In the front Dick and Derek discussed petrol consumption and the putt Derek had sunk the previous Saturday.

"Talking of golf," Dick said, "did you get your bill from the club this morning? I really can't see why they have to increase the subscription every year."

"Rising costs," Derek said. "Two hundred pounds! It's getting ludicrous."

"And there are we scrimping and saving in the shops," Irene said, "It hardly seems worth it. I used to sling everything I needed into the trolley without a thought in the world. Now I stand there for hours looking at the price and wondering if it's essential."

"The nouveau poor," Dick said, manoeuvring the Jaguar round a corner. "Look at this old thing. I used to change it every year. If I hadn't married Harmer's paints I'd be in a right old state. Nobody worries about the doctors."

"What about the architects?" Derek said. "You at least will always have work. The only thing I can be sure about are the rates and the mortgage and the insurance premiums and Joey's school fees, they make the terms shorter and shorter, and the fuel bills…"

"We had the thermostat on sixty-eight all winter and it didn't make the slightest difference," Dick said.

"…not to mention the telephone and the electricity and the gas. Sometimes I can't even bring myself to open the post in the mornings."

"…A patient of mine has had locks put on the telephones…"

"Not a bad idea," Lorna said. "I swear Anne-Marie phones Switzerland every time we go out."

"It's not Anne-Marie, it's Cam and Joey…"

"Derek! That's not fair, they have to speak to their friends."

"Not for hours on end! They wouldn't do it if they had to pay the telephone bills."

"Estelle told me that she and Jonathan are cutting out prawn cocktails and only going to Glyndebourne every other year," Irene said. "I didn't know whether to laugh or cry."

"It's certainly no laughing matter. I shan't be able to retire, ever. I doubt if I shall even manage to pay off my overdraft before I die, at the rate things are going. Do you realize that I'm using my return ticket and haven't managed to save a single penny?"

"Cam thinks we're rolling in it," Lorna said. "She disapproves of us for having two cars, although she's never averse to borrowing one, she's got mine tonight, and makes comparisons with the starving half of the world…"

"Just talk!" Dick said. "If you wait long enough they come to their senses." He turned the car into the accommodation road.

"They grow up," Derek said, "and realize that the engaging idealism of theirs – higher wages all round, feeding the undeveloped countries – has one little snag. It has to be paid for. When they start opening their own wage packets and find that the taxman has nabbed half before they've even had a look in they'll change their tune. Put it over there, Dick, behind that Rover."

The Dolce Vita, where they were regulars, was in a parade of shops between the Browserie, which sold handbags, costume jewellery and photograph frames as well as books, in order to pay the rent, and a children's shoe-parlour whose foot-fitting service attracted mothers from miles around.

"Good evening, Mr Brown, Doctor."

" 'Evening Mimmo," Dick said.

"I am sorry I 'ad to let your table go" – Mimmo wrung his hands and Derek glared at Lorna – "but I 'ave put you over 'ere."

They usually sat by the window, which tonight was wide open. Mimmo showed them to a table by the wall, pulling the chairs out for Lorna and Irene.

"Its too hot over here," Dick said. "I don't like it."

"Oh, do stop grumbling, Dick," Irene said, picking up the menu which Mimmo had put in her place. "I know what I'm going to start with. Cannelloni. I've been struggling with my conscience all the way here."

"Me too," Derek said. "What about you Lorna?"

She opened the menu. "Give me a chance."

"You've had all day to think about it."

There had been other things to think about. Proust and Flaubert. Besides, what she enjoyed most about going out for dinner was that you did not have to decide beforehand what you were going to eat, not until the last moment. At home you had to plan, shop, prepare, cook. By the time you actually got to it you had, somewhere along the line, lost your appetite. She had tried to explain to Derek.

They usually went out on Wednesdays. For Lorna it broke the monotony of the week, although it could not exactly be called living it up. About once a month they went to the theatre. Lorna loved the plays, it didn't matter what, just to be taken out of herself, stimulated by other sights, other sounds. She didn't much like the claustrophobia of the West End theatres, the trail down into the bowels of the earth, too hot in summer, draughty in winter, the disturbing of everyone in the row to get to your seat, the lack of leg-room which made Derek fidget, the no sooner getting settled than it was time to struggle out for the interval; to stand in the smoke-filled tomb waiting, while the overworked barmaid grew extra arms to serve two hundred people with drinks in ten minutes; the struggle back; the rush for the exit when it finished, finding that the car had been towed away or waiting half an hour to emerge from the subterranean car park into the traffic jams of Shaftesbury Avenue. The National Theatre was an improvement. There was more space and sometimes they had supper in the buffet, queuing for quiche or smoked mackerel and cheesecake. If it was anything heavier than Alan Ayckbourn Dick fell asleep. He had slept through Robert Bolt and Ibsen and Peter Shaeffer and Shakespeare. They had usually reached Home Farm Close by the time Irene stopped shouting at him. It was always a jolt to go home after an evening out. The sterile kitchen and the jumping dog shattered the fantasy with which for a while Lorna had managed to surround herself. She was courtesan, collaborator, or movie star, according to the evening's entertainment. There was often a note from Joey: 'Don't forget I'm having packed lunch', and she'd have to detach herself from the Incas in Peru or Rosmersholm and get busy with the Marmite and the peanut butter.

Sometimes they ate in the West End club to which Derek belonged and where he entertained his clients. Dining celebrities gave the illusion of charmed lives, and the return to reality in Home Farm Close was harsher than ever.

"I'll have the antipasto misto," she said, knowing that as soon as it came she'd wish she had ordered gnocchi or minestrone.

"You've had your hair done," Irene said.

Armand had touched it.

"I don't know how you could be bothered in this weather. I stayed in the garden and even that was too hot. What did you do for the rest of the day?"

Sat in a squat discussing the novel.

"Ordered my new glasses, got a button for Joey's blazer."

"That can't have taken all day."

"Wandered about," Lorna said, wishing she was back with Armand. "Window-shopping."

"There's talk of another recession," Derek said, pouring Frascati for Dick. He was not interested in how she had spent her day. "Have you seen the trade figures?

"That's enough for Dick," Irene said. "He's driving."

"I had lunch with a client who claims to know."

Dick picked up his glass. "Not a chance, if you ask me…"

"Fortunately they don't ask you," Irene said. "The country would be in a worse mess than it is."

"…Not with all that lovely oil coming out of the North Sea."

"I heard it was running out," Lorna said, but couldn't think where she had heard it.

"I hope it's not true anyway," Derek said. "I've just bought some shares."

"Dick always buys at the top of the market and sells when they reach bottom," Irene said. "Anyone could make a fortune doing exactly the opposite to Dick."

Dick put butter on a breadstick and took no notice. It was water off a duck's back.

"You don't need all that bread," Irene said. "You'll spoil your appetite."

Lorna was tired from her day and from the heat. She ordered scaloppine but could not finish it.

"Anything wrong?" Dick said.

"Nothing."

Derek, enjoying his polpette, didn't notice.

Afterwards Derek and Irene had zabaglione, Dick – to Irene's disgust – torta, knowing the portions were enormous. Lorna waited for the coffee.

On the way out, past the Ashley-Joneses, to whom they stopped to say hallo, and the racks filled with Valpolicella and Chianti, Derek took her arm.

"Enjoying your dinner?"

A careful and considerate man, he had not noticed. Did not notice. Dick had been aware she'd only played with the meal. She did not care about Dick. It was important that Derek should be aware of her actions, her mood. Sometimes. It depended upon the time of the month. There were days when she could be satisfied in the knowledge of his overall caring; with the mere fact that she was important to him, as she knew she was.

"Yes," she said.

"The polpette were good." He did not know she had had the scaloppine; did not know that it mattered that he did not know; that there were tears in her eyes at his insensitivity, threatening to overflow.

Dick said if they hurried back there would be time for a quick game of Scrabble.

When they got home there was a note on the fish-tank from Joey. It said Armand phoned but not whether he had asked for her or Cam.

Nine

If the dog hadn't had diarrhoea she would perhaps not have made the decision. That and Joey's phone call. The Scrabble had gone on until midnight. In the first game she and Derek had won by forty points because Dick had challenged her 'kazoo', never having had one as a child. Irene got so angry with him that there was nothing for it but to have a return although they were all tired.

In the bedroom Derek said, "We really trounced them tonight!"

"I'm getting a bit fed up with Scrabble," Lorna said. She was already in bed, thinking of Armand, and watching Derek get undressed.

"Oh, I don't know – it passes the time."

She wanted to do more than pass the time. She watched him remove the stiffeners from his collar and put them in the black lacquered box which held nothing else. He took off his tie and rolling it neatly laid it in the drawer amongst the others, which were in serried ranks, each point to the fore. His socks and underpants went into the bin in the bathroom.

Naked, he leaned over the bed to get his pyjamas from under the pillow.

Perhaps it was thinking of Armand, but she wanted him. She held out her arms, "Come to bed."

He looked surprised. "Half a jiff!"

"No, now." She felt a rush of tenderness.

He straightened up, his pyjamas in his hand.

"Shan't be long."

He went into the bathroom and closed the door. She felt angry with him and the desire left her.

She heard enthusiastic washing and brushing sounds for what seemed, as always, an age. There was never any hurrying Derek. When he came back he had his pyjamas on and had brushed his hair. He put out the light in the bathroom, then double-checked that he had done so, made sure the window was open and switched on the floodlights which illuminated the garden for a moment to make sure there were no intruders lurking on the lawn.

"I didn't lock the front door," he said. "Cam and Blake aren't in."

"What's the time?"

"Twelve-thirty."

"She promised to be back by twelve. She's taken my car."

"Where did she go?"

"Sally's."

"Sally who?"

"Have you ever known any of her friends to have a surname? Her name is Sally and she lives in Harrow-on-the-Hill. Cam's not usually late if she says she's going to be in at a certain time. What do you think happened?"

"Nothing. She'll be in soon." He climbed into bed. "Hope she remembers to lock the front door and put the lights out."

"I shall be awake all night now, worrying."

He put his arms round her. "Of course you won't. Come here; I'll take your mind off it."

"No." She pulled away.

"Thought you wanted to?"

"Before."

"What made you change your mind?"

It was not a question that could be answered in precise, architectural terms. It had to do with moods, and moments. The mood and the moment had passed.

"I'm too tired."

"OK." He switched off the light next to the bed.

"Good night, darling."

" 'Night."

She turned over into her sleeping position but could not sleep. Her ears were strained for the sound of Camilla and Blake. She imagined accidents in which they lay bloodstained and mangled in the ruins of the car she should never have lent them. At four o'clock she got up.

The car stood outside in the moonlight. The porch light was off. She fell into a fitful sleep and was woken by a nudge in the ribs from Derek.

"Seven o'clock!"

"It can't be. I haven't slept a wink."

"Why not?"

"Worried about Cam."

"She came in soon after we went to bed."

"How do you know?"

"I heard her."

"Why didn't you tell me?"

"Thought you didn't sleep a wink?"

"I must have dropped off for a moment."

"Poor darling! Go back to sleep. I'll see to breakfast."

He meant it. As kind-hearted as he was considerate, and quite capable of getting his own breakfast. She was awake now and got out bed.

"I don't mind a bit," Derek said.

"I know. I'll do it."

She opened the kitchen door and stopped dead. Cassius had messed all over the floor. Great liquid brown patches, evil-smelling. He came to greet her, looking sheepish.

"Cassius!" As if it was his fault.

It was a thing she hated. She'd never minded cleaning up after the children when they were small, excrement and vomit. Not for the other people's children, though, couldn't do it, nor for dogs.

It was useless calling Anne-Marie, she was too sensitive a plant. Joey would be late for school and keep Derek waiting which would be no good for anyone.

She hitched her housecoat up above her knees and tied it with the belt. She opened the garden door for Cassius and went for newspapers and rubber gloves and the bucket and the mop and the Jeyes fluid.

By the time she had finished the tears were running down her face from the smell.

She put Joey's fried eggs on the table and called him. He came bounding down the stairs, his shirt hanging out of his trousers.

He embraced Cassius who jumped up to greet him.

"Good dog, good dog. What's that terrible pong?"

"Your 'good dog'. Or rather the disinfectant. All over the floor."

"Poor Cass. Got an upset tum-tum then? Will you take him to the vet?"

It was the first erosion of her day. Derek held the second in his hand.

"Did you see this note from Cam? It was on the fish tank. What's the smell?"

"Your dog." She took the note. 'Dear Mum, Exhaust manifold has packed up. Sally's boyfriend says that's what it is. Sorry about that. Cam.'

"What's an exhaust manifold?"

He explained to her.

"Is it serious?"

"No, but you'll have to get it fixed."

The day without a car loomed before her.

"Can I have yours? I'll take you to the station."

"Why? Where're you going today?"

115

She realized she had been going to see Armand.

"To Pam's." She saw her sister rarely.

"OK. And you'd better take Cassius to Mr Purly. Do you remember last summer? He had diarrhoea for three weeks."

She wrote to 'Mr Purly' and 'Garage re car' underneath 'Freezer man' on the memory-board.

Joey brought his plate in and added 'mauve button' in large letters followed by an exclamation mark.

She pulled her blue jeans and a sweater on over her nightie. She didn't mind going to the station in the summer.

In the forecourt she joined the fast-moving queue of chauffeuring wives. They got in the way of the buses and had to move off smartly.

Derek kissed her. "Thanks, darling, have a nice day. Sit in the garden or something. You might have a look to see if we need any oil."

She straightened Joey's tie.

"Don't forget my button!"

"No."

They disappeared. Anne-Marie was drinking coffee and reading her letter.

"The dog messed all over the floor."

"Poor baby!" She looked genuinely upset.

Lorna wrote 'Oil' beneath 'Mauve button', 'Garage re car', 'Mr Purly' and 'Freezer man', then she looked in the larder and added 'Haddock, lettuce, toms'. She would make a fish mayonnaise for Leonard and Clare, with crème caramel to follow. She would go to Armand in the afternoon, getting back in time to take Cassius to Mr Purly and meet Derek at the station. She would also try to make time to drop in on Pam as Derek would be sure to ask her and she hadn't seen her for some time anyway. They did not get on badly but she saw little of her sister, their life-styles separating them from each other.

Pam was known in the family as 'the clever one'. She had not left university to marry as Lorna had, but had stayed on to get her degree and afterwards her Ph.D. She had done various teaching jobs, one of them in America, and at the age of thirty, when her parents had given up hope, married Benjamin who was a Fabian and a humanist and a playwright whose work was produced in fringe theatres and seemed to Lorna totally unintelligible, as was Benjamin himself. Pam lectured for the WEA and produced turgid and esoteric prose for the *New Statesman*. They never had any money. With a bit of luck she would be out and Lorna's conscience would be salved.

She tried three garages. The first could do nothing for a week, one of their mechanics had fractured a wrist, the second had no mechanics at all, two weeks' annual holiday, the third agreed reluctantly to have a look if she brought it in but couldn't promise… She persuaded Irene to follow her to it and give her a lift back. The man for the freezer said 'some time today' and could not be talked into making it in the morning, everyone was breaking down owing to the weather and they had to deal with the emergencies first.

She was ready to go out, take the car to the garage, and do the shopping, when the phone rang. It was Armand.

"Lorna?"

"Yes?"

"You left something."

"I was coming to fetch it."

"This afternoon?"

"Yes."

"See you."

She thought she heard the click of the upstairs extension but then that perhaps it was her imagination.

The phone rang again. More pips. It was Joey.

"Mum?"

"Yes."

"Mr Snell says if the button isn't on by tomorrow I can't be in the three-legged!"

"Don't worry."

"I've got to go. It's break and I'll get caught."

She felt angry with Mr Snell, what right had he to blackmail her? What did he know of the difficulties attendant upon getting buttons in the right shade of mauve?"

Cam came down the stairs carrying blue jeans.

"Cam, I've got the machine on."

"It's not for washing. The zip's jammed. Are you going out?"

"Yes."

"There's that little alteration man behind the flower shop. He has a special gadget. I've got to wear them tomorrow. Do you mind?"

"And if I do?"

She held out her hand for the jeans. Taken and, she presumed, waited for or collected. it meant a separate park. The flower shop was miles away from the fishmonger's.

"I'm sorry about the car. It wasn't my fault."

"It never is."

"Things just seem to happen when I'm in it. Who was on the phone?"

"Joey."

"No. Some thing about 'this afternoon'. The voice sounded familiar. A bit like Armand but it couldn't be."

"The man for the freezer. Coming this afternoon. It's all iced up. We don't want it going wrong in this weather…"

She stopped. Cam lost interest and was contemplating the larder.

"Don't we have strawberry milkshake any more?"

"No, we don't."

"Look, I'd take the jeans but we've got masses to do and it would take hours on the bus. I don't know how you manage, stuck out here."

She usually defended Home Farm Close to Cam, but did not. She held out her hand for the jeans.

She had to wait for Irene who was sitting on her bedroom floor with a bust developer.

"I get more and more pear-shaped," she said. "I thought if I got the top hiked up a bit you wouldn't notice quite so much what went on below. Dick says it's a waste of time, the only way you can improve the boobs is plastic surgery. He doesn't care anyway. He's a bum man and I've always had more than my fair share of that."

"Are you nearly ready? I've got an awful lot to do today."

"Six more pushes." She was red in the face. "It's bloody difficult."

She did six more then stood up, throwing the bust developer on to the bed. Lorna picked it up. It was pink plastic. Two discs joined by a strong spring.

"Where did you buy this contraption?"

"Mail order."

It was a hobby of Irene's. She sent away for racks to keep her shoes tidy and personalized pencils and wheels for her suitcases.

"Actually, poor Yolande gave me the idea. She was trying to get a bit more bust for Leonard. Every time I look at the damned thing I think of her."

"Leonard and Clare are coming for dinner."

"They should have the result of the PM today."

"As if it mattered!"

"They have to go through the motions. How do we know Leonard didn't do her in?"

"Leonard? He wouldn't hurt a fly."

"Neither would Crippen. We won't be long at the garage, will we? It's my surgery day."

It was different for Irene, Home Farm Close. On two days a week she helped Dick at the surgery, got out of the house, mixed with other people.

She stood up and put on her bra. "Dick hasn't forgiven himself for challenging 'kazoo'. He's absolutely obsesessed. Do you know what he was reading in bed last night? The

119

dictionary. The last thing he said to me was did I know that to yaup was to yell or cry out like a child?"

She told Irene about Cassius' misdemeanour.

"I wouldn't have a dog if you paid me," Irene said.

"I'm taking him to Mr Purly,"

"Mr Purly has it easy. Two-fifty for two minutes and the patient doesn't talk back and ask stupid questions. No night work either."

In Irene's kitchen Michael, in shorts and singlet, was sitting at the table, both hands round a mug of coffee.

"I didn't know you were home," Lorna said. "Have you seen Cam?"

"Hallo, Auntie Lorna!" It seemed ridiculous from a bearded giant.

"He came to bring his washing," Irene said. "It's cheaper than the launderette. You get service too."

"You know you like it."

"Are you on holiday?"

"Ostensibly. I'm working as a hospital porter. Carting the bodies about."

"Seventy pounds a week!" Irene said.

"With overtime. I start my clinicals in January."

"He came top in anatomy," Irene said, dropping a Sweetex into her coffee."

"Mother!"

"Well, you did, didn't you?"

It didn't matter how old they were. The pride stayed. The first smile, the first tooth, the first step. The first day at school, the first report, the first prize. The first boyfriend, the wedding, the first grandchild. It would not end. Flesh of one's flesh. One's contribution to eternity.

"Can we go?" Irene looked at her watch.

"I've been waiting for you."

Pamela lived in Hampstead. NW6 not NW3. There was a world of difference. They had a garden flat in an old house in

Goldhurst Terrace. She had driven up, not being able to face the train two days running. There was nowhere to park, the street was lined with cars, on both sides. There was a space in the next road. She walked back, hurrying, aware of her time with Armand diminishing.

Outside she pressed the bell that said: 'Basement. Ryan.' There were dustbins in the front of the house. Her mother called it a slum. She hoped there would be no reply.

"Hallo?" Cheerful as always.

"It's Lorna." She hated speaking into the impersonal grilles.

"Stranger!"

"You sound like Mother!" she shouted. A girl walking by looked at her curiously. She heard Pam laughing. Then the buzzer which opened the door.

They didn't kiss, always a little strange with each other. Pam had a fringe and straight hair, which never saw a hairdresser, to her shoulders. She wore a loose Indian dress and Greek sandals, and took in Lorna's yellow linen suit with matching wedge heels at a glance. The hall was narrow and lined with books. The Victorian wash-stand was dusty and strewn with letters and circulars, the doormat dark with stains where the cats had weed.

She followed Pam into the kitchen. The table was covered with written pages scored with red ink. Among the sea of papers a milk bottle and a bottle of apple juice stood like twin lighthouses.

"I was marking some essays. 'The failure of Browning to provide drama for his times.' He lacked vivid, pulsating, dramatic expression, of course. So sad; too much the poet. He understood, really understood, mankind. He was undoubtedly the best qualified of all the poets, except perhaps Byron, to produce excellent plays, but he simply never made it. Magnificent dramatic lyrics but no sense of drama, no dialogue. He let the commonplace pass him by and drama must be about the commonplace or it's bound to fail. Do you want some lunch?"

"It's three o'clock."

Pam looked puzzled. She opened the fridge and took out a chipped earthenware bowl.

"There's some dhal from last night." She looked at it doubtfully. There was a crust round the edge.

"What is it?"

"Lentils."

She dug a spoon into it and cut a slice from the wholemeal loaf which was on the dresser. She spread the slice heavily with orange paste and handed it to Lorna.

"No, thanks."

Pam shrugged and looked under the piles of papers on the top of the fridge.

"I had some tomatoes somewhere." She found them in a brown bag underneath the cat who was asleep in the armchair. She wiped one on her dress and took a bite.

"Seen Mother?" It was their point of contact.

"She came to tea on Sunday." She remembered Sunday and Armand.

"I suppose I should ring her." She took a bite of bread with dhal, then put it down on the essays.

It was Lorna and Derek who did everything for their mother. Lorna spoke to her twice a week and sorted out her problems, took off for Dorset when she was ill. Derek helped in her battles with the tax man and with her shares. She was an avid reader of the city columns but only noticed the prices of the shares which she had sold. When they went up she rang up Derek and complained, as if it were his fault. Pam was unaware and uninterested in their mother's day-to-day problems. When she did decide to contact her their mother swelled with pride and never stopped talking about it. My daughter phoned today, the one who writes for the *New Statesman*, you know. But it was Lorna who took her to have a tooth out; find a dress for her godchild's wedding, to exhibitions at the Victoria and Albert. Pam had great green eyes like her cat but she had always been the blue-eyed girl. It was hardly fair.

"How are the children?"

Lorna doubted if she remembered their names. She certainly never remembered their birthdays although there was a calendar stuck on the wall which said 'Amadeus' and 'Progressive League'. She was a write-off as an aunt.

"Cam's down."

"Sussex, isn't it?"

"Warwick."

"Of course. And Joey?"

"He's fine."

"What's he going to do?"

"He's only nine!"

"Of course. I was thinking…"

Of someone else, probably. Pam was not going to have any children. She had never been good about people, feelings, cared only for cats. Lorna wondered when she had last washed the kitchen floor.

She ran a finger along the dresser, collecting the dust.

"Don't do that," Pam said, "It's what Mother always does."

"Sorry. I wasn't thinking." She sat down opposite Pam at the other end of the table, hoping that the chair was clean or the linen suit would have to go to the cleaner's.

"I'm thinking of leaving Derek," she said.

Pam looked at her. "I wondered why you came."

"No, it wasn't that. I hadn't intended to. I hadn't told myself really. Not in so many words. It was more of an idea."

"I don't blame you." She did not get on well with Derek.

"Why?"

"He's such a bore."

"I love him."

"Why then?"

"I don't know. I have to get out."

"I'm glad."

"Glad?"

"I didn't think you had it in you. You got married too young. It's a mistake."

"Possibly. I shall go back. But I just have to get out for a bit."

"Where will you go?"

She told her about Armand. Pam finished her doorstep of bread with the dhal and poured apple juice into a coffee mug.

"It has to do with the utility room and Yolande and the dog," Lorna said. "I don't expect you to understand."

"Does it matter?"

"No. I haven't told another living soul. Not even Armand. I'm just going to. They'll probably say it's my age. Perhaps it is. I've bought a book about it. I left it at Armand's. You'd better get on with your Browning."

"Read *Pippa*," Pam said. "You'll like it."

The cat whisked past her legs at the door.

"Keep in touch," Pam said.

"Love to Benjamin."

Pam looked at the man's watch, their father's on her wrist. "It's after closing time. He should be back."

Leaving Pam's she felt a lightness, a sense of relief, as if by verbalizing what she was going to do, almost before she knew she was going to, she had relieved herself of some of the anxiety.

She was aware of a quickening of the pulse as she came out by the side of John Barnes into the Finchley Road and headed the car in the direction of Regent's Park.

Ten

Armand opened the door. Knots of summer tourists were walking by on their way to the park. She had been longer at Pam's than she thought.

"I can't stay," she said. "I have to go to the vet."

He looked surprised.

"Cassius; he has an upset tummy."

She followed him upstairs, past the bicycle. He was by himself in the big room.

"Whose is the bicycle?" she asked, to mask the nervousness she suddenly felt.

"Mine. I don't ride it though."

"Why not?"

"You'd never believe me if I told you."

"Tell me."

"Come over here then."

She sat on his bed. He lay down and put his head in her lap. She stroked the long hair.

"There was this man in Wales," he said. "A neighbour, although he lived three miles away. Nobody saw much of him. Kept to himself. Everyone called him the 'hermit'. The only people he spoke to were Ted the post, Owen Evans the potato man, and my father. One morning Ted the post found the hermit hanging by a wire from the ceiling of his front room. No one knew why he took his life but there was a letter. A kind of will. It turned out there was not very much to dispose of. Only his climbing boots, his motor-bicycle, and his bicycle. He left his climbing boots to Ted the post, his motor-bicycle to Owen Evans, and his bicycle to my father for 'the boy'. That was me. It was winter when they found the hermit hanging. That spring, at the start of the climbing season, Ted the post lost his footing on quite a small mountain and broke his neck. He was wearing the hermit's boots. Six month's later Owen Evans rode the motor-bicycle into an articulated lorry. He left eight children."

"I don't believe it," Lorna said.

"It's true then. I swear to God it's true. Now you know why I won't ride the bicycle."

She reached down and took his hands. "Don't. Don't ever ride it. Promise me?"

"Don't worry, I won't."

He was looking at her with desire. She thought of the vet and collecting Derek from the station, Leonard and Clare coming for dinner, and that she hadn't made the crème caramel.

"I don't know how I came to leave my shopping bag."

Armand grinned. "I do."

"How?"

"I hid it. I was afraid you wouldn't come again."

"You wanted me to?"

"I keep thinking about you; when I'm trying to work. It gets in the way."

"And I've been thinking about what you said. About Steve's bed...did you mean it?"

The answer was on his face. He began to unbutton the jacket of the yellow linen suit.

"There's no time," she said, not stopping him. "I'm meeting Derek at the station, he hasn't got the car because of my exhaust manifold, it was Cam's fault, she borrowed the car, something always happens, and I have to collect it and take Cassius to the vet and Leonard and Clare are coming to dinner..."

He stopped her words with his mouth.

"…I'll have to open a tin of peaches…"

When she looked at her watch it was four-thirty. She'd hoped to be at he vet's by five.

He lay naked, watching her button the yellow suit.

"When will you come?"

She thought. The next day she was driving Cam and Blake to the airport and it was Joey's Sports Day. They were spending Saturday on the boat with Lois and Geoffrey. On Wednesday she was taking her mother to the specialist about her varicose veins. When Joey broke up he was going on an exchange and after that they were all going on holiday together. When they came back there would be Joey's winter uniform to get, last year's would certainly not go near him…

"It doesn't seem very practical," she said.

He said nothing. Waiting.

She fastened her skirt.

"I'll come on Wednesday."

She wondered if Pam would go with Mother to the specialist, then dismissed the idea. There would be a lecture or a deadline to keep.

"Do you realize," she said, "that I'm old enough to be your mother? People will laugh."

"I don't bother too much about people, what they say."

She thought. It would certainly be no laughing matter for Derek. How would she tell him? When?

Far away she heard a familiar sound.

"What's that?" she said, listening.

"What?"

"I thought I heard a child cry?"

"There's a baby. Opal's baby. They live upstairs."

"It isn't going to be easy," she said, thinking of Derek.

"What is easy?"

He was right. There was nothing that was easy. She moved to the long window that looked out on to the park. She was beginning to love this huge, high-ceilinged room with its green view. She looked at her watch, forcing herself to think of Mr Purly.

Armand was stepping into his jeans, hopping with the agility of youth.

He brought out her nylon shopping bag. It swung from his finger. Taking it, the duck pâté which probably had not survived, the buttons for Joey's blazer, her book, she felt Home Farm Close closing in on her. She didn't want to go; to the garage to collect her car, to Mr Purly, to cook dinner for Leonard and Clare. She thought suddenly of Yolande and shivered.

"Cold?"

"Of course not." She told him about Yolande, delaying the moment when she must go. "I keep wondering where she is," she said. "Perhaps in some enormous Home Farm Close in the sky."

Armand put his arm on her shoulders and looked into her eyes.

"The grave's a fine and private place, But none I think do there embrace."

He kissed her mouth. His mouth was young, soft.

"She isn't in her grave," Lorna said. "The PM's today."

Joey heard the car and came to meet her.

"Did you get my button and can I go under the hose?"

"Yes."

"Which?"

"I got your button."

"Thanks, Mum. And I can go under the hose?"

The request seemed simple but was not. Like many of the decisions she had to make *qua* mother, there was more than one factor to be considered. Firstly, she wanted to please him, he looked hot and tired and what he had asked seem not unreasonable. On the other hand, each time he went under the hose he seemed to get a sore throat which meant a visit to Dick and days off school and sometimes antibiotics.

"No."

"Oh, come on!"

"You know you get a sore throat."

"I go swimming, don't I? And have a bath? What's the difference?"

She didn't know. Only that the sore throat seemed to follow. They wore you down, children. She neither wanted to incur his displeasure nor seem unfair. A thought occurred to her.

"We aren't allowed to put hoses on."

"That's to water the garden. I'd only use a dribble. I'm sweating."

"Joey, shut up!" It came out as a scream. She felt like a shrew.

He stared at her, open-mouthed, then stalked upstairs, offended. She thought she heard him say, 'I think you've gone potty,' but couldn't be sure. She was dying for a cup of tea and to get her sticky clothes off but Cassius was lying limp beneath the table in the kitchen, looking decidedly unwell. She rang the garage – her car was ready and would be twenty-six pounds – and Irene about collecting it, and told Anne-Marie to get the table laid, and searched for the lead which was supposed to hang on a hook in the hall. It was nowhere to be found. She called Joey but there was no reply. He was sulking in his room and told her sniffily he had no idea where it was. After wasting another five minutes she found it in the pocket of his blazer. She put the blazer on the bottom of the stairs to remind herself about the button.

In Mr Purly's waiting-room she sat down next to a woman with hairy legs in a sun-dress. She held a small dog to her shoulder like a baby and was crooning to it. "Poor Oscar," she said to Lorna, "he hasn't stopped shaking since we've been here. Don't you worry," she addressed the dog, "Mr Purly going to make Oscar all better."

Lorna turned away to discourage the woman from confiding in her further. She had her own problems. She pretended to study the notices. 'Rabies is a killer'; 'The new dog-wormer your dog will like'; 'Is your pet in love?' She looked at Cassius who sat at her feet. He didn't look particularly amorous. There was a boy with a tortoise and a fat woman with something in a basket before her. She hoped it wasn't going to be too long. A man sat with his hands between his knees but appeared to have no animal unless it was in his pocket. She wondered if that meant four before her or three.

There were plastic marigolds on the central table. The waiting-room was as clean as any doctor's, cleaner than some she had seen. The smell of disinfectant was intensified by the heat, which was unrelieved by the open door and windows. Joey should have been doing this, would have come with her if she'd asked him, but he was upset because she had shouted at him about the hose. He sulked, like Derek; too easily assumed hurt feelings. There were magazines to read, dog-eared, ha!, and copies of *Your Dog's Dinner* which reminded her that Leonard and Clare were coming and of Yolande and the private hell she must have gone through, for she couldn't believe her death had been accidental. Death was something she had not managed to come to terms with, certainly not her own. The word itself made her go cold. Not death in wars, wherever the fighting happened to be, where the enormity was mitigated by numbers and she was unable to identify with the suffering. Single deaths, in prison cells, pop stars in road accidents, friends and acquaintances from coronaries and cancer. Unable to tolerate the thought of 'unbeing', it was easier to imagine herself immortal, that she, Lorna Brown, of everyone, was going to be different, to outlive them all. Sometimes she put a finger on her pulse or a hand to her heart and thought how incredible that it just went on pumping, pump after pump, for sixty, seventy, eighty years if you were lucky. It really did seem a long time when you thought about it like that, but not in terms of actual living. That went fast. She still wasn't sure how it had happened that she had moved up from daughter to mother and it was not beyond the realms of possibility that a few years would make her grandmother, when grandmothers had always seemed so old, so remote from oneself. Life was both relentless and unfathomable.

She had been only half-aware of the door opening and closing, people and animals padding across the linoleum floor and out into the stifling evening.

It was her turn. Cassius' rather. He had gone to sleep. The girl in the white coat was waiting. She pulled him to his feet. "He's a lovely fellow," she heard someone say, and "Aristocratic face" came from another corner.

She explained the symptoms to Mr Purly, who was short and fat like the wobbly-man.

"Not his fault, not his fault," Mr Purly said when she told him about the diarrhoea. "Mustn't be angry with him; not his fault."

He straddled the dog and felt his belly with expert, sausage-like fingers. Afterwards he washed his hands at the basin in the corner.

"Not uncommon at this time of year," he said to Lorna. "What do you feed him on?"

She explained about the tinned dog food.

"Change of diet," Mr Purly said "Change of diet. Fresh meat or chicken, cooked, and a couple of slices of bread, wholemeal bread, mind you, baked in the oven…"

She stared at him. What about a nice lemon meringue pie for dessert, she wanted to say.

"…That should do the trick. Plus some granules I'm going to give you now." He was measuring white stuff from a huge tin that said 'Strep…' something, into envelopes. "One sachet a day, Mrs Brown. I'd advise you to mix it with half the feed to be sure he gets it all, then you can give him the other half." He wrote in his ledger. "What did you say the dog's name was?"

"Cassius."

"That'll be two pounds fifty. He may not be clear of it by the morning but he'll certainly be well on the way. If you've any more trouble, let me know."

Fresh meat or chicken; to be cooked; every day. Wholemeal bread, baked in the oven. The alternative was to clear up after him in the mornings. It wasn't fair. She'd never wanted a dog in the first place. Derek and Joey had said they'd look after it. Children were one thing... part of the bargain. Not dogs. She was not prepared to cook for the dog. Not in this heat, not even for one day. I will go to Armand, she thought, tomorrow. Pam will have to take Mother about her veins. I will go tomorrow; after the Sports.

She realized that she was standing in the middle of the waiting-room, by the table with the plastic marigolds. A child with a gun in one hand and a kitten in the other was staring at her.

Cassius snarled at the kitten. She pulled on the lead. He stood his ground. There were other dogs who began to get restless. She pulled harder. "Cassius, come on!"

She got him out to the car. It was almost time to meet Derek. She still had to get to the garage and had not started dinner. Dinner. Sometimes she had caught herself wondering what would happen if Derek came home and she said, 'Today there is no dinner'. She had not, after all, signed a contract to provide three hundred and sixty-five dinners a year for, say fifty years, less holidays. Eighteen thousand dinners, not to mention the planning and shopping. Some women she knew had their husbands home for lunch as well, bringing the number to thirty-six thousand meals. Not that Derek was unreasonable. She knew very well that if she told him one night she was too tired to cook dinner or was not feeling very well, he'd say in a flash, 'OK, I'll take you out,' or go out with Joey, leaving her to a boiled egg. That wasn't the point though. Why should she plead illness or fatigue, why not just the fact that she did not want to provide dinner, had never contracted to do so? To love and to cherish, yes, it seemed so long ago now, to honour and obey. Nowhere was there anything about eighteen thousand dinners. It was only her generation. The youngsters either didn't want to get married at all or arranged things differently. They started as they meant to go on with Chinese take-aways or Kentucky fried chicken fetched when they felt like it, not at seven-thirty each night, give or take a few minutes, as if life itself depended on it. Pam, too, had opted out, but then she hadn't married Derek who went regularly to an office to earn the daily bread and expected, reciprocally, to be sustained in the manner to which he was accustomed when he came home. And then there was the time it took to eat compared with the effort involved. It was an equation at which she never ceased to be appalled. Especially with casseroles, which Derek liked in the winter. All that cubing and frying, with fat spitting in your face, and browning of onions and simmering gently and watching and tasting and then in minutes with a swab of bread for the gravy it was gone, as if it had never existed, been created, with patience and with concern and with care. It was not their fault, who ate it. If anyone's, it was her own. She knew there were certain standards within herself to which she had to live up. They had to do with looking after her man and her family as her mother had looked after her father and herself and Pam. There had been much talk about 'standards' and 'duty' and much, to be fair, teaching by example. But somehow for her mother there had never been anything else. She was not discontented. Her father's last days on earth had been distinguished by the amount he had been persuaded to eat each day. He made a lovely lunch; half a bowl of soup and a little mashed potato; only a few grapes, seeded and skinned; barely a mouthful of gruel. You won't catch me getting married, Cam said. Lorna wondered about the new-style partnerships and if they would last. The mutual shopping and visits to the launderette. The fusion of the roles. The emancipation of the women, an emancipation which was more important somehow than the achievement of the vote, touching something more fundamental. Carried to its logical conclusion the family, the extended family at any rate, was doomed. The family was said to be the world in miniature; was the world itself then doomed?

Hers seemed very much alive. Joey, appearing to have got over his sulks, was feeding the fish in the hall, Cam and Blake were unpacking their rucksacks over the floor.

She stepped over Joey's tins and feeding rings and the T-shirts and knickers and boxes of Tampax from the rucksacks.

"Do you have to do that in the hall?"

"We were having a try-out," Cam said. "Do you think I've got everything?"

Lorna looked at the one skirt and the espadrilles and water bottle and one warm sweater, two or three shirts and a pair of shorts, and thought of her own holiday packing, which had to do with half a dozen pairs of trousers and as many things to change into in the evenings and various shoes and bags and cardigans and beach cover-ups and swimsuits and sun-creams and after-sun-creams and scarves and belts and other accessories.

"It seemed very little to me."

"I haven't got the sleeping bag on yet. You try carrying all that on your back?"

"What did Mr Purly say?" Joey asked. "About Cass."

She told him.

"What have we got for dinner?"

"Fish mayonnaise."

"What about the chicken or beef for Cass?"

She shut her eyes. "He can have dry biscuits for tonight."

Joey stared at her. "Dry biscuits! How would you like it?"

"That's what he's going to have," Lorna said. "And you can get that mess cleared up," she said to Cam. "I want to start the dinner, Uncle Leonard's coming with Clare, Aunty Irene's taking me to fetch my car, and I have to collect Daddy on the way back from the garage."

"What do we say," Cam said, "to Uncle Leonard?"

"How do you mean?"

"About Auntie Yolande."

"I don't think he expects you to say anything at all really. Just make him feel at home; and Clare."

She understood Cam's difficulties in the presence of the bereaved. It was an awkwardness relieved only by age and the acquaintance, as Derek wryly put it, of more and more dead people.

She prided herself on her ability to do more than one thing at a time. She flaked the fish and had the mayonnaise going in the blender and made the dressing for the salad while the new potatoes were bubbling in their skins. She wondered who would cook when she'd left. Anne-Marie? Hopefully she'd stay, her time wasn't up until Christmas. She adored Joey and would do anything for Derek. She couldn't boil an egg though. Her mother waited on her hand and foot at home. Derek certainly wouldn't cook, turned the whole kitchen upside down when he had to make a cup of instant coffee, although he had been known to take a turn in the gallery on Geoffrey's boat. They would just have to manage. Get a cook perhaps, a housekeeper. Anne-Marie was filling the water jug for the table.

"Not yet, dear. Not in this weather. It's far too early."

It was the same every day. They did things like automatons; no thought, no sense. Anne-Marie poured the water out into the sink, admiring the cascade. She dried the jug, which had been bought with Green Shield stamps, slowly, carefully, as if it were hand-cut crystal, then put it away in the cupboard.

"You could leave it out."

She took it out of the cupboard again and smiled at Lorna. Her teeth became whiter and whiter as her face grew daily more tanned. She really was a very pretty girl, although her lips were thin and her face, Lorna thought, slightly hard and predatory.

The bell rang. Irene, to take her to the garage. It was the man for the freezer. He held the door of the cabinet wide open and she saw herself having to defrost it again soon. He gazed at the bulge of ice as if he had never seen anything like it before.

"Got a scraper, love, and a bowl?" he said to Anne-Marie.

Anne-Marie smiled at him, not understanding a word of his cockney accent.

Lorna gave him a plastic scraper and a bowl.

"And some newspaper."

He chipped away at the iceberg, whistling. His face was red and damp from the heat.

"Would you like a drink?" Lorna said.

"Wouldn't say no."

"Can you make some orange squash, Anne-Marie?"

She watched Anne-Marie pour half a glass of undiluted squash at thirty-five pence a bottle, then top it up with water.

"It's your seal," the man said, mopping his brow. "How long have you had her?"

"The Christmas before last."

"Out of your guarantee, then."

"Shouldn't it last longer than that?"

"Not today, they don't. Don't make anything like they used to. I'll have to fetch one along. Be a couple of weeks on account of them being on holiday. We got them on order, I know, because I needed one for another customer."

A couple of weeks. She wondered who would deal with it.

"Look, darling, it's my surgery night. If you want me to take you for the car…"

She looked at her watch. "Yes." She took off her apron. "It's nearly time for Derek anyway. You'd better order one," she said to the freezer man.

"Best not open it," he said.

She wondered how she was supposed to take anything out.

He left grubby finger-marks on the white porcelain.

Irene dropped her in the forecourt of the garage. She went into reception.

"I've come to collect my car."

"Ah, yes. Mrs…?"

"Brown."

She hated saying her name. Brown. It was so desperately ordinary. Lorna Brown even more so. One had to struggle to rise above it. Sometimes she said it slowly, beautifully, as in 'How now brown cow', but it didn't really help. Brown was Brown. Her single name had been Allardyce. She had liked that. Names were important. She felt that the man in the white overall with the blue collar was judging her because her name was Brown.

He was totting up figures.

"Forty-five pounds fifty, please, Mrs Brown." He twisted the invoice round on the counter so that she could see it.

"You told me twenty-six on the telephone."

"Yes." He leaned over patiently, as to a child, pointing to the figures with his ballpoint. "That was your parts, then there's your labour, and that little lot's for the government." He smiled at her, amused. She could see nothing funny. This week had seen the waste-grinder, the car, and the freezer. That was just for starters.

She wrote a cheque and produced her bank card. She was going to be late for Derek.

She joined the queue of wives in the station forecourt, and hoped Leonard and Clare would not have arrived before she got back. She wanted to shower and change before dinner, get out of the yellow suit which had lain on the floor at Armand's. She wondered how many of the other wives had spent the afternoon in adultery. How many of the husbands for that matter. She watched them through the window. Coming out of the station, in shirtsleeves mainly because of the heat, jackets slung over shoulders, evening papers and briefcases. Their first look was an anxious one in case their wives were not there, delaying the oasis of the cool garden, the Campari. You could divide them quite neatly into the kissers and the non-kissers. She passed the time away guessing and giving herself points for the correct answer. She remembered her first kiss. She had been fourteen-and-a-half at the time and had gone to the pictures with the brother of one of the girls at school. They had held hands during the film. She remembered feeling embarrassed because hers had been clammy with anxiety and wondering whether he would notice. There had been the problem of when to take the hand away. At one point she had been trying to get to her handkerchief, yet dare not move her hand for fear of offending him. Later she'd got cramp in her arm from the awkward position of it along the plush arm of the seat, but had gritted her teeth rather than fidget. He had taken her home and suddenly, walking along the dimly-lit street, had pulled her into a hedge and fastened his mouth on hers. She'd stared at him in amazement, until he said, 'You're supposed to close your eyes, silly,' and found her lips again, but this time she was prepared although he'd caught her mouth at a slightly awkward angle and she hadn't been quite sure whether she was supposed to move it. At the third go she'd found it came easier and generated a curious glow throughout her body which she was convinced was love. They'd stopped at every hedge after that, kissing, and when she'd finally got home she'd thought she would die of happiness.

'You're late dear,' her mother had said. 'I was getting worried. Was it a nice film?'

Lorna had stared at her.

'The film, dear? Was it nice? I remember seeing it years ago. Myrna Loy was in it then. Is anything the matter, Lorna?'

Matter? When she was floating on air. Divested of her body. Soaring, floating, madly, passionately in love.

'Why don't you have some cornflakes before you go to bed?'

Later there had been different kisses. Kisses involving the tongue and other parts of the body. There was the kiss of passion and the station kiss. The English, on the whole, did not kiss.

She watched the heads of the couple in the car ahead come together briefly and switched on her engine so that she could move up a place. Outside the station a woman sold flowers to conciliatory husbands, and a man evening papers to town-going ladies.

She watched Derek blink into the sunshine. He smelled of trains, the city. He kissed her.

"Had a good day?" she said.

"Hot. What have you been doing?"

"Nothing much." She thought of Armand and how easy it was to deceive.

"Did you remember to look at the oil?"

Eleven

Leonard said: " 'Death due to barbiturate poisoning.' Glad that's over. The inquest is tomorrow."

"Poor Yolande," Lorna said.

Leonard said: "I still can't believe it. I go home at night and I can't convince myself she's really not there. Out in the garden perhaps, or on the phone in the den, Yolande was always on the phone. I look in all the rooms; hopefully. It's the same in the mornings. I put out my hand. They say one does get used to it."

"It's a question of time," Derek said.

"What about Clare?" She was upstairs talking to Joey.

"Very strange," Leonard said. "Very self-contained. I keep trying to talk about Yolande but she changes the subject. She'll have to face it. The funeral's on Monday."

She would be with Armand. She did not want to miss Yolande's funeral. They stood by each other in Home Farm Close. Births, engagements, weddings, funerals. She wondered if they'd talk about her. Have you heard about Lorna? She's left Derek. You've got to be kidding! Not Lorna! Mayonnaise-making, button-sewing Lorna. Gone to live in a squat. Has she gone crazy? Crazy? No. Just served her sentence and out on parole. They let her out. Opened the gates of Home Farm Close and she walked away a free woman.

Crazy? At certain times of the month. This was one.

Leonard and Clare had been late. Changing, she'd thought Biological Lib was a fact. The pill had given a woman control over her fertile years. The monthly build-up of unbearable tensions remained. How little the men understood the state of mind at that time, the changing of perspective. Those you loved became hate objects. You could cheerfully murder. Guilty but insane, my lord. The tiniest criticism, implied or overt, became a federal case provoking anger and tears. Fingers became clumsy, memory failed. The future seemed blank if it could be seen at all. Life itself barely worthwhile. Fluid was retained in the body which felt heavy, swollen. The breasts became tight, lumpy, painful to the touch. She had felt the crags as she fastened her bra. She had been angry with Derek for asking about the oil, as if she had had nothing else to do. Another day she might have let it go.

"I have had other things to think about."

"I only asked you, Lorna. There's no need to get so excited."

She edged out into the main road.

"There's a car coming. Look out!"

"I know there's a car coming. I manage to drive all day long on my own. I spend my life in the car."

"You're not careful enough."

"You impair my judgement because you sit there criticizing."

"I only said there was a car coming. It's better than having an accident."

"Who's having an accident? I've been driving for nearly thirty years without any trouble."

"What about the mini?"

"I wasn't feeling well. Besides, I didn't know the post was there. What on earth are you dredging that up for now?"

"It was you who said you'd never had an accident. I was just... Lorna, it's too hot and I've had a busy day..."

"I suppose I haven't! I suppose you're the only one to have a busy day! That I've had nothing else to do but to look at the oil gauge every five minutes."

"Not every five minutes. Just once. I would have thought the one thing I'd asked you to do…It doesn't matter anyway."

It mattered. His face had the closed expression which came over it when he was angry.

"Leonard and Clare are coming to dinner," she said to change the subject.

"I hadn't forgotten."

"I suppose I'm the only one who forgets things!"

"Lorna, shut up!" He rarely grew angry with her. She could see he was hot and tired. Coping with the heatwave alone in the city was enough to exhaust one.

"Don't tell me to shut up!" The demon inside was driving her.

"Well, shut up then. It doesn't matter about the oil. I'll check the gauge myself when I get home."

She overtook a car too close.

"If we get home!"

She stopped the car. "That's enough. I'm not driving any more."

He put a hand on hers. "I was only joking."

She snatched her hand away and got out of the car.

In the shower she cried. She hated Derek, herself, everybody.

Derek brought her a drink upstairs. She hated him for that too.

"It's the heat," he said. "We'll eat in the garden."

"Typical! When it's all laid up in the dining-room!"

"I was only trying to help."

She'd watched him through the window, hoeing the parched earth round the wilting flowers. She did not deserve him. Perhaps he would be glad to be rid of her. She wasn't always as she was tonight.

Leonard said, "Cheers," when Derek gave him his drink. Could one say 'Cheers' to a man who had just lost his wife?

"Well…" she said, raising her glass and hoping he would realize that she was sorry, so sorry about Yolande.

She wondered who would die first, she or Derek. It didn't matter now that she was leaving, although she had the feeling she would be coming back. It would be a sabbatical really. One that she would award herself for outstanding services to housekeeping. She hoped it was not Derek. Society was not kind to women on their own, despite the inroads of the liberation movement. A single man was welcome anywhere. A woman lacking the alibi of a husband was either shunned or offered up to every unsuitable acquaintance, no matter how fat or stupid or old, provided he wore trousers. It was the way of the world. Leonard, she knew, would never be short of a meal, small treats brought round by the women of Home Farm Close. They would vie for his company. Introduce their most suitable unattached friends. Include him in everything, anything. Look after his children. He would become a social asset.

Leonard said: "Yolande and I have known each other since we were sixteen. It was love at first sight for both of us. There has never been anyone else. Never will be."

Lorna knew differently. She had seen it happen. He would, for a time perhaps, be inconsolable. They had been right together, he and Yolande. Of all of them in Home Farm Close, perhaps the most right. Because they were different from each other, and from their differences admiring, respecting. Leonard stolid, legal, ponderous, intellectual. Yolande a beautiful butterfly with scarcely a thought in her head. Often you would see Leonard watching her from behind his pipe, pride in his lively, lovely, scatterbrained wife apparent. She swam, danced, prattled, gave parties. Leonard watched, participated within his limitations. She had her head. Giving it to her, he adored her. Or so it seemed. There would be a time of mourning. He would begin to confide then in other women, in another woman, mitigating the loneliness. It would be pleasant. He would find himself unable to live without the companionship of a woman. Yolande would not be forgotten but Yolande was dead. He would discover that life had to go on, to progress. Others had discovered it. Why should it be different with Leonard? She looked at him. Hurt still, bewildered. Teddy-bear fat, his white shirt straining across his belly, pebble-thick glasses. She tried to imagine him at sixteen, then gave up. It was more difficult with men, the change precipitated by the ageing process more radical. Women were generally mature versions of their younger selves. Not so men. It wasn't merely a question of hair receding and greying, of facial furrows and blurred outlines. There seemed always to be some structural change of contours. It was hard to reconcile the middle-aged man with the lad, although she was never quite sure exactly at what point the change took place, so subtle was the metamorphosis.

When Clare came out on to the terrace with Joey, it was as if Yolande had walked through the sliding windows. They all felt it. The stick-thin paleness, the fiery hair like a flaming mop on a broomstick. She said, "Joey's got some super fish, Daddy. He's going to give me one."

"Two," Joey said.

Lorna recognized the gift as a nine-year-old's gesture of condolence. His fish were his babies. She was proud of him.

"Is that all right?" Clare said.

Leonard said, "You'll have to ask..." But there was no Mummy. They all felt uncomfortable except Clare, who refused to feel and said, "I'll keep them in my room. Joey's going to give me an old tank."

Looking at her in her blue denim skirt and white shirt which said 'Keep Smiling' across her undeveloped chest, Lorna felt angry with Yolande for abandoning her at such a crucial and uncertain time. Simon, it was true, was only eleven, but a girl at fourteen needed her mother. Not necessarily to confide in but to be there like a rock to cling to while you were savaged by the storms of adolescence.

Cam and Blake had gone out for a farewell drink. She wondered whether it would have been easier to go to Armand if Cam had been staying at home. Not really. Lorna could not see her rallying round, replacing her, running the house. She was too disinterested, too wrapped up in herself. She was glad Cam would be away. She did not particularly want to face her ridicule.

At dinner she sat Leonard next to Anne-Marie, pairing them off, as if it would be in the slightest bit suitable. She felt as if she were being unfaithful to Yolande. He asked Anne-Marie about Switzerland, discovered places of mutual interest. It was not unknown for second wives to be half the age of the first one. Changing a forty for two twenties, so the joke went round Home Farm Close. Nobody would think it in the least strange, yet she and Armand...She never thought of a similar situation herself without ridicule. What could a young man possibly see in a woman old enough to be his mother, apart from his mother?

Uncertain of the duck pâté, she had thrown it away.

The fish mayonnaise went down well with the Sancerre Derek had opened. When they'd finished and Anne-Marie was clearing the plates Derek said, "What's for pudding? I expect Lorna's made one of her creations for you, Leonard. What is it, Lorna? Honey and banana sorbet? She makes them in her sorbetière."

She brought in the tinned peaches. Derek looked embarrassed, "I suppose it was too hot to cook?"

Why should he suppose any such thing? Why should he not suppose she had spent the pre-dinner hours in bed with her lover?

"Wasn't it?" he said, giving Leonard the last of the wine.

"What?"

"Too hot."

"Not really." She did not expand. She knew she was letting him down. It was the agonizing tenseness inside her. The wish she had to hurt him. The cloud settled on his face for the second time that evening.

Lifting the spoon on which was perched a tinned peach-half, like an orange dome, to his mouth, Derek let the syrup drip on to his tie.

"You've spilled it on your tie," Lorna said sharply, as if to a child.

"Where?"

"There." She pointed.

He put down the spoon and picked up his napkin. "Blast!"

" 'Ot water?" Anne-Marie said, pushing back her chair.

"No. It'll make it worse." He looked at Lorna. "You'll have to take it to the cleaners."

She felt the wire, which had been pulled tightly inside her head, snap. She had wiped the memory-board clean for today and already it was filling up for tomorrow. 'Derek's tie to cleaners.' Waiting, while those in front of her laid their soiled garments on the counter, collected others, smelling of cleaning fluid, swinging from wire hangers under plastic shrouds.

'One tie.'

'And the name, please'

'Brown.'

'Ready on Monday.'

She would be with Armand in Regent's Park. She wondered if she would send the pink cleaning ticket to Derek by post. Who would fetch the tie? Anne-Marie? Irene?

He was still rubbing at it.

"Blasted nuisance."

She saw Leonard looking at him as if equating their problems. Death relegating such trifles to their proper place.

She gave them coffee in the garden, Leonard and Derek. The air was still and warm, the temperature in the seventies, an evening more like the tropics. They discussed the possibilities of war in the Middle East as seriously as if either of them had the capacity to resolve the problem. Leonard said, "Thank you, Lorna," when she gave him his cup, like a lost child grateful for any consideration. She wanted to put her arms round him, to console.

The tensions which had been mounting within her all day erupted when they went to bed.

When Derek came into the bedroom she was brushing her teeth, the bathroom door was open.

"What a mess in the back of my car," he said. "Cassius' hairs all over the place."

"I took him to the vet, remember?"

"You could have cleaned it up."

"I could have done. But I didn't."

"No need to be snappy. I only mentioned it. I don't know what's the matter with you today, Lorna. Must be the heat."

He took off his tie.

"I'll leave my tie here." He laid it across the back of the chair instead of rolling it up and putting it in line with its mates.

She closed her eyes, thinking of the enormity of it. He would leave his tie on the back of the chair, just leave it, no more effort than that, and when he wanted to wear it again, in one day's time, or in two, he would expect to find it, cleaned and in good order, once more in its place. Great tears slid down her face and mingled with the saliva and the foaming toothpaste which she spat into the Sahara Beige bowl. She wiped her mouth and tears tasted salt within it. They were still rolling down her face when she went into the bedroom.

Derek saw her tear-stained face as it was intended he should.

"What's the matter, Lorna?"

He had taken off one shoe and he sat on the armchair with it in his hand. "Is it because of Yolande? I must say it was a bit sad-making having old Leonard. One feels so sorry, yet there's so little one can do. Anyway, crying won't help."

"It's not Yolande."

"What then? If you tell me what it is about, maybe I can help."

She sat on the bed, sniffing, and thought that perhaps the moment had come to tell him about Armand, although it wasn't because of Armand she was crying.

"You never could take the hot weather."

He was putting a shoe tree into his shoe.

The storm which had been brewing all day within her erupted.

She turned to him. "It isn't the weather and it isn't my age. How is it possible for you to live so close to me, to share a bed, to go to sleep in my arms, and not to know me? To blame everything on to the weather and my age?"

"Take it easy, Lorna." He put down his shoe. He never lost his temper, not Derek. He came to sit on the bed beside her, bringing with him the smell of Leonard's cigar. He put an arm round her.

"Tell me what it is then, what's the matter?"

She didn't answer.

"There must be something." He handed her his handkerchief which she blew into. "Tell me."

Perhaps she should. She put the hair back where it was stuck to her cheeks with tears.

"It's the memory-board and all the little things, and taking Cassius to Mr Purly and forgetting about the oil and you reminding me and having to take your tie to the cleaners tomorrow and, oh God! I still haven't sewn the button on Joey's blazer and Cam and the mess she makes and Anne-Marie's so stupid…"

"I know," Derek said suddenly. "I recognize the symptoms, it's the time of the month!"

"And the time of the day and the time of the week and the time of the year…" she said hysterically.

"Perhaps you should have a chat with Dick; maybe you need some pills or something. I'll come with you if you like. Is it too late to give him a ring?"

"I don't need pills," she said. "I need…"

She looked at his face on which there was nothing but kindness, concern. If she told him now that she was going to leave him it would dissipate her resolution. She would never go. She loved him too much.

"You need a good night's sleep to start with. You look exhausted, Lorna. This heat's not good for anyone."

"Please leave the heat, my age. It has nothing to do with anything." She started to cry again.

He got up from the bed and, folding up the tie which was stained with the juice of the offending tinned peaches, he put it into his briefcase.

"Derek, what are you doing?"

"I'll take it to the cleaners. There's one near the office." He looked at her disbelieving face.

"There's no need to do that."

"It's no trouble to me."

"It's no trouble to me either."

"But you said, I distinctly heard you, not two minutes ago…"

"Why do you always listen to what I say?" she shrieked.

He looked at her. "You wouldn't like it if I didn't."

She laid her face in her hands. I don't mean to what I say, you listen to that, you don't listen to what I mean, the plea for sympathy and understanding, the dog and the tie and the oil are only symptoms, symbols if you like, of what is going on inside me, your wife, your woman, there was no understanding, no communication, it was not possible, never would be, not a real coming together of what was important, only the day-to-day trivia, I'm going to leave you, Derek…

"Why don't you come to bed? I'm exhausted if you're not. You'll probably feel a lot better in the morning."

He went into the bathroom and shut the door. She hadn't felt so wretched for a long time. She wanted to close her eyes and for it all to be over. Perhaps that was what Yolande had felt. Perhaps it wasn't such a mystery after all; nor all that difficult either. She dried her face on Derek's handkerchief and took the nylon shopping bag which Armand had hidden from the table beside her bed. She took out the book she had bought, the menopause book. There was a picture of a jolly-looking forty-year-old on the front. She was smiling brightly as if she had overcome all the problems attendant upon her age very nicely, thank you. There was a quotation from Byron inside the front cover:

> Though her years were waning,
> Her climacteric teased her like
> her teens

The phrase 'her years were waning' made her cry again, blurring the opening paragraph. 'The changes that affect both the body and the mind at and after the menopause are immensely complicated…' She heard the flush of the lavatory and put the book into the drawer in which she kept her sewing equipment. There was no reason why she should not be reading a book on the menopause, yet she felt distinctly touchy about it as if she, of all women, was to be different, not admitting to its oncoming. She took out the card of mauve buttons from the bag. They were in a blister pack, ten of them. She dug her nail into the plastic bubble, hurting herself but making no impression. She looked for her scissors in the sewing drawer and remembered Cam had been sewing. She felt renewed rage well up within her. She had borrowed the scissors and, of course, not put them back.

"Blast the thing," she said and hurled the packet at the bathroom door. It caught Derek as he came out.

"I can't open it."

"What is it?"

"Buttons for Joey's blazer. They pack everything in those silly plastic bubbles and it's impossible to open them. God almighty, why is life so difficult?"

"Not life, Lorna. A packet of buttons."

"Open it then."

"Hang on." He held the packet in both hands and examined it carefully. Turning it over he discovered a perforation down the back. He opened it and shook out one button. It sat, a mauve circle, on his extended palm.

"You get so worked up."

She looked at him and took the button.

"Thank you."

"Don't mention it." He was trying to restore her good humour.

The other button was sewn on with mauve thread which matched the mauve of the mauve and black striped blazer. In her box of cottons, their ends tangled, were reels of yellow and green and black. She decided upon the black and, unwinding a length, made a double knot in it. There was a hard stump of atrophied thread in the place where the buttons were off and where she had to sew on the new ones. It was impossible to remove them without scissors. She put the blazer and the needle and cotton down on the bed.

"Where are you going? Derek was in bed.

"To see where Cam's put my scissors. She drives me mad."

"She's going away tomorrow."

"Thank goodness."

"You know you like it when she's home."

"You must be joking!"

If she hadn't known where Cam's room was, she would have found it by following the smell of stale smoke from Blake's cigarettes. She found it revolting. Cam's room was unbelievable. The beds were unmade, not stripped, abandoned, just as they had crawled out of them. The eiderdowns were on the floor. It was her fault, Cam said, for not providing duvets at home as she had at college, nobody had sheets and blankets any more, it was too much of a bore. The rucksacks and their spilled contents, like sordid cornucopiae, were on the floor. Passports and air-tickets and student cards lay half-buried in skirts and shirts. She wondered how they would ever be ready by eight o'clock in the morning. There was no inch of the orange carpet which wasn't covered with knickers, records, speakers, with attendant wires and leads, record deck, amplifiers, cardboard boxes of books, feather boas, African drums, empty cigarette cartons, full ashtrays, dishes with encrusted dried cornflakes, and cups of cold undrunk coffee. Every cupboard was open, the jumbled contents spilling out into the general river below, every drawer erupting with unsavoury-looking contents. It was too bad. You don't have to look at it, Cam said. But what about the scissors? In term-time she reclaimed the room. Sorting and stacking, tidying and organizing until it was sweet and fresh. Only the labelled champagne bottles on the windowsill, the books in the bookcases, and the various weird garments she had hung on the walls indicating it was Cam's. She had been such a tidy little girl. Start-rite sandals side by side beneath the bed each night, clothes folded and laid neatly on the chair. She even had to get out of bed before she went to sleep to close a drawer or cupboard if it was open. She knew it didn't matter; that the chaos was indicative of something going on within Cam herself. It did matter. Disgusted, revolted her. Glad to see them come. Glad to see them go again. It was the battle cry of Home Farm Close. They all suffered from it, like some disease.

She wondered why young men on white chargers no longer came and snatched them away. It could be thirty years, horror of horrors, before they became someone else's responsibility. She had seen it happen and wondered whether it was the pill or political cynicism. She moved a burned-out candle and a teddy bear with her toe in an effort to find the scissors. She wondered what would have happened if she had ever left her her room in similar condition when she was young. It simply couldn't have happened. She was afraid of her father and had to strip her bed and make it before she went out. She did as she was told. Cam's generation did not, as they did not accept what they were told, which was healthy. She rummaged among the dried-up deodorant bottles on the dressing table and screwed-up tissues like solid snowballs. The scissors were among the dismembered parts of a desk lamp Cam had been trying to repair. She had been using them as a screwdriver. The end of one of the blades was blunted and bent. Lorna was convinced that had Cam been in the room she would have lunged at her with them, wishing to hurt in her fury at such inconsiderate and selfish behaviour. If she told Derek he would say, 'They're good kids, what are you carrying on about?'

He was in bed, the *Architect* propped on his stomach. She told him about the scissors, Cam's room.

"I don't know why you keep on," he said without taking his eyes from the article he was reading. "She's a good kid..."

She removed the knot of cotton from the blazer.

"If I died, or left you," she said, putting in the first stitch of black cotton, "would you marry again?"

"Yes."

She knew it was true.

"Why?" The black cotton did not look too good against the mauve button. She did not care.

"I like being married."

She hoped Mr Snell would not look too closely at her handiwork.

"Look," Derek said, putting down his journal. "Stop thinking about Yolande. You're getting morbid."

She stared at him. He was going up the down escalator again. "Yolande?"

"It upset you having Leonard. Come to bed."

She wound the cotton round the base of the button tightly so that it would not come off, for who would there be to sew it on again? She would it so tightly that she did not leave herself enough to make the few final fastening stitches. She had to unwind some again. She did it slowly, knowing from the way that Derek had said 'Come to bed' that he wanted to make love.

Perhaps some odour of that day's previous sexual encounter had aroused him. Poor Derek. It would be the last time. Tomorrow he would lie alone in the king-sized bed between the percale and cotton sheets.

Twelve

She woke suddenly at six, aware that things were not the same in either mind or body. The body first. She felt her breasts. They were no longer taut, turgid, but detumescent, only the left one still had its premenstrual nodules. Inwardly there was a sensation of peace. Today she loved the world and realized that the onset of her monthly period was responsible for her altered view of the universe. If women were in charge, man's destiny would be dictated by their biology. Today everything would be good. She would be kind, gentle, loving, giving, understanding, beautiful. She knew that when she looked at her face in the mirror the looks she had lost in the past weeks behind a mask of tension would have returned. Careful not to disturb Derek, who slept unaware of the dynamic changes being wrought so close to him, she went into the bathroom.

When she got into bed again she did not want to sleep in the hour that remained before she must get up to take Cam and Blake to the airport. She felt too happy and decided just to lie and enjoy her thoughts and where they took her.

Her state of mind reminded her of the glow she had felt after the births of both Cam and Joey. Its manifestation had been noted by the poets. 'No man could smile it,' one had said of the seraphic look on a woman's face after parturition. You could not describe the sensation any more than you could convey the quality of a painting or the evocations of a Beethoven sonata. It compensated for the agony; expunged the pain.

Today she loved Derek, who was breathing regularly near her. Last night, unable to abandon her tensions, she had merely submitted while he made love to her. Shut her eyes and thought not quite of England but of how she was going to make the transition, in practical terms, from Home Farm Close to Armand. He had put her lack of response, with everything else, down to the heat. She could have murdered him in the marital bed. Derek, everybody. Now she put out her hand. His chest was cool. He had thrown off the sheet in the heat of the night. He looked gentle, vulnerable. Today she loved him but was going to leave him because she wanted out. From what? She looked round the room in the light that filtered through the Colefax and Fowler curtains. Very Derek. Very Home Farm Close. White unit furniture; inside, the smoothly running drawers, the well-fitted cupboards, a place for everything. White, space-age television. Squashy brown leather chair with chrome legs. Sugary pastels of Cam and Joey when they were small. A photograph of her mother and father beneath an apple tree in the garden in Dorset. Walls and ceiling covered with the same wallpaper, stylized brown tulips on a biscuit ground, Colefax and Fowler again, it had been the vogue when they had decorated.

Peace, calm, nothing. Nothing that was her, if there was anything that was her. She was going to Armand to find out. She would have liked to get up and go now, just like that, but there was the day to get though. Only one more. She hoped that Cassius had not had diarrhoea in the night. A door slammed, then the sound of Blake coughing as if she hoped to eject her lungs. She wondered if they'd finally managed to pack their rucksacks from the chaotic shambles of their room.

She never felt very energetic on the first day of her period and would willingly have lain there letting the world carry on without her. The day had to be faced, however. This one in particular. It was a turning point in the non-event that was the life of Lorna Brown.

Downstairs the kitchen was clean. Cassius wagged his tail. She could have hugged him. She let him into the garden, which was dappled with the early sun, put the kettle on, and decided to take Derek his breakfast in bed. First she went up to wake Joey.

The stereo was pounding in Cam's room. She went in to tell her to turn it down before it woke Derek. Cam was on her knees stuffing things into her rucksack, Blake was pulling a greyish T-shirt over her naked body. Lorna was sure there had been no washing.

"Can you lower it?"

"What? Cam said.

"It's too noisy."

Cam put out a hand and the sound abated slightly.

"Will you be ready at eight? Don't forget it's the rush hour."

"You're always fussing."

"Yes," She realized suddenly that when Cam was gone she would not tidy her room. It made her laugh.

"What's funny?" Cam said.

"Nothing. I must wake Joey."

He was her only problem. The others could manage. Used her simply as an accessory. Joey was only nine. Had he been a girl she would not have gone to Armand. Derek, she suspected, could be both mother and father to Joey. The sheet was tightly wrapped round his body. He looked like a small mummy and was deep in sleep, his long eyelashes against his cheek tanned from the summer. She sat on the bed and put her cheek against his, wanting suddenly to cry.

"Be good, Joey."

He opened his eyes.

"Time to get up."

"Have you sewn my button on?"

"Yes."

"Thanks, Mum." He closed his eyes again.

"Come on, it's Sports Day."

"You're coming?"

"Of course."

"Bet I win the three-legged."

"Bet you will."

She prepared Derek's tray with care, scrambling the eggs just as he like them.

"Breakfast!"

He opened his eyes, puzzled.

"What's this in aid of? It's not Sunday."

"No."

"Well, then?"

"Just felt like it."

The condemned man ate a hearty breakfast. Condemned to manage without her. To face the world a cuckold; a Feydeau farce.

"It's funny you should have brought me breakfast."

"Why?"

"I think I've got a cold coming on." He felt his neck. "I've a bit of a sore throat."

With Derek a cold was a major production. He really did get them badly. Something to do with his tonsils. It was always a matter of two or three days in bed and hot drinks and aspirins. She hoped he wasn't going to stay at home today, of all days.

"Perhaps it will go away."

She knew it wouldn't. It always started with a sore throat. She would not put on her nurse's hat. She would be with Armand.

"Don't forget to wish Joey luck."

"What for?"

"The three-legged."

"Stupid race. What's wrong with the fifty metres?"

"He can't be good at everything."

"Why not? Irene and Dick coming round tonight? I've a marvellous word using five vowels."

"Not tonight." Nor any night unless they wanted to play three-handed Scrabble with Derek.

"Give them a ring."

She changed the subject. "I'd better hurry. I'm taking Cam and Blake to the airport."

"We shall be quiet again. When Joey goes on his exchange there'll be just the two of us."

Just the one. She refused to think as far ahead as the exchange. He was going to Brittany for three weeks. If she started to consider the implications of her action she would never go. Never get out of Home Farm Close. Derek would manage. He could stay at his club.

She saw them into the car, Derek and Joey. Joey with all three buttons on his blazer, two of them secured with black cotton. For the first time she felt afraid.

" 'Bye, Lorna."

"Goodbye."

" 'Bye, Mum. Don't be late." He meant the Sports. "Wish me luck."

"Good luck!" She meant when she was gone.

She wondered when she would next see Derek.

In the kitchen Anne-Marie, the long hair twisted into a neat bun on top of her head, was drinking coffee.

"I am going to town."

Lorna stood still. She had forgotten it was Anne-Marie's day off. There would be problems about Joey getting in. She would have to leave the key. She hadn't reckoned on his coming back to an empty house. She would get some dinner ready and leave it for him and Derek. The last supper. Cold meat and salad. She was not going to extend herself. A shutter in her mind had closed down as if she had already gone.

159

In the car Cam said, "If Sally phones tell her her records are in my room if she wants to come and get them. And I've left my lamp. Can you take it to be repaired? I tried to do it myself…"

With my scissors.

"… but I couldn't. I shall need it for next term."

"No," Lorna said.

"Thanks, Mum." She hadn't even heard. Or if she had, simply not registered. "Sorry about the mess in my room…didn't have time…"

She wasn't sorry at all. Just confident that when she came back from Israel it would be cleared away. By magic. By Lorna.

She left them with their rucksacks outside Terminal 3 and parked the car in the multi-storey car park. She didn't like multi-storey car parks. There was something of Brave New World in the concrete artificiality of them. She was always doubtful of finding the car again and was certain when she walked towards the exit, footsteps echoing, that someone was following her like in a TV thriller.

Inside Terminal 3 they stood at the check-in amidst a huge crowd. El-Al was taking no chances. There had been too many hijackings recently. She left them to go upstairs and buy chocolate for them for the journey as if they were small children. She had always bought Cam and Joey chocolate bars when they travelled.

She looked down through the glass of the gallery to where Cam and Blake were waiting. An elderly man in a skull-cap had opened his suitcase on the counter. It had been carefully packed. The blonde girl in her smart uniform removed every single item. There was something obscene about the public display of the inside of a packed suitcase. Others in the gallery watched as if it were a peep-show.

She went down again. It was Cam's turn. She heaved Armand's rucksack up on to the counter before the handsome young man in the white shirt. He had curly black hair.

"Open it, please." He indicated the rucksack.

It had taken Cam half an hour to get it closed. She opened it.

"Please remove everything."

She began to spread the things on the counter: Tampax, documents, clothes, books.

The young man picked up a book. "You like Herman Hesse?"

"Yes."

"Me, too. Why are you going to Israel?"

"Holiday."

He nodded to Blake. "Your friend too?"

"Yes."

"Where are you staying?"

"On a kibbutz."

"Which one?"

She told him.

"It's very nice. I live not far from there." He was examining the contents of the rucksack as he spoke. "Do you have any relatives in Israel?"

"No."

"Are you taking any gifts or presents?"

"No."

"How long are you staying in our country?"

"Six weeks. More if we like it."

"You'll like it." He undid a tube of toothpaste. "OK." He helped her put the things back in the rucksack.

When the strap was done up he looked at her passport before handing it to her.

"Camilla Brown. Next week I'll be in Israel. I'll come to see you on the kibbutz. We'll talk about Hesse. Enjoy your stay in Israel." He looked at Blake. "May I see your rucksack please?"

There was a rapport among the young today. It was their world.

She walked with them to the entrance of the departure lounge.

"Thanks for everything, Mummy. I know you're pleased to see me go. To have the house to yourself. I can't help it."

Lorna wasn't quite sure what it was that she couldn't help.

"Thank you for putting up with me, Mrs Brown," Blake said.

Lorna hugged Cam, suddenly wanting to cry into the woolly hair. She held her tightly.

"I'm only going for six weeks," Cam said.

But I am going. She did not want to make a scene and released her, unable to speak suddenly.

Overcoming her revulsion at the pallid face, the dull hair, she kissed Blake.

"Look after yourselves. And write." She wondered if Derek would forward the letters.

They disappeared into the departure lounge. It seemed important that Cam was taking Armand's rucksack.

Driving in the three lanes of traffic that flowed towards the exit of the airport, Lorna had the strange sensation that it was she who had left. She felt a happiness, a lightness creeping upon her although there was still two-thirds of the day to get through before she was free.

She stopped at the supermarket and bought luncheon sausage, a lettuce, a cucumber, and some tomatoes, and two peaches. Lois was at the check-out with a trolley-load of groceries. She looked at Lorna's basket.

"Your family left home?" she said.

Lorna smiled. Lois would say, I met Lorna at the super-market, it must have been the day she left. I must say she was acting most strange. As if half a pound of luncheon sausage, some salad, and a couple of peaches was strange. She pitied Lois with her loaded trolley.

"Must rush," she said. "It's Joey's Sports Day."

At home there was only Cassius to greet her. She gave him the granules the vet had given her.

She went into the den which she hated almost as much as the utility room. It was fitted with rosewood. Bookshelves, a desk with a pull-down flap, drinks cupboards, concealed TV, a special shelf for Derek's golf cups. The carpet was shaggy and cinnamon brown, the armchairs oatmeal tweed.

She sat at the desk and took a piece of the die-stamped notepaper whose print matched the shaggy carpet. Underneath the address, Home Farm Close – Her Majesty's Prison – she wrote, 'Friday. Dear Derek.'

Like the bank manager. My darling Derek. Derek. If she started crossing out now she would never get it done. At best it wasn't going to be easy.

DEAR DEREK,

You won't understand so please don't try. I have gone away for a bit. I am quite well. It's not the heat and it's not my age and there's no one else who's important to me. The most I can produce by way of explanation is that I feel that living the life I do in the place that I do is like living in a sort of open prison. The warders are very kind indeed and I can get out but it is only on parole. I always have to come back. Perhaps I want to. I don't know. I have to get away for a while to see what it is I do want. Life is so short that it seems foolish for people to jog along doing all the things they are not really happy doing day after day until they get the screaming abdabs which is what I have. I love you. If I didn't I would have told you instead of writing. I have tried to discuss how I feel with you once or twice but we no longer seem to be on the same wavelength. Perhaps I am too impossible for anyone to be on the same wavelength as me. That remains to be seen. I have to get away to sort it out. I am sorry about Joey but he is immensely resourceful and I know you can take care of him, you get on so well together. Cam is another matter but she has gone away and does not need me anyway. I need her but must learn not to. Tell Mother whatever you like. The only person I have told, or intend to tell, is Pam. In a funny way, although we are worlds apart, she understands. If you have anything important to say to me tell Pam and I will keep in touch with her. Please don't come after me with tracker dogs, that would demolish me. I have to have time. I am so sorry, my darling. None of this is your fault, you have always been a good husband and I hope you will understand that I really do still love you. I am sorry about Yolande's funeral. Tell them all what you like. I shall be there in spirit. Please don't forget Cassius has to have fresh meat or chicken and wholemeal bread. Perhaps it is the heat. And my age. And Yolande. And Thelma Barrington. I don't know. Just that I have to get out and the only sadness is hurting you. There is luncheon sausage in the fridge for supper... Oh, my darling

…LORNA.

She wrote 'Derek' in large letters on the envelope with a felt pen and put it on the fish tank where he could not fail to see it. She refused to imagine how he would feel, reading it, and went upstairs to pack her case.

The case itself presented the first problem. In the top cupboards was the set of matched luggage with the triple stripe which she and Derek used when they went on holiday. It seemed wrong somehow to break the set; cheating. In the loft there was an old case, battered, one of the locks gone. She used it for jumble. She would take that.

She got it down and opened it on the bed which she had not made. In her wardrobe were clothes for every occasion: round the house, coffee mornings, informal entertaining, dinners in town, theatres, grand evenings, country weekends. Not a thing for squatting. As far as she remembered there was nowhere to hang anything anyway, she would probably have to keep her possessions in the case. She thought her jeans, like an ageing hippy, and some sweaters and shirts that were not too new. She took out a classic Italian cotton knit dress that did for anything and was tempted to take it. Looking at it, she realized that it represented everything she was running away from.

She heard a noise and spun round from the wardrobe. Irene was standing in the doorway.

"I let myself in the back."

She looked at the case. "Where are you going?"

For a moment Lorna wondered about telling Irene but she knew she would put on her doctor's wife's act as if she were sick and telephone Dick and Derek and raise the alarm generally.

"Oh, that!" Lorna laughed as if she had suddenly noticed the case. "Jumble."

"It's not till October!"

"I thought I'd have a clear-out."

Irene eyed the Giovanozzi dress she was holding. "You're not giving that away?"

"Certainly not." She hung it back in the cupboard. "I thought it might perhaps need a wash."

Irene sat on the bed looking into the case which was packed too neatly for jumble. Lorna wished she wouldn't.

"There's a mysterious-looking letter for Derek in the hall. In your writing. Don't you speak to each other any more?"

Lorna laughed. "It's about the...about Cassius' dinner, he's on a new diet... in case I'm not back from Sports Day."

"After Yolande I'm suspicious about everything. I don't want to come round here one day and find that you've gone."

Lorna realized she meant taken her own life.

"Not that you would," Irene went on. "People like you and I, Lorna, keep on keeping on until we drop dead in our tracks. Who was it said on his death bed: 'Is that all?' That'll be us. No suicides, no dramas. Home Farm Close, then put to grass in a bungalow or filed away in a flat until the reaper comes to get us."

"What about Yolande?"

"Yolande was different."

"We didn't think so. Before."

165

"You're not Yolande. I know you too well."

Lorna looked at her swinging her bare brown leg complacently. "What about Thelma Barrington?"

"Thelma and Yolande were not you and I. There is a certain dumb, accepting stability about us. Are you coming round to us tonight? Dick thinks he now has the Scrabble word guide by heart. He's been memorizing words like 'tolyl' and 'britska' all week. They take things so seriously, men; golf and Scrabble and cars, which road to take. It seems to matter so dreadfully."

"You come over here," Lorna said. "Derek wants you to come." It would be company for him.

"If you insist. How were Leonard and Clare? I'm really worried about that child. She's too controlled."

Lorna wished she would go away so that she could pack her sponge-bag and her beauty-case with her cosmetics.

"They were fine. Considering."

"It's strange, how life goes on. Come and sit in my garden and I'll give you some home-made yoghurt for lunch."

Lorna looked at the unmade bed. "It's Anne-Marie's day off."

"I'll help you with it," Irene said. "I'm feeling energetic this morning." She got off the bed.

"No, really! I've got a bit of a headache anyway and one or two things to do…"

"Please yourself. I must go and get into a swimsuit. It's too hot even at this hour. Sure you won't come?"

"Positive."

"See you tonight then."

"I expect so," Lorna said.

"It'll be gone by then," Irene said, meaning the headache. "Take a couple of Veganin." She almost tripped over Cassius who lay across the doorway.

"That ruddy dog! I don't know how you put up with him. I shall fall over him and break my neck one of these days."

She heard Irene go, knowing that she would kick herself with hindsight. 'She was actually packing,' she could hear her say to

Derek, 'and I didn't have the sense to realize. She told me it was jumble when I physically saw her Fiorucci jeans.'

She finished quickly now, deciding against her heated rollers and the hand-dryer she considered indispensable. She put in the new Margaret Drabble and the *Harpers and Queen* which had come that morning and which she had not read, and closed the one lock of the case thinking that she had never travelled anywhere so light.

Looking at the unmade bed and thinking of Derek getting into it that evening, she had a fight with her conscience, part of which was already in Regent's Park, then decided to make it. She made Joey's too, knowing how fussy he was and how he would hate to come back to an untidy room. No one was allowed to dust the treasures with which he surrounded himself. A collection of vintage cars, books, mainly about fish. On his armchair lay the threadbare panda he had had as a baby. It seemed to look reproachfully at her with its one eye. She covered it with a sweater and left the room which was redolent with small boy and with sunlight. Stopping at Cam's room she picked her way over the debris to open the windows because of the smell of staleness and of smoke, then remembered she had to leave the house locked up. Cam had a picture of herself on the windowsill in a glassless frame. Derek had taken it. She had been Joey's age, a fresh-faced schoolgirl in a striped cotton dress and blazer. Cam, Cam, what will become of you? The opened bed with its daisy-strewn sheets looked cold, despite the sunlight, as if it knew it would have no occupant that night. She wondered who would clean the room, feeling sorry for Derek, for Anne-Marie, for herself.

'Goodbye, Cam,' she said, as if she were going to Australia instead of Regent's Park. She shut the door and as she did so heard a voice in her ears. 'Mummy, I want a drink of water'. It was the inevitable cry as she had shut the door at night when they were small. And she heard it. Cam's voice. She opened the door once more on the desolate, abandoned bed and the silent, resting speakers.

In the hall she put down the case and went round the ground floor touching things like a blind man, the leaves of the ficus, the soapstone knife they had bought in Mexico, the silver cigarette box from a grateful client of Derek's.

As she moved, from the hall to the den, to the living-room, to the dining-room, Cassius followed her, stopping and starting as she did, a look of reproach on his sad face as if he knew.

In the kitchen she touched the Magimix which chopped onions in moments and the cooker with its speed broil which grilled both sides of the food at once. She filled Cassius' bowl with water and he got excited, thinking it was dinner-time. She left the key outside on the fuse-box for Joey, who would know where to look for it.

She picked up the battered brown case. Cassius stood in the hall, waiting to see whether it was 'walkies'.

"Stay," she said. "Good boy!"

He blinked at her.

"Joey will take you out," she said. She always thought that people who talked to dogs were idiotic.

She shut the front door and locked it and put the case into the boot of her car. Home Farm Close slept in the sultry afternoon. There was not even an au pair to be seen. Everyone, she imagined, except Yolande who was still in the cold morgue, would be supine on their garden beds, asleep, or listening to 'Woman's Hour.'

She got as far as the carriage drive when she saw Lois running as fast as her fat would allow her; running and waving. Damn Lois.

"Thank goodness I've caught you." She was out of breath and leaned against the open window of the car.

Lorna waited, thinking if she was as fat as Lois she would certainly make more of an effort.

"My battery's flat," Lois said. Confined to prison. "Can you bring me a small brown?"

Lorna looked at her.

"We've got smoked trout and my in-laws are coming."

"I'm not coming back," Lorna said.

"Later will do," Lois said, misunderstanding her. "They won't be here till eight. I'll send Andy round. Thanks."

The fact that she wasn't going to get the small brown troubled her more than anything. Something to do with the picture of Lois and Geoffrey round the table with their in-laws and no brown bread and butter cut thin with the smoked trout.

The main road was almost as deserted as Home Farm Close. She felt as excited as if she were going on holiday. Whenever she left the house to go on holiday she worried about what she had left behind, forgotten to pack. She thought of the poor suitcase in the boot which Irene had thought was jumble, and realized she had forgotten to take her knitting.

PART TWO

Thirteen

The trees in Regent's Park dripped soddenly into the swollen lake. Since October the rains had come with a vengeance, swallowed up like a thirsty man by the parched earth and washing away all evidence of the long, hot summer. Those who walked through the park hurried, avoiding the puddles and holding their coats around them against the damp, penetrating cold. At no season were the benches that bordered the lake quite deserted. No matter what the weather they came, to rest the feet, refresh the body or the spirit, to sit and think, or just to sit. The man who swept up the leaves had seen them all, thought nothing of them, more of the leaves which were wet, and wasn't bothered that each could tell a tale of life with a capital 'L'. He liked his own company and knew every stick and stone of the park where he had worked for thirty years. He wasn't bothered by the people on the benches who came and went. The only thing that bothered him was the dogs turds; as if the paths were his particular Persian carpet. Even after thirty years his blood boiled. He said 'Good morning' to the woman who sat on the bench with the suitcase with one lock by her side. He always said 'Good morning', then waited to see if there was to be any more chat. It was up to them. He wasn't going to intrude. The woman had frizzy hair and a cloak wrapped round her. Her feet were in a puddle but she seemed not to notice.

"Wet," he ventured. Some of them needed a little encouragement. "After the summer." He remembered the ice-cream papers and the Seven-Up cans and the lolly-sticks that were so difficult to pick up. The paths that were dusty and dry and the girls with next to nothing on. It made them brazen, the heat. You wouldn't believe some of the things he had seen, in broad daylight.

"After the summer," she repeated.

She looked at the ducks in their wet element but did not see them. She saw a green meadow.

"More to come," the sweeper said, looking at the sky.

She didn't hear him. Her ears were full of laughter of small boys and her eyes were narrowed against the sun.

They sat in deckchairs around the field which had been marked out into lanes for the sports. Mothers, and a smaller number of fathers, holding mauve-and-black striped blazers all with the appropriate number of buttons securely attached. The women wore cotton dresses, with bare legs and the high wedge sandals that were in fashion that summer. Their sunglasses had initialled frames. Some of them had brought parasols against the sun.

For Lorna the Sports Field of Priory House School was a transit camp between Home Farm Close and Armand. She longed for the afternoon to be over so that she could continue her journey. She looked at her programme but he they had only got as far as the egg-and-spoon. Whoever had thought up such a daft race? There was a page and half of events to get through before the three-legged. Then there were another half-dozen races, after which, of course, there would be speeches and the giving of the prizes. Joey would go into school for tea and she would go to Armand. She looked at the woman next to her. She did not know her but was testing to see if she had written on her face that she was running away to her lover.

"It's impossible," the woman said, meaning the heat, and fanning herself with her programme. "There seems no end."

Lorna nodded.

"Not that we should grumble. We shall look back in the winter, I suppose. We're never satisfied."

"No," Lorna said, thinking of Home Farm Close.

"Are you in the egg-and-spoon?"

"No," Lorna said, "The three-legged."

"Egg-and-spoon," came the important voice of Mr Snell who was so concerned with blazers and with buttons. A dozen very small boys, no more than babies really, took their places behind the white line, china eggs balanced upon spoons.

"On your marks," Mr Snell said. "Get set, go!"

They wobbled purposefully, in line at first, towards the tape. A few moments sorted the wheat from the chaff. Two eggs were dropped, sending their owners scurrying back to the start, pink with embarrassment and heat. The middle registers ploughed on steadily, two boys pulled ahead, one with black hair like a scrubbing brush, and a blonde angel, determination written all over him. A leader of men, Lorna thought, you could tell even at six. Half-closing her eyes she could see him, sober-suited, in the Cabinet, or possibly knighted for climbing Everest. The black-haired one she saw as a surgeon or playwright, his face was full of humour, but he would always be second-best, he lacked the streak of audacity and tenacity that was bringing the blonde angel, utterly absorbed in his egg and his spoon, up to the winning post.

A burst of clapping erupted and only then did the winner's face relax into a broad, gap-toothed grin as he looked round the field for his mother. If life was a race, he was going to win. He had started already. He did not spare a glance for the stragglers who were still wobbling up to the tape. *Summa cum laude*, he waited for his laurel wreath.

173

"That's young Dalloway," the young woman next to Lorna said. "His father's our man in Brazil."

She watched young Dalloway watching his mother. Our futures are mapped out, she thought. We are free to do as we wish but we are not free in our wishes.

The afternoon stretched on. She sat sweltering through the obstacle and the long jump and the high jump and the sack race. At one point she got up to buy a drink from the trestle table Mr Snell had thoughtfully provided. It was sticky and warm and could not be called refreshment. The sports were a punishment, like carol concerts and Speech Days. They seemed to go on for ever. She was always surprised, on looking round, to find that some parents were actually enjoying themselves. She never could understand it. Today, particularly, she wanted to continue her flight. She shut her eyes and thought of the suitcase in the back of the car. When everyone else went home to tea, to start thinking about the dinners they were going to provide, she would be with Armand.

"The next race is the three-legged." Despite the heat and the length of the programme, Mr Snell lost none of his enthusiasm. It was a thing with games masters, enthusiasm. She remembered her own schooldays and the bullying hockey mistress bouncing enthusiastically about on the frozen ground, her breath coming in great misty swirls. 'Run, Lorna, run!' When all she wanted was for the whistle to blow and to get inside into the warm somewhere and collapse.

Joey, lock of hair over his forehead as usual, was tying his ankle to that of Wainwright Major. They had been practising in the garden for weeks, shrieking with laughter each time they collapsed on the lawn and generally ending up with a fight over whose fault it had been.

Joey was not good at games. Like Derek, he lacked the killer instinct. He was perfectly happy to struggle along in the three-legged with Wainwright if he had to compete in anything at all.

At the starting line he put his arm around Wainwright and looked towards Lorna to make sure she was watching. She had a moment of agony wondering who would be at the carol concert, the next Sports Day; how stupid to think of running away when Joey needs you. He will manage, of course, it's nicer if you have your mother there but many parents are divorced, the boys manage, but who said anything about divorce anyway?

"Three-legged!" Mr Snell in his white shirt and white trousers was becoming slightly dishevelled as the afternoon wore on. He looked at the boys. His boys. Whose blazer buttons must be sewn on.

"On your marks, get set, go!"

She told herself it was only a silly little race but her stomach contracted and she fixed her eyes on Joey and the Wainwright boy, slightly urging them to win. They were going in fine fettle, striding steadily, leading the field, many of whom had already fallen, when Joey looked across at Lorna and the rhythm was lost. They stumbled and staggered but managed to stay up while the second and the third pair of boys cantered past them.

"Come on, Joey! Come on!" She did not realize she spoke aloud until she saw the woman beside her smile sympathetically.

They didn't regain their lead and her heart sank in disappointment as they limped across the finish in sixth place.

How ambitious we are for our children. Even in the three-legged. Joey was searching for her face, smiling ruefully. She smiled back, angry with him for losing and angry with herself for feeling angry.

She paid little attention to the relay, hearing merely the thump of plimsoll upon grass as they sped by, the hurdles, and the fifty metres. She wished herself in the garden with a cold drink, then realized there would be no more garden. She wondered if Joey would mind if she didn't stay for the prize-giving and the speeches. He wasn't going to get a prize and he had to stay at school for tea anyway.

A big boy, already boasting a slight moustache, won the hurdles.

She thought of Joey going home to the empty house; no one to talk to about Sports Day; about how Wainwright had nearly pulled him over; about what had happened at tea. For a moment she thought she would take the case with the one lock home and unpack it. Destroy the letter she had written to Derek. She thought of Armand and stood up, exchanging a smile with the woman with whom she had been chatting.

The field was dry, burned from the summer. She felt it hard beneath her feet, conspicuous as she walked away from the marked-out ground away from the deckchairs, groups of fathers standing behind, away from the small boys and the waves of clapping.

The cars stood hotly in rows, glimmering, shimmering. She gave the man who was looking after them fifty pence and agreed it was a scorcher.

She heard a burst of applause, like gunfire, as she drove away, from the field, from Joey.

On closer inspection, the park sweeper thought, the woman wasn't as old as she appeared. Anxious really, as if there was a problem, drawn about the face. Looked as if she could do with a nice hot cup of tea. Shouldn't be sitting with her feet in the puddle. Only had plimsolls on beneath the blue jeans, catch her death, all right if you keep moving. She was looking not at the ducks but out over the lake as if she was miles away. He was about to have another shot at conversation. It was a dreary day and there was no one else about and not likely to be, too cold and wet, when she stood up and picking up the case with one lock, a poor, battered case, she set off towards Baker Street. Strange, he thought, she seems not to notice the puddles. The paths were awash with them. More puddles than path really.

"Fine weather for ducks!" he called after her.

But for Lorna it was high summer.

Carrying her case, slowly, because of the heat, she walked towards Cornwall Terrace.

'I am come,' she thought, 'Armand I am come' and wondered if she was really out of her mind.

She stood uncertainly on the step, noticing it could do with a good scrub, then reprimanding herself for thinking in terms of Home Farm Close which already seemed far away. If he does not open the door himself, she decided, I shall go home. She was uncertain whether she wanted him to or not, beginning to feel afraid, anxious about Joey going back to an empty house, the unreality of it all.

Armand opened the door. Behind him she saw the bicycle, like a talisman, comforting.

He looked at the case with one lock.

"I came today," she said. "Is it all right?"

He took the case from her.

She followed him, not sure whether he minded that she had come. "I took Cam and Blake to the airport," she said to his back. "Joey didn't come anywhere in the three-legged. They fell over."

She was just talking.

He opened the door and the music hit her like a tidal wave. It was like Cam's. She hadn't reckoned with the music. Nor with Eugene. He was sitting cross-legged on Armand's bed, grinning.

"He's really out of it," Armand said, following her glance. "Steve's bed, or are you going to share with me?"

She wondered about Eugene and if he was always going to be there.

"Steve's," she said, raising her voice above the sound, "for a few days. It's necessary." She hoped he understood.

He put the case down next to Steve's bed.

"The music…" She waved her hand towards the speakers. It was beating into her head.

"Listen to those words," Armand said.

She tried but could not distinguish them.

177

"Aren't they far out?"

"Far out." She wanted suddenly to go home. To Home Farm Close. If she hurried she would be back before Joey got in.

The music stopped, suddenly, the silence falling like an avalanche. Eugene went out and left them.

"He sleeps upstairs," Armand said. "He comes down for the music."

The windows were open on to the park. It was cool in the room; quiet now. She stood in the middle of it uncertainly.

"I didn't think," Armand said, "I was going to survive until Wednesday."

"It was because of Cassius. Fresh meat or chicken. I didn't know if you'd mind...coming today."

Armand looked at her, "*Croeso*," he said.

"What's that?"

"Welsh for 'welcome'."

He had only to speak in his gentle voice and her resolution melted. She would do what he wanted. She was his slave. She was smiling at him.

"You smile with your eyes," Armand said, "You will wear out your face."

"You say such astonishing things."

"It's not original."

"It makes no difference."

They sat on his bed amongst the pages of his novel and she told him about Joey's sports, about her day.

"I wrote like the wind," he said. "I knew you would come. Listen to this, Lorna." He took a page and started to read. At first she didn't really listen, not liking to be read aloud to, then she did, despite herself. It was about a young man who sat on an empty, pebbled beach, throwing stones into the water and watching them skim across the winter waves. He is full of his own thoughts as people are who throw stones into water. After a while the young man is joined by another. They don't speak but soon both are throwing stones into the water. The young men select their stones carefully, each according to his mood. Great grey rocks, tiny white pebbles, smooth brown discs, the size of small potatoes. For each stone they choose they reject a dozen, black and sharp, pink and gritty, amber and cream. It is serious business. The winter sun sets on the water, pearling the grey with pink and orange until suddenly everything is grey and the spume of the waves a white clarity. It is cold now and the two young men clamber up, stiff from sitting on the damp stones. They scrunch their way up the sloping beach, feeling their feet slip and slide beneath them. When they reach the path at the top they part. One goes to the right, one to the left. Not a word has been spoken but the two young men would remember each other for the rest of their lives.

"You love the sea," she said when he'd finished reading.

"And the valleys," he said. "I was brought up in the valleys. I'll take you one day. Show you where I live. It took courage to come, Lorna." He touched her face. "I'm going to make you happy."

She smiled.

"What's so funny?"

"Sometimes you sound very Welsh."

She felt Home Farm Close slipping away and tried not to wonder which one of them, Derek or Joey, was going to wash the salad.

The traffic woke her. Shooting round the Outer Circle of the Park. She stared at the chandelier, dulled with dust, and tried to think where she was. She put out her hand for Derek, then remembered. Thinking to feel strange, remorseful, guilty, she waited for the sensations they would bring. There was nothing. Only a complete, vast, tranquil happiness seeming to emanate from the fact that today there was no memory-board; nothing that she must do; except please herself. Meals were not an item. Last night at midnight they had fetched food from a Chinese take-away and eaten it from the containers, on the floor.

She had slept like a baby. Not even the hardness of the parquet floor through Steve's mattress had kept her awake. Across the room Armand still slept, his long hair floating across the pillow. She savoured the feeling that there was nothing she must do, turning and twisting the idea, holding it to her. Her watch under the pillow. She felt for it and squinted at the black figureless dial with the neat gold hands. It seemed to be eleven o'clock but that could not be right. She was always awake at seven. Perhaps it had stopped. Not possible. They hadn't gone to bed until one and she had wound it up. No one seemed to be moving in the house. She turned over and went back to sleep. When she opened her eyes again, Armand was sitting cross-legged on his mattress, intent upon what he was doing. She watched him. He had on jeans but no shirt. His feet were bare and clean. He took three cigarette papers from a packet and laid them on his thigh. He removed one cigarette from a packet of Marlborough and unrolling it took out the tobacco. Neatly, carefully, he spread the tobacco on the papers on his thigh. He stretched out a hand for one of his boots and reaching into it removed a small plastic bag. Taking a pinch of something from it, he sprinkled it on top of the tobacco. He tore a cardboard strip from the Kleenex box next to his bed and rolled it into a small cone. She watched, fascinated. He rolled the cigarette papers, ran his tongue along them to stick them down, and inserted the paper cone into the end of the roll. The matches were in his jeans pocket. He felt for them and lit the cigarette, inhaling deeply, not letting it out. When he did he saw her watching him. Getting up slowly he came over and sat beside her. He offered her the cigarette.

"I don't smoke."

He bent down and kissed her mouth. She was transported. Long moments later she sat up and took the cigarette.

"Like this." He showed her how to hold it. "Inhale."

She drew at it shallowly, nervously, puffed out the smoke.

"You have to hold it."

"What will happen?"

"You'll feel great."

She felt nothing.

The wide door to the room opened and Eugene staggered in. He was barefoot and not smiling. He put on a record then sat on the end of her bed. Armand handed him the cigarette. He inhaled, his eyes closed, and handed it back.

Lorna felt afraid. Afraid and curious. She wanted to see what would happen, felt daring and adventurous yet was unwilling to let herself go.

"I don't want to become an addict," she said.

Armand smiled. "I wouldn't let anything happen. Not to you. It's only grass. Everyone does."

Not in Home Farm Close. It seemed far away. She took the long, thin cigarette from Armand and drew at it, this time more deeply. Eugene was nodding his head in time to the music which she could have done without so early although it wasn't, she didn't know what time. She wondered whether Anne-Marie was cleaning the house and about the shopping and what they were going to have for dinner.

"You can't get it down on the paper," Armand said.

"What?"

"What's in your head. You have it there as clear as a bell, neatly laid out. Your head is on your shoulders to which your arms are attached. At the end of your arms you have your hands. Your fingers, which are at the ends of your hands, are on the keys of your typewriter which at the move of the muscles will imprint what you will on the paper. It is an unbroken line. You would think it possible to transcribe exactly what is in your head on to that paper. Not at all. I don't know where it gets lost. In the brain, in the arms, in the hands. What you see on the paper is not what was in your head. Not at all. It is all written in my head, you see. If one could bind and sell heads, in rows, on shelves, mine would be a best-seller."

It was Lorna's turn. She drew on the cigarette. Not feeling a thing. She imagined rows and rows of heads on the shelves in a bookshop. I'll have that one, please, she said, pointing to Armand's. And mind the hair.

"I went to Italy with this bloke," Armand said. "He sat for a week trying to paint this mountain. He took blue and green and black and grey; he could see those colours as clear as anything on the mountain. He put it down on the canvas exactly as he saw it. At the end of the week he chucked the lot into the ravine and went on a long trip."

Lorna had tried painting once. Evening classes. She'd got the prospectus thinking to get out one evening a week. Derek had been enthusiastic, encouraging. 'Painting for Pleasure', it had been called. She'd enrolled and got the list of required materials. She remembered standing in the Artists' Materials shop with it. Flake white, yellow ochre, cobalt blue, ivory, black; big fat tubes of them. Four brushes, round, flat, and filbert, hog bristle, Russian or Chinese. Special paper, not canvas, not for beginners. She'd packed it all into a plastic bag with an overall, gone off like a child on its first day at school. They had to start with a wine bottle and an apple on a table. It looked simple. The teacher told them how to apply a colour wash first to the paper, to spread it evenly. There were elderly, dumpy women with grey hair in the class. This was their second or third year. She was the new girl. She couldn't even get the colour wash right. It was dirty, messy. After three weeks her bottle and apple were still unrecognizable. She tried a chair, what could be more simple than a chair? Then a guitar which was in the corner of the classroom. She tried every bit as hard as the others but the knack seemed not to come. She washed the overall and gave the paints and the brushes to Joey.

"I couldn't write a book if I tried for a million years," Lorna said. "I'd never get past the first page. Am I supposed to be feeling anything?"

Eugene was drawing at the cigarette. He handed it to Armand who dragged at it and handed it to Lorna. She inhaled, more relaxed now.

"I can't even write letters. I wrote one to Derek. I ought to go and see Pam to see if he's been in touch. I left the car in the street outside her house. Pam's a funny one. Quite different to me…"

"From," Armand said.

"What?"

"From. Different from me."

"Yes. You'd like Pam."

"Does she look like you?"

"She's dark and thin."

"Then I wouldn't."

"She writes for the *New Statesman*. Pamela Allardyce."

"That your sister?" Armand looked impressed. "She's good."

"She had all the brains. Went to Oxford. Takes life very seriously."

"It's a serious business."

Eugene held out his hand.

"When we went to parties Pam used to sit with the grownups. We had to recite, do a party piece. Children don't do that these days. It was excruciating. I used to say…"

"The joint," Armand said, taking the cigarette from her fingers and giving it to Eugene.

"I used to say…" She couldn't remember what it was she used to say. Her hands felt clammy. "I was always jealous of Pam. She was so sure of herself. So right. Knew exactly what she wanted from life. I'm still not sure what it's all about."

"About living," Eugene said. "You've got to concentrate on it. Very hard. Try to do a bit every day."

"He's right." Armand took Lorna's hand and held it reassuringly.

Eugene nodded towards the window. "Take those people," he said, "out there. Going to work. They're so busy they don't bother about living. Got no time for it."

"What do you mean by living?"

"It isn't easy," Eugene said. "You have to practise every day. It can take years."

He moved closer to her. "You have to sit very still. Listen to your own breathing, try to think of nothing."

No memory-board.

"You want me to help you live?" he asked Lorna.

"All right." She was in a mood to agree to anything.

"Nobody feels anything any more," Eugene said. "We're all too busy. Have so much on our minds. We're so impatient that we don't realize what we feel. You've got to wait and listen. Get to know your own feelings. Take you, for instance. You know a lot of what you don't think you know. What do you know?" His eyes were sparkling and he was beginning to look happier.

"Nothing," Lorna said. "If I did I've forgotten it all except cooking…"

"I like people who cook," Eugene said. "Time people. You can't hurry a soufflé. You have to have a life-loving attitude before you can cook. Do you have that? Can you stand by and watch things grow, slowly…?"

"Only children."

"That's right. And plants. A plant takes its time about growing. You have to watch and wait. Like babies. Women know what it's about. It takes a long time. Look at nature. There's a lesson to be learnt. Everything goes slowly. We have to learn to be."

Lorna thought of the memory-board and the cleaning and washing and mending and taking and collecting.

She took a drag of the joint.

She would learn to be.

Fourteen

The case was heavy and her feet, through her plimsolls, were wet. It hadn't been necessary to go into the park at all but she'd wanted to, remembering the summer, the hot, endless summer, which had started with Derek desperately watering the parched lawn, before they'd put a ban on hoses, and ended with the roses in Queen Mary's Gardens where she'd sat for patient hours practising learning to be. She never had liked the autumn, feeling it was a season of death and despair, the wind, sighing through the trees it was stripping, bringing winter in its wake. It was Derek's favourite season. He saw the golds and the reds of the leaves as breathtaking auguries in the cycle of the year. Spring was what pleased Lorna most. It was a time of hope, of rebirth. She loved to see the delicate tracery of green on the bare branches of the trees, certain they would burgeon into leafy fullness. It was a time of watching and waiting to see what would come forth. A season full of hope when anything might happen. There were spring as well as autumn people.

The junction of Baker Street with the park was always a cold spot, open to the winds. Today it howled from east to west, whipping her cloak around her and sending a damp chill through her body which was already cold with fear.

At the bus stop there was a long queue, orderly, patient, holding their collars about their throats and occasionally stamping their feet against the cold.

She wondered how long they would keep her in. She hadn't been in hospital since Joey was born. Joey. Her heart lurched. The panorama of his nine years ran through her mind. A baby in blue bootees. Pulling himself up to the kitchen table demanding biscuits. Play group. Nursery school where he'd howled when she'd left him, determined to take no interest in the nice plasticine. First day at school, his grin determinedly brave beneath the too large cap. Dirty football shorts. Grazed knees. With Derek, serious over his chemistry set; hours with his guppies, the three-legged...

The bus stopped, sending a great shower of dirty water on to the pavement. The queue shuffled forward, each watching the other to be sure he took his turn. When it was Lorna's she picked up the case she had been shunting along the wet pavement with her foot. The conductor was black as coal and put his hand across the entrance, barring her way.

"Full up now!"

He rang the bell.

Behind her two women in furs and boots with three-inch heels stepped from the queue and hailed a taxi. She knew the feeling of enveloping warmth that would engulf them when they stepped inside, sank down into the seats, their furs about them, out of the cold. If they saw the woman in the grey cloak with the wet plimsolls standing by the case with one lock, they did not notice her.

"Well, you've really done it!" Pam said, opening the door. "I was wondering when you were going to show up."

Lorna followed her into the kitchen which smelled of cats and which had, she swore, the same loaf of bread on the dresser which had been there a week ago.

"Where on earth have you been? I'm surprised Derek hasn't had the police round."

"I asked him not to come after me." She perched on the edge of the armchair, taking care not to sit on the cat.

"Push him on to the floor," Pam said. "Come on, Totty. It's his favourite chair."

Her cats were called Socrates, Plato and Aristotle, on whose chair she had been sitting.

"It's all very well asking him not to, but the poor man was out of his mind."

"I tried to tell him," Lorna said. "Did he say anything about Joey?"

"Nothing. He wants to see you. He says he won't try to make you go back if you don't want to but he must talk to you."

"I'm not going to Home Farm Close. I couldn't."

"Anywhere you like. I'll tell him."

"What else did he say?"

"He couldn't understand what he'd done to upset you. He said he had no idea you were unhappy. You'd seemed the same as usual, except for being a bit irritable and weepy which he'd put down to the time of the month and the weather..."

"What about my age?"

"How do you mean?"

"Never mind." Pam was six years younger. She'd keep the book for her.

"You look years younger, anyway." Pam lit a cigarette.

"Aren't you afraid of lung cancer?" Lorna thought of their father with his chain smoking.

"Probably. Poor Daddy. I can't seem to relate the two though. I couldn't stop if I wanted to. Ben's always on at me. He hates it."

It was the first time in years Pam had let her hair down. It was as if they had suddenly grown closer.

"How do you mean, younger?"

"I don't know. It's sort of fallen away."

Lorna looked down at her jeans.

"Nothing to do with clothes. Your face. Happy. Relaxed. Should have done it years ago. Derek..."

"I know what you think of Derek. You've never understood."

187

Pam shrugged. "Where are you living?"

"Regent's Park."

"Trust you."

"In a squat."

Pam stared at her.

"It's true."

"No wall-to-wall carpets? Ben always swore they were germane to your existence."

"No memory-board."

"No what?"

"Memory-board. You write things on it. Things you have to do."

"Like what?"

"Waste-grinder man…" She looked round Pam's kitchen, void of machinery. "I don't think you'd understand."

"Is that why you walked out? Because of the waste-grinder?"

"Partly. Did Derek say anything else?"

"Something about a funeral. He seemed upset."

"Yolande. She took an overdose. We were all upset."

"I can't understand people taking their own lives."

"Do you never get depressed?"

Pam thought. "Never." She waved her arm over the papers on the table. "Too much to do."

"That has nothing to do with it."

"What has then?"

"Perhaps it's because you've no conscience. You never have had. Not as a child. Did you take Mother, about her veins?"

"I had a deadline… She's perfectly capable of getting a taxi from Paddington and it wasn't exactly a matter of life and death."

"What did the surgeon say?"

"I haven't had a moment to ring her."

"See what I mean?"

"I don't know if she even kept the appointment, she was in such a tizz about you."

"What did she say?"

"You'll have to ask Derek. What shall I tell him?"

"I'll meet him. Any day. It doesn't matter. I can hardly tell one day from the next."

Pam looked at her.

"Don't look at me like that. There's nothing the matter with me. Just don't say anything about where I am."

"Why *did* you marry Derek?" Pam said.

"How do I know? How does anyone know? I was nineteen, Pam, when we got engaged. One changes. Instead of living your life you get to the point where life lives you. That's why I had to get out. Did you know I've always been jealous of you?"

"You! Of me?" She stubbed out her cigarette on a saucer where there were already a dozen ends.

"For not needing anything," Lorna said. "For being happy with..." she looked round the kitchen, "...this."

"Who said I was happy?"

"You are, aren't you? Ben..."

"We get along. Only the ignorant expect happiness."

"I envied you for your selfishness."

"Am I selfish?"

"Don't you know? When did you last do something other than to please yourself? That's what I'm doing now. Pleasing myself. I don't do anything. Not even read a newspaper. It's surprising how you can exist without newspapers. I used to be under the impression that the day could not proceed without them."

"Will you go back? To Derek?"

"I don't know. I haven't thought. I don't think of anything, except perhaps Joey and whether he's changing his underwear."

"You really have opted out," Pam said, "for the moment."

She had the key now and already felt that it was home. As the front door in Cornwall Terrace opened on to the black and white tiled floor she was aware, as usual, that for a moment she was waiting for something and that it was Cassius, rushing eagerly to greet her. Glad to be in from the heat, she walked past the bicycle upstairs. She'd got used to the music, no longer noticed it was there, changed the record when it was her turn. She could even distinguish some of the words. She'd grown used to the other things too, used, well tolerant perhaps was a better way to describe what she felt for the kitchen, the bathroom, the house in Cornwall Terrace and its inhabitants, living together yet each in his own orbit, a separate entity.

Opal was coming down the stairs clutching the bannister as if she depended on it. Her dark hair was lank and greasy, almost obscuring her face. She went out rarely, seeming to hold court in her room to an endless stream of visitors. Lorna had seen her mainly in the kitchen when she came to make feeds for the baby.

"Hallo," Lorna said, and would have walked by, eager to see Armand.

"Hi!" Opal put a thin hand on her arm, stopping her. "I suppose you couldn't lend me a fiver?" she said. "Until Friday."

"I'm sorry," Lorna said; she had been warned by Armand.

"It's for the baby. He needs some Paddi-pads and things."

Lorna glanced up the stairs to see if anyone was looking. There were two five-pound notes in her wallet. She gave one of them to Opal.

"I'll pay you back." She was already at the front door.

"Of course," Lorna said.

She wasn't sure how she was going to manage about money. Derek paid her housekeeping money and personal allowance into her bank quarterly. She was dependent on him. She knew she would not see the money she had given Opal again and that she was not going to buy Paddi-pads. It wasn't the first time. To Opal, Armand's lady was a soft touch. She always thought there but for the grace of God goes Cam. Jed had brought her home and Armand and Eugene had let her have the room out of pity.

Above the music only Lorna was bothered by the frequent crying of the baby.

It was eight o'clock and the sun still shone through the three sets of full-length windows. The sheer pleasure of coming into the room had not diminished. Often she thought of the times it had seen when first built, a drawing room in Georgian England when Upstairs was upstairs and Downstairs downstairs. There would be cribbage and bezique, the ladies and gentlemen correctly dressed, instead of Armand, Eugene and Jed sitting cross-legged on the uncarpeted floor playing three-card brag. The smoke would be cigar, not grass. She wondered if the previous inhabitants were turning in their graves, which made her think of Yolande, thoughts of whom were never very far away. They had both left Home Farm Close. She thought her method the better of the two. Perhaps Yolande had not considered that there was any other way. If Cam hadn't brought Armand that Sunday, if it hadn't been hot, if she hadn't gone upstairs for a shower…She looked at Armand, who met her eyes for a brief moment while Eugene laid a card. It had been a week of happiness such as she hadn't known before, never mind what Pam said about happiness. She'd grown to love the great, bare room with its dusty chandelier where she learned to 'be' under Eugene's tutelage, for hours at a time. He'd taught her to know and be aware at every moment of the day. When you sit, know that you sit; when you eat, know that you eat; when you drink, know that you drink; when you brush your hair know that you brush it. It was surprising how the time went by if you thought about, really thought about, the simple tasks you happened to be doing and that alone, instead of the dozen things she had tried to do and think of simultaneously in Home Farm Close. She began to understand why Cam was appalled at the meaningless hustle and bustle of her daily life, in which there was little time for thinking, let along contemplation. There were no demands on her. Not from Armand. Not from Eugene. She existed in a kind of limbo where there was not a time for

191

anything. She'd brought her bedside clock from Home Farm Close but she hadn't wound it for days now. Like Cam, she no longer wore a watch. Although her conscience was not salved on the principal of the squat itself, she managed not to think about it too much. Cornwall Terrace had become home. A home in the true sense. She was free to come and go. It did not wrap her round with tentacles as did Home Farm Close. It was a refuge from the storm, a place to lay her head at night. She slept now with Armand. They made love by night and day. It was as though she was first married. She was accepted by Eugene and Jed and Opal as Armand's lady. They accepted her as they accepted everything, easily, gently. There were no pressures. There were others living at the very top of the house. She knew them by sight only as they came and went. They had their own kitchen and there were no frictions. The house was so built that they did not even hear each other's music. Sandwiched between two layers of music was Opal and her crying baby.

They played cards most nights. Three-card brag or whist; Lorna, Armand, Eugene, and Jed, until it was time for Jed to go to the café. They looked as if they had been going for some time. The ashtray was full of pennies and the air heavy with smoke.

"See Pam?" Armand laid a card, drew on the joint he was holding, and handed it to her. For Lorna it was the first smoke of the day. She only needed a few drags to get off on it now.

"Derek wants to see me." She inhaled deeply.

"Droit de seigneur," Armand said. "In Home Farm Close?"

"I told Pam anywhere but there. She's going to fix it up."

"My lady," Armand said, his eyes glinting, "lives in a palace. They have a room where they keep the dog's brush. A special room." He laid a card.

Lorna took another drag of the joint, thinking of the utility room.

"To everything there is a room," Armand said. "A room to be born and a room to die, a room to eat and a room to sleep, a room for the wellingtons and a room for the flower vases…"

"…It's the same room!" Lorna laughed.

"There are also nineteen bathrooms…"

"Three," Lorna said.

"Sometimes people get confused and use the wrong one." He leaned over and touching Lorna's chin turned her face towards him. "It can have devastating consequences."

"My father's house has many mansions," Eugene said seriously. "I'll see you." He laid down his cards.

Armand showed his hand and picked up the pot. Jed shuffled and dealt, including Lorna in the game.

When she next looked up she saw through the uncurtained windows that night had fallen across the park.

Armand stared at the cards. Eugene yawned. His jeans needed washing, so did his hair.

"Do you realize," he said, "that they have put some quiet music on?"

He looked gravely at the deck, where the arm had long gone back to its rest position, then at Lorna.

She smiled, floating on air.

"My lady," Armand said, "is not to lift a finger."

"What about my lady's bloke?"

"Resting." He pointed at Jed. "Those with dosser's degrees must expect to do the menial tasks of this world."

Jed yawned. "You forget I have to devote the rest of the night to scrambling eggs. I have no conserve my energy. Eugene!"

Eugene grinned but did not move.

"If we had a tape," Armand said, "we could have music for hours and hours and hours without lifting a finger. My lady's husband has a tape."

"In a special room?"

"Of course."

"Can't you rip it off?" Jed said.

"It is built in," Armand said. "You would have to rip off the whole house."

"That might present problems."

"Such as?"

"It would leave a nasty great hole in the road. The neighbours might object."

"Would the neighbours object?" They turned to Lorna.

"I think they might. Pauline Pearson is very proper."

"She sounds like Peter Piper."

"Or the pheasant plucker."

"Whosoever fails to complete the saga of the pheasant plucker puts the record on," Jed said.

"Brilliant," Armand said. "I, as the most – or should I say only – literate member of the wedding will begin. 'I'm just a pheasant plucker said the pheasant plucker's son, so I'll pluck pheasants till the pheasant plucker comes.' "

"Anyone can do it if they say it that slowly. That's cheating."

Armand repeated it at speed. "Eugene."

" 'I'm just a pheasant plucker said the pheasant plucker's son, so I'll pluck pheasants till the pheasant plucker comes.' I used to have elocution lessons because of my lithp."

They looked at Jed.

"Nothing to it." He took from his mouth the end of the joint, which was all that remained, and stubbed the roach out in the ashtray. " 'I'm just a pheasant plucker said the pheasant plucker's son, so I'll phuck pleasants…' Bloody hell. I can't even keep awake. I must snort a line if I'm going to get through the pheasant plucking night."

"Well, change the record while you're up."

They sat and watched him through the haze.

He was a giant of a man. Sometimes they used him as a bouncer in the café. He left the room. They heard him go upstairs. When he came back he had a small tin, a mirror, and a knife. He sat on Armands' bed, trying to keep eyes open long enough to concentrate on what he was doing. Using the knife

194

blade he took a tiny quantity of powder from the tin and put it on to the mirror, painstakingly forming it into a white line.

"Anyone got a quid?"

Armand and Eugene did not move.

"I have a five-pound note," Lorna said.

"Nothing like doing things in style."

She looked in her handbag and with difficulty located her wallet. She handed him the five pounds. The ticket for the shears fell out. She replaced it carefully.

Jed rolled the note up into a narrow tube. He placed one end over the powder on the mirror, blocked his nostrils and snorted on the tube along the line with the other. He repeated the operation until every speck of powder was gone.

"What about the music?" Eugene said plaintively.

Sniffing, Jed picked up a single and sat staring at it as if he couldn't remember what it was for. His eyes were watering.

"What about my fiver?" Lorna said.

She could never understand where the evenings got to. At home, whether it was Scrabble or television or friends, the kettle was put on at ten for coffee and at eleven Derek would start to yawn and mutter about having to get up in the morning. Now they sat up, sometimes half the night, and often it was midday before any of them surfaced. She thought of nothing, consciously, allowed herself to be carried along in an endless half-life with Armand and Eugene. Sometimes it was hours at a time now before she gave a thought to Derek or Joey or Home Farm Close.

Into the small hours of the morning Armand said: "I've got the munchies. There's great hollow where my stomach used to be."

"Mine," Lorna said, "is making noises."

"Jed would make us bacon and eggs," Eugene said.

"I feel more like chicken, Peking-style, with pancake rolls."

"Pancake rolls!" Lorna said.

Eugene yawned. "A cup of tea would go down nicely."

"I," Lorna said, enunciating carefully, "will make a cup of tea."

"There's no milk."

"Opal had a tin. For the baby."

"It tastes like piss."

"I'll put the kettle on," Lorna said.

She stood in the kitchen. Well, kitchen. A small reception room really, behind the drawing-room. There was a gas-cooker with some dried-up bean mush in a saucepan, a pedal bin which was overflowing. The cat had not eaten her dinner. The empty milk carton stood next to the open bag of sugar and the packet of tea in which there were only a few leaves. She looked in the leaning cupboard whose doors would not close. The shelves were covered with cracked oilcloth. She remembered the table in her grandmother's kitchen. Yellow and white. Like lace. There was woolly stuff on the other side; flannelette. Her grandmother had had flannelette sheets too. They were warm. There was a tin of beans and a tin of pilchards. She could just remember eating pilchards in the war. In tomato sauce. Like large sardines, only more meaty. If there were any eggs she could make an omelette. Or scrambled. There was an advert on the television for eggs. Boiled or fried, the landlady said to the lodger at breakfast-time. Or quiche Lorraine. She had a special quiche dish. She couldn't remember where. With fluted edges. In the cupboard. The Poggenpohl cupboard which opened at the touch of a finger in Home Farm Close. There was a pull-out larder full of things. Full. Tins of tuna and salmon and sardines and luncheon sausage. If that larder was here she could make something in no time. That was a thought. Her mother had a pantry with slatted shelves. You would walk into it and it was cold. Her mother kept things under umbrellas made of wire netting. Because of the files. Cakes. And looked meat. If there was cold meat she could cook that. Well not cook. Cold meat was cold. Cooked, one meant. Cooked meat was cold. Something like that anyway. She remembered Armand and Eugene were waiting. She took the beans and the pilchards. It wasn't going to be easy. There was the question of the tin opener to start with. She looked vaguely round the kitchen.

Armand and Eugene were leaning against the wall when she came in with the tray.

"My lady," Armand said, "is a supercook. She can stuff eggs. We had them. In the garden."

"Anyone," Eugene said, "can stuff an egg."

"You try it," Armand said. "You just try and stuff an egg."

Lorna put the tray down on the floor. Beans and pilchards and fried bananas.

"A super-cook," Armand said. "What's in the gravy-boat?"

"Marmalade," Lorna said.

The baby woke her, crying. She had always been sensitive to the cry of a child. Derek used to laugh at her. She slept like a log, unrousable almost, yet at the first whimper of Cam or Joey when they were babies she would be out of bed like a shot. A mother's reflex. Armand was sleeping. He had a Christ-like face, she thought, the long hair flowing. So Jesus must have looked on the cross. She put her head on his shoulder and went back to sleep. When she woke again it was light and the baby was still crying. It was getting hoarse now. She would have to get up.

"Where are you going?" Armand said.

"The baby. It's been crying for hours."

"It's always crying."

"I know. It's never gone on for so long, like this."

He went back to sleep.

She stepped over the remains of the beans and the pilchards and fried bananas.

Jed was sitting on the stairs, his head in his hands. "God!" he said. "I ache all over. I don't know how I got home."

She tried to go by, up to the baby.

"My whole body's seized up."

She didn't know what to say. "Why don't you go to bed?" she suggested.

"My head's like a bloody merry-go-round. No point going to sleep until I've done a downer."

She went on up the stairs.

She had never been in Opal's room.

She knocked on the door but knew she would not be heard above the noise of the baby. She opened it and went in. She looked round the room and her heart sank.

Opal was lying fully dressed on the bed. She seemed to see Lorna come in but her eyes were glazed, the skin on her face was green, or pale grey, Lorna couldn't be sure, only that she looked ill.

"You need a doctor," Lorna said above the noise of the baby.

There was a low table by the bed. On it were ampoules, full and empty, a hypodermic syringe, and a belt.

"Oh, God!" Lorna said and remembered the money she had given her.

She looked at the baby, not enjoying the smell of dirty nappies and ammonia-tainted urine that came from the cot. The baby had kicked off its blankets and was covered only by a vest which stopped at his umbilicus. His legs were purple with cold and there was a crust of saliva round his mouth from crying.

He looked at her, his arms and legs going with the sobs. He was skinny, not nicely rounded like a baby should be. Overcoming her distaste she picked him up. The bottom sheet was sodden.

In a drawer there were a couple of what had once been terry-towelling nappies. They were yellow and hard. She took them and the baby to the bathroom.

He did not stop crying while she cleaned him up. She put him against her shoulder. He no longer smelled evil. In the kitchen she held him with one hand and put the kettle on with the other.

It was a long while since she had fed a baby. Nine years. This little scrap of Opal's had fallen upon the teat as if he were starving, hardly able to draw the breath to enable him to suck.

"Slowly, slowly," she said.

She hadn't been too happy about the hygiene of the operation. The bottle, with stale milk, had been on the floor next to the cot, the teat still in it. She had washed it as best she could. Cam and Joey's bottles had been sterilized in bowls of Milton, the teats floating like rubber nipples. There had been no such thing as a bottle brush but she didn't suppose Opal used one anyway. The baby looked quite healthy apart from being hungry. He was quite sweet now that he was clean. She would like to give him a proper bath.

He dozed off over the last ounce, exhausted from crying. She cradled him in her arms, enjoying the feel of him, and went back to Opal who had not moved.

There was a towel on the chair. She put it in the bottom of the cot. The blankets were smelly but dry. Remembering, she put the baby on his side and tucked him up, smoothing his hair.

She sat down on the bed next to Opal and realized with amazement that she was younger than Cam. She had on a man's shirt, one sleeve was rolled up. The inside of her arm was covered with scabs.

"I've fed the baby."

She wasn't sure whether Opal had heard.

She tried again. "What's his name?"

After a long time and with a great deal of effort Opal said, "Rory. Rory St John Heyward."

From the recesses of her mind Lorna recalled a newspaper sensation. Heiress elopes with hairdresser. Opal Heyward. Distraught father, mother crying on television.

"How old are you, Opal?"

"Eighteen."

"I have a daughter your age. Well, a bit older. Do your parents know where you are?"

It was a stupid question. She knew there would be no answer.

"How old is Rory?"

She waited.

"Five months? Six?"

Opal had drifted back into lethargy.

"I don't suppose you've even had any breakfast."

Opal stared at her. Stupid. She wasn't with Cam in Home Farm Close.

Jed was asleep on Steve's bed.

"He's done some Valium," Armand said. He had the typewriter on his lap and the papers strewn over the bed.

"Do you know who Opal is?" Lorna asked.

He looked at her. "If you want to live here," he said, "you have to mind your own business. We all do. That's how we survive."

Fifteen

The vestibule of the hospital was busy. Like an airport or an hotel. To one side were rows of canvas chairs where people sat waiting, patiently, expectantly, as if for a film to begin. Opposite, long desks had men in white coats behind them. Lorna went up to one of them.

"I've come to be admitted."

He pointed to the far end. "You want reception."

She walked down the line. A young girl in a white coat sat at a desk.

"Can I help you?" She was deliberately cheerful, encouraging. It helped.

"I've come to be admitted."

"Name please."

"Mrs Brown." There must be a hundred. "Lorna."

The girl looked through a stack of index cards and half-withdrew one. She looked up at Lorna.

"Aren't you Camilla Brown's mother?"

"Yes."

"I thought I recognized you. I'm Polly. Polly Jarvis. Cam and I were at school together."

"Of course." A picture of Polly Jarvis and Cam in green tunics and Panama hats flashed into her mind.

"How's Cam?"

"She's fine."

"What's she doing?"

"She's in her final year at Warwick. Philosophy."

"She was always clever. Will you give her my love?"

I haven't seen her. Not for four months.

"Of course."

Polly looked at her notes.

"I see you've moved from Home Farm Close. Such a beautiful house. Have you still got Cassius?"

She was writing on a narrow strip of paper. She folded it and enclosed it in a band of clear plastic which she sealed with a machine.

"I have to give you this."

Lorna held out her hand.

"No. Your left arm, please."

She fastened it round Lorna's wrist.

"In case we lose you."

Lorna wondered how many times a day she said that. She felt like a convict wearing her number.

"You're in Harvey Ward. I'm afraid you have to wait over there." She pointed with her pen to the rows of canvas chairs. "It shouldn't be too long but we seem to have a big rush on today. I hope all goes well for you."

"Thank you." She was a kind girl.

"And to give my love to Cam."

"I will."

She picked up her case and sat down next to an elderly man with a muffler round his neck and a veined purple nose.

She looked at her new plastic bracelet. 'Lorna Brown. No. 8564720. Harvey Ward. Mr Gillespie." Dear God, she thought, what am I doing here?

She felt anxious and frightened meeting Derek. As if he were a stranger. He'd said Wheelers, Old Compton Street. It had been one of their favourite places. He was already in the bar. She knew he was angry by the closed look on his face. Agitated too.

The empty dish of nuts, olives and potato crisps told that he had abandoned his diet. He stood up, making no attempt to kiss her.

"What'll you have?"

"Vodka." She had been drinking it neat in Cornwall Terrace.

"Bloody Mary?"

"Yes. Please." She sat down on the banquette next to him. He was a stranger in his city suit. He paid for her drink and tipped the barman.

"How's Joey?" she said.

"Never mind Joey." He was not going to make it easy. "I want to know what's going on."

"Don't be angry," she said. "I can't talk to you if you're angry."

"Not angry! I come home one day, a perfectly ordinary day as far as I'm concerned, to find my son alone in the house because my wife has pushed off; vanished. Leaving me a note, an unintelligible note. I don't suppose you even gave any thought to the effect it would have on me. I'm surprised I didn't have a heart attack there and then. I couldn't believe it."

She drank the Bloody Mary, not trusting herself to speak. She hadn't imagined it was going to be like this. Derek was rarely angry.

"What did Joey say?"

"You didn't seem all that concerned about Joey at the time."

He wasn't going to tell her.

"I'm sorry about the letter. There didn't seem to be any other way."

"We could have discussed it like civilized human beings."

"I tried to tell you how I felt. Two or three times. It didn't seem to work."

"Your table is ready, Mr Brown," the manager said, inclining towards them from the waist. "First floor."

"We'll have dinner," Derek said. "You have a lot of explaining to do."

They sat at their usual table and the waiter, who had been there for years and was part of the fixtures and fittings, asked how they were and commented that there was no let-up in the heat. Through the open window the lights of the cinema opposite flashed on and off.

He put their napkins on to their laps with a flourish and gave them the big shiny menu with the lobster on the front. Lobster was Lorna's favourite but she was not hungry. She did not know how she was going to get through the evening with Derek so angry. She didn't know how she had imagined him. Hadn't, she supposed, given it too much thought. Unhappy perhaps, a little annoyed, concerned about her, anxious to have her back...

"What are you going to have?"

"I don't mind." The names of the dover soles cooked in a dozen different ways swam before her, one into the other.

The waiter in his white apron stood with his pen poised.

"The salmon is still very good; hollandaise sauce and few new potatoes."

"All right," Lorna said.

"I thought you liked lobster," Derek said.

"She could not allow herself the lobster. It was a kind of self-inflicted punishment. "Salmon will be fine."

"Make that two," Derek said.

"Anything to start?"

Derek looked at her. She shook her head.

"That's all. And bring a carafe of house wine. Very cold."

"Yes, sir. Rightaway, sir."

Lorna looked the mat on the polished table with the picture of the hunting scene on it. She had seen them so many times before on birthdays, anniversaries. *A Perfect Day, The Ford in Flood, Dogs Drinking.*

"Don't you think you owe me an explanation?" Derek said. "Or do I have to go crawling to Pam to enquire what has taken possession of my wife?"

He was demolishing the French bread from the basket on the table.

"There's nothing more than what was in the letter. I'm sorry. I just had to get away."

"I suppose you didn't think how humiliating it would be? Yolande's funeral and everyone asking where you were and giving me funny looks. Irene coming round especially to tell me she saw you packing, something about jumble…inviting me to dinner. Me and Joey with Leonard and Clare!"

"I hadn't thought," Lorna said, "it would be like that."

"How on earth did you think it would be?"

She was conscious of the American woman in the pants suit at the next table staring at them. She had always thought the tables too close. Derek did not notice.

"I don't know." She spoke in a low voice, hoping he would follow suit.

"I don't suppose you gave it a moment's thought. Too wrapped up in yourself."

She started to cry, the tears dripping on to the hounds and horses.

"I'm waiting," he said, "to hear what you have to say, Lorna."

The salmon arrived, giving her a breathing space. She willed the waiter not to go away. Derek picked up his knife and fork. It was obvious she was going to have to speak.

"You remember that Sunday," she said, plunging in at the deep end, "when Cam came down with…with her friends, and Irene and Dick had that couple from Guildford and the Pearsons came in for drinks?

"Yes?"

"Well, it started then, although it wasn't really the beginning. It had all been festering away in me for a long time…"

She tried to explain, choosing her words carefully, about Home Farm Close and the utility room and her life. He listened but did not speak, dipping forkfuls of salmon into the hollandaise sauce and pouring wine for both of them.

"What I dislike most," Derek said, "is your dishonesty."

She stared at him. "What do you mean?"

"Well, all this nonsense about Home Farm Close and utility rooms when you just don't love me any more."

"That's not true. I didn't expect you to understand. That's why I had to write the note. Believe it or not, I still love you. Just as much."

"Looks like it. What about this fellow?"

"Armand?" She realized he did not want to say his name. "It's different. It's all different. Cornwall Terrace, the life…"

"I think it's disgraceful," Derek said. "The whole damned thing. You're behaving like some mixed-up adolescent. Like Cam…"

"Have you heard from Cam?"

He ignored her. He was going to punish her with the children.

"…I suggest that you just forget all this nonsense and come home with me now. I'll take you round to Dick and he'll fix up for you to see someone."

"I suppose you've already discussed it?"

"Of course."

"I'm not coming back, Derek. Not tonight."

"We'll forget all about it."

She looked up. Something in his voice told her that if stopped being angry he would break down. He was terribly upset. His hand was on the table. She wanted to take it, to comfort him. He would see it only as duplicity.

"I can't come home. Not yet. I have to sort myself out."

"You need help to do that."

"Is that what Dick says?"

He didn't reply.

The waiter, friendly as always, took their plates. She thought he couldn't have helped hearing the conversation in the small room and wondered how many domestic dramas he had witnessed over the years. He flapped at the crumbs on the table with his white napkin.

"A little Brie?"

When there was no answer he said: "Fruit salad, black-current sorbet?"

"Coffee," Derek said.

"Certainly, sir." He left them alone.

"Look," Lorna said, "I'm sorry. For everything. It was a terrible thing to do. I know that. But I had to do it. I just had to. I couldn't go on…day after day…"

Derek took her hand.

"Was it so bad, Lorna? I thought we had something good going. We've always understood each other, you and I…"

"Nobody understands…anybody. We do our best."

"We did our best then. I gave you everything you wanted, didn't I?"

She closed her eyes.

"You never had to ask me for anything twice. If you wanted to go on holiday we went on holiday. Bed was OK. I thought so. We've had our patches. Bad patches. But then everyone does. You can't expect to be married for twenty-four years and not have a few rough stretches. We've always come out of them though."

"Do *you* love *me*?"

"Black or white?" the waiter said, hovering with the silver pot.

"Black, please."

"A little cream for me," Derek said.

She thought of his cholesterol but had no right to say 'don't'.

He stirred the coffee in the tiny cup, making patterns with the cream. She thought he wasn't going to answer.

"You know I do, Lorna. That's what hurts."

She thought he was going to cry. He looked vulnerable for a moment like a small boy, then the closed look took over his featurse again. He took his notepad with his initials DB and the rolled gold edges out of his pocket and his architect's pencil which was always sharp.

"You'd better give me your address."

She was afraid. She did not want him to come round. To make trouble for Armand.

"I don't really want to. Pam knows where I am."

He put the notepad back in his pocket, abruptly.

She wanted to cry out, all right, I'll tell it to you. She said nothing. It was best.

"Bill, please!" He called the waiter. She was being dismissed. There was silence while he paid.

He preceded her down the narrow winding staircase, through the packed tables on the ground floor, and out into Old Compton Street.

"Taxi, sir?" the doorman said.

"No." He turned to Lorna. "I'm not asking you again."

She knew he meant to come home.

"That's all right."

"Throw twenty-four years down the drain if you want to."

"It's not like that."

"Well, I'm not listening to any more of your nonsense. Goodbye."

"Goodbye."

He was about to go.

"About Joey," she said desperately.

He put his hand into his pocket. "He wrote you a letter."

She took it. When she looked up Derek had gone.

DEAR MUMMY,

My report was quite good except for chemistry talks too much and Maths. could do better if he tried but you know Miss March she says the same about everybody. Grandma gave me two new Guppies and a pocket chess and is coming to stay for the weekend. Anne-Marie makes muesli every day and shrank my socks. Daddy says to get some more and gave Anne-Marie the money. Heatherington's parents are divorced and the judge said which one do you want to stay with and he said his father because his mother can't play football. Anne-Marie won't let me watch television on school nights. I told her it wasn't fair you let me.

Love JOEY x x x x x x

At Cornwall Terrace she read and re-read the letter until Armand took it from her.

She spent the night in his arms.

In the morning she wrote:

DEAR JOEY,

Thank you for your letter. I'm glad you had a good report. I knew you would. Don't worry about Miss March and try not to talk so much in class. Be good for Grandma and for Anne-Marie, she means well about the television and there are always weekends. Tell Daddy I get them at Pullens, you have to for school. The socks, I mean, and I always get size eleven, which are a bit big to start with. I am having a nice rest and a holiday and will come and see you in a few weeks. Look after Daddy and be good.

Lots and lots of Love,

MUMMY x x x x x x

PS Give my love to Cam when she phones.

PPS Sorry to hear about Heatherington's parents.

She looked at the letter.

"How do you put your heart down on paper?" she asked Armand.

He stopped typing. "I've been trying for years."

"I think you are a kind of Svengali."

"How?"

"Making me come here. Leave Joey."

"Did I make you?"

"I don't mean that."

"Just the catalyst."

"What's that?"

"The agent. I made it possible."

"And if you hadn't come along? If it hadn't been hot? If you hadn't used the wrong bathroom?"

"Who knows? You might have met someone else."

"I think that moment was important. Derek didn't understand about the utility room."

"Did you expect him to?"

"No."

She put her letter to Joey in the envelope and went to sit on the bed beside Armand. He handed her the joint he was smoking. She inhaled deeply.

"We're out of skins," he said "And cigarettes."

"I'm going out. I'll get some."

"What are you going out for?"

"Some things for the baby. I promised Opal."

"I told you not to get involved."

She didn't answer. The events of last night were beginning to get less painful.

"Don't buy them in the same shop," Armand said. "The skins and the cigarettes."

She looked at him questioningly.

"It wouldn't go down too well in Home Farm Close if we were busted."

"Local lady in drugs raid!" Lorna said. "Next to 'Public Protest over Bus Service' and 'Traders Up in Arms over Yellow Lines'. I don't suppose you've seen our local paper?"

"I'm not joking. You wouldn't like it."

"I don't suppose I should. I'll be careful, though." She was still preoccupied with Derek. "I told Derek that I loved him. He didn't believe me. I don't know if it's because he's Derek or because he's a man. In his mind, if I run away it's because I don't love him."

"Do you?"

"Of course. I'm very fond of him."

"That's not the same."

"What is love?"

Armand put the typewriter on the floor and leaned against the wall beside her.

"You want me to show you?"

"Tell me."

"You ask difficult questions."

"Try."

"To define love? Has anyone, ever? It can be so many things."

"Such as?"

"Fondness, warm affection…"

"Then I love Derek."

"…Sexual passion…"

"Not lately."

"Delight in, admiration for…"

"Yes."

"Look, you *know* if you love him. The other is just words."

"I could not tell him," Lorna said, watching the smoke drift in lazy circles towards the high ceiling, "that I was being strangled by the wall-to-wall carpets. How, Derek would say, can you be strangled by wall-to-wall carpets? Go and see Dick, he will sort you out. Send you to a psychiatrist, he meant, it's all the rage in Home Farm Close. Yolande was seeing one, he gave her the tablets. I know Irene has been, and Lois goes to a hypnotist because she can't stop eating. It's got to be like going to the dentist. He would give me coloured pills which I would take by the handful, like Yolande, in a bad moment. What ails you, Mrs Brown? He would say. Oh, doctor, I am being strangled. Yes? Strangled. He would make a note. And who is strangling you? Not who, I would say, what. I am being strangled by the wall-to-wall carpets. Yes, he would say, humouring me. Go on. I would go on, oh yes, how I would go on. Strangled by wall-to-wall carpets, garrotted by double garages, raped by the rubber plants. Most of all I am being throttled, slowly but surely, by life itself. Life? Not life. My life. Tell me about your life, Mrs Brown. And I would bring it up, vomit, regurgitate it all over him. The television and the au pairs, burglar alarms and barbecues. Birthdays and birthday cards. Christmas and Christmas cards. Green Shield stamps and coupons for sundae glasses from the garage. Petrol and oil and air in the tyres. Hoovers and health foods and yoga and diets, the banana and milk, the cottage cheese and grapefruit. O-levels and A-levels, Marks and Spencers and static bicycles, tennis and the garden, Glyndebourne and the National, pocket money and rotating parties, boxes of chocolates with pre-packed guilt, evening classes and hairdressers and holidays insulated in the best hotels where you might be anywhere, Sunday supplements and Scrabble and *en suite* bathrooms, clothes and commuting and belonging to the AA. He would listen. I am paying him to listen. How many people get paid just to listen? When I'd finished, when the stream had dried up, he'd say: How about your sex life? in a tone of voice that would not offend, like doctors when they're enquiring about your bowels. My sex life? Fine, I'd say. At least twice a week, sometimes three when Derek's been at the wine. And always in the same position? Certainly not. We've read Masters and Johnson, it's required reading in Home Farm Close. We know about orgasms, clitoral and vaginal, most of us indulge in do-it-yourself jobs in the afternoon, we know about premature ejaculation and putting it in your mouth and not to shout at our men when they can't get it up. You seem very well adjusted, he'd say. Remarkably well. Then what is wrong? What is ailing Lorna Brown? Women of your age, he'd say, and closing my eyes I would hold out my hand in the darkness for the prescription I could exchange at any chemist for a bottle of coloured pills."

Taking the joint from her Armand put his arm round her shoulders and looked at her.

"You are the only one, Armand," Lorna said. "I could drown in your eyes."

"But you love Derek."

"Love! There are as many kinds of love as coloured pills."

"I am the green," Armand said, "take me."

It was a long time since she had bought Paddi-pads, anything for a baby. On the shelf there were pink plastic bottles of baby lotion and shampoo, zinc and castor oil cream and baby powder, items without which it would be unthinkable to rear any self-respecting infant in Home Farm Close. She wanted to buy them all for Rory, and a wicker basket to put them in. There would be nappy pins stuck into the lining. Dotted organdie. Her mother had made it for Joey. It matched the cradle, swathed in frills. Baby supermarkets were new. Minute garments hung in rows, handled lovingly by incipient mothers. Blankets, light as air, delicate shawls, knitted jackets. She fingered them, wondering if Opal would mind knowing she was in no fit state to. Armand had told her not to get involved. He didn't understand how it was with women and babies. How could he? She walked past the tiny garments, the lemon plastic potties and took her fishnet basket to the pay desk standing between two hugely pregnant girls who looked no older than Cam.

She bought the cigarettes and the skins in different shops. When she asked for cigarette papers she thought the tobacconist had looked at her strangely. She put them into her nylon shopping bag with the Paddi-pads, thinking of the duck pâté and the mauve buttons it had held what seemed a lifetime ago.

She walked home through the park. It was a novelty having it so near. At Home Farm Close there was the common, grass and trees the same, Cassius liked it, but it was dead. Like a village in the war, the young and the able-bodied had gone, during the week that was. A few elderly men, walking slowly, housewives like herself dutifully walking dogs. In the park you could believe that there was life. Lovers on the dry ground abandoned in the heat, children in boats, toddlers shrieking at the ducks and throwing bread, an animated painting, subtly coloured and dappled with sun wherever you looked.

She sat down on a bench, drinking in the light, the movement. She was not yet used to these moments, a reprieved prisoner, eyes dazzled by the new experiences, by the world outside Home Farm Close. From across the water she could hear the band; they were playing the 'Gold and Silver Waltz'.

They had taken her to hear a band one night, Armand and Eugene. In front of the club small groups of young, like themselves, like Cam, sat like limpets on the narrow pavement in the tepid night. Inside they drank warm Guinness then insinuated themselves into the packed cavern, the joints like glow-worms punctuating the dark, to hear the music which came from a stereo, speakers like small pantechnicons, on the stage. The bodies were jammed tight, swaying in unison to the rhythm, cemented together by the beat. Next to Lorna a girl with green hair and chalk-white face undulated with the changing mass, joining in the dirge, 'I wanna be a machine', through plum-purple lips which did not move. She could not have been more than fifteen. Beneath the painted face you could discern the innocence that went with the age. Somewhere, Lorna thought, an anxious mother sat waiting. She had imagined that in Cornwall Terrace she had grown used to the music. It was as nothing.

"The band's coming on in a minute," Armand said and as he spoke the noise from the speakers stopped abruptly, leaving a black lake of silence for no more than thirty seconds. Then a group in muscle-tight satin trousers hurled themselves and their instruments on to the suddenly floodlit stage, filling the room with sound of such intensity that what had gone before seemed now a lullaby.

In the spotlight the lead guitarist, a lesson in perpetual motion, flung himself into the music, on to the music which erupted with such passion it carried everyone in the room with it assaulting the eardrums with a great tidal wave of sound.

She'd never understood when Cam had said it was an experience. It was not one she wanted to repeat. Afterwards Jed served them bacon and eggs in his café and she sat, limp from the noise, and thought of Fortnum's Fountain Restaurant where she always went with Derek after a show.

"Please could you tell me the time?"

A young girl with a pram had sat down on the bench and was talking to her.

Lorna smiled at the golden-curled baby, feeling sorry for the girl who thought her troubles were over now that he was sitting up.

"I'm sorry," she said into the sunshine, "I haven't a watch."

Sixteen

It seemed to Lorna that she waited hours, the hands on the clock opposite with the roman numerals seeming not to move. The man with the muffler had gone, escorted by a nurse, and in his place sat a thin, nervous-looking girl wearing the previous day's mascara. She spent the time trying to make herself believe that it was really she who sat there waiting. Waiting to be told where she had to go, what she must do. At the doors of the hospital an invisible being took your will away from you. You sat like a zombie waiting to be manipulated, to be pulled and pushed this way and that, to be slid, unprotesting, between sheets, probed in intimate places, plied with personal questions, divested of free will. Like sheep they sat in rows, silently, patiently awaiting the will of the gods in the white coats and striped dresses with red belts or with blue according to rank. You could not tell from looking who was ill or how seriously. Livers, kidneys, lungs; it sounded like the butcher's, disgusting really, eating all those organs, more and more people were becoming vegetarians, particularly the young, although perhaps with them it was the price of meat. You had only to look at the health food shops. When they started they had been few and far between, frequented by a few cranks, now they had sprung up everywhere. Vegetarian restaurants too, where they served not just nut cutlets and a bowl of soup but gourmet menus. Lois' husband, Geoffrey, had had a coronary thrombosis and had been warned that he might have another, yet to look at him you would have said he was the picture of health, you could never tell with people, never thought about it really, until something got fouled up in your body, just took it for granted, like the washing-machine and the dishwasher, until they started leaking water, only you didn't call in a urologist, they fitted new parts, but so did they hearts and kidneys, she'd never believed in life after death but like daffodils and crocuses you flowered and when your time was up you withered and died, unless you were cut down before your time like Yolande or Thelma Barrington. Why should men and women be any different from the plants when everything belonged in the natural rhythm of things? She had never believed in the Resurrection either, and had kept in her room with no food for a day for saying so; this business about the soul, there was not a shred of evidence, not one shred. She wanted to go to the lavatory, it must have been because of the cold wind, she was only just beginning to thaw out, and wondered whether there would be time or if they would come for her. She watched a nurse go to the desk and exchange words with Polly Jarvis. You could see the backs of her black-stockinged knees when she leaned forward. She watched as they pointed her out and grinned like an idiot as the nurse came towards her across the hall.

"Mrs Brown?

"Yes."

The nurse picked up the case with the one lock.

"Sorry you had to wait so long. We're ready for you now."

Harvey Ward was going about its business. It smelled like all wards in all hospitals. The nurse, a pretty girl with a tiny waist and a big bust, put her case on the bed and drew the curtains around it in a continuous and fluid movement.

"If you'd like to get undressed, slip into your nightie and pop into bed, Doctor will be along to see you shortly. Put your clothes into the case, you won't be needing those for a bit and your husband can take them away. I expect he'll be coming later."

"No."

"A relative then?"

"Nobody knows," Lorna said.

"Well, never mind," the girl said cheerfully. She was a cheerful girl. "I'll pop them in our cupboard for you. Sister keeps it locked. You can put your slippers and any other bits and pieces in your locker here. This bag is for rubbish and you can switch your reading lamp on here. Be back in a jiffy. Three going down to theatre this morning and only two of us on duty…we're going bananas…"

She was gone with a swift movement, mauve and white striped dress disappearing through the floral curtains.

Lorna stood immobile, holding the iron bars at the foot of the impersonal, uninviting-looking bed, staring at the thermometer on the wall in its slim tube of pink fluid.

Opal did not thank her for the money she had given her, for her attentions to the baby, which became more frequent. She tried to do as Armand suggested and not become involved, not to hear the crying. When she could stand it no longer she climbed the stairs, knowing that as like as not she would find the baby filthy, Opal tripped out. Sometimes she thought of telling the NSPCC about the baby, Opal was certainly in no fit state to look after him, but she knew it would lead to all kinds of trouble for others in the house. It would not do to introduce authority. The first time she had seen Opal shoot the mixture of morphine and pethidine she was mainlining she had vomited. She had been feeding Rory, softly singing nursery rhymes, when Opal came in with a saucepan. She did not look at Lorna, at Rory. She sat down on her bed and tied a black leather belt round the top of her arm. Taking the syringe and needle from the saucepan which they used in the kitchen to boil eggs, she jabbed it into an ampoule and withdrew the plunger.

"Please don't," Lorna said. "Opal!"

She turned her head away as Opal flexed the scabbed arm, its fist on the table. She moved the baby, not wanting him to see. She heard Opal put down the syringe, the belt, lie back on the bed. Unknowingly, Rory finished the bottle. Lorna hurried to leave the room. There was nothing she could do for Opal, the baby.

As she closed the door she heard Opal say: "Wow, this rush is really amazing!"

"Can't you do anything?" she said to Armand. "About Opal?"

He was caressing the cat. "Like what?"

"Where does she get that stuff?"

"A dealer, I suppose."

"Where does she find them?"

"Don't worry, they find her. They know their customers."

"Shouldn't she be in hospital?"

Armand shrugged. "There'd be a dealer waiting when she came out."

"It's frightening! Her parents must be worried out of their wits. Think of all the time and money and love they've spent on her. And what's going to happen to Rory?"

Armand held out his arms. "Come here, little mother," he said.

It was true. She had turned to mother them. It had begun with the baby. For the first weeks in Cornwall Terrace, released from her responsibilities, her household chores, she had flopped, mentally and physically. She spent her days sleeping, they never got up till noon. She did not like to think how many times she had shouted at Cam for just that. They sat dreamily with joints, watching the smoke drift up to the ceiling, drinking endless cups of tea, talking, making love, sitting in the park. She had wandered round the Wallace Collection, the British Museum, and the Tate, revelling in the fact that she had no tugging children in tow. She hadn't felt so free in years, since before she was married. She had only herself to please. Armand, Jed, Eugene, and Opal came and went. No one asked where are you going? What time will you be back? Shall I wait dinner? For one thing there was no dinner. They ate when they felt like it, whatever was in the kitchen, which wasn't usually much, or else went out. They fetched take-aways, Indian or Chinese, or sat in the Felafel house. Once, when Armand wrote a short story and sold it, they went with Eugene to Poon's in Lisle Street.

They had Won-Ton soup and wind-dried duck and had got up to leave when Irene and Dick came in and sat down at the next table. Irene stared at her uncertainly, taking in the grey roots, the hair tied back in a pony-tail with an elastic band, Armand's shirt which she was wearing.

"Lorna!"

From her tone Lorna knew she was no longer the Lorna who had left Home Farm Close.

"Hallo, Irene." They stared at each other for a moment.

"Dick, it's Lorna!"

He was reading the menu. "Hallo, Lorna." He did not look up.

"This is Armand" – Lorna then remembered they had met a lifetime ago – "and Eugene."

They stood in an awkward tableau.

"You look different," Irene said, staring up at her, "Thinner...different..."

"What are you going to have, Irene?" Dick said, as if Lorna did not exist.

Irene picked up her menu. "I must talk to you," she hissed from behind it at Lorna. "It's important. Ring me tomorrow."

Lorna smiled. Irene was wearing a Giovanozzi dress and her false eyelashes.

"Promise?" she said, putting her hand into Lorna's.

"I'll try."

"Please."

Lorna glanced at Dick.

"Take no notice," Irene said. "They stick together, men!"

She did not ring Irene. It had something to do with the Giovanozzi dress. They were a uniform in Home Farm Close. Chic and Italian and you could wash them. You could recognize them anywhere. She took her washing to the launderette. She liked the atmosphere after the sterility of the Poggenpohl kitchen. Usually she went in the evenings when it was cool and busy with students. She had watched more than one liaison take root and blossom. It was nice to sit and watch the kaleidoscope of scenes through the porthole. Sometimes the machines broke down. It was not her problem. She did not have to send for the repair man. Just used another machine. She liked putting her money in the slot for the cup of soap powder. She did not have to order more when it was getting low. She enjoyed merging into the street scene of Camden Town. Sometimes she walked along Bond Street or Knightsbridge, quickly turning her head away when she saw someone she knew. In the jeans and sneakers she would never had gone further than the end of Home Farm Close in, she watched mirror-images of her former self in expensive cottons and high-heeled sandals, peering in the shop windows, pondering whether this went with that and anxiously wondering whether they would find what they wanted before it was time to make tracks for home. Avoiding or fighting the rush hour, they would prepare dinner in their kitchens which were operating theatres, remembering before they went to bed, if Ingrid or Claudette had not done so, to turn the dial on the milk-bottle carrier to the correct number of pints for the milkman in the morning. In Cornwall Terrace there was no milk. They bought milk in cartons when they needed it. There were no empties to be rinsed self-righteously, as if you were in line for a medal from the dairy. If you wanted a cup or a spoon you generally had to wash it. The system was merely reversed. You washed up before you ate instead of afterwards.

It was when she started to feed the baby on a regular basis, she had nothing else to do and could not stand to hear him sobbing his heart out, that she began to do things to the kitchen. She washed the tea towels and, because she could not get the dirt out, bought an enamel basin and boiled them. She wiped the cracked oil-cloth in the cupboard and stacked up the few tins. One day she scrubbed the kitchen floor.

She went to see Pam.

"For God's sake," Pam said when she opened the door. "About time!"

She followed her sister into the overgrown garden. A doll with no arms lay next to a doll's pram with no wheels. The garden was shared with the other tenants of the house.

Pam brought chairs from the kitchen.

"Your husband," she said when they were sitting down, "is driving me mad. To tell you the truth, Ben's fed up with it."

"What's Ben got to do with it?" Lorna asked.

"He comes round."

"Derek?"

Pam nodded. "They go to the pub. Come back tight as tics."

"Derek?"

"Right."

"They never had two words to say to each other."

"Things are not the same. You have put the cat among the pigeons, Lorna. Derek thinks that Ben understands such problems as errant wives because he writes plays about them. He thinks that Ben can find solutions. That he understands the human condition."

"And does he?"

"As far as it makes good theatre."

"What advice did he give Derek?"

Pam looked at her. "Stop panicking. That you'd be back. To leave you alone for a bit."

"What else?"

"Find a girlfriend."

Lorna laughed. "Not Derek."

"Why?"

"He's too moral. That's why he's so angry with me."

"Would it worry you?"

"It's a daft thing for Ben to say."

"I think he was a bit fed up with Derek badgering him. There are letters. I was going to post them."

"From Joey?"

"And Cam. From Kibbutz Something-or-other." She drew on her cigarette. "Derek wants you back, Lorna. He needs you."

"Like he needs his clean shirt before he can go to work."

"That was the message. I promised to pass it on. What are you doing with yourself?"

Lorna shrugged. "I'm happy."

"You look it. What about the boyfriend?"

"He's gentle."

"I don't think men appreciate how important that is. Gentleness, tenderness. They think it unmanly. Women will do anything for gentleness."

"Is Ben gentle?"

"Within his limitations."

"Derek is kind but not gentle. Sometimes I sit for hours at a time. Doing nothing. Just being. Aware of my heart beating, my soul, my mind, my eyes, my big toe. Doing nothing but being Lorna Brown. I sit in the park a lot. I really see. Sometimes just one rose. Or a leaf. Or think about a line from a poem Armand had read me."

"My, my!" Pam said.

"I suppose you think I'm being stupid?"

"Not at all. Just growing up at the wrong end of the day. You did well to get out."

"We've never really talked all that much. Not for years."

"I can't talk Magimixes," Pam said. "I'll get the letters."

223

There was a card to say her bi-focals were ready. The house-wife bi-focals. She tore it up.

Cam said:

It's so beautiful here. I think I might emigrate. We are right on the border with Lebanon. Kibbutz life is very stimulating although the kibbutzniks don't think much of the volunteers and keep themselves to themselves. There are people from all over the world, Dutch, Scandinavian, German, South American. At night someone always plays music and we sit for hours under the stars. We eat in this big, communal dining-room, soup and stringy chicken, the noise is indescribable. At first I was picking apples. We get up at four (me! Can you imagine?) and the truck comes to take us to the orchards. By the time we get back Blake and I have to support each other we are so exhausted. We don't realize what a soft life we lead at home. Now I have to take my turn in the kitchen. I peel mountains of potatoes (I'm not exaggerating) and clean saucepans so huge that we almost have to crawl inside them. The Israeli women shout at us. Some of them spend their whole lives in the kitchens, they are really dedicated. Blake is on cleaning the bedrooms and lavatories so I think I'm quite lucky with the saucepans. You think the summer is hot in England but you wouldn't believe the heat in these kitchens. The sweat just runs off you. I don't think I could stand it for long. We shall work here for about a month then go off and see something of the country. I met this boy from North Africa. He's really amazing. His name is Simon. We speak French. Blake is involved with a guy from Tel Aviv. I've got a feeling she might stay. Home Farm Close seems so far away. Why do we always imagine the centre of the universe is where we live? It's not like that at all. I think of you and Daddy and Joey and Anne-

Marie and Cassius and send love. 'L'Hitraot'! (That's Hebrew), Your loving CAM.

Joey said:

DEAR MUMMY,
I am being good. I am going to France tomorrow. Anne-Marie has packed my case. I wonder if Jean-Paul plays chess I am taking it anyway and Mastermind. I couldn't find my mask and snorkel but Daddy says I can buy one there he's in a bad temper most of the time because of the weather he says. Auntie Irene and Auntie Lois and all the others keep asking us for dinner but Daddy doesn't want to go. I'll send you a postcard.

Love JOEY.

She sat on Steve's bed reading the letters.

"Do you think I'm a wicked mother?" she asked Armand. "Abandoning my children?"

"Cam is grown-up."

"Joey then? He never says he's missing me. When am I coming back? I miss him. I don't even know what Derek has told him."

"Cheer up." Armand was reading.

"I've made a mess of things, haven't I? My life. The trouble is, I don't know what I want. Only that I can't go on living in Home Farm Close. I think it's the generation I was born into. There's this enormous army of women totally untrained for anything, children grown-up or no longer needing them, alone and tranquillized in the suburbs. Just think of all that wasted manpower, womanpower, whatever you want to call it; all those untapped resources; all that potential dissipating itself in coffee mornings and bridge afternoons. There are battalions of us, wasting away, frittering our lives, except for a bit of occupational therapy perhaps, evening classes where we learn to tat or decorate cakes. What are we to do? What are we to do? I suppose I could go back to college. It's the in thing now, get a piece of paper saying how clever I am, but then what? There are too many teachers already. I was thinking, if I'm going to stay here much longer I shall have to get a job. I can't expect Derek...and Derek! What am I to do about him? You're not listening to a word, are you, Armand?"

"I'm listening."

"Well?"

"Well what?"

"What do you suggest?"

"Nothing, my love. You have to work it out for yourself. I can provide the sympathy. Not the solution. It's what most people want."

"Where did you learn to be so wise?"

"You mistake silence for wisdom. It's a common error."

"You know what you want. It's important."

"What's that?"

"To write your novel. All I can write is a grocery list. It's frightening. I don't know if you've noticed but I've been tidying up. Rory, the house. I had a shock yesterday. I didn't tell you. I was messing about in the kitchen. There were no tea bags and the washing-up brush has only one whisker left. Do you know what I did, Armand?"

"You tell me."

"I looked round for the memory-board. I wanted to write 'Tea bags', 'Washing-up brush'. I wanted to. I've been upset all day with the enormity of it."

He looked across at her. "Are you crying, Lorna?"

"Yes."

"Why?"

"Self-pity. I've made a middle-aged fool of myself."

"No."

"Yes. You know it. You're too polite."

"That's not something I suffer from."

"You wouldn't hurt anyone."

"No."

"What am I doing here?"

"We like having you."

"We?"

"Eugene, Jed, Opal. We need you."

"It's not enough. What about you, Armand? You only need me like Eugene, like Jed?"

They looked at each other across the vast room.

Armand pointed. "You see that door? Each time it opens I hope it is you who will come through it. Each time it is you my heart sings. You're still crying?"

"You've made it worse. Nobody has ever said anything like that to me before. Not for a long, long time, at any rate. When I first met Derek. Back in the dark ages. We were in the garden with my mother. He said: 'Mrs Allardyce, if only you knew how much I love your daughter'. I thought I would die of happiness. It wears off."

"The happiness?"

"The love."

"Or changes; matures."

"Could be. I've never said this to anyone. Sometimes I sit across from him, Derek, at the table. I look at him, double chin, pot belly, going a bit thin on top, and wonder when I fell out of love with him and how devastated he'd be if I told him. He hasn't done anything. Been just the same as always, but something between us has gone. I feel full of guilt and self-recrimination and usually go out and buy his favourite supper."

"I thought you loved Derek?"

"I do. Love, but not in love. You think I'm crazy?"

"No."

"I am. Crazy. It's my age."

"Rubbish. You look" – he put his head on one side – "like a young girl."

227

"I wish I was. Starting again. I think I kidded myself. Coming to you. That I could. Start again. It was a mistake, wasn't it? A big mistake."

"You are going round and round in circles," Armand said.

"I spend my life…"

"If you come over here I will wipe away your tears."

She crossed the room and knelt by him. "With such an incentive…"

He dried them.

"Women of my age shouldn't cry. It does diabolical things to the face."

"Forget your age."

"I do with you. I could fall in love with you quite easily, Armand. That would be disastrous."

"I love you. There's no disaster in that."

"Think you do."

"Know. You are all woman. Soft."

"My body perhaps."

"You. Mother earth. I want to crawl into you."

"You can do whatever you like with me, Armand. You bring out the best in me. I like it."

"I often dreamed of a woman like you. Now I have her. Not many people achieve their dreams."

"I hope you're not disappointed."

"Never, in you."

"I could lie here with you, warmed by the sun, to the ends of the earth."

There was no one to tell her it was the time of her optimum happiness.

Seventeen

She got into bed aware that she was shaking, although it wasn't cold in the ward. Funny how hospitals made you afraid. The mattress was hard and unyielding, the sheets rough, and the weight of them light, no wool blankets or eiderdowns here, no duvet as at Cornwall Terrace. The light shone through the floral curtains, outlining the orange poppies with the black stalks. Some Ladies Guild or other had made an effort to cheer the place up. It needed more than orange poppies. The curtains were swept back brusquely, no warning. What had she expected? A knock? The right to privacy had been relinquished with her clothes. She no longer belonged to herself.

"There we go!" Nurse Cooper rewarded her with a smile for getting herself so skilfully into bed. She picked up the case.

"Get rid of the body! Doctor will be along any minute."

"Nurse Cooper!" An imperious call came from the end of the ward.

"There's Sister. See you later then." She patted the curtain where she had drawn it back into place and was off.

There were a dozen beds in the ward, with pale blue cotton covers. Hers was the only locker not overflowing with flowers and fruit and boxes of Black Magic and packets of biscuits and bottles of lemon barley water and tonic wine. She felt like the new girl at boarding school and wanted to run away.

A waif in a striped towelling bathrobe appeared at the foot of her bed. She looked about fifteen and had unkempt, straggling blonde hair.

She stared at Lorna. "That's a smashing nightie!"

It had come from the White House. Her mother had bought it for her when Joey was born. The girl was wearing some kind of flannelette shift beneath the robe.

"Bet it was expensive!"

She was sorry she'd put it on.

The girl produced a box from behind her back and came to stand next to Lorna.

"Like a chocolate?"

"No, thanks." It was the last thing she wanted.

The girl peered into the box. "I like the caramel. And the nuts. Can't stand the marzipan. Nobody seems to like the marzipan." She sat down on the bed. "I've got syphilis," she said with pride.

Lorna made a slight retracting movement, not sure whether it was catching.

"And" – she leaned forward – "guess what?"

"What?" Lorna wished she'd go away. She was in no mood for confidences.

"I'm pregnant!"

"Oh dear!" What was she supposed to say?

"I have injections every four hours. You'll see them coming round. They're going to take it away."

"The baby?"

"Yes."

"Doctor to see you," Nurse Cooper said. "Off you go dear!"

The girl stood up but didn't move.

"Run along now, Annie."

She backed away, not taking her eyes off Lorna.

The doctor looked no older than Armand. She wasn't sure what she had been expecting, but it caught her on the hop. When she thought of Doctor it was middle-aged Dick or Mr

Gillespie, the surgeon. This was a boy with scrubbed hands and pimples, playing at doctors. He sat on the bed.

"Hallo."

"Hallo," Lorna said, smiling. She wanted to make it easy for him.

"I'm just going to ask you a few questions." He took the cap off his pen and opened the folder he was carrying. "Mrs Brown, isn't it?"

"Yes. Lorna."

"How old are you?"

"Forty-five."

She felt ridiculous. He was taking it all very seriously, writing in a neat, tiny hand on the ruled paper. He asked her about her appetite, her weight, her periods, her bowels. Whether she got up in the night to pass water. She wanted to ask him if he hadn't got all the relevant information from Mr Gillespie. It must surely have been in her notes.

"How much do you drink?"

"Very little."

"Smoke?"

"No." The joints were past now and irrelevant.

"Do you take tablets of any kind?"

She thought of Yolande.

"Asprins?" He was helping her.

How thorough he was. She was getting tired. He filled two pages with his neat notes. When he had finished he read them through then put the cap back on his pen and slid it into the pocket of his white coat.

He stood up and removed the pillow from behind her head.

"Let's have a look at you then, shall we, Mrs Brown?"

She slid down the bed. The nurse helped her to remove the White House nightie. It was eau-de-nil with coffee lace.

She lay feeling ridiculous, ashamed, with bared breasts.

He did not touch her. Standing, staring at them, arms folded.

"When did you first notice the lump, Mrs Brown?"

She'd been in the bath. The rust-stained bath in Cornwall Terrace. She'd never really got used to the austerity of it, thinking often of the Sahara Beige suite in Home Farm Close. Usually she didn't linger, getting in and out again as quickly as possible, trying not to notice the grime round the taps, the walls which wept with the steam. She had been idly feeling her breasts. The lump in the side of the left one seemed not to have gone away since her last period. Or was it the period before? She didn't know. She did know. Had been aware of it for some time yet knowing ignored it, dismissed it, glossing over, in her mind, the significance, the ramifications of it which she knew very well yet did not allow to penetrate her conscious mind where she could examine and act upon it. Not till she saw with horror the puckered skin like a deflating balloon above the lump which seemed now to be quite large beneath her fingers.

'I have a lump,' she said aloud, in the bathroom. 'I have a lump in my breast.'

She tried to pick up the soap and couldn't. She forgot whether or not she had washed. She knocked her knee on the side of the bath trying to get out. She was trembling so much she couldn't unfold her towel. 'I have a lump in my breast,' she said. 'Dear God!'

They had discussed it often. She and Irene and Lois and Estelle. Talking of women they knew, one of them knew. 'She found this lump and they took her in straight away, the next day, wouldn't let her wait a second longer. Had to remove the lot but the doctor said she'll be all right now. They caught it in time.' But there was always the doubt. She tried not to look when women she knew had had mastectomies, saving them the embarrassment of the stare at the front of their dresses to see if you could tell.

Her mother's best friend had had both removed, then died a horrible death from secondaries in the spine. It could not, could not, be happening to her.

She dressed quickly. There seemed to be no time to lose. Not a moment. She was going to see Dick and if she hurried would be just in time for the end of the morning surgery. She could have gone to a strange doctor, someone with his name on a shop window in Camden town, there was a Dr Mukajee and across the road a Dr Rosenberg, she'd noticed them. It did not seem to be the moment for strange doctors. There was another reason. She suddenly felt the need to go back to Home Farm close. A frightened child running to Mummy.

"You're in a hurry," Armand said.

"Yes."

"Could you bring me some bank paper? A4?"

She stared at him. "What paper?"

"Bank. Copy paper. I didn't realize I'd nearly run out. Do you know I've written eighty thousand words?"

"Eighty thousand." She realized she sounded like a parrot. "I don't know. It doesn't mean anything…"

"Eighty thousand out of a hundred and twenty-five thousand!"

She fastened her skirt. "That's marvellous!"

"Something's wrong, Lorna. What is it?"

"Nothing. Really. I'll get your paper."

He stood by the window. The sun was shining across the top of his hair, turning it chestnut.

"Come back soon!"

Today it meant nothing. Like a stranger speaking.

"As soon as I can."

Outside the door she stopped. The baby was crying. In the horror of finding the lump she had forgotten his feed. She usually did it at ten. It depended what state Opal was in. She went up. Opal stared at her.

"Opal, you must get up and feed Rory!" she said with authority, as if she was talking to Cam.

Opal stared at her from the bed.

233

Lorna shook her shoulders. "Come on, dear, make an effort. Don't let him cry like that. Will you?"

"Right," Opal said.

"Sure now?"

There was no reply.

"Please!"

It was not her baby, she told herself at she ran down the stairs, not her responsibility. She had assumed it lately. Loved it. Loved the soft, clean feel of him when he was bathed and changed and in her arms. Armand teased her. Little mother. She didn't care. When she cradled him she was holding Joey. Holding her son. Joey had gone to France. On the day he left, she had cried, wanted to run home but did not. Not then, not when Derek had begged her, meeting at Pam's. She could not. Was not ready.

Home Farm Close slept. It seemed always to be asleep, the houses offering their noncommittal faces to the sun. She had to drive past her own house to get to Dick's. She remembered it was Friday and Anne-Marie's day out. There would be no one in but Cassius. She wondered if he would still know her. She could wait, she supposed, until after she'd seen Dick but did not want to mix the two issues. Perhaps what Dick would have to say would not be pleasant. Perhaps she would want to run straight back, to Armand, perhaps to Rory, the sound of his crying was in her ears. Knowing it was what she was going to do, she turned the car into the drive.

The step was dirty, Anne-Marie had not cleaned it. She felt the old anger and frustration rising within her before she had even put her key into the lock. Her hand was trembling. Cassius barked and jumped at the door.

"OK, Cass," she said. "It's only me."

He fell upon her, crying like a child. His paws were on her shoulders.

"OK. OK. Down, boy. Good boy. Down Cass." She would have to take a few minutes to calm him. When eventually he sat, whimpering, shivering, at her feet, she looked round the hall. It was all there, the fish staring at her accusingly as they swam back and forth, there but unloved. There were finger-marks on the doors. The fringes of the rugs were tangled, the leaves of the ficus and the monstera were dulled with dust. She moved on to the kitchen, knowing that if she stayed any longer she would have to get out cotton-wool and milk and leaf-shine and attend to the plants. The tops in the kitchen were dull too, and littered. Bills and papers, needle and cotton and scissors. Another button off Joey's blazer? The coffee jar, instead of in its place. An empty flower vase. The shopping basket, when it had its own hook. There was a casserole soaking in the stainless steel sink which too looked dull, the tea-towels were grey. She picked up one and put it down again. There was a hole burned in the oven gloves, a saucepan with some crusted mashed potato was on the cooker. She sat on one of the tall stools, then got up. If she lingered for more than a moment she would not be able to leave. Would start busying herself, putting the house to rights.

The living-room was tidy. Too tidy. As if no one had been in there. There were no flowers. It was like a hot house. Shut up. No one had put the blinds down on the terrace. The chairs had been left out, not that they were likely to have any rain. The lawn was browner than ever, the patches larger. The dining-room looked desolate. No centrepiece on the table, which showed ziz-zags of dust in the sunlight where Anne-Marie had swiped at it with her duster. She went into the den. Cassius followed her. The evening paper was on the armchair, some grapes in the bowl. Derek had obviously been sitting in there, cosier she supposed when on his own than the living-room. The thought of him, on his own, all evening, made her sad. It all did. What had she done in her foolishness? Derek! She said his name aloud. Cassius cocked his head on one side.

"Not you!" She patted him and went upstairs.

Someone had tidied Cam's room. Well, tidied. They'd picked up the rubbish she had left and stowed it neatly into cardboard boxes. It was the best anyone but a mother could do. The room had been dusted and hoovered. She went quickly, not wanting to remember. There was no change in Joey's room. Dear Joey. So full of him. It could not have belonged to anyone else. The panda stared at her. She picked it up and kissed it, hoping Cassius would not think her daft.

The door to her bedroom, hers and Derek's was shut. She opened it, knowing that the full blast of the sun would envelope her, it faced due south. It did, blinding her for a moment. When she got her vision back she looked round, touching the familiar landmarks with her eyes. When her glance reached the king-sized bed it stopped. There was the new John Le Carré next to Derek's side of the bed.

Next to hers was a maroon leather Swiss radio and a maroon leather travelling clock.

She did not remember leaving the house, locking the front door, driving back to Cornwall Terrace. She did not remember to buy the paper Armand had asked her for.

She ran up the stairs, past the bicycle, through the open door, and flung herself into his arms.

"He's sleeping with Anne-Marie," she said. "With the au pair!"

"Who is?"

"Derek. In my bed. She's been sleeping in my bed. Her clock and her radio were on the side. Little bitch! Bloody little bitch!"

"You did run away from him. Left him alone," Armand said. "You can't really be surprised."

She stared at him.

"You don't begin to understand," she said. "She's the au pair!" He had let her down. Derek, reliable Derek, had let her down.

236

She arranged to meet him at Pam's. There was a thundery storm brewing and the air was heavy. He had a blue open-necked shirt on which flattered his garden tan. He looked fit and well.

"You've been sitting in the garden," she said. "You look as if you've been on holiday."

"More than I can say for you," he said. "You look terrible, Lorna."

"I haven't been sleeping."

"Nor eating, by the look of you."

She stared out into the unkempt garden, the grim backs of the houses opposite.

"Why did you want to see me?" Derek asked.

"I've been thinking, about Anne-Marie."

"Yes?"

"I think I should get a housekeeper. A proper housekeeper for when Joey comes back. Irish or something. A capable woman."

"What's wrong with Anne-Marie? She's managing very well. Joey adores her."

"What about Joey's father?"

"We get along. She's an obliging girl."

"I bet she is!"

"Meaning what?"

Lorna sat down in the brown moquette armchair with the protruding springs. "I came home, Derek; to Home Farm Close."

"I know."

She looked up. "How?"

"Pauline Pearson saw the car outside the house. She told Lois who told Irene."

"Neighbours!"

Derek sat down opposite her. Somehow he looked younger, had the air of a young man.

"What did you expect me to do, Lorna?"

237

"Not sleep with the au pair. It's disgusting. And in our bed. I don't know how you could."

"One law for the Medes and another for the Persians?"

"It's quite different, as you know very well."

"I know no such thing."

"What about Joey?"

"What about him?"

"What can he think? I suppose you didn't consider that!"

"Lorna! Joey doesn't know. It's only since he's been away. We were alone in the house. Anne-Marie and myself."

"I always thought you had so much self-control. Always admired your self-control. She's a child."

"She's a woman. Warm."

"I suppose I'm not."

"Lorna, you weren't there. And when you were there you weren't there. Haven't been, not for months."

"What do you mean?"

"Oh, you've been going through the motions. Running the house and being a mother to Cam and Joey. A wife to me. Do you think I didn't know that every time we made love you did it for the momentary satisfaction it brought you? I could have been anybody. It was insulting."

"You never said."

"What was the point? I hoped it would pass. We haven't been getting on too well for some time. You've been tolerating me. I don't much like being tolerated."

"That's not true."

"Of course it's true. I tried to make you happy but everything I did seemed to be wrong. You were never satisfied. With anything."

She said nothing.

"Am I right?"

She nodded.

"I know you don't like Home Farm Close but do you think it would be different anywhere else? After you'd got over the excitement of the change, when you'd have other things to think about, it would all come back. You'd be just as dissatisfied. It's not Home Farm Close. I'm not even sure that it's me."

"What is it then?"

"How do I know? I suggested you went to talk to someone before you went running off. Making a fool of yourself. Of me."

"You don't like being made a fool of. I'm sorry for that, Derek."

"Does anyone?"

"I mean I'm sorry you see it like that. I had to think of myself."

"Do you ever think of anyone else?"

"Meaning?"

"Me."

She opened her mouth but he held up his hand. "Please, Lorna. Don't insult me by cataloguing the evidence of your solicitude. I know my meals are cooked, my house kept in exemplary condition, my clothes cared for. A housekeeper, as you say, could do that. Do you care, though, how I feel? About losing the South Bank contract? About the fact that there is no work about? That my creative talents are being stifled? That I have to build tacky houses on a shoe-string and ugly office blocks, and fight – trampling on other people's faces sometimes – for every contract? Do you know how it feels not to have job satisfaction? And if you know, do you care?"

"You never talk about your work."

"Right. I used to. Sometimes you said. 'Oh really?' as if I'd told you it was raining. Other times you never even bothered to look up from what you were doing. I stopped discussing it with you. And then the children."

"What about the children?"

"Whatever I said you overruled me. If I tried to discipline your precious Joey you got between us. It's not good for a boy. And Cam. You let her walk all over you. Cam wants this and

Cam wants that. And you give it to her. You let her take you for a ride."

There were beads of perspiration on her upper lip. She felt stifled.

"I didn't know you felt like this."

"How could you? You were so wrapped up in yourself."

"I tried to talk to you. Often."

"Always about yourself."

"I never stopped you…"

"I gave up trying, long ago."

"I never realized," Lorna said, "I simply never realized that you weren't happy, Derek."

"You didn't give it a moment's thought. You were far too busy."

"Thinking about myself? Perhaps I was. You were never very sympathetic. Always laughing. The heat, my age."

"I'm nearly fifty, Lorna. There are problems too. Life turning out not quite the way you expected it to do. Having to pull in one's hopes, fears, dreams, aspirations. Sometimes it is not very comfortable. One needs loving arms, reassurance."

"I had no idea."

"No."

There was a crash.

"What's that?"

"Thunder," Derek said. He got up and looked out of the window. "It's been threatening all day. We can do with a good downpour for the garden."

"I had no idea you were unhappy."

"Not unhappy, Lorna. I didn't say that, I loved you."

"Loved?"

He turned to face her. "Look, there's something I have to tell you. There's no easy way. I want to marry Anne-Marie!"

There was nothing Armand could do to comfort her. Nothing he could say.

The lump in her breast became unimportant against the background of Derek's pronouncement. It became buried in the turbulence of her thoughts that erupted from the volcano of her mind. She went over and over her talk with Derek in Pam's sitting-room until, like an old photograph, it became tattered and blurred. She took it out and looked at it a hundred times during any one day. She could feel the heat, see the rain that fell in stair-rods on to the pram with no wheels, the doll with no arms, in Pam's garden.

"Marry? Anne-Marie?"

"I want you to give me a divorce."

She could not have got up from the chair if she wanted to. It was as if she sat there, limp within her skin, no muscle, no bone.

"I don't believe it."

"I'm sorry, Lorna. It's been a shock. It's true."

She looked up. The storm had darkened the room. He was a silhouette against the window, against the rain.

"It was going on then. Before...?"

"No. It just happened suddenly. We fell in love."

"Love!"

"You fell in love with Armand."

"No. I love you, Derek."

"You've a funny way of showing it."

"Armand was the excuse, the catalyst, for running away."

"Perhaps it's what we both need. I can't describe to you how I felt when you left, but perhaps it was fortuitous. We were suffocating each other."

"All that life," Lorna said. "The shared life. Everything we've done, the children..."

"I'm sorry about the children. About Joey. We'll do whatever you like."

"Heatherington went to his father because his mother couldn't play football..."

"Are you feeling all right, Lorna?"

"...Sometimes I think children have second sight."

"What are you talking about?"

"Nothing. It doesn't matter."

There was a flash of lightning. It lit up the room. Derek had always held her in his arms during a storm, like a child, a frightened child. Perhaps, she thought, it would wash away the long, hot summer. That after the storm all trace of it would have gone. That it would in its wake take the day that stood out from the rest like an outlined picture in a child's pop-up book, Cam and Armand, Irene and Dick, and the Pearsons, eating curried eggs in the garden. It was a dream, a foolish nightmare, she would go back with Derek, back to Home Farm Close, back to her life.

"You weren't happy," Derek said. "Haven't been for a long time. I'm too dull for you."

"No."

He turned round. "Oh, come on, Lorna, that's what you thought, admit it."

"I don't know what I thought," Lorna said. "What I think. Not any more."

"I'll get Pam," Derek said. "We need a drink, if they've got anything."

Eighteen

It was July when she'd first noticed the lump. It was now November. The young doctor nodded, surprise only in his eyes.

"Anyway, you're here now," he said reassuringly.

"Yes. I'm here now."

She didn't like to tell him that she did not really care if she lived or died. It was immaterial. She who had once been so afraid.

He felt her neck, under her arms. Looked at her eyes, her tongue. Listened to her heart, her chest. He made her sit up and stared at her first from the end of the bed then from the side. Then he was feeling her breasts, the breast, gently, with the flat of his hand, touching the lump, holding it in his fingers. Finished with the breast, the poor breast she knew she would not see after tomorrow, he pulled on a white rubber finger-stall.

"Turn round to face Nurse," he said. "I'm going to examine you. I'm sorry. It won't take a moment."

She wanted to tell him that he need not have apologized. That she no longer cared about such minor indignities.

She blamed Pam.

"It was you who told him to find another woman," she said when Derek had gone home.

"Not me. Ben."

"Ben then."

"You know very well you can't make people do things. Not anything they don't want to do."

"Ben put the idea into his head."

Pam picked up the whisky bottle and held it to the light. The rain was easing up now, falling in light, slanting needles. She held the bottle over Lorna's glass. Lorna did not protest.

"You can't go round blaming other people." She shut the door to the garden, the air was fresher now, cooled by the storm, and sat down opposite Lorna. "Anyway it's probably for the best."

"What do you mean?"

"You know what I feel, have always felt, about Derek. You'll probably make a great career for yourself when you've got over the shock."

"Doing what?"

Pam shrugged. "I don't know. Something will turn up. You're not a stupid girl, Lorna. Not by any means. Once you've learned to stand on your own feet. My God, Lorna, you carried on enough about Home Farm Close, Womb Farm Close, about Derek. Now you're going to be free. It's what you wanted, isn't it?"

"What about Joey?"

"Is Derek trying to take him from you?"

"No."

"Well then. He's still Joey. Don't act as if he'd died or something. Children are very adaptable."

Lorna stared at her. "How on earth do you know," she said, "about children? About anything? You think you know about children, about life, you always have, Miss Smarty-Boots. You always were a Miss Smarty-Boots. You always were a Miss Smarty-Boots, going round with that superior face of yours as if you knew it all. And you know nothing, nothing! Less than nothing. You think that because you mix with all those egg-heads you know all about it. But you know nothing. Oh, I know you 'lived your own life' in the ten years before you married Ben. 'Did your own thing' as they call it today, but what did you really do? Casual encounters with this one and that one, nothing deeper than a puddle in the street, talking and writing, observing from your ivory tower. People think you're very clever, I know, Mother especially, but you're not clever enough to keep Ben from the pub every night, to make a decent home, look at this filthy mess, a decent meal, I don't suppose you've cooked one since you've been married. Do you make him happy in bed? I doubt it. Ben doesn't have the look of a man who is happy in bed. Life, Pam? You make me laugh. You've never known what it's like to conceive, the utter joy, the shared joy of knowing you are going to have a child. The secret that binds you together, closely, so closely, until you decide, the two of you, to share it with the world. Have you experienced birth? I assure you, ask anyone who has, that you cannot call yourself a woman until you do. I don't care how many times you've been to Tibet, Peru. It doesn't matter how many aborigines you've lived with, interviewed for the Third Programme, any woman who has spent one night, one night, in the labour ward knows a million times more what life is all about than you with your second hand views which you parcel up in clever language and ram down people's throats. You've sat up all night watching the Aurora Borealis but when have you sat with a sick child, wishing you could give him your life, your breath? You've watched the Samoans dancing but not your own flesh and blood playing, in his own little world, in the sunlight. And when they grow, and you begin to see yourself as a child, to recognize a little here, a little there, that you have reproduced yourself, made your contribution to eternity, how does that compare with the fifty quid that they pay you for an article, a couple of columns of sterile newsprint? Your words won't jump up off the page, Pam, when you're old, won't care for you, bring joy into your life. How can you sit there, bloody sit there" – her voice was rising – "you, a dried-up old stick, and tell me children are adaptable! Joey. My Joey! Half the time you can't even remember his name..." She was sobbing, letting the tears run

245

down her face, unchecked. She was crying for Derek, for the lump she was nurturing in her breast to punish him with, for what she had done.

Pam picked up the whisky bottle. "There's a drop left." She poured it into Lorna's glass. "You'd better have it."

When she was calmer she said, "I'm sorry, Pam. Really sorry."

"No," Pam said. "It's best to say what you feel."

"It wasn't very fair." Lorna took a mirror from her handbag. "To take it out on you."

"It doesn't make an iota of difference. Really."

She looked into the tiny square mirror. "What a bloody mess. I didn't mean all those things."

"If you did or if you didn't," Pam said, "it doesn't really matter. I'm sorry there isn't any more whisky. When Ben gets back…"

Lorna got up. "Don't worry. I'm going."

"Are you sure you're all right?"

"Super," Lorna said. "Just super."

"Just a couple of forms for you to sign," the house doctor said, "then I'll leave you in peace."

She read the form giving her consent to a preliminary investigation and to 'any other surgical procedures which seemed necessary'. She signed her name, Lorna Brown, and found that her hand was shaking. The young doctor wrote his name beneath hers. The signature was illegible.

"I'll leave you in peace now," he said. "I'll be bringing Mr Gillespie to see you later; and I expect Dr Cox will be along."

Lorna raised an eyebrow.

"The anaesthetist. He'll want to talk to you." He picked up the notes from the bed and smiled. "See you!"

He was a nice lad. Perhaps Joey would be a doctor. A fish doctor. She wondered if there was a name for them.

"Never a dull moment," Nurse Cooper said, tidying the curtains where she had pulled them back so that Lorna could see the ward again. "Here comes Miss Dobson."

She wore a white coat and held a clip-board.

She smiled brightly. There seemed no shortage of bright smiles. "Just a few questions," she said. "Let me see." She looked at her notes. "Mrs Brown, isn't it?"

"Lorna." She shut her eyes for a moment. She was tired, wanted to be left alone.

It was not the same with Armand. She began to see faults in him, in Eugene, Jed, the squat. She seemed no longer able to sit for hours learning to be. If she tried to concentrate on her hands, her breathing, her thoughts went to Derek, to Anne-Marie. She picked up a twig in the park and brought it back to study it. Her mind was filled with Joey and the effect a divorce would have on him. The twig seemed to be an old bit of stick. She threw it in the rubbish bin.

She quarrelled with Armand.

He was sitting on his bed, typing, around him was a sea of papers as usual. They floated on his discarded clothes.

Lorna came in with the broom and started sweeping the floor that had once been polished parquet.

"For Chrissakes, Lorna!" Armand said, his fingers poised over the keys. "Look at the dust you're raising!"

"It's about time," Lorna said. "It hasn't been swept properly in years."

"Leave it alone then," Armand said, "there's a good girl. There's no need to disturb it now." He went on typing. Lorna went on sweeping, enjoying the grey lines of fluff she was collecting in front of the broom.

When she got to where Armand sat she pulled the discarded clothes from beneath his papers, disturbing them.

"Lorna, please!"

"I'm going to the launderette," she said. "I'll take your washing."

"I'll take it myself."

"It'll save you a journey. I'm going anyway."

"I'll take it myself. Leave it alone."

She ignored him, pulling a sock from beneath a pile of paper. The pile scattered over the floor.

"Lorna, please! That was all in order."

"Sorry. I was getting the sock."

"Damn the sock!" Armand said. It was the first time she had heard him raise his voice. "You're getting on my nerves lately. I can't work with all this tidying and sweeping. It's disturbing. You're getting on Eugene's nerves too, and Jed's."

"What do you mean?"

"Organizing the kitchen. They can't find anything. Every time they get something out you put it away. Just leave us alone."

"You've been talking about me?"

"The subject did come up."

"Perhaps you'd rather I left?"

He looked at her. "Lorna!"

"Well, it sounds like it!"

"Just stop trying to organize us." He collected his typewritten pages from where they had floated across the floor.

"There's another sock somewhere under there."

"Well it can stay there!"

"I'm not leaving one sock! That's how they get lost."

"Shut up!"

"Don't tell me to shut up, Armand, I'm old enough…"

"Yes?" He looked at her.

She left the room, slamming the door.

They ignored each other studiously for the rest of the day. That night she slept in Steve's bed. In the morning she was wakened by Armand getting in beside her. They made love

248

without speaking. For the first time when with Armand she felt detached and wondered if he knew.

"It's because of yesterday," he said afterwards.

He knew.

"I'm sorry."

"It was my fault," Lorna said. "I'm getting on your nerves, on Eugene's nerves. Most of all I'm getting on my own. I'll try. I will."

He kissed her. "That's my girl."

"Perhaps I should go."

He sat up on one elbow. The sun glinted through his lashes. "Don't ever do that."

"Never?"

"Never."

She knew he did not mean it. Only his book was important. It was growing daily. His relationship with it formed a partnership she could not penetrate. She was careful not to disturb him, confining her activities to the kitchen, to the baby. She didn't mind upsetting Eugene, Jed. She smoked herself into oblivion or found tasks round the house, not leaving herself one moment to dwell upon Derek, upon Anne-Marie, upon Joey. Spending money recklessly she bought romper suits for the baby, two feather-light blankets which she washed regularly and hung in the bathroom to dry. She stocked up the cupboard in the kitchen with food and in her mind began to call it the larder. One day she went to John Lewis and bought canisters, blue and white, which said 'sugar' and 'coffee' and 'tea'. On her way out through the store she passed the haberdashery. It seemed a lifetime ago that she had bought the mauve buttons for Joey's blazer. She stopped by the revolving button-stand, wanting to cry.

"If you're not choosing anything can you get out of the way?" a woman said. "I'm looking for green buttons."

She imagined a small boy who went to a school with a green blazer and wondered if he'd been in the three-legged.

"Address?" Miss Dobson said. She sat on the bed and wrote on the clip-board with the pen which she kept slung round her neck.

"They have my address downstairs," Lorna said. "On my card."

"Yes. That's for the admission. This is for the records."

She couldn't see the difference. She gave her address.

"How old are you?"

"Forty-five," Lorna said.

Miss Dobson filled in the appropriate box on her form.

"The same age as me," she said. "Do you have problems?" She relaxed her professional manner.

"What do you mean?"

"Dryness. And I keep shouting at everyone. My husband thinks I don't love him any more. But I do. It's just that everything seems so difficult. I'm thinking about hormone replacement therapy but there seem so many different opinions."

"Yes," Lorna said. She was not concerned about the state of Miss Dobson's vagina.

"I suppose we shall get over it," Miss Dobson said, allying herself with Lorna. "Religion?"

"Well… nothing really. Not any more."

"I don't mean practising. C of E?"

"Yes."

"We have to put down something. Sex? Female. Next of Kin?"

Lorna looked at her. "In case I die?"

"It's just a formality."

It was no use putting Armand. Her mother would only fluster. Pam would probably have a deadline to meet.

"Husband?" Miss Dobson suggested.

"I've left him. We're not divorced. He doesn't even know I'm here."

"You still see each other though?"

"Oh yes. I love him. He wants to marry the au pair."

She hadn't meant to blurt out her problems. It served Miss Dobson right for her dry vagina.

"He's still your next of kin then?"

"I suppose so. It is just a formality?"

"Of course. What's his name?"

"Derek. I know it sounds stupid but I left him to save our marriage. I had to get out."

"We all need to get out at times. I know I do."

"You have your job."

"Yes. I'd go berserk otherwise. Does he have a telephone number where he can be reached during the day?"

Lorna gave his office number.

"Evenings and weekends?"

She gave the number. Her number. Home Farm Close. Anne-Marie would answer it. The telephone was on her side of the bed.

"I think that's the lot," Miss Dobson said, handing her the clip-board. "If you'd just put your name there…"

Lorna signed her name again. So much red tape.

"And the date," Miss Dobson said, pointing. "Just there."

She filled in the little box neatly, noting with surprise that only six weeks remained before Christmas. They spent Christmas Day in Dorset with her mother. Her mother loved acting the queen, seeming not to feel the tensions. Cam went under sufferance, preferring to spend the day with her friends than with Grandma. Derek objected to the journey. Pam always had a long face and Ben got drunk. Only Joey really enjoyed it, because of the presents and eating until he was almost sick. Boxing Day was an endless round of drinks in Home Farm Close. Lois and Geoffrey, Irene and Dick, Leonard and…well, last year it had been Yolande. Lorna remembered she had worn a new red trouser suit with a plunging neckline showing her bony, freckled chest. She'd darted like a flame. In the evening, they'd done it for years, they had a rotating party. A Home Farm

Close party. Last year they had had drinks at the Pearsons'. Lorna had provided the first course, Irene the main dish, then they had all trooped round to Leonard and Yolande for the dessert, fabulous flans and savarins for which Yolande was famous, had been famous. By the time they got to Lois and Geoffrey for the coffee and liqueurs they had all been roaring drunk, but that of course was the idea. It was, after all, Christmas. Things would not be the same this year. She wondered if there would be a rotating party and if Derek would take Anne-Marie. Perhaps Anne-Marie would give them muesli. Lorna smiled at the thought.

"Not long to Christmas," Miss Dobson said.

"No," Lorna said. "Not long."

She thought the canisters looked nice in the kitchen. She stood them on the narrow marble mantelshelf and put plastic scoops from Rory's dried milk into the sugar and the coffee. Inspired by her own efforts she decided to give the others a treat. She would make them a dinner party. The only table they had was in the kitchen. It wasn't very big and it was covered with an assortment of objects, there not being anywhere else to put anything down in the kitchen. She pulled it into the middle of the room and half-closed her eyes. If she cleared it and found some sort of tablecloth it would do. A bit small but that would add to the fun, the intimacy. She would buy a couple of candles, then they could have the light off and you wouldn't notice the paint peeling off the walls.

Jed lurched into the kitchen.

"You're home early."

"I'm dying," Jed said.

It was the same every morning when he came back from the café.

"I'll give you some coffee," Lorna said, filling the kettle, "and a couple of Mogadon."

"I don't know what we'd do without you," Jed said. "You look after us."

"I'm making a special dinner," Lorna said. "A sort of party. Tonight."

"Anyone's birthday?"

"No. I just feel like it. What time are you going to work tonight?"

"Ten."

"I'll make it eight o'clock."

"Great."

"I'll try to get Opal into shape. She never has a square meal."

She poured his coffee and went to find Armand and Eugene.

Armand was writing. His book was going well and the mornings were spent in the full flood of production. Music filled the vast room, drowning the noise of the typing. Eugene sat cross-legged on Steve's bed.

"I'm making a special dinner," Lorna announced. "Eight o'clock tonight. It has to be early because of Jed. Everyone's invited. OK?"

There was no reply.

"Armand?"

"OK. OK." The typing didn't stop.

"Eugene?"

He nodded, grinning at her.

It wasn't exactly enthusiasm.

There were no recipe books. She tried to think herself into Cordon Bleu, Elizabeth David. To remember some of her more successful dinner parties.

She would start with minestrone; with everything in it. Vegetables, pasta, garlic, oregano, of course you really needed courgette leaves but there was no garden, no courgettes.

Afterwards they'd have veal escalopes fried in egg and breadcrumbs and garnished with anchovies and hard-boiled egg and capers. For dessert she'd give them a soufflé put into the oven when they were starting the main course. Grand Marnier if she could get one of those miniature bottles. She found an envelope and started to make a list.

She enjoyed the day, not thinking once of Derek, of Anne-Marie; shopping and cooking and accepting the challenge of the kitchen which was not a kitchen and where she had to chop and mix and peel by hand, no gadgets, no Anne-Marie to help her. By two o'clock the preparation was over. By two o'clock the preparation was over. She went up to fetch Rory who was crying, and to talk to Opal.

She held Rory on her shoulder, comforting him.

"Opal, dear, I'm cooking a special dinner. Tonight. Eight o'clock. Armand, Eugene, Jed, you and me? Do you think you can be up and about?" An idea came to her. "How would it be if I washed your hair for you? And you could put a dress on. Get out of those trousers. We'll make it a real party?"

"Fine," Opal said.

"There's not much room in the kitchen but we'll manage." She looked at Opal. "You won't let me down? I don't want to be the only woman."

"I'm looking forward to it," Opal said. "The last time I went out to dinner was before Rory was born. My mother and father at the Mirabelle. They were trying to get me to leave John."

Lorna remembered the headline in the newspaper: 'Parents plead with heiress'.

"I threw up in the Roller," Opal said. "Mother thought it was the oysters but of course it was Rory; I didn't tell them. They weren't terribly impressed. I think they sold it soon afterwards and bought a Caddy. It seems such a long time ago."

"Have they ever seen Rory?"

Opal was rarely so chatty. Perhaps it was one of her good days.

"They don't know about him."

"A grandson! It seems hard, Opal."

"They would use him to get at me."

Lorna held him up. "Such a beautiful baby. What about bathing him this morning?"

"You do it," Opal said.

"Come on. It will do you good."

"I'm too tired. I couldn't. You do it so nicely."

"Flatterer."

"Well you do. Rory loves you."

It was true. He smiled at her now when she bent over the cot. Busy with him, she was able to yearn less for Joey. She went to the door.

"No trips before tonight?" she said.

Opal looked at her and shook her head. "No."

"I think you'll enjoy the dinner. It will make a change for you."

By seven-forty-five the kitchen was transformed, the minestrone steaming in a saucepan on top of the cooker and the veal keeping hot in the oven. She was as excited as a child.

Armand was coming out of their room.

"Where are you going?" Lorna said.

"Why?"

"The dinner. Eight o'clock."

"I'll be back."

"It's quarter to. It won't keep. And Jed…"

"Won't be long." He went down the stairs.

She bathed and changed, splashing herself with the remains of the one bottle of toilet water she had brought with her. There was not much she could do with her hair. Apart from the two inches of grey roots it was now shapeless and needed cutting.

Jed was asleep on Steve's bed. She nudged him with her toe. He was full of Mogadon and didn't stir. Eugene was nowhere to be found. She hoped he hadn't forgotten.

She checked the soup and the mixture for the soufflé. She had only to whip the egg-whites when they started eating. It all looked good. She went to fetch Opal.

255

There was not a sound in the room. Rory was sleeping beneath the new blankets she had bought, fluffy and blue. She sighed, recognized Opal's pallor and accepting the fact that she was going to be the only woman at the table. Opal was tripped out. She would not wake for hours.

She went down again and shook Jed.

"What the hell?" he said. "Is it ten o'clock?"

"No, eight. I've made a special dinner, remember?"

"F— off!" Jed said. "Wake me at ten."

It was like the ten little niggers. She sat on Armand's bed with a joint and waited for him and Eugene.

At eight-thirty she helped herself to some soup. She wasn't hungry for the veal which was beginning to look dried up. At nine-thirty she switched the gas off in the oven. At ten she left the house, slamming the door behind her. The tears were streaming down her face, streaking the mascara she had put on for the occasion. She walked round the Inner Circle of the park, not knowing where she was going but crying for Joey and Cam and for Derek and for Home Farm Close and her spoiled dinner and most of all for herself.

It was midnight when she got back. There were two police cars outside the house.

Her first thought was Opal and that she'd taken an overdose, but Opal was in the hall, Rory in her arms, sitting against the wheel of the bicycle. Armand was in the hall too, so was Eugene. There were police on the stairs.

She came in out of the night and stood in the doorway.

"What is it?"

"We've been busted," Armand said.

Nineteen

Annie was waiting for Miss Dobson to go. She sat on Lorna's bed. Lorna closed her eyes, wanting to sleep.

"What you in for?"

She wanted to tell her to mind her own business but she was only a child. Probably lonely.

"A lump. In my breast."

"Cancer?"

"I don't know."

"You won't. Not till they have a look. You don't need to worry though. They have special bras. Fill them with bird-seed. My baby would 'ave been black."

That's nice? What a pity?

"At least, I think so. There was this fella, see, worked in Berwick Street, that's where I live, Berwick Street, only then he went back to Trinidad. It's nearly lunchtime. There's nothing else to do here. They have lovely custard. Like custard. Do you like custard?"

"Not terribly."

"Well, never mind, there's generally jelly. And ice cream. What time they doing you?"

"Tomorrow. I don't know."

"Hope it's early. It's rotten when you got to wait. Can't have anything to eat, see, because of the anaesthetic. Not worried, are you?"

"No."

"There's nothing to worry about. I had my appendix out. I'll sit and talk to you if you like, until they come for you. How old are you?"

"Forty-five." It was easier to answer.

"My mum died when she was forty-five. There was this fella she was living with. Great big fella. He used to 'it 'er. They found her in the hall one day. 'E said she fell down the stairs but I know 'e 'it 'er. Great big fella 'e was. You can have jelly *and* custard, if you like. Sister doesn't mind. She's ever so nice. Have you met Sister yet? Smashin' red hair. My mum had red hair. Well, not really, but you know... 'Ere's Miss Baker. She coming to see you?"

Lorna followed her gaze. At the entrance to the ward a tall young woman in a white coat, pushing a trolley, stopped to talk to Nurse Cooper, then walked down the ward towards Lorna.

"Mrs Brown? What are you doing here, Annie?"

"Keepin' 'er company."

"Well, off you go, there's a good girl."

"Don't you want any blood off me?" Annie said wistfully.

"Not today."

"I don't mind."

"I said 'Off!' "

Annie backed away.

"I just want a little blood from you for cross-matching," Miss Baker said.

She picked up Lorna's arm and smoothed an expert finger over the veins. "Splendid," she said. "Shouldn't be any problem there."

Taking a needle and a syringe from her trolley she tore open the packets.

In the Panda car Lorna thought of the skins and cigarettes she had bought. "I got them in separate shops," she told Armand, "but I thought the man looked at me strangely."

Armand took her hand. "It wasn't you. It was Opal. She was dealing!"

She sat between Armand and Opal. Eugene was in the car in front. Opal looked as if she was about to pass out. Her face was green. Lorna took the baby, who was sleeping. She did not protest.

"What will happen?" Lorna said. More than anything she wanted to go to bed, to sleep. The car shook with every bump, sending them bobbing up and down. Rory did not wake. She wondered whether she was dreaming. Armand looked at the policemen who was young and fair and the other who had a big, dark beard.

"It's the first time. For me," Armand said. "Not for Eugene."

"You'll spend the night with us, I dare say," the blonde policeman said chattily. "We'll have quite a few questions for you."

"All night?" Lorna said.

He looked at his watch. "What's left of it. About six months, is he?" he said, chucking the baby under the chin. "Mine's three-and-a half months. Never stops crying."

She thought of all the movies she had seen.

"Am I allowed to telephone a lawyer?"

"You are. Don't reckon he'll be too pleased though, this time of the morning."

The car drew to a halt.

"Everybody out!"

The one with the beard let them out and escorted them up the steps.

It was cold in the charge room. She'd come out in the thin cotton dress she had put on for her dinner party. A police-woman brought her a grey blanket. She'd been in police stations before. In the front entrance. With the au pairs to register their address. To claim Cassius when he got lost. They tied him up in the yard. He hated it and was always howling pitifully when she went to fetch him. Once she had been to tell of a bracelet she had lost in the street. The sergeant wrote the particulars carefully in a ledger but it was never found. She had the baby on her lap and he was wet. He had soaked through her dress and on to her lap. Opal was in the corner, sleeping. The boys had been taken to another room.

She had phoned Leonard. The phone had rung for a long time and she guessed he had taken a sleeping pill. He was surprised, amazed. She told him not to tell Derek. He said he would come. Immediately. The room was the colour of margarine, bare except for a table and a few chairs along the wall. She closed her eyes and tried to imagine she had committed some terrible crime; one which would keep her in prison for years, for life; or that she was a political prisoner in solitary confinement. People survived. She had read their stories in the newspapers. Even horrible torture. Unimaginable things they thought up to degrade the human body, warp the mind. She would crumple at the first hint. Tell them whatever they wanted, give away her comrades. She was not brave. The worst would be the time. The months, the weeks, the days, the hours, the minutes. She never had been any good at waiting. People recited poetry to themselves; she couldn't remember any except '...the King asked the Queen and the Queen asked the dairymaid...' which she had last read when Joey was about four. Something about some 'butter for the royal slice of bread'. Meditation, too, or reciting chapters from the Bible. Yoga. The best she could do would be Ilse's exercises and she didn't think the 'Happy Marriage' would be terribly suitable. She would go crazy; crazy. Before the first day was out, was not the stuff heroes were made of. Home Farm Close was a prison and she had left it and now was in one. Well, not prison exactly, the police station, near enough. I will open my eyes, she said, and be in bed, with Derek, with Armand... She opened them. There was only Opal, and the baby heavy and wet on her lap. She pulled the blanket more tightly round her. A horrid blanket, stiff and grey. The ones in her bedroom at Home Farm Close were sand-coloured, matching the walls; she put fabric conditioner in the water. She had bought some for Rory's blankets. The new blue ones. He was wrapped in one and it was wet. She wondered what was going to happen to her and if she would really go to prison. At the least, she supposed, it would be a fine, together with Armand. About Eugene and Jed she was not so sure. She presumed they would pick up Jed at the café. It was Opal who would be in dead trouble. Poor Opal. Dealing was serious. It explained the constant stream of visitors to her room. Perhaps it was all to the good. Perhaps she would have to go to her parents for help. She looked at the sleeping Rory and wondered if he was already affected by his mother's addiction to heroin. What a way to start. Who would have kids these days? "Joey," she said aloud, "Joey!"

"Lorna Brown?" A policeman put his head round the door.

"Yes?"

"Will you come with me?"

She followed him along the corridor, holding Rory. She wondered which was the torture chamber and whether it would be a lighted cigarette or electrodes applied to her genitals.

"In here, please."

In another bare room, there seemed to be an endless supply, Leonard was waiting.

He helped her into the Daimler Jaguar and closed the door. It smelled luxurious, of new leather. There was a polished wooden fascia with enough dials for an aircraft. The smell engulfed her like amniotic fluid. Leonard got in beside her.

"It was nice of you to come, Leonard."

"For God's sake don't start thanking me."

He turned the key in the ignition. There was a soft purr.

"Where are we going?"

He pulled the lever into drive and looked at her.

261

"I hadn't thought."

"Not Home Farm Close. And not back…not for a minute. I don't know."

"Tell you what," Leonard put his foot on the accelerator. The car slid forwards. "I'll take you to my chambers."

She was surprised at the modern furniture. The white carpet. Then remembered that Derek had designed it for him. There should have been antiques, an old desk, not the black and chromium monstrosity.

"You're shivering," Leonard said. "I've got some whisky."

"Because my dress is wet. From the baby. I probably smell too."

He got the whisky from a cupboard and a mohair rug. He held it out.

"I have a nap sometimes. After lunch. You could take your dress off and put it round you."

He had his back to her, pouring the whisky. She took off her dress and wrapped the rug round her, sarong-fashion. She sat down on the edge of the black leather sofa.

He came over and gave her a glass. He had one for himself. She drank, shivering. He sat down beside her and pulled the rug up higher in the back.

"Lorna, Lorna!"

"I know. I've got myself into a bit of a mess, haven't I? I mean generally."

"I suppose you have."

"What will happen? About the drugs?"

"It depends how much you were involved and what with."

"Only cannabis. It was just Opal and Jed on the hard stuff."

Leonard took off his glasses and rubbed his eyes.

"I'm not very well up in these matters but I presume it will mean a fine."

"I feel a bit mean walking out on the others."

"Do you?"

"No. I don't really care. What will happen?"

"It depends if they've been up before. Fines, probation, suspended sentences possibly. Treatment somewhere perhaps for the girl with the baby." He took his glass and stood up.

While his back was turned she said: "Do you know about Derek and Anne-Marie?"

He did not answer for a moment. When he turned round the glasses were refilled.

"Yes. I'm sorry."

She took the glass from him. "I brought it upon myself."

He sat next to her again and put his jacket round her shoulders. His eyes blinked behind the pebble glasses. She hadn't noticed before that he wore a wedding ring.

"Why did you leave Derek?"

"It wasn't so much Derek. More Home Farm Close."

"What's wrong with it?" He looked puzzled.

He would never understand. Not Leonard.

"It's hard to explain. I can't explain. Not really. In a way it was me. The way I felt about my life."

"Felt?"

"Felt. Feel. I don't know any more. I know it doesn't make sense to anyone, leaving Derek, Cam, Joey. It was just something I had to do. I didn't reckon with Derek and Anne-Marie. It simply didn't occur to me…it was as if I'd walked out leaving the door open and could walk back at any time."

Leonard crossed the room and fetched the whisky bottle. He filled their glasses and sat down again beside her, putting the bottle on the floor.

"It was very foolish," Lorna went on. "Yet do you know, I believe if I had the time over again I would do exactly the same thing. I just had to get out. There'd be one difference, though. I'd pack Anne-Marie off before I left. I suppose he's been parading her round the district?"

"No. I haven't seen them. I wouldn't have known if Irene hadn't told me."

"I can understand him sleeping with her." Lorna realized that her voice was beginning to get slurred and that the whiskies had been on an empty stomach. "But he wants to marry her!"

"Isn't Derek an all or nothing man?"

"I suppose he is. Sort of uncomplicated. Black or white. Me, I see all shades of everything and everybody's point of view. It's quite exhausting." She put her head on his shoulder and held out her glass.

"Where's Clare? Have you left her on her own?"

"Staying with a friend."

She held up her glass. "Cheers!" She drank. "Do you know, Leonard, I am so very tired. I don't even know what time it is."

He looked at his watch. "Two-thirty."

She held his wrist. His watch was paper thin. "Armand hasn't got a watch…"

"Armand?"

"My…my…my lover! My lover. Do you know, Leonard, he is twenty-two years old? Twenty-two. He has long, long hair right down to…do you think it's disgusting? Would you think it disgusting if your wife…"

Through the mists she remembered Yolande and began to cry. "I'm sorry, Leonard. So sorry. Here am I just talking about my problems and you…" She put an arm round him. "You poor, poor old thing. Old Leonard. Poor old Leonard. I'm sorry, Leonard, but I didn't have any dinner. I made a dinner party but nobody came. There was a poem Cam used to recite. 'Miss Smartie gave a party…' I can't remember how it went. Nobody turned up. At Miss Smartie's, I mean. And not to my party. Not a single, solitary…I am so tired. Do you mind if I lie down?"

She stretched out on the sofa, putting the rug over her. It felt soft and warm. She was warm now.

"I'm afraid I'm going to sleep."

"Go ahead, Lorna. You've had a rough night."

"Leonard?"

"Mm?"

"Did you know you're a teddy bear? A fat, cuddly teddy bear?"

"No."

"Everyone in Home Farm Close knows." She raised the rug. "Come and lie down. I want to cuddle the teddy bear."

He didn't answer.

"What are you doing?"

"Taking my shoes off."

He lay down beside her beneath the rug. She put her arms round him.

"You are a teddy bear. Aren't you?"

"If you like."

"I like… A fat, comfortable teddy bear…"

She woke in the night, her eyes snapping open suddenly into the dark. Leonard was feeling her buttocks, breasts, moaning, "Yolande. Yolande." Her shoulder felt warm and damp beneath his head and she realized that he was crying in his sleep for his dead wife. She stroked his forehead. "All right, all right," she said soothingly. He caressed her body, tenderly, gently, beneath the rug. She stared up into the darkness of the high ceiling, wondering what she should do. Before she had decided the hands ceased their movement, their searching. She fell asleep.

The bar of sunlight through the window woke her. Her head was throbbing. For a moment she could not think where she was, then she saw Leonard. He was standing over her, a cup of coffee in his hand. He looked pale, tired.

She sat up on her elbow, pulling the rug over her breasts, and took the coffee. He went back to the window, stood with his back to her. "Lorna…?"

"Yes?" The coffee, black and strong, was too hot to drink.

He scratched the back of his neck, the roll of fat where it came over his shirt.

"I don't know how to put this…" He turned to face her. "I had a dream – in the night – I'm not sure…"

"It's all right," she said. "Nothing happened. It was my fault anyway for behaving as I did. I think I was very drunk."

"Me too. I've been drinking lately. Too much."

"Poor Leonard."

"Poor Lorna."

"We're not very happy, are we? You through no fault of your own."

"It doesn't really matter whose fault it is, does it? It doesn't help if you're unhappy."

"I suppose not. Anyway, you don't need to worry about last night. You had a dream and called her name."

"I dream every night. And call her name. In the day too. I say it to myself aloud. Yolande. As if it will bring her back."

"Why did she do it?"

"She'd get depressed. Suddenly. Like that!" He snapped his fingers.

"She seemed so happy."

"She was. Most of the time, then quite suddenly she'd...just change. Start talking about life not being worth living, no future, worried that she was a bad wife, bad mother..."

"Yolande! She could teach us all a thing or two."

"It wasn't real. Just in her head. Real to her, of course. I never did understand. The doctor tried to explain it to me, several times. Perhaps if I had understood..."

"Leonard, no. You absolutely mustn't blame yourself."

"If I'd tried a little harder to understand...I will blame myself to the end of my days."

"What a cross to bear."

"I will bear it, Lorna. Believe me, I will bear it."

"Leonard?"

"Yes?"

"You won't tell Derek? About last night? About...any of this business?"

"No."

"That's nice of you. I can trust you. I feel you're my friend. It's nice to have friends. We've known each other for ages, you and I, yet we've never really spoken all that much. In Home Farm Close the women talk to the women and the men to the men."

Leonard turned to look at her, leaning against the window.

"Let me take you home, Lorna?"

"Why? Why do you say that?"

"You look…you look as if you need caring for."

She put a hand to her forehead. "It's just my roots. I don't go to the hairdressers, you see, no need. I'm sorry, I know I look a bit of a mess. I could do with a bath too…"

"It's not your hair. I hadn't even noticed."

"What then?"

"I don't know. I had quite a shock when I saw you. Are you eating?"

"You sound like a doctor."

"You haven't answered my question."

"Of course. Will you hand me my dress? My smelly dress. I hope they look after Rory."

She put on the crumpled dress and, folding up the rug, went to the cupboard from which Leonard had taken it. "In here?"

"Yes."

"When will the case come up?"

"It depends on how busy they are. I don't know."

"Will you come with me?"

"Of course."

She put her arms round him, feeling the solid bulge of his belly against her.

"Thank you again, friend."

He kissed her cheek.

When Miss Baker had gone she lay back on the pillow, tired. She was always tired lately. Through half-closed eyes she examined the ward. Three ladies were sitting by their beds in quilted nylon dressing-gowns and furry slippers. One of the beds had the curtains drawn. In another a woman with a white face lay deathly still while blood dripped into her veins from a suspended bottle. Two beds were neatly empty, the lockers testifying to their occupancy. A woman with glasses on the end of her nose sat up reading the *Daily Mirror*. Another was being helped out of bed by Nurse Cooper.

"It's no good," she said. "I can't. I'll get up tomorrow."

"I'm afraid you have to," Nurse Cooper said firmly. "Just take a deep breath, Mrs Forster, and let me take your weight."

"My stitches will burst," Mrs Forster said. "I can feel it."

"Not at all. Put your feet on the ground."

"I can't," she gasped. "I can't. You don't understand. I only had the operation yesterday."

"We all 'ad to do it, dear!" A voice came from another bed. "It's best in the long run. Think of something else. Your old man on a Saturday night!"

There was a sniggering round the ward.

"That's enough, Mrs McNee," Nurse Cooper said. "Mrs Forster is going very nicely. There's a good girl. Nearly there. Yes, I know it hurts. It's early days. But we don't want complications, do we?"

"You might get a clot if you don't," Annie said.

"Ow!" Mrs Forster screamed. "I'm coming apart!"

Lorna closed her eyes and wondered what she was doing here in bed in Harvey Ward, sharing a room with a bunch of strange women she neither knew nor wanted to know.

The last time she had been in hospital was to have Joey. It had been a private room, Derek subscribed to an insurance scheme, everyone in Home Farm Close did, and it hadn't been like this. It was small but her own little cell with private bathroom. Afterwards there had been flowers and grapes and chocolates and bottles of Champagne she wouldn't drink because of her milk, and her friends, wrapped in furs against the cold winter, coming to visit. At night, when they'd all gone,

Derek had sat on the bed and they'd watched the television, happy in their closeness and the wonder of their new son who would grow up to be Prime Minister or an Olympic champion at the very least; not sixth in the three-legged.

There was a clang and a rattle like a tube train arriving in a station.

"Good! I'm starving," she heard Annie say.

There was a clinking over her own bed.

"Time for dinner," a voice said. A vast woman in a pink overall was pushing her bed-table up to where she lay.

She sat up, knowing she must.

The red-headed sister in her dark blue dress came up to Lorna.

"Mrs Brown," she said, "I'm sorry. I haven't had a minute. I'm Sister Donovan. We're short-staffed and three for theatre this morning. You came in too late for the menu but I think they've extra fish. It's plaice today. Is that all right?"

"Fine."

"Tomorrow you can choose, there's usually fish or meat or a salad dish, not that you'll feel like eating for a couple of days. Mr Gillespie will be in to see you later on. Have you everything you want now?"

"Everything," Lorna said.

"That's grand." Sister Donovan patted the sheet. "I'll see you later."

She was off like a little automaton. Such women made you feel humble. They ran the ward and the nurses and the patients, probably the doctors too. They ruled with rods of iron yet when there was suffering, as there had been when she'd had Joey, they knew what to do, what to say, for comfort.

The fat lady ambled across holding a wooden tray which she set on Lorna's table. There was a bowl of pale soup with vegetables swimming in it and a plate with a curl of fish, brown at the edges, a dollop of instant mashed, and some tired sprouts. There was a pale blue plastic salt and pepper.

Fodder, Lorna thought, and could not. She lay back against the pillows.

Twenty

The candles had dripped wax on to the kitchen table. It was still laid for five, dinner for five, although someone had left a milk carton in the middle of it. She had arranged roses, garnet roses, in a jam-jar. The man with the barrow had cheated her. The buds had not come out as promised, but died with tight, dark red, drooping heads. In Home Farm Close the roses bloomed from May to October, November sometimes, and even Christmas. The soil was good, according to Derek, for roses. Taking the buds she dropped them in the rubbish bin. So much for the dinner party. For the night. The house was quiet. No music. No baby. She wondered how long they would keep them at the police station. But for Leonard she would still be there herself.

She opened the oven. Curled and dried, the escalopes of veal lovingly garnished with capers and anchovy and egg lay on their plate. The petits pois with tiny onions and carrots were coldly encrusted in their dish.

In Home Farm Close, when you asked someone to dinner they came. They brought boxes of chocolates wrapped in gift paper or bottles of wine which they left on the hall table. Opening them afterwards, when the guests had gone, you thought perhaps, after all the effort that had gone into it, the evening had been worth while. It was an effort. Deciding whom to ask in the first place. Dinners were generally for eight. A

271

comfortable number round the table. She kept a hostess book. Cam had given it to her for her birthday. In it she wrote the dates of her dinner parties, who had come and where they sat, what she had given them to eat, and what she had worn in the space that was headed 'gown and jewels'. After the laying of the presents, like votive gifts, in the hall, they would go into the living-room for drinks. Sometimes she salted almonds. They would comment on the weather and the time of year and if they'd travelled any distance discussed how long it had taken them to get to Home Farm Close, the traffic, and the route. Drinks over, they'd come into the dining-room and coo over the table she had made such efforts with. If it was eight to be seated there was inevitable twittering over how it was impossible for one to alternate the sexes if she and Derek kept their traditional places at top and bottom of the table. Over the soup or pâté there were children, universities and schools and the waywardness of them. With the main course, they served only three these days, politics or religion, the cinema or theatre. The dessert brought forth diets and fitness and means of keeping fit and holidays in 'undiscovered' places. There were jokes, Irish and Jewish, with the coffee, as well as marshmallows and After Eights, and Derek offered cigars and liqueurs with the business and financial news while Lorna and her friends disposed of the price of everything and au pairs. At eleven-thirty the husband and wife telegraphs began to work across the room as the men remembered they had to be up in the morning. Coats were fetched and compliments about the dinner and the company and the delight of it all heaped upon the host and hostess. In the car, before the goodbyes had faded away, they'd say what a frightful evening or what a bore old so-and-so's become and didn't you see me signalling to you no I thought you were only scratching your head. The next morning, putting away the silver and the best china was interrupted by the thank-you phones. Such a lovely evening and how did you know beef wellington was my favourite when they'd probably been up all night with indigestion and pretended not to notice that the syllabub had separated.

Lorna wondered if Anne-Marie would give dinner parties. She took the dish of veal from the oven. Picking up one piece and shredding it in her fingers, she put it into the cat's dish. It seemed a shame. Veal was so expensive. She would heat the rest up in tomato sauce and eat it herself if no one else would. They could keep their vegetable mushes.

There was a noise downstairs. In the stillness she heard the front door open and close. She went on to the landing and leaned over the banisters.

"Armand?" she said.

A girl's voice said: "It's not Armand."

She came up the stairs. She was six feet tall and had the figure of a showgirl. Her straw-coloured hair was wound into a casual bird's nest on her head. She wore drainpipe jeans tucked into boots and an off-the-shoulder blouse through which you could see her breasts. She stopped when she saw Lorna, studying her with electric blue eyes ringed with long, separated black lashes.

"Who are you?" She seemed to eye Lorna's stained cotton dress, her face unwashed since the night.

"Who are you?" Lorna returned.

The girl was carrying a suitcase which she rested on the stairs.

Somewhere Lorna knew that she did not want to know the answer.

"I'm Fiona Stevenson…"

Lorna stared at her.

"…Steve."

"You'd better eat it," Annie said. "It's nice. You won't get any tomorrow."

Lorna opened her eyes. "No." She pushed the table down the bed. "It's all right. I'm not hungry."

Annie picked up the plate and looked at it with her head on one side. "Seems a pity. Never mind. Jelly and custard, I'm doing the puddings today, Sister's busy, or ice cream?"

Lorna opened her mouth.

"I'll bring you some ice cream," Annie said. "It's good for you."

From across the ward Mrs Forster in a blue Pyrenean-wool dressing-gown looked at her.

"It's not so bad once you're out," she said. "It's the getting out. I thought I was going to break in half. Honestly. Did you have fish? Anything's nice when you don't have to cook it yourself. I shan't be in a hurry to go home. I like a nice piece of fish. My husband and the boy won't touch it. Think you were trying to poison them. They'll eat a kipper; or come to that, a fish-cake. Do you think it was frozen? Everything's frozen these days, especially in a place like this."

Annie stood by Lorna with the ice cream.

"She's a good little girl, aren't you, Annie?" Mrs Forster said.

Annie put it on the tray with a spoon Lorna knew would taste of tin.

"Eat it," Annie said. "It's vanilla."

Steve humped her suitcase up the stairs.

"I thought you were in Germany," Lorna said.

"I was. Modelling. I got the sack. I was ten minutes late one morning. Ten minutes! It's not like England. I stashed away enough bread for a bit anyway. Where's Armand?"

Lorna didn't answer, not knowing whether to say about Opal, the police. She followed Steve into the drawing-room. She put her case down by her bed, which was now littered with Lorna's belongings.

"I see," she said looking at it.

"It's all right," Lorna said. "I'm going."

"There's probably a bed upstairs," Steve said. "Is Opal still here? And the baby?"

"No, honestly," Lorna said. "I'm moving out. It was only temporary."

She wasn't sure when she had made the decision. It had to do with the dinner she had prepared and the police and the mess in the kitchen and the smell of cats and with Steve.

"Where did you say Armand was?" Steve said.

"I didn't."

She told Steve about the events of the night, how they had been busted because of Opal.

"I brought some stuff back from Germany," Steve said. "It's really amazing. Is there any food in the house?"

"Minestrone soup. Escalope of milanaise with a bouquetière of vegetables, and Grand Marnier soufflé."

Steve stared at her as if she was mad.

"Tea and a piece of toast, I meant."

She was sitting on her bed, Steve's bed, writing a letter to Armand, when he came back. She seemed to spend her life writing notes to people. The shabby case with the one lock was on the floor. There were dark circles beneath his eyes. He looked at the case.

"What is it, Lorna?"

"I'm going. Leaving. I was writing to you."

He took the letter.

"It doesn't say anything. I've only just started."

He sat down beside her and pulled her down, kissing her. "Don't be ridiculous, Lorna. Just because of last night?"

"It isn't that."

"What then? You were all right yesterday."

"Steve's come back."

"Steve!"

"Yes. But it isn't that either."

"You don't need to worry about that. Steve and I …"

"I told you. It isn't that."

275

He leaned on one elbow, looking at her, stroking her face, "I need you, Lorna."

"I expect you do."

"Do you know how much I've written since you've been with me?"

"I don't belong here. You know that."

"You belong with me."

"No. The fantasy of a menopausal woman."

"You stick too many labels on things. Youth, age...how many times have I told you...it doesn't matter. Please don't go, Lorna."

"You'll have Steve. It's far more suitable. She's a lovely girl. Young..."

"I told you, you don't have to worry about Steve. I'm just one of many. We have fun. That's all."

"She makes me feel...I don't know. I was going anyway."

"I love you, Lorna. Stay."

"I love you too, Armand. In a way."

"What way?"

"You're kind. Gentle. I just melt when I see you."

"Where's Steve now?"

"In the bath."

He got up and locked the door.

"Perhaps I can persuade you to change your mind."

After lunch she slept. The whole ward slept, heavy with dried-up fish or boiled mutton, instant mashed, jelly and ice cream. She dreamed about the last time with Armand. There had not been such love, such powerful intercommunication of feeling, since the early days of her marriage with Derek. When it was over she was crying. Armand wiped away her tears but did not speak. It was not a time for words.

"She's crying," Sister Donovan said, "in her sleep. Poor soul. Worried about tomorrow, I expect." She shook Lorna's shoulder gently. "Wake up, dear, here's Mr Gillespie to see you."

They both slept, tired from the night. When they woke Armand said: "Are you going back to Derek?"

"You know he doesn't want me."

"Do you want him?"

Lorna put her arms behind her head and looked up at the chandelier with its thousand diadems, beneath which she had been happy for a while.

"Quite honestly, Armand, I don't know what I want. Do you?"

"What?"

"Know what you want."

"To finish my book. Get it published."

"Of course. It must be nice to know exactly what it is you're aiming for. To have the path from A to B neatly mapped out in black ink, no deviations, I used to think I knew what I wanted – no, that's not true, I never knew, I was just too busy to think. I suppose it started with Cam going away. The feeling that everything I had worked for, towards, for eighteen years, was no longer valid. Cam no longer needed me, you see, not in the same way."

"What about Joey?"

"I suppose I saw, foresaw, the same thing happening. Only it would be worse in a way. Joey was the baby. It was then I began to pick holes in Derek, in Home Farm Close, to thrash about, searching for direction, to discover what it was all about." She looked at Armand. "I'm just talking. Don't expect to follow the tortuous outpourings of my mind. You're too young, to start with."

Armand held her hands, stroking her thumb with his.

"It isn't enough, you see," Lorna went on. "Just reproducing yourself. You feel there must be something more to contribute."

"My mother doesn't feel like that. I don't think so anyway. She's too busy."

She let the fact that he equated her with his mother go by.

"You don't want to worry about it, Lorna. Why should you have to justify your existence?"

"Because I feel the need."

"You were doing a job, Lorna, in Home Farm Close."

"I was running my home…"

"Excellently. I think no one praised you for the excellence. You were using your natural skills…"

"Making chocolate cake?"

"Look, the only difference between you and other women in the caring professions is that there is no pay packet at the end of the week."

"Oh God, Armand! I know the arguments. I used to tell them to myself a million times a day in Home Farm Close. It's no use being rational about it. It's how one feels."

"You left your open prison. How do you feel now?

"As confused as ever. More."

"You don't think, Lorna, the prison is inside yourself?"

"Maybe it is. Is there to be no escape except as Yolande escaped, Thelma Barrington?"

"One day I'll write a book about you."

"About me? There would be nothing after the first chapter. Your readers would die of boredom."

"Not so."

"You see something in everything. I see nothing."

"Where will you go?"

"I don't know."

"You see, you have nowhere."

"I was thinking of getting a room. And a job." She'd just thought of it.

"You'll be lonely."

"Yes."

"What sort of a job?"

"Don't ask me anything, Armand. I don't know. I can't stay here, though. It's finished here. You know it's finished. Some things have a beginning and an end. This is the end. I made it happen with my stupid dinner party. Trying to force you all into a mould. My mould. I knew very well...some-where...Armand, let me go while I have the courage."

"I'll come with you."

"No, I'll come back if I get stuck."

"You really don't have to worry about Steve. It was just someone to hold in the night."

"Everyone needs someone to hold in the night."

"What about you?"

"I don't know. I think I need to be quite by myself for a bit. I have enjoyed you, Armand. You have added richness and perspective to my life. Your book will succeed. You will be famous. You deserve to be. There's someone at the door."

"No."

The handle rattled.

"What are you doing in there?" Steve said. "Hurry up, I want to get my knickers."

Sister Donovan pulled the curtains round the bed. She was getting to know the orange poppies with the black stalks.

"You were crying," she said, "in your sleep."

Lorna felt her cheeks. "Was I?"

"There's nothing to cry about," Mr Gillespie said. "You've had an operation before."

"It wasn't about that."

"What then?"

"Nothing. Something in my dream."

"Good. I expect you're glad I woke you up, in that case."

"Oh no!" She wanted to get back to Armand, that last time with Armand since when she had not been happy. "It doesn't matter."

Mr Gillespie looked baffled. He never had understood women. "About tomorrow," he said.

She took a room in Kentish Town. A shared flat with two girls, Christine and Clare. She had heard about it through a friend of a friend of Steve's who had vacated it. It was the only way. Accommodation in London was impossible. She would not let Armand come with her. Already he belonged to the past. The last she had seen of him was sitting on the floor with Steve and with Eugene and Jed playing Yatzi, the rattle of the dice scarcely audible above the music. She'd looked at him fondly through the haze of smoke, thought of the hours of contentment she had spent in the high-ceilinged room beneath the chandelier, the green of the park opposite. He was hurt, withdrawn, could not understand why she was abandoning him. I will dedicate my book to you, he said, to Lorna Brown. People will say you are crazy. Who is Lorna Brown? And he said, I will remember. That day in the garden at Home Farm Close. The curried eggs and the heat and Cassius and the utility room and upstairs in the bedroom. Don't you think that was fate? I don't know. I don't know anything any more, Armand. Really. Only that I don't belong here either and that I must go. Let me come with you then. We'll get a room. I'll write my book. No, I have to be alone. To think. To think it right through. You and Derek and Anne-Marie and Cam and Joey. I have to be by myself. You belong here. You will write your book and one day I will open the Sunday papers and it will say Armand Morgan, great new English novelist…Welsh, he had said. Welsh then. And you will be on the best seller lists for weeks and interviewed on television, I can see it, I can really see it, and I will be so proud. But you must let me go. Walk in and out of my life? he said. Yes, leaving no trace. Everything leaves its trace, everything. You'll go far. I know. Promise me one thing. Anything. Don't ever ride the bicycle.

It was the last thing she had seen in the hall on the black and white tiles. She looked at it for a moment, touching the saddle, then shut the door on the music, on Armand.

There was no high ceiling. A small, ugly room almost taken up with a bed and a wardrobe. It was years since she'd had a wardrobe. In Home Farm Close everything was built-in so that you never got dust underneath, dust on top, as if dust itself was evil. Each time she opened the door of the wardrobe it threatened to fall on top of her. She had to remember to lean against it with her shoulder. It was the ground floor back with a door on to the garden for which she paid extra. It was dry and brown and choked with weeds. She thought, she would clear it, care for it, plant it, with thyme and with chives and with sorrel and things for the kitchen. At Home Farm Close she had done nothing in the garden except pick the dahlias and the roses and sow parsley which never came up. She watched while Derek mowed and pruned and swept the leaves but never offered to help, never wanted to, hating the voracity of the garden which ate seeds and plants and manure and the lawn fertilizer and weed-killer and anything you cared to give it. Visitors said what a super garden to Derek, so completely secluded, do you do it yourself? And he said yes, modestly, conveniently forgetting Mr Lavender who came once a week to do the donkey work and who had to be fuelled with tea and biscuits at ten and lunch at twelve and tea and biscuits again at three and a little something before he went home until Lorna thought it was hardly worth it having a gardener and then having to wait on him although Derek was never there to see how inconvenient it was.

This garden, outside her room, was different. A little barren patch. A challenge. Her challenge. Perhaps because Derek wasn't there. He considered the garden his province. Hers was inside the house. His outside. She would buy a trowel and some seeds, not now, it was the wrong time of year, coming up to autumn, but she could prepare the ground, dig a little, get rid of the weeds. There was a frayed carpet and a small table under the leg of which you had to put a wad of paper to keep it steady. It was the most basic room she had stayed in and not very clean. That too she regarded as a challenge. She swept and washed under the bed and shook the dust off the curtains out in the garden and polished the wardrobe, inside and out, and the table, and bought violets and stood them in a Marmite jar which she had never realized before had such an attractive shape.

Her flat-mates were Christine who was black and had a white boyfriend and Clare who was white and had a black boyfriend. Christine worked at Harrods and offered to get her anything she needed at the discount which was allowed to employees. Lorna wanted to say what about a grand piano or a mink coat but did not, knowing she meant soap or tights or cheese. Clare was a super secretary and spent most of the time when she was home painting or repairing the nails which were the bane of her life and seemed to be terribly important. From the beginning she mothered them and they did not object. She kept the flat clean and took their washing to the launderette and ironed it. When they came home in the evening there was a meal waiting although they were going out and did not eat it. She tried not to get annoyed, to reproach them as she would have Cam. The kitchen, really the curtained-off end of the corridor, had contained some sour potatoes in a bowl of water, a blouse Christine was dyeing in another bowl, a few Ryvitas and some mouldy cheese when she arrived. Now it was transformed. There were always milk and eggs in the tiny fridge, and vegetables which she bought fresh each day. On the wall was a memory-board. She had bought it in Timothy White's. It said 'peanut butter' (for Christine whom she was trying to fatten) and 'yoghurt' (which Clare seemed to live on) and 'Mansion polish', of which since her arrival the whole flat smelled.

Once she had cleaned the place up the days hung heavy on her hands. There was no Armand to talk to, to make love with.

No Jed or Eugene in and out, no Opal with a child to care for. She took to going to the cinema by herself in the afternoons, sitting through documentaries about the Eiffel Tower and hang gliding as well as the main feature. Once a man next to her had exposed himself, another had put a groping hand on her thigh. She learned to be careful where she sat.

It was an Indian summer. The real one had passed, going down in history as the hottest on record, something to remember, to recount to your grandchildren. It had finally broken. The weather became dull for a while, a summer such as they were used to, rainy days and cloudy, brief intervals of sun when people sat on walls or by open windows offering their faces to it. In the mornings you never knew whether to take coat or cardigan, scarf, layers you could shed, or umbrella. It was more familiar. Suddenly one morning it was summer again. Indian summer.

She sat in the park and watched it die. Sat among the banks of marigolds, of geraniums, and late roses. Sat by the copper carpets of leaves, watching the nannies and the dogs and the children and listening to the flap, flap, flap of the pigeons' wings. Sometimes there were boys on the grass, fighting, rolling over and over, locked in each other's arms. Her heart bled for Joey. She wrote to him and fetched his letters from Pam. They were shorter now as if he couldn't be bothered, full of Anne-Marie and what they had done together.

She threw bread to the pigeons and watched the lovers. They seemed to be foreign and middle-aged, finding themselves, re-finding themselves. Their love was more poignant than young love. It had endured. Survived the doubts and the greying hair, the angst and the thickening waists. They did not notice her throwing the bread to the pigeons, sitting by the trash bins full of coke tins and crisp bags, a woman who had let herself go. She had. With no exercise classes to keep it in trim her body had spread, slackened. Her hair cried out for the attentions of Clive. She wore no make-up.

One day she picked up an evening paper left on the seat, her seat, she generally sat on the same one, looked at the Situations Vacant. She had looked before, thinking she must get a job for money, to pass the time, for her own self-respect. None was suitable. She was too old. Had no qualifications, could not even type. The world seemed to have no need for Lorna Browns. The advert asked for help with an antique shop. She had always been interested in antiques although she didn't know much about them. The shop was in Camden Passage. She rang up to make an appointment. They asked her age. She told them thirty-nine.

The appointment was for one. She arrived too early and had a great wedge of quiche she would once have eschewed as too fattening, and a cup of coffee, in a wine bar.

The shop was a large one with great tables and polished chests in the window. She'd imagined something smaller selling Wedgwood and Lalique.

A trendy girl with a big mouth and a Peter Pan haircut gave her a friendly smile and a cane-bottomed chair when she said she'd come about the job. She seemed occupied ticking things off on a list as if she was taking an inventory. Justin would be down in a moment, she said, he was on the phone. She followed her glance up towards the gallery which ran round the shop. A young man was sitting at an old desk, writing. A telephone receiver was tucked beneath his chin. She couldn't hear what he was saying. After a while he came down looking harassed and pushing his hair back when it flopped into his eyes. He wore a navy blue roll-necked sweater. He sat down at the table, which seemed to be part of the stock and on which there was a list of names, though even by straining her eyes she couldn't read it.

"We've been inundated with replies," he said.

Her heart sank and she began to feel ridiculous.

"You can see the type of stuff we sell," he said, waving his arms. "Good stuff. Mainly export. You'd have to deal with buyers from abroad…"

"I could cope with that," she said. "My husband is an architect and..."

"And there's another thing..." He wasn't interested in the fact that she was used to playing hostess to business people, had a beautiful home herself in Home Farm Close, was an intelligent woman. "...you'd be alone here a good bit of time, I'm buzzing in and out. If anything needed shifting, you'd have to shift it."

She looked at the large tables, the heavy chests, and thought of her back which was liable to go if she lifted anything which was too heavy, like the pet food for Cassius from Cash and Carry.

"I could manage," she lied.

"You'd have to rearrange the showroom as you thought fit. I'd give you a free hand with that." He looked at his list. "What did you say your name was?"

"Brown. Lorna Brown."

He traced a path with his gold Biro.

"Ah yes. I said I'd see everybody. It seemed fair."

"I have a confession to make," Lorna said, seducing him with her eyes. "About my age. I'm forty-five."

"It doesn't matter," he said. "We'll ring you. I have to see everybody. It's only fair."

"Of course." She stood up, wondering how she could have put herself in such a humiliating situation. The girl with the big mouth smiled at her sympathetically. She was polishing the top of a chest with antique wax.

"Joanna is getting married," the young man explained. "If you'll excuse me..."

He disappeared. Lorna knew there would be another Joanna. London was full of them. The bell rang as she let herself out of the door into Camden Passage.

She remembered seeing the window of the shop opposite, decorated china Buddhas and umbrella stands, before the blackness enveloped her, submerged her. She cried out into the darkness but could not be heard.

The friendly shop owners of Camden Passage opened their doors, came out to see what the disturbance was about, left their wares to help the woman who lay motionless on the ground.

Twenty-one

Mr Gillespie felt her breast. He had pale eyes beyond which you could see nothing.

He turned to his houseman. "Has she signed the consent form?"

"Yes, sir."

"Splendid. Thank you, Sister."

Sister Donovan covered her with the sheet.

"We'll soon have that out," he said to Lorna. "No trouble."

She would buy a bra with bird-seed inside.

"See you tomorrow then." He looked at her over his half-glasses. "Don't worry, Mrs...er..."

"Brown," Lorna said.

"Brown." He stared at her, fingertips together, seeming to go into a trance.

"Brown," he repeated, and turning on his heel walked up the ward, followed by his retinue.

"I'm all right, really." She sat in the shop with the china Buddhas and the decorated umbrella stands, drinking a cup of hot, sweet tea.

"I'd take you home myself but I'm alone in the shop. You look terribly pale."

"I'm much better." It was true. The black mists were clearing, but she doubted whether she could stand up. The last time she had fainted was when she was about twelve. She had been watching a hockey match. One minute she had been cheering for her house, then the pitch had suddenly faded into mists, the cheering grown quiet, she found herself on the ground. She stumbled up, ashamed, leaned against the girl next to her. Her name was Priscilla. 'Lorna feels faint, Miss Jones.' Priscilla said. 'I fainted,' Miss Jones had eyes of steely grey, and pink cheeks. 'Nonsense. Just felt a bit dizzy.' She realized no one had seen her on the ground. She felt angry with Miss Jones 'You'd better take her home Priscilla. You girls don't eat enough breakfast.'

The antique-shop lady had dangly earrings and a bun. She wore a quilted waistcoat and a long silk scarf.

"What about a taxi?" She looked at Lorna doubtfully. Lorna realized that she did not see a Home Farm Close lady. "I'd be only too pleased…" She meant to pay.

"No. Honestly. I feel much better now. It must have been the heat."

She was talking rubbish. It wasn't even hot.

"Not like it was," the woman said. "I hope we don't get another summer like that. I was one hot flush from beginning to end. Thought I was going to die."

She finished the tea. There was sugar, undissolved, in the bottom of the cup. She tried to focus on a blue and gold Buddha. He kept splitting into two, then swaying back into one again. Perhaps the taxi would be a good idea. She didn't want to be a bother. Just to crawl into bed and lie very still. The bed she imagined was in her bedroom in Home Farm Close with the Patience Rose sheets. Derek would hover, anxious, solicitous. He would telephone Dick, tell Joey to be quiet, Mummy doesn't feel well. There'd be supper on a tray.

"…But it's much cooler now."

Lorna stared at the striped silk scarf, the quilted waistcoat, the dangling earrings. When the Buddha seemed to be staying fairly steadily in one place she stood up.

"Thank you for being so kind."

288

"Are you sure…" The woman looked at her.

"Sure." She managed a smile. It felt as if it were on someone else's face. As if she were the Buddha and would dissolve into two.

"Take care," the woman said at the door. It sounded as if she spoke from a distance. A telephone call, the line not very clear.

"I will." She presumed it was she who had answered, smiled again. She put one foot in front of the other in the passage. If she concentrated very hard she would get to the bus stop. She wished she were dead.

The doctor was black. He was Christine's doctor. She watched the black fingers with the pale, manicured nails crawling over her breast, her white breast. He seemed to take a very long time. She wanted to tell him that the waiting-room was full of people. That it was nearly time for the surgery to end. She put her arm on her hip, pressing deep, her elbow on his hand as he felt under her armpits. She was to get to know the routine.

"How has your weight been?"

"I haven't been eating very much lately."

"Have you lost any weight?"

"I haven't any scales."

"What about your skirts?"

She knew he meant doing them up.

"I suppose I might have lost a bit. But I haven't been eating…"

"You can put your clothes on, Mrs Brown."

He sat at his desk, writing. She sat down opposite and waited until he had finished. Until he looked up. She knew that when her opened his mouth he would put a long chain in motion, a long, wearying chain of events which she didn't much want to have anything to do with.

He wrote a name on an envelope and handed it to her.

"I want you to take this to the hospital. I'm going to ring and ask for you to be seen tomorrow."

"I can't go tomorrow." She stared at the envelope. It said 'Breast Clinic'.

"I'm afraid you have to. You can't neglect yourself any longer, Mrs Brown."

"I have to appear in court."

He stared at her.

"I'll go on Wednesday."

"The next clinic is on Friday." He shrugged. He had done his best. "I'll tell them to expect you." He looked at his watch. "Ask the next patient to come in, please."

In was always a relief to see Leonard. He was waiting for her on the step of the Magistrates' court.

He kissed her. "How are you, Lorna?"

She wanted to say, not terribly well. I have this lump in my breast, my poor little breast. I knew but I didn't do anything about it because of Derek and Anne-Marie. I neglected it. Neglected myself. I knew the consequences but it was as if I was doing it to somebody else, not to myself at all. I have to go to hospital on Friday, I should have gone today.

"I'm fine."

He held her at arm's length. "You're not eating enough. Not looking after yourself. I'm going to lunch after this. You'll come with me?"

She looked down at her bare legs, the worn sandals she'd bought one happier summer in Italy.

"I'm not dressed."

"It doesn't matter. Not these days."

The vestibule was busy with comings and goings. Offenders waiting anxiously to be called, policeman without their hats, barristers in striped trousers, passers-by examining the lists to see which court would provide the best entertainment for the morning. Armand came in with Jed, Eugene, and Opal. They seemed embarrassed when they saw her with Leonard. Looking at them she felt alien, wondering how she had ever belonged.

She looked at Armand, surprised to feel her heart leaping as his gentle eyes found hers. She took Leonard by the hand.

"This is Armand, Jed, Eugene, and Opal."

Opal looked ill, seemed scarcely able to raise her head, her hand to take Leonard's. She felt him appraising Armand, tried to put herself behind his eyes, wondering what she saw in him.

"How's the book going?"

He looked straight at her. "Not well."

"How's Steve?"

"In Denmark."

Anyone breaking the code would read do you miss me and how happy are you, yes I miss you and my work is suffering, I want you to know, to care, the room is free now, no one shares it with me and I want you to come back.

Leonard asked him about his book, good Leonard, Lawyer Leonard, used to talking to people. Armand answered softly, Welshly, linking his little finger into hers.

She hadn't realized the court would be so ordinary. People one might meet in the greengrocer's in the queue for the cinema. But of course it was, people.

There were three on the bench. She looked to see if it was anyone she knew. They were strangers. Half of Home Farm Close were magistrates, puffing themselves up with pride in their own importance. Always the wrong people, she thought. Aubrey Gardner who was thick as a post and thought they should bring back hanging; Dorina Summer whose daughter of sixteen kept leaving home and coming back pregnant, you'd think Dorina's time would be better spent looking after Sue. They always talked for hours, the magistrates, at the Home Farm Close residents' meeting, holding forth about the squirrels and the rabbits and pot-holes in the road and people driving over their grass verges, as if they were addressing a meeting at the National Temperance Hall instead of a couple of dozen neighbours in someone's living-room. One of the ladies had grey hair and looked kind, the other was Lorna's age, smartly dressed. The man in a navy blue suit with a waistcoat looked serious, as if it mattered.

They stood in a line while the charge was put by the sergeant. She'd thought it was going to be like on the television, taking the Bible in your right hand… There was no television in the flat she shared with Christine and Clare; there had been none in Cornwall Terrace. She suddenly realized how long she had lived without the tyranny of television, swallowing the shows like the potato crisps one munched while doing so, passively, contributing nothing. Derek looked forward to it when he came home. It was like a drug. Drug! Ha! That was funny in the circumstances. He liked pressing the button, watching the picture come into view, into focus, sitting back, his feet up, falling asleep before the programme had ended. Relaxing, he said, particularly the golf. He liked cowboys and westerns too, with plenty of shooting. A lot of men did. She didn't know why, unless it was to rid themselves vicariously of their desires to shoot their secretaries, their partners, their wives.

She felt that the bench, in particular the man, looked at her curiously. They understood Armand, Opal, Eugene, Jed. They saw them every day. Lorna Brown made them uneasy. Twenty-five pounds, they said. She did not much care. Armand was fined the same. Forty pounds for Eugene. Jed fifty pounds and a suspended sentence. It was not the first time. Opal was put on probation. Her face did not change.

"Come back with us," Armand said when it was over. "I want to read you the last few chapters."

Come back. Come back. She thought of the great calm room and the ugly ground floor back of the flat she shared with Christine and Clare.

"I'm going to lunch with Leonard," she said avoiding his eyes.

She had crossed the Rubicon. She knew she would never again touch the long hair, the hard thighs. He put his arm through Opal's leaving her standing on the steps with Leonard.

The woman in the next bed was sitting up, knitting. She met Lorna's eyes, watching her. The knitting was yellow. Bright yellow like Bird's custard.

"It's to be a tea-cosy," she said, although Lorna hadn't asked her. "In the shape of an owl."

She knitted with long needles tucked beneath her armpits and wore pink National Health glasses.

"It's good to have a hobby," she said, "when you've to be in hospital. Takes your mind off yourself. Mine's owls."

"Owls!" Lorna said, despite her wish not to be drawn to other people and their problems.

"Owls." The knitting didn't stop. "I'm dippy about them. I've got owl tea-towels, owl egg-cups, owl sheets and piller cases, owl cushions, owl spoon-rest, owl table mats, ooh, umpteen."

Lorna stared mesmerized, wondering if she was in the right hospital. The woman looked sane enough.

She leaned towards Lorna, the rhythm of the yellow knitting unchanging. "Would you like to know the name of my house?"

Lorna nodded. There seemed to be no alternative.

"Toowit Towers," the woman said. "Nice, isn't it?"

"Very," Lorna said weakly. She lay back with her eyes closed. You certainly met some strange people in a hospital ward. Different people. She decided to keep her eyes closed to discourage the owl woman and hoped they would leave her alone for a bit instead of waking her each time she dropped off with more questions, more probings of her mind and body. It was only mid-afternoon, yet already it seemed a lifetime since the morning. She had woken early in her small room with a sense of excitement, anticipation, like a child going to a party. She had packed her case, the case with the one lock, the night before. Unable to sleep, she got up and fried bacon and eggs and bread for Christine and Clare.

She had confided in them because they were nothing to her, told them where she was going and why. Christine had given her a cake of Floris soap, sandalwood, and Clare a bottle of toilet water. They were kind girls. They said they would come and visit her and wished her luck. They went to work, leaving her alone in the flat. She had left it clean and tidy for them, hoping they would remember to buy more loo paper, and shut the peeling front door behind her. In her anxiety, she was too early to go to the hospital. In all probability they would not be ready for her. On an impulse she went to sit in the park, although it was wet and windy, cold too, no day for sitting. There were dreams there, though, of Armand, or Cornwall Terrace. She went to pick them up.

"Brown bread and butter or a currant bun?" The voice brisk, cutting across her thoughts. A young ward maid with acne stood, one hip extended, by the tea trolley which was at the end of her bed.

"No. Thank you," Lorna said.

"Got to keep your strength up, dear," the owl woman said. "The buns aren't bad."

"No, really. Just a cup of tea."

"It's on your table," the girl said. Lorna hadn't noticed the steaming cup. "I put sugar in."

"Can I have 'er bun?" Annie's voice came from across the ward. "I love buns."

"Wonder you're not fat as a pig," the owl woman said. "I don't know where you put it."

" 'Oller legs," Annie said. "That's what me mam used to say."

"Well, I wouldn't like to 'ave to keep you fed. I must say. I'd have me work cut out."

This led the owl woman on to a discourse on how difficult it was to keep a family fed anyway these days, what with the price of everything going up each time you went down the supermarket, and two of the children were earning good money but only gave her two pounds a week because they were saving up to get married and her husband wouldn't let her ask them for more.

The tea was hot and sweet and tasted more like an inferior brand of tinned mushroom soup. Lorna drank half, sitting propped up on her elbow and letting the vapid, comfortable talk flow over her head, then she slipped down again between the sheets which smelled of laundry soap.

"Wake up, love," the tea girl said. "There's someone to see you. 'Ave you finished wi' your tea? You haven't drunk it!"

She made it sound like a crime. A young man with a beard in a white coat was standing by her bed dangling a stethoscope.

"Just check you over for the anaesthetic," he said cheerfully. His label, blue with white letters, said Doctor Fox. Nurse Cooper pulled the curtains. The orange poppies swayed and were still.

He took her blood pressure and listened to her chest. So young, she thought as she breathed in, breathed out, it really doesn't seem possible. He tapped her back with his fingers, one hand on the back of the other. It made a sound like a drum.

"Right." He wound the stethoscope up and put it in his pocket where it lolled over like a black snake. "Any asthma or hay fever?" he asked. "Are you allergic to anything you know of, or to any medicines?"

She shook her head.

"Right, no problems then. I'll see you tomorrow. You'll get some pre-medication about an hour before you come to theatre so you so you'll be nice and drowsy."

They thought of everything.

"Cheerio!"

"Cheerio!" she said.

He was like the freezer man, the waste-grinder man, the man to fix the slipping frame on the telly. She had come full circle.

"He's nice," the owl woman said. "Mind you, they are all are, but he's my favourite. I've got this asthma, you see, well I've had it ever since I was a child, it started during the war, my doctor said it was more than likely something to do with the bombing, we lived at the Elephant then, that was before your time, it's quite different now, you'd hardly recognize it, and by rights I should have gone to Sunderland where my mother's sister lives, he's in the building, when I say building I mean painting and decorating..."

Surely, Lorna thought, punching her pillows into a more comfortable position beneath her head, there can't be anything else they want to know about me before tomorrow.

She sat opposite Leonard at a corner table. He had been right. It mattered not at all that her sandalled feet were bare. Anything went these days in London, the last decade having taken with it most of the pretensions of formality, in dress at any rate.

She had bought the sandals in Italy. It seemed a lifetime ago, Joey had only been four, or was it five, she was never very good about dates, didn't need to be with Derek who remembered everything, every day, every date, the year this, that or the other had happened. It was in the south. A long beach. Rows of deckchairs and a wind that got up at tea-time. Joey had spent the day, days, in the water, Cam sulking because there was no one her age at the hotel. It was a family hotel, young children mostly, Joey was in his element. She could see him now, head above the waves, cheeky grin, standing shivering, spraying her with water, waiting for money for Coca-Cola. They had played bowls, hired bicycles to ride in the evenings. She had bought the sandals in the market. They were hanging from a stall and she had tried them on, standing on one foot in the heat while Derek walked ahead, stood impatiently with his hands in the pockets of his shorts while she wondered if they would wear, as if it was important for what was the equivalent of an English pound. They had bought serviette rings too. Tooled leather, in a different colour for each of them. They still used them, or rather they did in Home Farm Close. Such family holidays were the pearls on the string of life, although one never recognized the fact at the time, too preoccupied with stomach upsets and mosquito bites and the prices of the English newspapers.

"Not a very large fine," Leonard said. "Twenty-five pounds."

How to tell him that she didn't care, couldn't think any further than Friday.

"What will happen to Opal?"

"Her probation officer will probably advise her to go into hospital. To get her off the drugs. Not that it will help. Her friends will be waiting for her when she gets out."

"And the baby?"

"They could take him into care."

"I'm sure Opal's parents would have him if they knew. Do you think I should try to contact them?"

"I'd keep out of the whole business if I were you. What can I tempt you with?" He looked through the pebble glasses at the menu. "Artichoke, butter or vinaigrette, crab cocktail, whitebait, a few oysters? Afterwards there's steak, fish. What do you fancy?"

She was thinking of her appointment at the Breast Clinic.

"You order for me. I'm not terribly hungry."

"Being in court," Leonard said sympathetically. "I expect it upset you. Anyway, you're out of all that now, aren't you? No more pot?"

"No."

She missed it sometimes. In the evenings in her small back room. Would have liked a joint, to relax, forget.

Leonard ordered whitebait and fillet steak charred on the outside and raw in the middle; with spinach.

There seemed to be a shoal of whitebait. She ate three, thinking of Joey. 'How could you?' When he'd seen them for the first time. 'Those tiny little fishes. Whole?' Tears had come to his eyes. He loved fish. It had started with a goldfish bowl won at the fair and two miniscule goldfish in a plastic bag. Now he was an expert. She had to give him fish-cakes or fish-pie so that he wouldn't notice.

"I'm thinking of moving," Leonard said. "From Home Farm Close."

"I wish you'd persuade Derek," Lorna said. Then she remembered. Derek was no longer hers. Belonged to Anne-Marie. It didn't matter if he moved or not.

"I don't know what to do with the thing's she's grown in the garden. Whether they need taking up, putting in the greenhouse for the winter. There are cucumbers. And stuff hanging upside down in the boiler-house, drying. She used to do something to the leaves and bring it in for the winter when there were no fresh flowers."

"Honesty," Lorna said. Of all of them, Yolande had been happiest in Home Farm Close. She loved growing, making. Lettuce and tomatoes. Fat raspberries she brought round in a breadbasket. Jams and preserves and dried flower arrangements. She even had a vine with grapes.

"It's too painful," Leonard said. "She's everywhere. I hear her voice. I really do."

"Where will you go?"

"I don't know. It doesn't matter much. Just me and Clare and Simon in the holidays. Something quite small. Nearer to my chambers."

Lorna pushed away the plate with the whitebait. The waiter removed it and served the steak.

She looked at it with horror, its pat of butter starting to ooze. She could no more eat it than fly. She tried to remember the days when her biggest treat was eating in restaurants, gourmet dishes she did not have to cook.

"I found this photo," Leonard said. He had it in his wallet. It had been taken with a Polaroid camera and was not very good. It showed Yolande in the garden shading her eyes, the green eyes that went with red hair, from the sun.

"That's nice."

The tears were forming in Leonard's eyes behind the pebble glasses. She wondered if Derek would cry for her. If anyone would cry.

"It was taken last summer. In the garden. Is anything wrong with your steak?"

Twenty-two

"There we go!" a cheery voice said.

Lorna snapped open her eyes to see Nurse Cooper standing by the bed, feeling the cool, light touch of her fingers on her wrist.

"What now?" Lorna said, aggrieved at being disturbed again. She had been in the middle of a dream.

"Temperature and pulse, then you can hop out and have a little wash and we'll straighten your bed. Soon be supper-time."

She closed her eyes against the cheeriness. She didn't want to wash, her bed didn't need straightening, she had hardly moved, and she certainly didn't want supper at this nursery hour. She knew it was no good protesting.

"You are a sleepy one then," Nurse Cooper said. "Won't have any difficulty getting you off tomorrow." She made a note on Lorna's chart, took the thermometer from its pink liquid, shook it, and put it between Lorna's lips. It tasted of disinfectant.

"Had your bowels open today?" They always expected you to speak when something was in your mouth. Like dentists.

She nodded.

"Good girl." The thermometer was whipped out. It could not possibly have had time to register.

Nurse Cooper consulted her clip-board.

"No breakfast for you tomorrow, I'm afraid. Nothing to eat or drink after twelve o'clock tonight. Sorry about that."

She took hold of the corner of Lorna's sheet and pulled it back.

"That's a pretty nightie. That didn't come from M & S. Just look at the tucking. Off you go then."

"Do I have to?" Lorna said.

"You lazy thing." She attacked the pillows.

Annie was in the lavatories. She clutched her towelling robe round her with one hand and in the other held a metal jug.

"Twenty-four-hour urine," she said, raising the jug as for a toast. "They have to measure my output."

She wasn't interested in Annie's output. Wondered what she was doing in these prison-like lavatories with the wooded sink and brushes in jam-jars, piles of plastic bed-pans. The Sahara Beige bath and bidet on the shaggy carpet in Home Farm Close swam before her eyes. No smell of disinfectant there.

She let herself into a cubicle and locked the door.

"Can't wait for me supper," Annie said through the partition. "Macaroni cheese. My favourite. Do you like macaroni cheese?"

Lorna didn't answer.

"Macaroni cheese. Do you like it? It's my favourite. I like the brown on the top."

"Yes," Lorna said.

"So do I. It's my favourite."

They came out simultaneously, Annie holding her jug of amber liquid.

"Wonder what's on telly tonight?" she said. "I like 'Sale of the Century'."

Her bed was cold, impersonal again, the bumps and furrows she had made smoothed out. There was a smell of cabbage and in the distance the rattling of trolleys. A man in a blue cardigan and a money apron appeared at the end of the ward, selling newspapers.

" 'Evening, ladies!" he said and stopped at the first bed.

There was a scuffling in the lockers for purses. He passed by the three beds with the sleeping ladies who had come back from

301

theatre and came to the owl woman who stopped knitting long enough to open her purse.

"Me bedsocks nearly ready," the newspaper man quipped.

"Cheeky!" the owl woman said. "What's it like outside?"

"Raining."

"Makes a change."

"Better off where you are." He came towards Lorna. "Paper, love?"

"*Standard*, please." She held out the money.

"Thanks, love."

She looked at the headlines. 'English volunteer killed in border raid on kibbutz.'

"I see the bread men are threatening to strike again," the owl woman said.

She sat shivering in the curtained cubicle in the Breast Clinic. 'Undress to the waist,' they'd said, handing her a dressing-gown, 'and put this on.'

Tying it round her she found that her hands were trembling which was odd because she was not afraid. She examined the thought. She could not be afraid because she had brought her present predicament upon herself, so how could she be? She had read enough articles. Every time you picked up a magazine there was one, warning you; advising you. For years she had examined her breasts for abnormalities. All of them had. But when it came, she had done nothing. Not true. She had been going to see Dick. It had been the shock of finding out about Derek and Anne-Marie. It seemed stupid when she thought about it now, rationally, but she had managed, neatly, adroitly, to relegate the problem to the back of her mind, to a place where she was aware of its existence but did not have to deal with it. As if by ignoring it it would go away. But of course it didn't. It was a behaviour pattern she recognized in herself, generally pertaining to things far less important. Problems she ignored. They did not go away but there had been Derek to sort them out. The overdraft at the bank she knew she had and which, as if it did not exist, she let mount up until Derek had to pay it off then give her the increase in her allowance she had been too diffident to ask for. Another time she had driven her car, ignoring the strange noise it made, putting the sound in the recesses of her memory until she could no longer shift the gear lever, and it was merely for want of oil in the automatic transmission, and because of her neglect – wilful, Derek called it – she almost had to have a new gearbox. He didn't understand. It wasn't wilful, but something in her which got in the way of dealing immediately with problems as they arose. One could not, she knew, equate a lump in the breast with an overdraft or a gearbox. Yet they had the same feel. All three were problems which she had managed to blot out, not hearing the tiny, insistent squeaks they made from the corners of her mind. They were drowned by the trumpets of her every day life. Serves you right. It was a phrase from her childhood. It did not serve her right. They would take it away. The doctors. The people in the white coats. With their pills and their potions, their machines which send the powerful rays bombarding into your very soul. With their knives.

The curtain of the cubicle was opened.

"Ready for you. You can leave your clothes there." The girl was young, with a clean, shiny face above the white coat.

Lorna stood up. It would probably turn out to be mastitis anyway. She had always had a tendency towards it.

She stared at the newspaper. The owl woman was carrying on about nobody wanting to work these days and what we needed was another war. She saw a patch of desert and Cam sprawled in the dust. A bullet wound through her head. Only, of course, it wasn't desert. Apples, she had said, on the kibbutz. She had been picking apples. Of course, she should be back. Term had long started now but there had been no word. Three letters which she had collected from Pam's, speaking of hitching lifts through the Sinai Desert, sleeping on the beaches at Eilat, a

303

Norwegian boy, with whom she had fallen madly in love... Of course, she had long left the border kibbutz, but what if she had decided to go back? She put on her glasses to read the small print. 'In an incident last night at a kibbutz on the Golan heights, an eighteen-year old English volunteer from Newcastle upon Tyne...'

A reprieve. Perhaps there would be others. The lump in her breast would turn out to be benign, nothing at all. There had always, throughout the whole of Lorna's life, been reprieves. The horrid things happened to others, to Yolande, to Thelma Barrington. They had not managed to catch her yet and would not. "...They need to give them stiffer sentences," the owl woman said.

She took off her glasses and lay back. In Newcastle upon Tyne a mother was weeping. She wanted suddenly to see Cam. To touch her.

They had kept her all morning in the Breast Clinic. The worst part had been the long needle they had plunged into the lump. She had not been prepared; nor for the dye they had injected into the nipple so that they could X-ray the soft tissues. Not that they were unkind. You'll have to come back, they said when they'd finished with her, there will be bone scans and liver scans. Dutifully paying attention now to her lump, she went back.

"Soon be visiting," Annie said. "Did you tell yours seven o'clock?"

"I shan't be having any," Lorna said.

"Oh dear," Annie was unable to cope with this state of affairs. "Well, never mind." She looked down the ward. "Here come the cocktails."

Nurse Cooper and another chubby little nurse in a mauve striped dress were pushing a bureau on wheels round the beds and handing out pills and tablets and small drinks in medicine glasses.

When it was Lorna's turn they consulted her chart.

"Two Mogadon," Nurse Cooper said, shaking two out a of a giant dispensing bottle. "Check, please, Nurse."

Eyeing the bottle, Lorna thought Jed would have been in his element. Enough Mogadon to last him for a year. She thought suddenly of Armand and how at visiting time he would walk into the ward with flowers. For her. But of course, he did not know. Nobody knew. Except Christine and Clare.

Nurse Cooper put the two white tablets on her locker. "You're lucky," the owl woman said, eyeing her medicine glass with distaste. "I've got the Molotov cocktail. What've you got, Annie?"

She had begun to feel at home in the Breast Clinic. Mr Gillespie sat with her notes before him. He studied them through his half-glasses for so long she began to wonder if he was still alive. When he finally looked up and stared at her over the tops of them he said: "I'll operate on Wednesday. Sister will fix it up."

She stared at him. "This Wednesday?"

"Yes." He made a note at the bottom of her notes. "I shall remove the lump, then wait for a frozen section. I may have to take away the breast." He put his pen down on the desk, her breast disposed of.

"Is it...?"

"Malignant?" He looked at his watch. "It's impossible to tell without a biopsy."

The waste-grinder man had brought a replacement machine. The freezer man a new flange. Mr Gillespie offered nothing but a biopsy.

"I shall have nightmares," the owl woman announced. "Cheese last thing at night." She looked across at Lorna. "What are you having?"

305

"Macaroni cheese," Lorna said. "The same as you." She played with it with her fork.

"I meant tomorrow!"

"I've got a lump. In my breast."

"My sister-in-law had that. She couldn't use her arm for months and months. Can't use it now properly. Of course they took the whole thing off. You having the whole thing off?"

"I don't know. They don't know until they start."

"Well, don't worry. My sister-in-law wears a special bra. I can always tell, though, looking at her. Mine was a hysterectomy. Should have had it years ago. They took everything. Brings on the change. Early. No more mucky caps, though. One blessing. You started yours?"

Lorna looked at the rapidly congealing elbows of macaroni.

"Change, I mean."

She had picked a right one in the owl woman. Wondered if it was possible to move one's bed. Probably not. Might get someone worse anyway. She would have to put up with it. It would not bother her tomorrow. Tomorrow she would be out for the count. She could use the sleep.

Annie's visitor had a T-shirt decorated with realistic looking blood, green stripes in his hair, and a safety-pin hanging from his ear. The owl woman's husband appeared to be weighed down by two plastic carriers. The half-hour after the remains of the sago pudding had been rattled away had been spent peering into mirrors and changing bed-jackets in preparation for the high spot of the day, which Lorna hoped was almost finished, although it was not yet seven. Annie, kind Annie had given her a Woman's Weekly to read, telling her there was a 'smashing story'. It lay on her chest. She had pulled the covers up to her chin and would sleep until it was time to take her sleeping pills.

She was wakened by a hand on her shoulder. A pretty nurse, the night nurse, looked into her face.

"Mrs Brown?"

"Yes?"

"Wake up, dear. You've got a visitor."

"No," Lorna said. "Nobody knows I'm here." She shut her eyes again.

"It's me," a familiar voice said from the foot of her bed.

Lorna opened her eyes, not believing.

"Irene!"

"Hallo."

Lorna struggled to sit up. The nurse arranged her pillows.

"How did you know I was here?"

Irene sat close to her on the chair the nurse had put by the bed. She had been to the hairdressers and was wearing her Saint Laurent blazer.

"Michael told me."

"Michael. What's he got to do with it?"

"He's working here as a porter. He told you, remember? He doesn't start his clinicals till January."

Lorna waited, remembering Michael in Irene's kitchen light years ago; in the summer.

"Well, Michael's going out with Polly Jarvis and Polly told him at lunch-time, they have lunch together in the canteen when Michael isn't busy in theatre, that Cam's mother…"

She was aware that Irene was talking fast, too fast, gabbling to hide what she felt.

"…and to cut a long story short Michael phoned me to see what was wrong with you, thinking I knew, and of course I didn't know a thing and came flying. What is it, Lorna? You look terrible. Why didn't you tell anyone?"

"I've got a lump," Lorna said.

"Breast?"

Lorna nodded.

"It's nothing these days. They just nip it out if they catch it soon enough. You know that."

Lorna was silent.

"What's the matter?"

"I've had it for ages."

Irene stared at her. "Not you, Lorna! Not after all that Sunday supplement business."

"I just...didn't bother." She wanted to know about Derek. About Anne-Marie.

Irene handed her a Fortnum's bag. "Choccy and almond biscuits. Your favourite. Don't suppose you'll get anything special here. When are they doing you?"

"Tomorrow."

"What time?"

"I don't know."

"Haven't you asked?"

"No."

Irene looked at her, troubled. "You should have come home. I've been so worried about you. We all have."

"How could I?"

Irene stood up.

"Don't go!" Lorna grabbed her hand. There were tears in her eyes.

"I only popped in for a minute. I brought someone to see you, He's parking the car. I'm sure you'd much rather."

"Derek?" Lorna said.

Irene nodded. She kissed her cheek, holding her close. "Good luck, darling. For tomorrow. And don't let's have any more of this nonsense."

She wanted to comb her hair, do something about her face. She didn't want Derek to see her like this. She reached towards her handbag, her locker, but he was walking down the ward.

He looked splendid, bronzed still from the summer, in an impeccable grey flannel suit and a pale tie, impeccable Derek.

He moved the chair and sat down on the bed. She looked into the familiar face, the worried face that told the extent to which she had let herself go in the past weeks. She tried to say hallo, how's Anne-Marie? but the words stuck and tears came instead, of relief, of despair, of feelings she had kept in a locked compartment. She flung herself against his shoulder, wetting his grey flannel. His face was against hers. He stroked her hair. She didn't care. About the owl woman. About Annie. Finally she raised her head and sniffed.

"I've no Kleenex."

He took the handkerchief from his top pocket. She mopped herself up with one hand. The other was in his as if she would never let go.

"I thought I was going to be so brave. I'm not brave at all."

"I just saw Irene. She told me. You should have come home. I shall never forgive myself."

She stared. "You? For what?"

"For everything. The summer. For neglecting you."

"Derek, you didn't. You didn't do anything. I ran away."

"I was hurt. In my pride. Huffy. You made me look a fool. You know I have never been able to stand being made to look a fool."

"It doesn't matter now. I brought it upon myself. All of it. How's Anne-Marie?"

"I don't know."

"Don't know?"

"She's gone back to Switzerland. Bernard came. With her mother and father. We both saw how foolish we'd been. They took her back with them. She's going to marry Bernard."

"Who's looking after Joey?"

"Your mother. She's going to stay. Until you come home. When you're better. She's going to look after you."

"Come home?"

"Do you want to, Lorna? I want you to. We'll move. Do anything you like. I can't manage without you, Lorna. I never realized. How much I love you, I mean. Perhaps it was my fault. I never said. Not for years."

"Perhaps we didn't really talk. To each other. Feelings, I mean. Both of us."

"It was my fault. I took you for granted."

"No. You work so hard. For all of us. I only thought of myself."

"We both did that. But it's going to be different. I promise you it's going to be different. You will come back?"

"You wanted to marry Anne-Marie. Before Bernard turned up."

"Not really. I was out of my mind. Hurt. Anne-Marie was there." He looked straight at her, holding her hand tight, tighter. "I love you more than anything in the world."

He took her in his arms. She didn't care about her face, about the grey roots, about the owl woman, about Annie. About Armand, she thought what a fool I've made of myself, what a stupid fool.

When she'd composed herself Derek said, "I'll take you out of here. Somewhere private. You'll be more comfortable. Dick will fix it all up."

"No. It's fine here." The ward already had begun to seem like home.

"Are you sure?"

"Sure."

"What time are they doing it?"

"I don't know. Will you be here? When I wake up?"

"I'll always be here."

"I'll probably have to have my breast removed. I shan't look terribly pretty for you."

The pressure on her two hands, his suffused, suffering face, told her it did not matter.

"Irene says," Derek said, "you told her Home Farm Close was a prison. I want you to be happy."

"I think the prison was in my mind. When women get to a certain age…"

Derek smiled, easing the tension. "I'm not allowed to say that!"

"Most probably you were right. A sort of panic sets in. Rushing against the weir. You see the end in sight and get frightened."

"For us it will be the beginning. I promise you that. I'll try harder to understand. I've missed you so much, Lorna. Tell me where you've been."

She told him everything. About Armand and the huge room, the trees of the park, the pot and the three-card brag, about Steve and about Leonard, about the small back room and how she'd tried to get a job in Camden Passage, about Christine and Clare.

When she stopped talking Derek said, "It isn't enough. I realize now. Home Farm Close. Stuck in the house all day."

"The children don't need me, you see. Nobody does."

"I need you, Lorna. So much. When you're feeling better I'll take you away. It'll be like a second honeymoon. We'll talk. And when we come back we'll find you something to do. Outside the house."

"Like sweeping the leaves?" She smiled.

"You know what I mean." He stroked her cheek. "It's good to see you laugh." He stood up.

"You're not going!" She looked down the ward. "Don't go. It's still visiting time."

"I'm going to get some coffee. I'll be back. They only allow two at a time. There's a notice. I brought Joey and Cam."

The owl woman was putting away the loot that had come in the plastic carriers. A bottle of apple juice, a box of Dairy Milk, half a dozen Kit-Kats, a bunch of grapes, two skeins of yellow wool, a mauve brushed-nylon nightie.

"You're a crafty one," she said to Lorna. "Thought you wasn't having any visitors. You had more than anyone. Come far, did they?"

"Not very."

"Ah well. It's nice to have a bit of company. Lovely children. My boy used to look like that. He's married now. In the surveyin'. Be glad when termorrow's over I expect. Like a grape?"

"No. Thank you," Lorna said.

"Nervous, I expect. Never want to eat when you're nervous. Nothing to worry about, though. They give you something before you go down. You're ever so woozy. Mrs Forster was fast asleep. Weren't you, Mrs Forster?"

Mrs Forster was putting in her curlers. "What's that dear?"

"Fast asleep. When they took you down. I was telling Mrs Brown."

She took the pink plastic pin from between her teeth. "Ooh, fast! Never knew a thing. Not till I was back in me bed. Knew something then all right!"

"Don't frighten her," the owl woman said proprietorially. "Never touched 'er supper as it is. What time they doing you then?"

"I don't know," Lorna said.

"Well, not to worry. Get a good night's sleep. Best thing. Got your tablets, have you?"

They were on her locker.

"I should take them and go to sleep. Termorrer's another day."

Twenty-three

She opened her eyes, expecting to see the Colefax and Fowler wallpaper, then the grime-laden chandelier, then the cracked ceiling of the small back room. When there were none of these, she raised her head and looked around. Sleeping women and a silent ward. In the night there had been coughing and snoring, hoarse calls for nurse, and the swish of curtains, the pouring of water and rattle of glasses. The doctor had been once to the bed opposite Mrs Forster. The curtains were still drawn. After that she had slept, the sleeping tablets overtaking the merry-go-round of her mind, first slowing it down, finally stopping it. A feeling of panic overtook her. She looked at her watch, five-thirty, wanted to call Nurse, Nurse, like a child in the night needing to be comforted, but what could she say? She was not ill, not yet, needed no attention. Could not even have a drink, a cup of tea. She must lie there, try to go to sleep again, next to the owl woman, opposite Annie, finally silenced, both of them. There had been operations before. Appendix. Dilation and curettage after Cam. She had been afraid then. A mixture really of excitement and fear, like a bride getting ready for a wedding, a star for a show. She would be happy, was in a way, if you discounted fear, the apprehension. Had seen Joey, had seen Cam. Derek wanted her back. She would go back. To Home Farm Close and the utility room. To Cassius. To Irene. To her Poggenpohl kitchen, the ficus and monstera and the goldfish.

Would go back, to swim back and forth and back and forth until… She had been happy for a while with Armand. What had happened to Opal? Poor Opal. And the baby. Rory. What had happened to Rory? What chance did he have? Probably already addicted to heroin, Leonard had said. It had been good of Leonard to come. Good Leonard. Dear Leonard. It was important to have friends. Leonard, Irene, Yolande, no not Yolande, not Thelma Barrington either. Joey had been embarrassed. Standing by the bed.

"Hallo, Mum."

"Joey." She held out her arms. They had cut his hair too short.

"We've started Latin."

"Of course. You're in a new form. You've got a new blazer." They had bought it too small. It wouldn't last.

"Who's your form master?"

"Mr Jellicoe. Jelly."

"Is he nice?"

"All right." He looked round the ward.

"Give her the flowers," Cam said.

He brought a bunch of anemones from behind his back.

"They're lovely," Lorna said. "Thank you." She smelled them, although there was no scent. "If you ask the nurse for a vase," she said to Cam, "we can put them in water."

When Cam had gone she patted the bed. "Sit here, Joey."

He sat down gingerly. Not looking at her. Looking at his knees which no one had scrubbed.

"When I come out of here," she said, "after the operation, I'm coming home. Everything will be all right. Like before."

"Grandma's at home. She makes pastry every day."

"I know. She's going to look after me."

"Anne-Marie gave me her radio."

Maroon leather.

"She gave Cam her alarm clock."

"That was nice of her."

314

"She's not going to be an au pair anymore. She's going to marry Bernard. She says I can go and stay with them in the holidays."

She took his hand, gingerly, afraid. "You'll like that." He did not withdraw it.

"She's going to teach me to ski. She lives right by the mountain."

"I've missed you, Joey."

"They've got one of those mountain dogs."

"A St Bernard. How's Cassius?"

"All right. Grandma doesn't like him. He gets under her feet. He sits by your bedroom door all day."

"He wants me to come back. I expect. Do you want me to come back?"

He stared at her locker and waggled his foot.

"Joey!" she said, pulling him to her. "Baby Joey!"

Cam had put the anemones on the locker. She had not cut the stems and they were all lengths. She would do them later. Her shoulder, her pillow, were wet with Joey's tears. She knew he did not want to sit up for shame of his face, his red eyes. He never liked anyone to see him cry.

She stroked the too short hair. He was quiet after the sobbing. "There's a television," she said. "In the day-room. Why don't you go and watch it?"

You would have thought he hadn't heard. She knew Joey. Remembered Joey. After a few moments he got swiftly off the bed and with lowered head walked down the ward, his eyes on the polished linoleum.

"What's biting him?" Cam said.

"Come and sit down." She patted the place Joey had vacated and which was still warm.

Ignoring her, Cam sat on the chair and crossed her legs primly.

"How are you feeling?"

"Fine."

315

"Does it hurt?"

"No."

"The flowers were from both of us."

"They're lovely. Thank you. How is it you're at home?"

"I only came down for a couple of days. I'm going back in the morning."

"How was Israel? The Kibbutz?"

"Fine."

Lorna put out her hand. Cam did not take it. Her head was lowered. She addressed the bush of hair.

"If you don't want to talk to me, Cam, why did you come?"

"Daddy made me."

"You're angry with me. I'm sorry. There are things you can't understand."

"If you want to know, I think you're disgusting!"

Lorna looked around to see if anyone had overheard.

"You mean because of Armand?"

"If you don't mind I'd rather not discuss it. I think I'd better go."

"Cam…?"

"Good luck for tomorrow," Cam said.

When Derek came back he said, "She'll get over it. Don't be upset. It'll take a while. I told her not to upset you."

"She'll never forgive me," Lorna said. "Never."

Lying there, before the ward was awake, she knew it was true. Cam might relent sufficiently to have some kind of a relationship with her but she would never forgive her for Armand. It had to do with mothers and daughters. She could not expect Derek to understand. It was the price; of Armand.

"Lovely hair," the owl woman had said as she went down the ward.

In Cam's eyes she had crossed the barriers to taboo. She realized that. The penalty was excommunication. She must try not to think about it, although it left an open sore on the surface of her mind.

"Cuppa tea!" Annie said. "Ooh, sorry. You're not allowed!"

Lorna opened her eyes. She must have dozed off again. The ward was bustling with activity.

"Good morning, Mrs Brown," Nurse Cooper said. "How are you today? Had a good night?"

She looked fresh as a daisy. Lorna wondered how she could be so jovial at such an unearthly hour.

"All ready for the big day?" Nurse Cooper said, taking her wrist. "Mr Gillespie is starting his list at twelve so you should be going down about one o'clock. I'm afraid you're to have rather a long morning. Never mind, though. We'll give you your pre-med at midday. Not nervous, are you?"

"No," Lorna said.

"That's my girl."

You had to answer their cheeriness with cheeriness. It was part of the game designed to stop you feeling sorry for yourself. She wondered how she was going to get through the morning. Until one o'clock. Twelve, rather, when they put her out. There was a sadness within her. A disease which she could not quite pinpoint but which had nothing to do with the operation. She remembered Cam. It would have been better if Derek had not brought her, had not made her come. When she went home she would have to try and make her understand. She would work on it.

"You can have a bath after breakfast," Nurse Cooper said, although she wasn't having any breakfast. "I'll give you some special stuff to put in it. You'll be nice and clean for Mr Gillespie. There you go." She put the chart back at the foot of the iron bedstead. "I should have a little snooze if I were you."

She had been snoozing all night. It was only seven o'clock now. Mrs Forster was protesting. They wanted to get her out of bed. One of the women who had been to theatre yesterday was leaning back against her pillows, deathly pale, looking very sorry for herself. A drip above her bed led into her hand which was strapped to a board. She would be looking like that

317

tomorrow. Minus a breast. She had tried not to think about it. Thought of it now, her hand going up to it. Up to the soft fullness of it with its mobile craggy lump shifting beneath her fingers. She had always been proud of the way she looked on the beach, for her age, always wore a bikini. Cam did not expect her to be vain, wondered why, at her age she bothered at all. Over thirty it did not matter. You might as well be dead. She remembered thinking the same at Cam's age. She had let Cam down. Children expected too much. Of their parents. What right had they? Why should the transaction be one-sided? She wondered how long they would keep her in, after the operation. She hadn't even asked. Stupid. A week or so, she supposed, although one never knew these days, things were different. It used to be a fortnight, with no getting out of bed, for a baby. Now it was forty-eight hours in hospital and home if there were no complications. She felt angry with Mr Gillespie for doing his list so late, wondering how she was going to survive with her thoughts until twelve o'clock. If Armand was there she could have had a joint, that would have been a good idea. What was he doing now, he and Steve? Just having fun, Armand had said. Her imagination ran riot. If he had started his list at nine, Mr Gillespie, it would be almost time for her pre-med now, then she could relax, would feel comfortably drowsy, her anxieties allayed. It wasn't fair really, making you wait. Especially with nothing to eat and drink. How comforting it was to eat and drink. That was why they all grew so fat in Home Farm Close, needing the comfort. She wondered if Derek would want her to sign a new contract, having broken the old one taken on her marriage. To love and to cherish and service your house and your children... It was too ridiculous, Cam had no intention, perhaps she was right. It was going to be difficult to talk to Cam now. What about everyone else in Home Farm Close? There was bound to be some embarrassment, some looking askance, well let them look, she had only done something each one of them would have liked to do. Got out. Not permanently like Yolande or Thelma Barrington, just for a while, to see what it was like in the outside world. Outside the prison walls, out on parole. Derek had been marvellous last night. She wondered whether he would really have married Anne-Marie if there had been no Bernard, and knew he would not. Not Derek. She had so much to be thankful for, to live for, and had almost thrown it all away. For the first time she felt upset that she had neglected the lump, the ugly thing growing within her, for of course it was growing, they were dangerous, these things, everyone knew that. How stupid she had been, pretending that it did not exist, that if she ignored it it would go away. She hoped that she had not left it too late. That Mr Gillespie would be able to remove every tiny bit and that there would be no more trouble. She was going to enjoy her life from now on, not always be hankering after something else, a will-o'-the-wisp. There would be a plan. She would make a plan, for the second half. For herself and Derek. Not just drift. That was the trouble. Drifting. Allowing yourself to drift without knowing where you were going. They would discuss it.

"Can't offer you a bit o' my bacon," the owl woman said. "It's a lovely bit o' bacon this morning. Isn't it a lovely bit o' bacon this morning, Mrs Forster? Never mind. Soon be over."

She hadn't realized that they were already having breakfast, although the smell of the bacon filled the ward. She wasn't hungry. Bored only, and frightened. Although there was no reason to be. It was not the first time she had had an operation. It seemed to have something to do with Cam and her rejection of her.

"Your old man, isn't it?" the owl woman said.

Derek was walking down the ward.

"I didn't think you were allowed," Lorna said.

"I'm not. I had to get round Sister. She said two minutes only."

"I'm so glad."

"I was on the way to the office. Are you all right?"

"Fine. You look tired."

"I didn't sleep. I was worried."

"There's nothing to worry about."

"Are you sure?"

"Sure. I slept like a baby. Until five-thirty. They gave me some tablets."

"One o'clock, Sister said."

"Yes."

"He looked at his watch. "Soon be over.""

"Yes."

"I'll go to the office, then come back. I'll be here." He took her hand.

"Thanks." She meant for having her back. Wanting her back.

"Good luck then."

She nodded, trying to bite back the tears, unable to think why they were coming.

"Don't worry."

She shook her head.

"You'll be all right, Lorna."

She nodded. They were brimming over her eyes.

"Don't cry. There's nothing to cry about. You know I love you."

She sniffed. "I'm not crying. I'm fine."

"You're not to worry...about how you'll look...if they have to remove it."

"I'm not."

"You'll look good to me. Always."

"He's ever so handsome," the owl woman said when he'd gone. "Like a film star."

"I still 'ad me curlers in," Annie said. " 'Ope 'e didn't notice."

She could not stop crying. Sobbing into her pillow like a child.

"Here's a hankie," the owl woman said, holding it out. "It's got an owl in the corner."

The bath was rough, scrubbed clean, reeking of the disinfectant Nurse Cooper had poured in and which made the water cloudy. She wished it was the Estée Lauder Irene had given her last Christmas. This Christmas would be different, sadder, without Yolande, without Thelma. If only things could be the same. Stay the same. You always thought you had caught the butterfly of contentment but when you looked round it had gone from your shoulder. She looked down her body. That too would change. The two breasts. Symmetrical orbs. They had suckled Cam. Joey. For the last time. She held the left one. What did they do with them? She pictured the dustman taking them away from the hospital. Bins full of them. Of course, there were incinerators. Horrible. She smelled the smell of burned flesh. Perhaps they'd put it in a glass jar and give it to her as they had with her appendix, for Cam who was doing biology at the time. It would look nice on the mantelpiece. A talking point, at any rate. Lorna's left titty, don't you know? She'd better get out before she went crazy. The smell of the disinfectant was getting up her nose, sickening her.

There was no fluffy bath-mat. A cork board which looked as if the mice had been at the edges. The towel was thin and not very large. She dried quickly and took her soap, her flannel, from the wooden rack across the bath, her dressing-gown from the hook behind the door.

Nurse Cooper was making the bed with the jolly fat girl.

"Roll on the end of the month," she said, flicking the sheet smartly into the air. "Only twelve more days to go."

"What's happening?" Lorna said, although she did not really care.

"Getting married."

"Congratulations."

"Thank you."

"Where are you going," Lorna said, "for your honeymoon?"

321

"Probably sneak off to Wales," Nurse Cooper said. "He's only forty-eight hours off. We'll have a proper honeymoon later. We're probably going to Tanzania for a year."

"What does he do?"

"He's a doctor."

"Here?"

"No. At the Central Middlesex. It's finding somewhere to live that's the trouble. My sister's got a room. We'll probably make do with that."

"Are you having a big wedding?"

"About thirty. My sister's doing it. She's already got a freezer full of sausage rolls and vol-au-vents."

"Wish I was getting married," Annie said, coming up to the end of the bed, bathrobe adrift.

"You behave yourself, then," Nurse Cooper said, banging the pillow energetically and putting it into place, "and you will one day."

"Is he good-looking?" Annie said.

"Mike? Good-looking enough."

"That wasn't my fella, last night," Annie explained to Lorna. "That was just a friend."

Lorna got into bed. While she'd been in the bath the news-paperman had been. She picked it up from her locker but could not read. The firemen were on strike. The electricity workers and the miners were threatening to strike. It looked like being a hard winter. It meant nothing. She put down.

"Like a date?" Annie said, holding out the box.

"No," Lorna said sharply.

The owl woman was already attacking the yellow knitting.

"You know, Annie," she said, "Sometimes you can be a little nuisance. Can't you find yourself something to do?"

"I'd help Nurse Cooper with the beds," she said. "But she doesn't like my corners."

"I'm not surprised. Go and look at the television or something."

"I'm not sitting there looking at the test card. Besides, Sister should be bringing my injection soon."

"Well, go away and leave Mrs Brown alone. She doesn't feel like it."

"I was trying to cheer her up."

"Well, she can do without you."

"She can be a little pest at times," the owl woman said when Annie had drifted off forlornly.

Lorna closed her eyes, not because she was tired but to discourage the owl woman, who was obviously ready to pass the next couple of hours with her chatter. She smelled the silicone spray and the tickle of dust in her nostrils as the cleaner polished her locker. Felt the bump-bump of the mop as it went beneath her bed.

The rattle of the cups brought and collected told her it was coffee-time. She would have loved a cup of coffee, although it wouldn't, of course, really be coffee, far too expensive, some sort of substitute made from figs and acorns with a coffee bean added here and there for good measure. From beneath her eyelids, so that no one would know she was not sleeping, she watched Sister come to Annie with her injection, the ward round, for which they all waited with their lists of complaints only to say 'Very well, thank you' when they were asked how they were, the changing of drinking water, the social worker for Mrs Forster, the nurses gathered round Sister like so many flowers at the table at the end of the ward, the smell of the cabbage that signified it must soon be lunch. Everyone seemed preoccupied with something, someone. Nobody with her. Everything, everyone, passed by her bed. She felt like a pariah. What had she done? She wished they would come for her. Put an end to the limbo. Each time she glanced at her watch only five more minutes seemed to have passed. She could not remember such a long morning. Perhaps they had really forgotten her. She opened her eyes.

"There we go then!" Nurse Cooper swept in like a tornado and closed the curtains, the poppy curtains. She had a white bundle under her arm. She put it down on the locker.

Having made the bed not two hours ago she made it again with Lorna in it. Not tucking it in this time but turning the foot back for easy access.

"Put this over your toes," she said, laying a cotton blanket across. "Not very warm today."

She shook out the white gown, the muslin cap, the cotton socks.

"Slip your nightie off, dear."

Lorna pulled it over her head, snatching a final glimpse of her breast. Nurse Cooper folded it, her hand smoothing the lace.

"I'd like you to have it," Lorna said, "for your trousseau."

"Oh, I couldn't!" She looked appalled.

"Please. I have several."

"You're a lovely lady," Nurse Cooper said. "Thank you."

She helped Lorna with the ridiculous gown, the socks and the hat.

"You look really smart."

Inside she was cold, shaking. The bed had grown cold. She wanted to cry. To run away.

"Any false teeth?" Nurse Cooper said. "Hairpins in your hair?"

Lorna shook her head, upset that Nurse Cooper thought her teeth might not be her own.

"What about your handbag? Would you like me to lock it away while you're in theatre? It's better all round. And any other valuables you'd like under lock and key?"

It was like prison. Lorna gave the handbag.

"Keep your change purse, for the newspapers."

Lorna put it on her locker.

"Back in a minute with your injection."

She felt as if she was in a shrine, a coffin, a mortuary, in her white garb. Hurry. Hurry, she said, but no sound came.

324

"There you go." Nurse Cooper pulled the curtain behind her. "Just a little jab in the bot." She pulled back the sheet. "Roll away from me a little more, dear."

She plunged the needle in.

"Ow!" Lorna said. "That hurt."

"Sorry dear." She sounded sorry and rubbed her buttock. "There." She smoothed the sheet, pulling it up to Lorna's chin. "Just relax now and you'll be off in no time. See you when you wake up."

It wasn't working. She was wide awake.

"…do nothing but eat," the owl woman's voice came, disembodied, through the curtains. "Not much else to do. What've you ordered?"

"Shepherd's pie," Annie said.

"I'm having liver."

"Liver makes me feel sick."

"I don't mind really. Anything's nice when you don't have to cook it yourself. First time in twenty-five years. My neighbour goes in to give him his tea. She's a terrible cook. Make him appreciate me."

"Hope she's not good-looking," Annie said.

"Don't be cheeky!"

"You can't trust them," Annie said. "Not any of them."

"You don't know my Arthur…"

They worked hard, the owl women of this world, Lorna thought. She saw them in the supermarket, trolleys loaded children by the hand, moiling and toiling. No meals at the Dolce Vita to break the monotony, weekends in the Cotswolds, weeks in Marbella. A few days in Broadstairs if they were lucky. Self-catering. Change of pattern only, on the crockery. Cam was always telling her she didn't know how the other half lived. Immured in Home Farm Close. As if she didn't know. As if that were not what the trouble had been, leading to Armand, leading to the shared flat with Christine and Clare. Cam was such a lovely girl. She understood why she was angry. She wondered what she'd do after she'd got her degree. The whole world was their oyster these days, the young. They were worshipped almost like the old in China. Venerated. Joey. He had a long way to go yet. Not over-bright. Pleasant but idle, Mr Snell put on his report. Pleasant, anyway, like Derek. She had not been very kind to Derek. He had come. That was nice. Probably not architect like Derek. Something fish. Chess or. Not for living. Boys different. Had to living something. Not drift. Doctors fine. Mr Gillespie. Christine's doctor. Left it too late. No everything all right. Happy. Happy. Great things achieve. Love Derek. Love Cam. Love Joey. Love Armand. Love Pam, Irene, Opal, love baby. Everybody. Floating. Poppies floating. Dancing on black stalks. Said make her sleep. Not sleeping wide awake. Orange poppies. Dancing. Dancing. Light. Airy. Poppies dancing. Hallo.

"Hallo!" Michael said.

Irene's Michael. Funny Michael in green gown. Hat.

"Take you to theatre, Auntie Lorna." Always called her auntie. "This is Rocky."

Hallo, Rocky. Words don't come. Eyes smile instead.

"Put you on trolley. You are sleepy thing."

No. Injection don't work. Wide awake.

"Off we go. Hold tight."

Remember Michael baby. Beard now.

"What's the matter with this lift?"

"Ladies' underwear, haberdashery. Basement."

Funny. To cheer up. No need. Happy. Very, very happy.

Swing door. Floating.

Put you here a minute.

Soon…

Soon…

Nurse hold hand. Eyes over mask. Blue. Kind. So kind.

"All right, Mrs Brown?" Big man rubber apron. Take arm. "Just a little prick then you count for me."

Big light. Round light. Floating up to light.

"That's it. You can start counting."

Smile. Nurse. Eyes. Blue. So kind. One. Two, three, four…

"OK."

In the ward lunch was over. Nurse Cooper took the sheets off the bed. She was crying, silently.

"What happened?" the owl woman whispered. She was no longer knitting.

"She never came round from the anaesthetic. Poor soul. She hadn't a great future anyway. Left it too late, you see. She gave me a nightie. She was a lovely lady."

Annie sat up, staring, silenced. The whole ward was hushed. Not because it was rest-time.

Nurse Cooper finished the bed. White. Impersonal. There was a patient waiting for it. She sniffed and wiped her eyes.

"Better take her bits and pieces," she said to the fat girl. "I'll give the purse to Sister."

She picked up the change purse from the locker and opened it.

"Nothing in it," she said with surprise. "Only a mauve button."

Rosemary Friedman

Golden Boy

This is one of Rosemary Friedman's best-loved novels. Freddie Lomax is a slick, work-driven city executive, popular and sociable, other eyes always drawn to the magnetic field of his charm. Utterly without warning he is given two hours to clear his desk at the bank and he finds himself joining the ranks of the middle-aged unemployed. His confidence that a new job will appear proves unfounded, and with all the time he now spends at home his marriage to Jane begins to suffer...until, when he thinks he can go no lower, he discovers that he is not the only one with problems and he applies his talents to a last attempt to save his relationship.

'What a story! What a storyteller!' *Daily Mail*

Life Situation

Oscar John has it all: a successful author, he has been married happily for sixteen years. But then everything changes when he meets Marie-Céleste, an elegant French doctor. When his sexual curiosity turns into passion and an all-consuming love, he is completely unprepared...

ROSEMARY FRIEDMAN

PATIENTS OF A SAINT

The doctor's practice, first introduced in *No White Coat* and again in *Love on My List,* is expanding. He finds himself buckling under the strain of an increased workload and the demands of his exuberant twins. His wife, Sylvia, persuades him to take a much-needed break and he realises that it is time to find an assistant.

This proves to be a difficult task, but once he has found the right man, the doctor has more time to devote to individual patients and to his family.

Into this busy environment arrives the doctor's alluring cousin Caroline. On a study visit from the US, she invites herself to stay for six months – a situation which causes much chaos and hilarity.

PROOFS OF AFFECTION

One year in the life of a London Jewish family at a time of great change: Sydney Shelton's business is not doing too well these days, but he has provided for his future and his worries are not about trade but about his own health and his children, now young adults. Sydney's wife Kitty knows how ill he is – but they cannot talk about it. The children openly flout tradition and go against his wishes. What will happen to them if he dies?

With a light satirical touch and great sensitivity, Rosemary Friedman explores the tensions and deeper feelings of a traditional family facing the pressures of change in a non-religious society. A thoughtful and moving novel.

ROSEMARY FRIEDMAN

ROSE OF JERICHO

Kitty's husband Sydney is dead, and eighteen months later she is still struggling to come to terms with his death. She takes comfort in the lives of her children, and the full comedy and crises of Kitty's circle of family and friends vividly unfold. On a package holiday to Israel, in between awe-inspiring visits to the Dead Sea and the dramatic desert, she gets to know Maurice Morgenthau, reserved New Yorker and survivor of the Nazi concentration camps. The friendship between them grows and Maurice helps Kitty gain a new sense of perspective on her life. In turn Kitty helps Maurice tell his harrowing story of survival for the first time.

TO LIVE IN PEACE

This novel pursues the story of widow Kitty Sheldon from Rosemary Friedman's delightful earlier novels *Proofs of Affection* and *Rose of Jericho*. Kitty has watched her beloved husband die, and her children grow to adulthood. She takes security from her role as family matriarch, but now her north London Jewish community is rife with dispute about the recent Israeli invasion of Lebanon. At the invitation of her gentlemanly suitor, Holocaust survivor Maurice Morgenthau, Kitty visits New York – where she learns to please herself and in so doing learns to *discover* herself too.

OTHER TITLES BY ROSEMARY FRIEDMAN AVAILABLE DIRECT
FROM HOUSE OF STRATUS

Quantity		£	$(US)	$(CAN)	€
☐	THE COMMONPLACE DAY	6.99	11.50	15.99	11.50
☐	AN ELIGIBLE MAN	6.99	11.50	15.99	11.50
☐	THE FRATERNITY	6.99	11.50	15.99	11.50
☐	THE GENERAL PRACTICE	6.99	11.50	15.99	11.50
☐	GOLDEN BOY	6.99	11.50	15.99	11.50
☐	INTENSIVE CARE	10.99	17.99	26.95	18.00
☐	THE LIFE SITUATION	6.99	11.50	15.99	11.50
☐	LOVE ON MY LIST	6.99	11.50	15.99	11.50
☐	A LOVING MISTRESS	6.99	11.50	15.99	11.50
☐	NO WHITE COAT	6.99	11.50	15.99	11.50
☐	PATIENTS OF A SAINT	6.99	11.50	15.99	11.50
☐	PRACTICE MAKES PERFECT	6.99	11.50	15.99	11.50
☐	PROOFS OF AFFECTION	6.99	11.50	15.99	11.50
☐	ROSE OF JERICHO	6.99	11.50	15.99	11.50
☐	A SECOND WIFE	6.99	11.50	15.99	11.50
☐	TO LIVE IN PEACE	6.99	11.50	15.99	11.50
☐	VINTAGE	6.99	11.50	15.99	11.50
☐	WE ALL FALL DOWN	6.99	11.50	15.99	11.50

ALL HOUSE OF STRATUS BOOKS ARE AVAILABLE FROM GOOD BOOKSHOPS
OR DIRECT FROM THE PUBLISHER:

Internet: www.houseofstratus.com including author interviews, reviews, features.

Email: sales@houseofstratus.com please quote author, title, and credit card details.

Hotline: UK ONLY: 0800 169 1780, please quote author, title and credit card details.
INTERNATIONAL: +44 (0) 20 7494 6400, please quote author, title, and credit card details.

Send to: House of Stratus Sales Department
24c Old Burlington Street
London
W1X 1RL
UK

Please allow for postage costs charged per order plus an amount per book as set out in the tables below:

	£(Sterling)	$(US)	$(CAN)	€(Euros)
Cost per order				
UK	2.00	3.00	4.50	3.30
Europe	3.00	4.50	6.75	5.00
North America	3.00	4.50	6.75	5.00
Rest of World	3.00	4.50	6.75	5.00
Additional cost per book				
UK	0.50	0.75	1.15	0.85
Europe	1.00	1.50	2.30	1.70
North America	2.00	3.00	4.60	3.40
Rest of World	2.50	3.75	5.75	4.25

PLEASE SEND CHEQUE, POSTAL ORDER (STERLING ONLY), EUROCHEQUE, OR INTERNATIONAL MONEY ORDER (PLEASE CIRCLE METHOD OF PAYMENT YOU WISH TO USE)
MAKE PAYABLE TO: STRATUS HOLDINGS plc

Cost of book(s): ——————— Example: 3 x books at £6.99 each: £20.97

Cost of order: ——————— Example: £2.00 (Delivery to UK address)

Additional cost per book: ——————— Example: 3 x £0.50: £1.50

Order total including postage: ——————— Example: £24.47

Please tick currency you wish to use and add total amount of order:

☐ £ (Sterling) ☐ $ (US) ☐ $ (CAN) ☐ € (EUROS)

VISA, MASTERCARD, SWITCH, AMEX, SOLO, JCB:

☐ ☐ ☐ ☐ ☐ ☐ ☐ ☐ ☐ ☐ ☐ ☐ ☐ ☐ ☐ ☐ ☐ ☐

Issue number (Switch only):

☐ ☐ ☐

Start Date: **Expiry Date:**

☐☐ / ☐☐   ☐☐ / ☐☐

Signature: ———————————

NAME: ————————————————————

ADDRESS: ————————————————————

————————————————————

POSTCODE: —————————

Please allow 28 days for delivery.

Prices subject to change without notice.
Please tick box if you do not wish to receive any additional information. ☐

House of Stratus publishes many other titles in this genre; please check our website (**www.houseofstratus.com**) for more details.